Orleans QUARTER

ST. ANN

DUMAINE

ST. PHILIP

URSULINES

HOSPITAL

BARRACKS

ORLEANS
BALLROOM

UIS
RAL

UARE

URSULINE
CONVENT

MARKET

N. PETERS

GALLATIN

P P I   R I V E R

72

THE RIGHTEOUS

RENÉE AHDIEH

putnam

G. P. PUTNAM'S SONS

G. P. PUTNAM'S SONS
An imprint of Penguin Random House LLC, New York

First published in the United States of America by G. P. Putnam's Sons,
an imprint of Penguin Random House LLC, 2021

Visit us online at penguinrandomhouse.com

Library of Congress Cataloging-in-Publication Data is available.

Book manufactured in Canada

ISBN 9781984812612 (hardcover)
1 3 5 7 9 10 8 6 4 2

ISBN 9780593407677 (international edition)
1 3 5 7 9 10 8 6 4 2

FRI

Design by Nicole Rheingans
Text set in Warnock Pro Regular

To Stacey Barney and Barbara Poelle, who opened
the door and took my hand

And for Cyrus and Victor, who are my sun, my moon,
and all my stars

—◆—

I seem to have loved you in numberless forms,
numberless times . . .
In life after life, in age after age, forever.
My spellbound heart has made
and remade the necklace of songs,
That you take as a gift, wear round your neck
in your many forms,
In life after life, in age after age, forever.

From "Unending Love"
by Rabindranath Tagore

—◆—

———◆———

Then I grew up, and the beauty
of succulent illusions fell away from me.

From **The Beautiful and Damned**
by F. Scott Fitzgerald

———◆———

———◆◆◆———

S he lay as still as death.

It unnerved Arjun to see her like that. As if he were listening to the final strains of the Sonata *Pathétique*. Waiting for the music to fade to the rafters before falling to silence.

It didn't suit her. Odette Valmont was a triumph. An "Ode to Joy," not a dirge.

As usual, he stood apart from his chosen family, now more from habit than anything else. Arjun Desai liked remaining along the fringes. He could see and hear everything. Ensure he was never caught unawares.

The candlelit darkness around them reminded Arjun of a painting by a Dutch master. Remnants of Odette's perfume— the citrus of neroli oil and roses—clung to the ivory silk drapes of her bed on the top floor of the Hotel Dumaine.

Arjun's gaze drifted to the five immortals gathered around the still figure of the first vampire he'd considered a true sister. He recalled the moment he'd realized it, not long after he'd arrived to New Orleans over a year ago. She'd brought him a cup of tea. The smell of cardamom and ginger and cinnamon and milk had warmed through to his soul.

"I thought you might like some tea," Odette had said.

Arjun had looked at her, unable to conceal his surprise. "You know how to make chai?"

She'd grinned. "J'ai appris à en faire. I hope it makes you feel at home, mon cher." Then she'd vanished without another word.

The last person who had made him a cup of chai from a place of love was his father.

A single tear slid down the cheek of the vampire standing before Arjun, as if he could hear Arjun's thoughts. A tear of bright red blood. When they first met, this vampire had disturbed Arjun the most. An assassin hailing from the Far East, Shin Jaehyuk kept a collection of razor-sharp weapons—honed from iron, silver, and steel—in a black box beside the coffin he used for sleep. Crosshatched scars marred his pale skin, and his black hair was styled long to hide his features from view. A look meant to engender fear. One Arjun found highly effective.

"Is there nothing more we might do for her?" Jae asked.

The fey with the ghost-white complexion and the long queue of auburn hair straightened. He turned away from Odette. "I never said we have exhausted all possible solutions. I said I have done all my skills will allow. Even a blood drinker as unimaginative as you should know the difference, Shin Jaehyuk." His disdain was clipped.

"Then what else must be done?" Jae demanded as he rolled up the sleeves of his linen shirt, preparing for battle. "Why has Odette still not awakened?"

The fey's eyes thinned, making him look even less human.

Even more like the dangerous creature he was. More like the warrior who'd served for years as Nicodemus Saint Germain's personal guard. He said nothing, the silence around them thickening.

Arjun sighed as he leaned his shoulder against the gilded fluting of the marble column separating the bedchamber from Odette's dressing room, the ornate furniture designed in the style of the seventeenth-century court in Versailles. He understood why Jae was always gunning for a fight. It was the place the vampire felt most at ease. Most in his element. Just like Arjun lurking in the shadows.

Madeleine would put a stop to Jae's penchant for violence. Or Bastien, if he were still here. Bitterness clouded Arjun's thoughts. Sébastien Saint Germain—the vampire who had inherited the Court of the Lions' crown after the recent demise of his uncle Nicodemus—abandoned them two days ago, chasing after Celine Rousseau's jewel-colored skirts. He'd left behind an unforgivably cryptic note:

I will return.

—B

The madarchod.

As Arjun had predicted, Madeleine blurred to Jae's side before wrapping her dark hand around his scarred palm. "Jae. Please," she beseeched. "We appreciate all you've done, Ifan." She dipped her head toward the fey.

"Appreciation is meaningless to me," Ifan said. "Honor your promise of payment in full for services rendered. That is all I require."

"If gold is all you desire, you shall have it," drawled Boone from the foot of the golden four-poster bed. "Mercenary till the end. Just like a goddamned fey." Even when he cursed, Boone sounded refined. Perhaps all wealthy young white men from Charleston were the same.

"Indeed," Ifan countered, an eyebrow crooking upward. "Why should the life of any blood drinker be worth more to me than my fee? My allegiance to your kind died with Nicodemus, and I have no use for gratitude." He placed a cork stopper in a dark blue vial as he spoke. "I have prevented Odette Valmont from succumbing to the final death, which was no mean feat, given the gaping wound to her throat. I have fulfilled my end of the bargain. My fee is due." With that, he began wiping his blood-stained copper tools with a length of bleached linen.

Boone crossed his tanned arms and pursed his lips to one side of his aquiline face. "How long will she remain like this?"

Ifan lifted a shoulder. "As long as she is undisturbed, she could remain as she is for decades to come, which is not much different from death, I suppose." A snide grin tugged at his lips. "I've heard that a vampire deprived of blood becomes a husk of itself after enough time passes . . . and often loses their mind in the process." His grin deepened. "That would likely rile this one's sensibilities beyond measure." The inhuman fey glanced from one gilded corner of the room to another. "Odette

Valmont was always such a vain creature. Perhaps you can keep her here. Another pretty piece of lifeless art. The Court of the Lions' very own masterpiece."

Jae all but snarled before he spoke. "*Tak-chuh*, you piece of—"

"I meant it as a compliment," Ifan said. "Beauty is the only thing worth living for."

Hortense stepped before him, her feet spread shoulder-width apart, her arms akimbo. "You cannot wake her?" She leaned closer, her dark eyes menacing, her French accent harsh. "Or you *will* not?" Though she bared her fangs at the fey, her jeweled fingers clutched tightly at a handkerchief stained with crimson tears.

They all loved Odette Valmont. Each of the blood-drinking demons Arjun considered family could not fathom a world without her. A lifeless Odette? It was like a sea without salt or a wine without taste.

"You may ask a million times in a million ways, Miss de Morny." Ifan matched Hortense, toe-to-toe. "The answer remains the same. I do not possess the skill to wake Odette Valmont."

"Then who does?" Her voice faded to a whisper.

Again, Ifan raised a shoulder. "Perhaps there is a healer in the Vale."

Hortense snorted, the sound filled with scorn. "Parfait! A healer residing in a realm to which vampires are prohibited from traveling. Idéal!"

"Not all of you are vampires," Ifan said. "Not all of you are prohibited."

A low groan split through the silence. Arjun couldn't prevent it from escaping his lips. His head struck the marble column once, twice, his jaw set.

There was no question that he would do it. He would do whatever they asked if it meant saving Odette. She was his sister. They were his family. But that didn't mean that Arjun had to like what happened next.

Five sets of immortal eyes turned toward him, their gazes expectant.

"Hell and damnation," he swore under his breath, his English accent harsh.

Hortense spun toward Arjun in a flash, her umber skirts swishing with her movements. "You do not wish to save Odette? I thought ethereals like you—"

"Ma soeur," Madeleine interjected with a warning glance at her sister, "please be patient." She blurred to Arjun in a whirl of turquoise silk. "Arjun, I know you have lived among us for the least amount of time, but we have long considered you one of our own, and—"

"Madeleine," Arjun interrupted in a soft voice. "You don't have to ask. Of course I'll go to the Vale to find a healer for Odette."

She blinked once, the lines along the brown skin of her forehead smoothing. With a nod, she said, "I know you do not relish traveling to the place of your mother's birth. I'm aware it causes you great pain." Her features softened further. "Go with our gratitude. Whatever you need, you have but to ask."

"Make him promise he will not return without a healer," Ifan said. "Even cursed ethereals like Arjun Desai should be bound by their promises. Halfbloods may lie, cheat, steal, or kill to do it, but their word is their bond."

Anger surged through Arjun's fists. But he held his emotions in check. Full-blooded fey like Ifan had been trying to provoke him from the day he set foot in the Vale as a boy of seven.

"A promise is unnecessary," Jae said. "Our brother will not fail us." He placed a hand on Arjun's shoulder. Though it was meant to be reassuring, Arjun couldn't help but wince at his touch. Fear was not an easy feeling to shed. Just like love.

"That remains to be seen." Ifan rearranged his sleeves. "He is an ethereal, after all. It would be foolish to trust one on faith alone. Do what you will, but I cannot bear fools."

Arjun shifted from the marble column and sent him a cool smile. "Apparently your mother could."

A muscle rippled in Ifan's pale jaw. He cast a threatening glance Arjun's way. One Arjun gladly returned.

Boone's laughter was soft. Weary. "One of us should go with you, Arjun."

"No," Arjun said. "They won't tolerate a vampire in the Vale. It's too much of a risk, for them and for you."

"Bastien would have gone with you." Sadness filled Madeleine's face as she spoke.

"Perhaps it is not in our best interest to follow in the footsteps of Sébastien Saint Germain," Hortense said, her eyes flashing.

All movement stilled in the darkness, save for the dancing candle flames. As if a sudden hush had descended around them. A hush of sorrow. A hush of rage.

Bastien had betrayed his family. Vanished in their hour of need. Left Odette to die.

No matter his excuse, it was unforgivable.

"If you ask your mother for her assistance, will she give it?" Madeleine studied Arjun, her back ramrod straight.

"It's unlikely," Arjun replied. "General Riya is the last fey in any realm who would provide assistance to a blood drinker, even when asked by her own son." Resignation set along his forehead. "I will do whatever I must to save Odette. She is family to me, every bit as much as each of you have become." His voice dropped further. "But the last time I crossed a tare into the Otherworld, I promised my service to a dwarf king in the Sylvan Wyld in exchange for our safe passage through the Winter Court. Once he realizes I have returned, I will be forced to honor it."

Ifan tsked as he continued cleaning his copper tools.

Madeleine inhaled with deliberation. "How much time do you think you have before the dwarf king discovers your whereabouts?"

"I promised I would return by the harvest moon. Perhaps less than two mortal months are left before then?" Arjun canted his head to one side. "Which is a mere week or so once I cross into the Otherworld. Time does not move the same there as it does here. I cannot imagine it would take long for word to reach the dwarf king after I am sighted in the Vale."

Boone sighed, his fingers raking through his head of cherubic curls. "A week or so? As in ten days? Twelve?"

"Ten at most," Arjun agreed after a moment of thought.

"Well then, enough of this talk," Jae said. "Go."

With a nod, Arjun reached for his jacket.

"What is the dwarf king's name?" Hortense pressed. "C'est possible he can be persuaded to forgive your debt? Or at the very least, we could send someone else to serve in your stead, non?"

Ifan's laughter was as cold and clear as a winter's night.

"The dwarf king failed to offer a name," Arjun said, sliding his arms into his caramel jacket sleeves. "And, alas, Ifan is correct. From what I know of the creatures in the Sylvan Wyld, he will be unlikely to forgive any debt, no matter the enticement. He's a bearded spitfire with a terrified blue hobgoblin in his service. His court did not rise to rule the Ice Palace of Kur by showing anyone mercy."

Hortense crossed her arms. "I can be very . . . persuasive."

The beginnings of a smile ghosted across Arjun's lips. "I don't doubt it."

Madeleine took him by the arm, her touch gentle. A sharp contrast to the bladed stare of her younger sister. "As the leader of this coven, I give you authority to entreat with those in the Vale by whatever means necessary so we may restore Odette from this deathlike sleep." She squeezed his forearm. "Go now, with all haste."

Arjun took her hand and felt her grip tighten, like a mother reassuring a child. At least, he surmised it was like that. His own mother had never been the reassuring sort.

"Arjun?" Jae sat on the edge of the jacquard divan at the foot of Odette's bed and unsheathed one of the many daggers concealed in his long coat to begin sharpening it, the skirr of metal against stone echoing through the darkness. "Leave the portal open to the Vale after you depart."

"It is usually open to Rajasthan," Arjun replied. "The secondary gate is concealed in a fountain on—"

"No." He peered through his long black hair. "Not the usual, ordinary portal. I meant a direct tare to the Vale."

Arjun faced Jae fully, his hazel eyes wide. "It's dangerous to leave a portal like that open to another realm. A direct tare to the Vale is a direct tare to New Orleans. If it is not properly sealed behind me, any manner of creature from the Vale could travel through it unimpeded."

Jae said, "If you are indeed confined to the Wyld in service to the dwarf king before you are able to secure a healer, we will need a direct tare so that we can do what must be done to heal Odette." He continued honing his blade as he spoke.

Boone grunted in agreement. "If you're worried that someone might abuse the magicked mirror, no one knows it's here in New Orleans. Nicodemus made sure to keep its existence secret from any immortals outside our circle, and your flat is warded against any unwanted intruders."

"There have been whispers that Nicodemus' court possesses a hidden portal," Arjun said. "I've heard them myself."

"Whispers are not proof, and I pity the one foolish enough to wander into the Sylvan Vale sans l'invitation," Hortense finished, the French words rolling from her tongue. "No matter how"—she gestured with her hands as if searching for something—"charmant those of the Vale are, I have no doubt they are just as cruel as our forebears in the Wyld."

"It will not be left open for long," Jae finished as he twirled the newly sharpened dagger between his fingers. "Of that you may be assured."

After a time, Arjun nodded, though the decision did not sit well with him. "I'll leave the silver open. But I'm not merely worried about those in New Orleans taking advantage. As I mentioned, I'm mindful of the possibility that a creature of the Vale might use the mirror to make its way here."

"An acceptable risk on both accounts," Madeleine said as she sat alongside Jae in solidarity. "Go now, Arjun. Godspeed."

Arjun almost smiled. God? He doubted God had very much to do with a coven of blood drinkers, especially this one, nestled in the heart of a city like New Orleans, teeming with ghosts and ghouls and goblins.

The Damned. The Fallen. The Court of the Lions. They were known by many names, and none were blessed, to be sure. It wasn't the way of it, not in this world of whispered curses, glowing wards, and changelings armed with poisoned trinkets. Funny how—despite being so different from the fey in the Summer Court—vampires behaved in the same dramatic manner, theatrical to the end. Boone, with his so-called Southern charm; Hortense, her elegant hedonism; Madeleine, her calculated control; Jae, his murderous frown; and Odette . . .

He feared most of all what none of them would say. To say the words might give them life. Odette Valmont was the one who held them together. And if she was not whole, then they would never be whole again.

With a final glance at the members of his family, Arjun

straightened his lapel and took his leave from the top floor of the luxurious Hotel Dumaine, moving swiftly into the damp darkness of a New Orleans summer evening. Resolve lengthened each of his strides as the plan he'd begun concocting in his mind began to solidify. He knew where to begin.

Five days. He had five days in the Sylvan Vale to persuade one of its famed healers to travel back to the mortal world with him . . . to save a vampire. Their sworn enemy.

This was not a game of chess. Arjun could not waste time anticipating the thoughts and actions of capricious fey. His father's mortal blood put him at a disadvantage in a world that prided itself on the purity of one's lineage. Arjun often thought there were only two kinds of humans who were safe in the Vale: one who was foolish enough to marry a member of the fey gentry and one who was dead. Most halfbloods did not fare much better. From the age of seven, Arjun had lived in the Summer Court of the Sylvan Vale. He knew their rules. He'd played their games. And he would do as he'd always done from a childhood spent as the half-mortal boy with an indelible target painted on his back . . .

He would lie in wait, like a creature on the bottom of the sea. He would let them pick at him. Let them tear at his flesh and gnaw at his soul. He would smile and keep still.

And he would never allow them to see the rage burning in his soul.

———— ◆◆◆ ————

S he was running out of time.

Only hours remained for her to uncover the truth. A mere seventy-two hours.

Pippa Montrose peered around the darkened street corner, her heartbeat thundering in her ears. She watched a trio of well-dressed young women exit the parfumerie in a flutter of chiffon and lace, the light of the waning dusk silhouetting their motions. The tallest of the three thrust her wrists beneath her friends' nostrils as they continued lingering just outside New Orleans' most popular fragrance shop.

"Is it too sweet?" she asked, her voice shrill, like a piano in need of tuning.

The plump girl in mauve shook her head. "I think it's perfect, Genevieve." The girl's eagerness to please reminded Pippa of her corgi puppy, Queen Elizabeth, who enjoyed bouncing around their flat, begging to be petted by anyone nearby.

Genevieve turned with an expectant gaze toward her other companion, a slight young woman in buttery yellow, who stood near the street curb, studying the flame in a gas lamp.

"You know I don't care for this sort of thing, Gigi," the girl said, raising a dismissive shoulder. "Your mother will—"

"Hang my mother. I need to know which scent will catch a suitor's attention, posthaste." Genevieve tugged the ivory satin ribbons of her bonnet taut beneath her chin. "I'm *twenty-two*, for God's sake."

The slight girl snorted. "Perhaps you should ask a suitor, then, instead of your *female* cousins."

An exasperated sigh flew from Genevieve's lips.

Pippa's left foot began to tap against the grey pavestones, her brow furrowing. In the distance behind her right shoulder, the clock tower of Saint Louis Cathedral began to chime.

Seven o'clock.

Valeria Henri's parfumerie was about to close.

Enough of this nonsense, Pippa thought to herself. She was running out of time. If something unseemly had happened to Celine, Pippa had mere days to provide aid to her dearest friend. Mere hours before Pippa's time was no longer her own to do with as she pleased. Her soon-to-be father-in-law, Remy Devereux, would never permit Pippa to gallivant around the Quarter like a heedless lady detective. It simply wasn't proper.

And a Devereux was, above all things, proper.

Her expression determined, Pippa marched past the three colorfully garbed young women toward the blue door beneath the swaying PARFUM sign and knocked three times, her knuckles taut.

No answer.

Pippa knocked again. Harder. Louder.

The plump girl giggled as if Pippa were a simpleton. "She must have closed up shop as we left, dear. A pity."

Pippa ignored her, her frustration mounting, her posture tense. She knocked once more. Tried the handle, only to find it locked. Her shoulders fell.

Blast it all. She wasn't ready to give up. Not yet. Pippa Montrose did not surrender that easily.

"Have you a perfume emergency?" Genevieve asked, her tone grating in Pippa's ears. Genevieve's cousins snickered behind their hands.

Pippa whirled in place, a retort on her tongue, her blue eyes flashing. She caught herself just in time. Smoothed her brow. No longer was she that angry young girl, seething by herself on the counterpane. She'd left that girl behind in Liverpool, and good riddance to her, for that girl had never given her anything but trouble. Pippa could not afford trouble.

After all, she was going to be a Devereux.

A patient smile pasted on her face, Pippa said, "I do, in fact, have a matter of pressing urgency with Madame Henri."

"Well, I'm sure she will be here tomorrow," Genevieve said with another sniff of her left wrist.

Tomorrow would mean Pippa had lost another day. One she could not afford to lose. Pippa raised her fist again, prepared to pound on the blue door until someone opened it. The instant before her knuckles struck against the wood, the hinges swung open with a sharp whine and a rush of scented air.

"What do you want?" demanded a young woman with brown

skin and a colorful headscarf folded like a crown, her features peevish.

"Eloise!" Pippa stammered, stepping back. She hadn't seen Eloise Henri since Eloise had voiced her strong objections to Celine's renewed relationship with Bastien and walked out of their dress shop in protest, never to return. Despite possessing a rather fiery temper, Pippa had never enjoyed confrontation. Her fingers curled into fists. "Hello. I . . . need to speak with your mother, Valeria."

"With my mother?" Eloise's slender eyebrows arched into her forehead. "¿Por qué?"

Pippa drew back, at a loss.

Eloise rolled her rich brown eyes. "About what?"

"About"—Pippa swallowed, her nerves tingling—"Sébastien Saint Germain."

"Sébastien Saint Germain!" Genevieve exclaimed, eavesdropping from mere inches away. Her plump cousin tittered with excitement, her pink chiffon sleeves trembling. "Isn't he missing?"

Her nervous puppy of a cousin nodded. "For almost two months, along with that pretty girl who lived at the Ursuline convent. The one with the green eyes and raven hair."

"Celeste was her name, I believe," the slight girl in yellow interjected in a bored tone.

Pippa bit her tongue. No, it wasn't her name. Not at all.

Eloise stared at Pippa, her arms crossed, waiting.

Pippa chewed at the inside of her cheek. Without a word, she withdrew a small square of thick ecru paper from the pocket of her pale green skirts and passed it to Eloise. A gust of summer wind kicked at their heels the moment the envelope exchanged hands. It swirled at the loose tendrils of Pippa's blond hair, cooling the sheen of sweat along her collarbone.

Eloise unfolded the paper. Took a single glance. Then stepped aside to usher Pippa into her shop. When Pippa failed to move fast enough, Eloise snagged her by the elbow, yanking her into the perfumed shadows in a single fluid motion. Pippa careened across the threshold like a ship tossed about in a storm, her shoulder smacking against the wooden door frame.

"Oi," Pippa yelled, biting back a curse worthy of an Irish sailor.

Before Genevieve and her cousins could follow suit, the blue door slammed shut, placing Pippa and Eloise in near darkness.

"When did you receive this?" Eloise demanded without preamble.

Pippa stood straight as a pin and rubbed her smarting shoulder. "Two days ago."

"And you recognize the handwriting?"

"It belongs to Celine. I haven't seen her since she disappeared with Bastien." Pippa nodded. "I'm certain of it. But something about it is wrong. It's all wrong, and everyone refuses to believe me."

A frown tugged at the Créole girl's smooth skin. "Coño. So . . . Celine Rousseau is as foolish as I thought. Lost to that comemierda—that *boy*—like a fly trapped in honey." She sniffed. "I hope she drowns in it."

"What?" Pippa blinked, outrage collecting in her stomach. "How dare—" She cleared her throat. "You have no right to—"

Eloise shushed Pippa with a click of her tongue. "You don't know this because we were not afforded the chance to become well-acquainted, but when Bastien and I were children, I counted him among my closest friends. By now, everyone in the Quarter knows about the disappearance of the foolish Celine Rousseau and the sole heir to the Saint Germain fortune. The Crescent City's very own Romeo and Juliet. Idiotas." Caustic laughter bubbled from her throat.

Fury sparked in Pippa's chest. "Now, see here, you can't—"

Eloise shoved her index finger in Pippa's face, then began muttering to herself like a madwoman, the words unintelligible to Pippa's ears.

Pippa took a step back, her anger tamped by unease. She'd heard from several people that Valeria Henri came from a family known to dabble in magic. That the Henri women moved about in occult circles, shrouded in mystery. That they brewed potions and fragrances that could enchant a young man or lull a young woman's rival into a stupor. It was the reason Pippa decided to seek out Valeria. And though Pippa and Eloise had worked together in the dress shop for a few short weeks, Eloise had never hinted at possessing any magical skill beyond knowing which scented oils were best for the hands or for the face.

If anyone in the entire city of New Orleans could help Pippa uncover what happened to Celine and the mysterious Sébastien Saint Germain, it had to be Valeria Henri. At least that was the consensus of anyone Pippa had encountered thus far.

She was tired of losing everything that mattered. She had already lost so much in life. Her home. Her family's name. Their wealth and good standing.

Lydia and Henry. Her dearest hearts.

She gritted her teeth. In a few days' time, she would have the means to get it all back. If she kept her head down and her features simpering, she—and those she loved with every fiber of her being—would never know want again for the rest of their lives. All she had to do was mind her temper, marry into the wealthy, powerful Devereux family . . . and ignore the fact that her best friend had vanished into a world of blood and mystery, where creatures moved faster than lightning and bared fangs sharper than scythes and changed into wolves beneath the light of the full moon.

Ridiculous. Impossible. But Pippa had seen it with her own eyes.

If she knew what was good for her, she would walk away this instant and not stop marching until she saw the altar and took hold of Phoebus Devereux's hand to pledge her undying fidelity. Until she lowered her eyes before the unflinching gaze of his father, a man who controlled the world around him with the precision of a maestro conducting an orchestra.

But . . . Celine. Her best friend. What had happened to her? Had Sébastien and the bloodthirsty demons in the Court of the Lions caused her harm, however unintentionally? Or had Michael Grimaldi and his pack of wolves taken her from New Orleans against her will?

Of one thing Pippa could be certain: the so-called farewell note her friend had left on her pillow two days ago may have been in Celine's handwriting, but the words sounded nothing like her, nor did they serve to mollify Pippa's worries or heartbreak.

Pippa Montrose had had enough of heartbreak. Enough of staying silent after losing the things she loved. Enough of smiling and pretending like nothing happened.

"If I could just speak to your mother for a moment," Pippa said, renewed in her convictions.

Eloise's eyes narrowed, focusing on the square of ecru paper in her hand. Her whisper rose in urgency, the words hypnotic. Unrecognizable. Pippa began to wonder if she might be in danger. She chided herself. Not once had she considered that she might be walking into a trap of her own making. She'd been assured by more than two individuals that Valeria Henri was not the type to consort with evil spirits. But nothing had been said about Eloise. In truth, Pippa had not expected to encounter Valeria Henri's only daughter at the perfume shop.

The ecru surface began to glow as if bewitched.

Pippa gasped and began backing away. Though she'd come to the parfumerie for precisely this reason, proof of their family's ties to the occult nonetheless took her off guard.

"Just what I thought," Eloise muttered. "This paper did not come from the mortal realm. It came from the Otherworld."

"Otherworld?" Pippa blinked.

"Throughout the years, it has had many names. At one point it was even called Eden, but it has always been the realm of the fey. The world we glimpse on the edges of sleep. A place where demons of light and dark reside. My mother's ancestors called them aziza."

"Aziza?" Pippa bit her lower lip. "Fey? As in . . . *fairies*?"

Eloise nodded, the square of paper still glowing at her touch.

"And they do not live in our world?" Pippa continued, her eyes round. "There is another entire *world*? Where?"

"How should I know?" Eloise snorted. "But if you're asking me how to find it, I suppose one could travel through a tare, which is a portal linking the two realms. Where those are is any fool's guess."

Pippa's heart trilled in her chest. Not only did demons of the night and manwolves exist beyond the pages of storybooks, but now she had to contend with the possibility of *fairies*? Exasperation cut through her stomach. Why was it that all the most dangerous creatures from her childhood tales appeared to be real? What about a unicorn or a talking flower or some other such benevolent being? Why couldn't those be real instead? A thought arose in Pippa's mind of a popular novel she'd recently read, about a girl named Alice. "Is it like . . . a world through a looking glass?" she asked. "A wonderland?"

Eloise's mouth kicked up on one side. "I read that book, too. I enjoyed the Queen of Hearts immensely. From what I've gathered, the Otherworld would make Wonderland seem like a frolic at a fair."

Pippa thought a moment. Was this the place where Celine had been taken? "Do you know anyone who might have a means to travel to this Otherworld?"

"I have my suspicions, but no proof as of yet." Eloise snorted again. "And if I were you, I would put an end to my curiosity." She flicked her gaze toward the entrance. "Best be on your way."

Pippa shook her head. "Can I send a letter there? Some kind of missive?"

"And postmark it to whom? Titania? Puck? Lord Oberon himself?"

Frustration collected in Pippa's throat like a knot pulling tight. Minding her temper was proving rather difficult in Eloise

Henri's company. "I want to make sure Celine is doing well. That she did indeed travel there of her own free will."

"It says right here that she is fine. Not to come looking for her. Not to ask any questions." Eloise stared at Pippa, unblinking.

"But wouldn't it say just that if something untoward had happened to her? Wouldn't her kidnappers want precisely for no one to inquire after Celine further?" Pippa stopped herself from grasping Eloise's hands in her own. Something told her the girl would not welcome her touch. "What if she wrote the letter under duress? What if one of these . . . fairy creatures has captured her?"

"What if, what if, what if," Eloise said. "Mira, I'll never understand your kind. Stirring up trouble when there's none to be found."

"I just want to know what happened to my friend!" Pippa said, her voice rising in pitch. "Why is that so hard to understand?"

"Basta," Eloise said, her eyes thinning. "I don't take kindly to colonizers who yell."

Pippa's cheeks flushed hot. "I'm sorry," she whispered, swallowing the need to continue shouting. "I just—I need to know she is safe. If she's safe, then I won't pursue the matter. Is there any way at all, any way we might be able to find some kind of . . . courier?" Even as she said these words, she knew how ridiculous she sounded. "Would someone in the Court of the Lions be able to help?"

"The blood drinkers in Nicodemus' coven will be of no service to you in this matter. There is no love lost between the demons of darkness and those who bask in the light." Eloise tilted her head to one side. "I suppose you could make a request of their attorney. My mother told me he has ties to the Sylvan Vale."

At the mention of Arjun Desai, Pippa inhaled sharply. Many of her most recent troubles seemed to be tied in some way to this sarcastic solicitor. Every corner she turned, he appeared from the shadows to offer his unwanted opinion. She was even plagued by dreams of his snide smile and ready quips. The way the moonlight struck his hazel eyes. Pippa hated how her pulse raced at the thought of him. She knew what it meant. The last thing she needed on the eve of her impending marriage was to be attracted to someone so insensible.

The mere thought vexed her. Immensely.

"I've sent at least five messages to Arjun Desai," Pippa said in a flat tone. "He has failed to respond to a single one."

"Then you have your answer. Perhaps you should wait until a better time." Eloise reached for the handle of the blue door. "Or perhaps you should, as they say, let sleeping dogs lie."

Sudden panic set in, causing Pippa's breath to catch. "I can't wait. I need to know now. I need to speak to Celine before it's too late."

Again, Eloise tilted her head to one side, intrigued. "Too late for what?"

Pippa sputtered. She hadn't meant to say that aloud. "I . . ." She searched for a plausible excuse. "I need to ask her for a favor."

"What favor?"

Of course the girl would ask for more information. Pippa's behavior at present was undeniably suspicious. Showing up at closing time asking for information so that she might request a favor . . . of a missing girl?

"My birthday is in three days," Pippa continued, her hands gripping her jade poplin skirts. "I'm to be married that day."

Eloise raised her brows and crossed her arms.

Pippa's cheeks colored. Her temper spiked, as it always did when she felt cornered. Her skin turned hot, her fingers flexing at her sides.

"The truth shall make you free, gringa," Eloise said.

The truth? Pippa thought. Her truths were too harsh for even her to face. She recalled the advice her fencing master had given her years ago. Mistress Egan had told Pippa she must stop wasting precious time calculating. That she simply had to do what was least expected to unseat her opponents. To catch them off guard and deliver the winning stroke.

"I don't want to marry my intended," Pippa admitted. "He is a nice young man from a respectable family. It is a wise decision for me. But I don't want to marry him, and I need to speak with Celine about it."

Surprise flashed across Eloise's features. "Why don't you wish to marry him?"

"Because he can never know who I truly am, and the thought of hiding myself for the rest of my life is . . . exhausting." Even as Pippa said the words, the truth of them shocked her.

"Claro," Eloise murmured. "How . . . fascinating. Gringa, you are much more interesting than I ever thought you were. To be sure, you were kind and sweet. But it appears there is more to you than meets the eye." A gold light glinted in her gaze. "So, tell me who the other young fool is. The one you really want."

Blood surged into Pippa's cheeks. "I don't know what you're talking about."

"Ayyy, qué mentirosa," Eloise said. "You know, anyone can tell a lie. It takes real courage to tell the truth. Just like that, you are not so interesting. Good evening to you." She indicated the door.

"If I tell you, will you help me?" Desperation forced the words from Pippa's lips.

Eloise smirked. "What makes you think I *can* help you?"

"I could . . . pay you."

Dry laughter echoed into the wooden beams above Eloise's head. "Tell me first who it is, and then I'll decide whether to help you."

"That"—Pippa balked—"hardly seems fair."

"I'll warrant it's a change of pace for your kind."

Pippa swallowed. She was running out of time. "Arjun Desai," she whispered through clenched teeth. "I am . . . attracted to the Court of the Lions' solicitor."

Eloise sucked in a breath. Then whistled. "How . . . terrible for you." Her smile stretched from ear to ear. "Bueno. I'll help you."

She'd acquiesced much too quickly for Pippa's comfort. "Why the sudden change of—"

Eloise clicked her tongue. "Understand, I do not work for you nor do I take orders. I am not your friend, nor am I a wise old mystic sent to give you guidance and advice. I'm providing assistance because this is the most interesting coincidence I've ever come across. And I don't believe in coincidences." She laughed to herself. "It appears the ethereal's time has come."

"Ethereal?" Pippa asked. "What is an ethereal?"

Eloise laughed. "¡Miércoles! This should prove amusing. Gather your things, gringa. Our quest has begun."

"Quest?" Pippa drew back. "Where are we going?"

Eloise ignored her and wandered behind the long wooden counter to the right, past the display of atomizers and filigreed perfume bottles and sachets of dried flowers in crisp linen pouches. Pausing before a small cupboard in the corner, she withdrew a summer jacket and a small bag fashioned of woven tapestry, its contents clanking within, as if they were coins or metal. She paused as she donned the lightweight brown jacket to eye Pippa's jade-green ensemble. "Do you have any clothing that doesn't resemble a flower in a spring meadow?"

"No." Pippa smoothed her hands over her poplin skirts. A hand-me-down from an elder cousin. One of many. "Why? Where in God's name are we going?"

"If I refuse to tell you, will you walk away this minute?"

Pippa paused in consideration, defeat causing her shoulders to slump. "No."

"I thought not." Another smirk took shape on Eloise's face. She glanced again at Pippa's dress. "I suppose this is just a lesson you must learn on your own."

"What?"

"You will see."

Ill met by moonlight.

A Midsummer Night's Dream,

William Shakespeare

———◆●◆———

The sun had sunk into the horizon beyond New Orleans. Pale blue light lingered along the edges, refusing to submit to the darkness. Everywhere Arjun walked, the sounds of the city coming to life clashed in his ears. The gaslights hissing in their iron sconces, the clatter of hooves against cobblestone, the music filtering through the balmy breeze, the cicadas chirruping in chorus, the sizzle of seafood simmering in browned butter and warm spices.

If it was any other night, Arjun might stop to listen and take in the air. New Orleans had a haunted quality that reminded him of Bombay. That feeling of a city emerging from a jungle, the wildlife deigning to make space for it, leaf by waxen leaf. Of nature threatening to take back these gifts at any moment, for any reason, without any warning.

Of life on the edge.

Arjun loved it in a way he'd not loved any place since he was a boy.

He thought about what he might need for the journey ahead. His talisman—a golden monocle dangling from a chain affixed to his waistcoat—went with him wherever he traveled. It enabled Arjun to see the color of the emotions swirling around any mortal before him. Whether they were angry or jealous or devious or pleased, each feeling had a color, like smoke. A haze of sentiment. Sometimes it was thick. Other times it was nothing more than a wisp of feeling.

His monocle was his most prized possession. One that enabled him to understand the true motivations of those around him, not just what they said or did, but what lurked beneath their heart of hearts.

Clothing was unnecessary. Those in the Vale held an affinity for mortal fashion, but they despised man-made fabric, unless it was pure silk. In any case, his mother would be sure to provide whatever garments Arjun needed. A fact that suited him well, as the most recent styles to whip the court into a frenzy reminded him a great deal of attire in his father's homeland of India.

Once Arjun crossed through the traveling silver from the mortal world into the Otherworld, of chief concern to him were the possible requests the angry dwarf king might make during the six weeks he'd pledged service. Arjun sighed. Offering himself in service to spare his life along with the lives of his friends had seemed like the only solution at the time. Alas, the diminutive regent would be sure to shame the half-mortal son of General Riya, leader of the Grey Cloaks and chief huntress of the Sylvan Vale, to no end, simply out of spite.

As was often said, there could be no love lost between those in the Sylvan Vale and those in the Sylvan Wyld. One could set his clock by this truth.

Arjun sighed to himself again. He should probably bring a cloak, at the very least. The Winter Court of the Sylvan Wyld would not suit the mortal side of his nature, the one that felt the cold deep in his bones.

In the end, he supposed the things he needed most were his papers. His books. The records he kept of each day, so that—if his memories were ever taken from him by the glamour of a vampire or a fey—he would at the very least be able to restore a semblance of who he once was. Arjun had sworn years ago that he would never allow himself to be treated like his father had been treated. To have the memory of his own family taken away, as Arjun had been erased from his father's remembrances in a pitiful attempt to spare them both pain.

He still recalled that night over a decade ago with startling clarity. How the moon had looked larger than life in the indigo sky. How the sound of swaying palm trees and the gentle lowing of cows had curled into his ears as he'd settled into sleep. The soothing smell of the ocean and the ghee on his fingertips from the roti he'd eaten. His father had called for him, his voice calm. He'd told Arjun to go with his mother. To never forget the love they felt for each other in their hearts. How their hazel eyes matched, which meant they could always see the same sky, no matter where they were in any world.

"As high as the sky, and as deep as the ocean," his father had said. "That is how much I love you." Then he'd taken a paste of red vermillion and pressed a mark into Arjun's forehead. A tilaka, meant to protect his young son from all sides.

Arjun frowned, his footsteps slowing, a familiar fear creeping under his skin. The same fear that eked its way into his soul every time he ventured into the realm of the fey. The first time he'd come to the Vale, the sensation had been sharp. He'd been a boy of seven, taken from his home in Bombay a mere hour earlier. Before that fateful night, Arjun had not even known his mother was fey, much less one of the most celebrated warriors in all the land.

He'd followed his mother into the Sylvan Vale, his hand in hers, his features trusting. Arjun wished he had known at that moment that it would be his home now. That he would reside among the fey with the feeling of walking a tightrope suspended above a sea of spikes. With the knowledge that—if he made a single misstep—the protection his mother's position as general granted him would be taken quicker than he could blink. Whatever happened next would be messy. Agonizing. Sharp.

If he failed to keep his detractors at bay, Arjun could become a plaything of the fey gentry in the Sylvan Vale, a fate settled on many unsuspecting mortals and halflings for centuries in the Summer Court. Even though Arjun himself was the son of a member of their court and therefore gentry in his own right, they could use him—toy with him—in every way imaginable, just as he'd borne witness to as a young boy. He could be made to sing until his voice was lost, to perform until his feet bled, to serve them food and drink until he collapsed in exhaustion, never to wake. Not to mention the things the more insidious members of Lady Silla's court enjoyed. The things Arjun could not bear to face. It was why he'd left the Summer Court for the mortal world the moment his mother had granted him leave to forge his own path. Her name might have protected him from their cruelty as a child, but that was not a guarantee now that Arjun had forsworn his position at court to build a life for himself in the mortal world.

He came to a sudden stop on the pavestones at the corner of Bienville and Royale, the two names painted in cerulean on aging, cracked white tile beside his feet. Jean-Baptiste Le Moyne de Bienville was among the founders of the French city of New Orleans, which he'd stolen from the Spanish, which the Spanish had in turn stolen from the Indigenous people, whose heritage they'd all but erased.

Arjun stared at the wrought-iron banister wrapping around the façade of the residence across the way. At the elegant black metal twisted into flowers and thorns and bars and spikes.

There were two more things Arjun should bring with him to the Vale. Things he rarely carried, as the fey around him could smell the scent, and it drove them into a rage. But these two items provided a means to ensure that his fey brethren would maintain their distance if his mother's protection was rescinded for whatever reason.

Yes. He would retrieve the iron jewelry and the iron bullets before he made the journey.

What did it matter if he made the journey minutes sooner at the expense of keeping himself safe?

Arjun Desai knew better than most how important it was to be prepared for whatever the future might bring. He would pause to retrieve these items from the hidden safe in his room. Perhaps he'd even bring a few silver bullets, for good measure.

For vampires were every bit as lethal as the fey. Every bit as conniving.

Every bit as sharp.

Curiouser and Curiouser!

Alice's Adventures in Wonderland,

Lewis Carroll

———◆◆———

S top!" Eloise demanded, not a second too late.
Taken off guard, Pippa lost her footing just as Eloise
grabbed the back of her skirt in an attempt to stop her from
touching the door handle. The sound of rending fabric emanated through the dark corridor beyond the entrance to the
pied-à-terre. "Ack!" Outraged, Pippa turned on Eloise, ready to
unleash the full force of her mounting temper.

"De nada," Eloise said while yanking Pippa straight.

"Excuse me?"

"You nearly touched a warded lock. You're welcome for saving
your skin."

"From what?" Pippa whispered. "What are we doing in this
place?"

Eloise rested her hands on her hips. "I suppose I've made you
wait long enough. We are standing outside the flat shared by
Shin Jaehyuk and"—she paused, a wicked grin settling on her
features—"Arjun Desai."

"*What?*"

Eloise's grin widened. "You're welcome again, gringa. Who

doesn't want to see the secrets their lover hides behind the doors of their private bedchambers?"

"He is not my lover," Pippa said, her voice shrill, the blood tearing through her body. Her tenuous control on her temper was fraying. "And why would you ever think I would agree to—"

"Because my mother and I have suspected for quite some time that there is a traveling silver inside this flat. You said you wanted to find your friend in the world of the fey. Or were you just llena de mierda?" Eloise asked in a matter-of-fact tone. She paused to check their surroundings. "Now, do you mind if I get back to work before someone sees us?"

"We shouldn't be here," Pippa muttered. "This is wrong."

"If you lack the stomach for light burglary, then you definitely don't have the cojones to travel to the world of the fey." As she spoke, Eloise knelt before the brass lock and began removing implements from her woven bag.

"Perhaps we should wait until they return home."

"Yes, by all means, ask them nicely. I'm certain the vampire assassin and the ethereal attorney will agree to let you use their magic mirror."

"Oh, bother," Pippa said. She watched Eloise work. Without warning, she yanked two pins from her hair and bent toward the lock. "You're doing it wrong. You should—"

Eloise slapped her hand before Pippa could reach the door frame.

"Blast it all," Pippa cried out. "Why would you hit me?"

"Coño, be quiet."

"I was trying to help you."

"Have you burgled before?" Eloise arched a brow.

"Well, not per se, but I have prized open locks on several occasions."

"How is that not burglary?"

"Because it was in my own home."

Eloise eyed her sidelong. "Will wonders never cease? You will have to tell me that story someday." She murmured a string of words and then blew a breath onto the innocuous brass lock set above the matching door handle. The metal fired red-hot in the darkness as if it had been placed in an ironworker's kiln, strange symbols flashing to life deep within the brass.

Pippa's gasp emanated into the shadows. "Is that why you wouldn't let me touch the lock?"

"Always do as I say," Eloise replied. "If your fingers had so much as brushed across the lock or lingered near the sill, you would have been badly burned or had your mind muddled so much that you'd be unlikely to remember your name for a week."

"*What?*"

Ignoring Pippa's dismay, Eloise began sprinkling what appeared to be finely milled salt along the door frame. When the powder touched the glowing lock, it began to flicker and wane. Unnerved by the sight of magic, Pippa bit her lip and looked around the landing. To her right, just beyond reach, large hanging baskets filled with overflowing fern branches swayed above an intricate wrought-iron railing. Honeysuckle and warmed metal wafted back at her, the breeze heavy with the scents of summer.

"Why do you and your mother suspect there is a traveling silver in Mr. Desai's flat?" Pippa asked quietly.

Using the contents of her woven parcel, Eloise set about constructing what appeared to be a slender chain of silver and iron braided together. "My mother told me Arjun Desai keeps a small garden along his balcony. It contains herbs from all over the world, the kinds one would be unlikely to find anywhere around Louisiana. Unless he happens to have a special knack for seed cultivation, she and I suspect he has brought them through a magicked silver." She blew another soft stream of air on the glowing symbols warded into the door frame, bringing them into sharper focus. A slow smile of satisfaction spread across Eloise's face as she recognized the etchings carved deep into the shimmering metal. "Whatever it is they've hidden behind this door, it's been warded against intruders." Eloise continued to exhale slowly, directing the air closer to the lock. More symbols began to blaze, their bluish-white light shimmering in the warmth of her breath, as if she'd stepped outside into a cold winter's night.

"These are strong spells," Eloise remarked. "It looks to be the work of Zohre." She sniffed. "That stupid warlock never could resist marking his work. Like a dog pissing on a tree." She laughed. "The good news is that I think I know how to fashion an amulet to weaken the effect of the wards." Eloise assessed the full expanse of the door a final time, then retrieved several small glass bottles filled with what appeared to be dried berries, acorns, and twisted thistles, alongside a needle threaded with silk twine.

To Pippa, it looked rather complicated, which raised the question: Why would Eloise go to so much trouble? She didn't seem to be the helpful sort.

Suspicion warmed through Pippa's stomach. "Why are you helping me?"

Eloise did not once look up from her work. "I have two reasons. The first is because I grew up with Sébastien Saint Germain. In fact, he, Michael Grimaldi, and I were inseparable as children. I'd like to know where in the hell he went and why." She began stitching small charms to the necklace. "The second, more important one is this: if there is a traveling silver inside this flat, I intend to blackmail the Court of the Lions into letting me use it."

"Even if it means angering them in the process?"

"They won't harm me," Eloise retorted. "Not if it means upsetting every bokor or caplata or houngan in the city. My mother is the only person this side of the Mississippi who can make them talismans to ward away the light of the sun. Besides that, do you know what it means to travel the length of the world in less time than it takes to brew coffee?" She sewed a dried berry onto a length of the braided chain.

Pippa blinked. "No."

"Imagine!" Eloise bit through the silk twine and proceeded to fasten a twist of something that resembled a dried blackberry to the necklace, a pattern beginning to emerge. "It took you how many weeks to travel from the land of tea and crumpets to our balmy shores? Just think if you could do that in a single afternoon."

Lydia and Henry.

Was it possible? Could Pippa return to Liverpool and retrieve her younger brother and sister from their aunt's home even sooner than she'd dared to hope? "Why have you never tried to prove there was a traveling silver in this flat before now?" Pippa pressed.

"Because my mother would tan my hide if she knew what I was doing at this moment. And if we get caught by someone with an unforgiving nature, I'm going to blame you. Pretty English girls with cornflower eyes and sooty lashes like yours can get away with murder." She glanced up at Pippa, a mocking light in her gaze. "So thank you for giving me the excuse I needed to defy my superior." With a flourish, Eloise ripped the last bit of thread off the necklace. "Come here, gringa," she ordered before she began fastening the silver-and-iron chain around Pippa's neck, just above the golden cross Pippa's grandmother had given her as a child.

"It's scratching my skin," Pippa complained as she tucked her chin to inspect the pattern of charms Eloise had affixed to the braided metal. "Are those . . . *thorns*?"

"Better they scratch your skin than set you on fire." From inside her woven tapestry bag, Eloise extracted another vial of what appeared to be black sand. She unstoppered it and proceeded to blow a trace amount of the dark powder onto the brass lock. The metal smoldered before clicking open. Satisfied, Eloise gathered up a handful of her skirts and used them to turn the still-warm handle. The instant the door swung open, she jumped back, as if anticipating an impending attack.

Pippa gasped, saying, "What are you—"

Without warning, Eloise shoved Pippa over the threshold into the flat.

A burst of electrified energy rippled over Pippa's skin, causing her shoulders to shudder and her teeth to chatter. It rumbled through to her bones, making her nerve endings feel alive, from the roots of her hair to the tips of her toes. As if she'd danced across the surface of the sun.

"What in God's name?" Pippa yelled.

"¡Cállate!" Eloise scolded. "Do you want the entire building to hear you? The old lady downstairs is an infamous carrier pigeon. She's better at spreading information than cholera is at killing the poor."

"Why would you do something like that?" Pippa spluttered, her fingers still tingling from the singe of unseen energy.

"I wasn't sure the amulet would protect a member of my family," Eloise said in a matter-of-fact tone. "And if someone was to be injured, better you than me. I'm not keen on sparing you pain at my expense."

"I'm not asking you to spare me pain," Pippa said. "I'm not that delicate."

"All evidence to the contrary."

"You should have told me it would hurt me!"

"You should listen more closely. I said it was better that the amulet scratch your skin than set you on fire."

"You know what I meant." Pippa frowned, her limbs still smarting. "You should have warned me properly before you shoved me like that."

"If I had, you would have hesitated." As she spoke, Eloise collected her vials and replaced them in the tapestry bag. "You always seemed like a hesitater. Hesitating isn't an option for people who are stealing into someone's home uninvited. Speaking of such, invite me in."

"There is nothing wrong with being intentional about one's decisions." The girl's admonitions cut Pippa to the quick. As a child, Pippa had suffered from constant indecision. She'd hemmed and hawed over trivial things, like which type of preserves to put on her toast. It was the reason her fencing master had pressed her to act spontaneously when sparring. "And why do you need an invitation to come inside?" Pippa asked.

"Coño, you are the most annoying girl I've ever met." Eloise rolled her eyes heavenward. "I can't cross this threshold without tripping the wards. Someone already inside must invite me in." She waited expectantly, her booted toes tapping on the wooden floorboards of the landing.

A part of Pippa wanted to make her wait.

Eloise smirked. "If you don't invite me in, I'd wager you will last exactly five minutes before your insides are burned to a crisp for touching something you're not supposed to touch."

"Please come inside, Eloise," Pippa said through gritted teeth.

"Thank you." Even with the invitation, Eloise stepped carefully into the flat, as if she were treading on thin ice. She studied a small gas lantern on a table beside the door before nodding in satisfaction and putting a match to its wick. The lantern caught flame, casting a shadow that resembled a pyramid along the plaster wall.

Trepidation spiked in Pippa's chest. They were *trespassing*. The last time she'd ventured in the darkness to a place she did not belong, disaster ensued. For a breath, she recalled the way the flames had licked at the curtains behind her father's desk. How she'd watched, frozen, knowing the outcome was inevitable. What was done was done.

It was true Pippa Montrose had done some foolish things in her life, but not once had she stolen into someone else's home uninvited. This sort of behavior was unbecoming, especially of a soon-to-be Devereux.

"Did you know," Pippa said lamely, "that the largest pyramid in the world isn't in Egypt?" The instant the words left her mouth, she regretted them. It had been a nervous habit of hers as a child, to recite obscure facts in moments of discomfort. Her father had disciplined the habit out of her by the age of twelve. Strange that it would return now, of all nights, in front of this oddly irreverent girl.

"Oh?" Eloise arched a brow. "And where is the largest pyramid in the world?"

"Mexico."

"Truly scintillating." Eloise snorted. "While sharing these useless facts, please search for any mirrored surfaces that catch your eye or look odd. Typically, a tare distorts reflections if one catches them at the right angle." She held the lantern higher, letting the flame cast across the pitch-dark space.

Pippa stifled a squeal when the lantern light caught their figures in a window across the way.

"Were you always such a miserable coward?" Eloise teased.

Outrage collected at the top of Pippa's throat. "I am not a coward. If you knew what I'd done to get where I am today, you would never call me such a thing." She paused to take stock of a silver platter, wondering whether it held any magic in its depths.

"Ah, that is actually interesting." Eloise held the lantern even higher. "Tell me what you did. I've been known to be wrong on rare occasions."

Pippa opened her mouth, then closed it the next instant. Her life story—her family's fall from British grace and the things she'd done to keep her siblings safe—was none of Eloise Henri's business. "Did you know that hired hacks in the city of London proper are required to pass the Knowledge test before they're allowed to accept fares?" Pippa said. "It can take years to learn, as it involves knowing all the streets and routes in town as well as extensive amounts of history."

Eloise laughed. "A noble attempt to change the subject. Yet I refuse to be deterred. Tell me what you did to get where you are today." As she spoke, she moved toward the bedchamber to the right of the entryway and pushed open the door, which was slightly ajar.

Pippa straightened. "Pardon me, but I don't need to prove myself to you."

"*Pardon me*, but I'm not the one who claimed to be brave," Eloise said over her shoulder. "As far as I can tell, you're just a pretty repository of useless facts."

"I didn't say I was brave. I said I wasn't a coward."

"¡Coño!" Eloise reemerged and rolled her eyes. "Whatever you are, I'd call upon those reserves now, for all I've seen in the last hour is a girl whose hesitancy is going to get her killed, especially if she insists on moving about in a world of demons and monsters. Take risks, gringa. Without them, life is a bore."

Risks? Pippa didn't possess the zeal for taking chances that other young women possessed. Ever since she was a child, she'd been careful. Calculating. She wasn't like Celine, who seemed drawn to danger like a magnet to metal. But Pippa wasn't a coward. Her life the last few months had been nothing but one continued risk. If she failed in any way, her entire family's future would be lost. And she might never see her little brother or little sister again.

What am I doing? Pippa thought. *Why am I here?*

Because when Pippa Montrose loved, she loved with all her heart and all her soul. And she loved Celine Rousseau as she would a sister. She was tired of ignoring her instincts and of being ignored in return.

Righteous indignation sprang to life in Pippa's chest, her heart pounding in time with it. Her anger began to boil over. An anger she'd held under tight control for weeks. She'd tried so hard to be the girl she knew she could be. The girl her grandmother had wanted her to be. The kind who held her emotions in check and did not allow them to dictate her choices, as they had her father. Pippa's father felt emotions deeply. Too deeply. He allowed them to rule his actions as the moon ruled the tides.

Pippa drifted further into the room's thick darkness, away from Eloise's chattering, her chest tight. She let the feelings race through her blood, willing them to pass through her fingertips.

Breathed them out in a slow and steady stream, relinquishing them like a handful of sand. With great care, she wrapped her palm around the golden cross settled in the hollow of her throat, her fingers brushing the warm metal of the amulet Eloise had fashioned only moments ago. She held the crucifix tight, praying without words for peace and guidance.

Once Pippa's blood cooled, she opened her eyes to find Eloise studying her from across the way, the girl's elegant features warmed in the lantern light. "You don't know a thing about me," Pippa said in a calm, careful tone. "I gave up everything to come here. And I wasn't trying to escape. I was trying to build something better for myself and my loved ones. I think anyone who leaves everything behind for a chance at something better is brave. Braver than you will ever know."

Eloise held up the lantern so the two young women could better see each other. For the first time since Pippa had knocked on her door earlier this evening, Eloise looked at Pippa with unvarnished admiration in her gaze. "Even though I still think you're a pathetic hesitater, you aren't so bad, Pippa Montrose." She grinned. "Actually, remind me again of your full name? I recall it being much longer."

Pippa sighed to herself. "It's Philippa Frances Jane Montrose."

"Philippa Frances Jane Montrose." Eloise snorted. "Sounds like the sort of name that follows 'milady' or 'duchess' or some other such nonsense. I always liked the name Philippa, though."

Eloise was too close to the truth for comfort. "I've always preferred for my friends to call me Pippa. My mother called me Philippa."

"Even better, as we are not really friends, are we?" Eloise turned in a slow circle, the light from the lantern catching on a large object propped against the far wall, close to the opposite bedchamber. A white sheet covered its surface, but once they drew closer, a flash of silver caught their attention. "Ah! There you are." She took a step toward the magicked mirror and halted in her tracks, her brown eyes huge.

It was then that Pippa heard it. A sound that clutched at her throat and stole the air from her body.

Footsteps emanated from outside the flat. With every second that passed, they grew louder. Moving up the steps toward the landing. Closing in on the door to the pied-à-terre.

"What are we going to do?" Pippa gasped, her voice more breath than sound.

Eloise blew out the lantern flame. "Hide, Philippa Frances Jane. And pray."

Through the forest have I gone.

A Midsummer Night's Dream,
William Shakespeare

———◆◆◆———

Arjun knew something was amiss the instant before his hand came to rest on the door handle of his flat.

The metal was warm.

Which meant someone—or something—had wandered too close to it. Once, not long ago, he'd found the shriveled carcass of a fly on the floor beside the threshold, its wings burnt to a crisp, the metal still pulsing from the spell warded within it.

If an intruder tried the handle, they would soon bear a burn mark on their palm and a muddled mind, meant to distort their memories. Meant to confound any manner of creature that tried to gain entry to the flat without an invitation.

Mrs. Buncombe, the elderly widow who resided in the flat below them, had sported such a mark just before the turn of the year. Thankfully she believed it to be the result of touching a hot frying pan unawares, for this particular woman was known to be the neighborhood gossip. Not to mention the fact that she suspected both Arjun and Jae of deeds befitting their foreign origins. Befitting their strange statues and stinking spices and unmistakable otherness.

Mrs. Buncombe's trust in those who did not kneel before the

Christian God was as nonexistent as her so-called Christian morals. Strange, that. From what Arjun knew of Jesus Christ, he had been the kind of man to hold out his hand to those in need of refuge. To offer the least among them the most of his love.

Alas, the God of Jesus Christ was not the God Mrs. Buncombe worshipped in truth. To her, the best foreigners were the ones sent back to their shores, regardless of whatever fate awaited them there. If they or their children died of hunger, warfare, sickness, or injustice, it was indeed a shame, but none of her affair.

It still gave Arjun perverse joy to hear her complain about the fragrant herbs he grew along his balcony. The ones that brought him back to his childhood, though Bombay existed half a world away. But he'd had his own revenge. The delightfully petty sort. The sort that gave him life, even on the darkest of days. After Mrs. Buncombe singed her hand on their doorknob, Arjun had offered her a healing salve he claimed worked wonders on burns in his "little village."

In reality, he'd given her a scented cream . . . mixed with pigeon excrement.

He laughed to himself. For weeks, that old bigot had rubbed bird shit on her hands before going to bed.

Sometimes it was the simplest things that gave him the greatest pleasure.

Arjun paused as he unlocked the door and wandered into the darkness of his flat. He remained still and silent for a moment, his eyes scanning his surroundings. Despite the fine hairs raised on the back of his neck, nothing seemed amiss. It was foolish to succumb to paranoia. He could neither hear nor see anything out of the ordinary. Of course, he did not possess the same heightened senses of a vampire. Jae was able to smell the blood of an intruder from across the room. An ethereal like Arjun was certainly faster and stronger than a mere mortal, but he would never possess the gifts of a full-blooded fey, a fact which had caused him no small amount of consternation as a child.

He exhaled. Let the sound reverberate throughout the flat. Though it was a large space, it was rather simple in design. One main room in the center bookended by two identical bedchambers. A utilitarian kitchen lined the wall to Arjun's right, a brick fireplace nearby. The door to Jae's room remained shut, as was typical of the vampire, who returned home on rare occasions, especially after the assault on their coven's stronghold almost a month ago. Now Jae preferred to sleep away the day on the top floor of the Hotel Dumaine, which had become the Court of the Lions' temporary refuge.

On the wing opposite Jae's chamber—the wing closest to the flat's entrance—Arjun saw the door to his room slightly ajar, which was how he left it. Neither Arjun nor Jae used the sitting room situated beside the kitchen, the shelves along the far wall stacked with well-worn books. The only other features of note were Jae's calligraphy scrolls and Arjun's statue of Ganesha, the god of beginnings, which he'd received as a gift from his father the night his mother took Arjun to the Sylvan Vale and erased his father's memory. The last item of note was an ornate, floor-length mirror propped against the wall parallel to the kitchen, its spotted surface cloaked by a sheet of white silk.

Maybe Mrs. Buncombe had earned a new burn on her palm tonight, for it did not appear as if anyone had managed to gain entrance to the premises. Yet Arjun could not seem to shake this strange sense of unease. As if he were being watched from afar.

Perhaps it was simply the apprehension he felt at what was to come. He should be satisfied that all was as it should be. So Arjun went to his room to collect a warm cloak, the iron and silver weapons, and the book of his most recent writings, upon which he'd dictated explicit instructions to himself, should he find his mind addled in any way. He concealed the small notebook in his left breast pocket. Secured the clip of his monocle. Then he studied the closed door to Jae's room, wondering whether he should check inside, just to be certain.

The vampire assassin would not take kindly to Arjun transgressing on his privacy. Jae's senses were the keenest of all the blood drinkers Arjun had encountered. It wasn't worth the chance of upsetting Jae. So with a final glance about the space, Arjun moved before the large mirror propped against the wall.

He wished Odette Valmont's fate had not fallen on his shoulders. The responsibility was almost too great to bear. It was much easier to care for himself and himself alone. At the age of fifteen, Arjun had voluntarily rescinded his role in the court of the Sylvan Vale and moved to England, where he studied law at Cambridge. For the next three years, he cared for no one but himself. Though a small part of him had longed for something more, this chosen solitude among academics suited him well. It was far preferable to a life held in thrall to the callous creatures in the Summer Court.

Then, a year ago, Nicodemus Saint Germain asked Arjun to come to Louisiana to manage the legal matters of his coven, known to those in New Orleans as the Court of the Lions. Upon Arjun's arrival, he'd been struck by both the sinister beauty of the Crescent City and the sense of belonging he found among this motley band of blood drinkers. For the first time since he'd left Bombay as a boy of seven, he felt a sense of home.

Until he came to New Orleans, Arjun had never known what it meant to be part of something. To trust that someone would fight alongside him, through thick and thin. The immortals in the Court of the Lions accepted Arjun into their fold in a way that those in the Vale never would have done. Slowly but surely, Arjun gained a family. The first real family he'd known since he lost his connection to his father almost twelve years ago.

True, it was easier to care only about himself. But his father used to say that the right thing to do was usually the hard thing to do. And the hard thing to do was usually the right thing to do.

Curse him for being right again, as always.

Arjun wrapped his cloak around the small satchel of iron weapons, slung the parcel across his shoulder, and stood before the mirror. With a single tug, he let the silk fall and paused to peruse its brass-framed edges. Sighing, he reached his right hand forward and pressed his palm against the cool surface. The silver began to shimmer at his touch, concentric rings spreading from his fingertips like pebbles dropped in a lake. His skin tingled as his hand sank into and through the mirror, the world around him giving way to the other behind it.

With a look of resignation, Arjun stepped into the looking glass and disappeared.

SHE GENERALLY GAVE HERSELF VERY GOOD ADVICE,
(THOUGH SHE VERY SELDOM FOLLOWED IT).

ALICE'S ADVENTURES IN WONDERLAND,

LEWIS CARROLL

———◆◆◆———

From behind Shin Jaehyuk's shuttered bedchamber door, Pippa clutched Eloise's hand in a death grip, her left eye pressed to the keyhole as she watched Arjun Desai *wander into a mirror and vanish from sight.*

Eloise squeezed back to the point of pain. Pippa knew what she would say even without having to hear the words:

Keep silent, gringa. No matter what you see.

The mirror continued to shimmer long after it had swallowed Arjun Desai whole, as if he were a faceless figure melting into the shadows or a creature of the sea disappearing beneath the waves.

Though Pippa trembled with shock and awareness, she managed to wait a full minute before jumping to her feet and yanking open the door. Eloise grabbed her by the arm to stop her, but Pippa wrenched free and bolted through the darkness toward the pulsing mirror.

"It swallowed him," she exclaimed in choked wonderment. "Like a gulp of air or a drink of water."

"I knew it." Eloise's whisper was loud. Triumphant. "Those

cursed vampires have been concealing a traveling silver this entire time. You'd think they would at least offer to let us use it, given everything we've done for them over the years." She clucked her tongue. "Criaturas ingratas. A traveling silver . . . in *our* city, all this time."

"Is a traveling silver different from a tare?" Pippa remembered the word Eloise had used earlier.

"A traveling silver connects places on the mortal plane, while a tare also possesses the ability to connect the earthly realm to the fey realm," Eloise said. "I don't think any of these blood drinkers would be foolish enough to leave an actual tare unguarded like this. That would be the height of stupidity, as they are forbidden from entering the world of the fey."

"Why?"

Eloise waved a dismissive hand. "The blood drinkers made some kind of mistake centuries ago. For it, they were banished to the mortal world."

"How awful," Pippa mused. "To be forbidden from returning home."

"Besides that, an open tare would mean that any kind of creature could use it as doorway from which to come and go. It's too big a risk."

"I thought you appreciated risk takers," Pippa said.

"Claro," Eloise said. "You'd still be foraging for fruits and nuts and lying naked in caves beside spiders if none of us took any risks. It's one thing to gamble with one's own life. But a risk to an entire city of innocents is not a risk at all. It's foolhardy."

Pippa continued staring at the surface of the silver, her gaze intent. "So, if this isn't a tare to the Otherworld, then where would Arjun Desai have gone?"

"Likely back to London, where the comemierda belongs." Eloise blew another stream of air along the gilt frame of the still-undulating mirror, as if she were attempting to draw any hidden wards to the surface, just as she had around the entrance to the flat. "If his clothing is any indication, he frequents Savile Row far more often than any man should." No wards appeared, and Eloise frowned, her fingers tapping along her hip.

"Look on the floor and around the frame," she muttered. "Tell me if you notice anything unusual." Then she knelt on the floorboards, undoubtedly to peer behind the mirror.

Savile Row. Celine had spoken to Pippa about the street in the heart of London, famed for its bespoke tailors. Was Celine in London now? Had she and Bastien taken this same silver and traveled across the ocean in the blink of an eye? Were they gallivanting on Bond Street and taking tea at Claridge's while Pippa fretted alone in the damp, sweltering darkness of the Crescent City?

London. A stone's throw from Liverpool. An ocean and a world away.

The idea that this portal could take Pippa so close to where her brother and sister were in a snap of two fingers tantalized her with possibility.

The damnably beautiful risk of it all.

Never mind that. Pippa had already taken several risks today. Despite the advice of her fencing master to act spontaneously, it was far better to weigh and measure each decision with care. Her grandmother had always said that the best choice was the most righteous one, and doing what Pippa needed to do to take care of her brother and sister—to ensure a future for them all— was the most righteous, God-fearing path.

Enough of this.

It was time for Pippa to honor the commitment she'd made to Phoebus Devereux. To marry him and become a member of his well-heeled family. To cease with any mischief and be a credit to her new name.

But if Pippa could vanish in one instant through a mirror, could she not reemerge a moment later, with none the wiser?

"I can hear the wheels turning in your head, Philippa Frances Jane," Eloise warned as she stood up and began perusing a scroll of slashing black script along the nearby wall. "I wouldn't risk it. Especially not if I were you."

That word again. Risk.

The higher the risk, the greater the reward.

"What do you mean?" Pippa murmured. "Why shouldn't I take this risk?"

Eloise snorted. "We've already established that you're a hesitater. Though in this instance, your sense of— *What the hell are you doing, you stupid gringa?*" She lunged a second too late.

Pippa walked through the surface of the shimmering silver without a single glance back.

¡Qué Hostia!

"My Favorite Curse,"

a poem by Eloise Henri

———◆◆◆———

For an interminable minute, Eloise Henri stared through the mirror's shifting darkness, watching it ripple like the surface of a lake. She didn't move. She didn't blink. She barely breathed.

But, coño, did she pray.

She prayed to God in Heaven. The Holy Spirit. The Blessed Mother. All the saints above. Prayed the gringa would reappear just as she'd disappeared. That not a single one of the blond curls framing the estúpida's heart-shaped face would be harmed.

Another minute passed in silence. Eloise listened to the rapid thrum of the blood racing through her body. The carriages outside as they trundled over the cobbles, the horses steadily clopping down the lane.

What time is it? Eloise wondered, trying her best to evoke nonchalance.

Her fingers nevertheless trembled as she reached for the small watch tucked into the pocket of her oatmeal-colored linen skirt. She fumbled for the gold trinket and would have dropped it, if not for the thin chain clipping it to her waistband.

Clenching tightly to the cold metal, she pried open the lid with her thumb, the sound of the spring clicking free echoing through the layered darkness.

Half past nine o'clock.

Again Eloise's eyes leveled on the magicked mirror resting against the wall parallel to where she stood. Its silver surface was starting to settle. A sight that would have been calming to anyone but her in this moment.

"¡Qué hostia!" Eloise swore loudly. "God. Damn. It." She tucked her watch back into her skirt pocket and spun about, her eyes darting every which way as she fended off a wave of panic.

"Basta," Eloise commanded. She stood tall. Straightened the front of her chocolate-colored linen jacket and adjusted the collar.

Enough, she said to herself. *Enough.*

She swallowed, her fingers curling into fists at her sides. ¡Miércoles! She was *hesitating.* Only moments ago, she'd mocked the gringa for doing just that. And here Eloise was, uncertain. Immobilized by ever-mounting worries. She needed to think. But first, she needed to take leave of this place. If the vampire returned to find her loitering in his home, she wouldn't have a snowball's chance in Hell of making it back to the parfumerie unscathed. Eloise had never met Shin Jaehyuk, but she'd heard tales of his past as an assassin. A *vampire* assassin.

Eloise almost snorted, her amusement taking a dark turn. Weren't all vampires assassins, of a sort? Whatever the case, she wouldn't advocate for any of them teaching Sunday school. But apparently Shin Jaehyuk's bloodlust exceeded that of a typical vampire. Eloise's mother had warned her to stay clear of the unsmiling vampire from the Far East, whose pale skin was covered with scars. Eloise shuddered. Men who didn't like to smile were like women who didn't like to eat. Eloise trusted neither of them.

Of course, if the vampire assassin did chance to return at this moment, she supposed her mother's name would protect her. Somewhat. But her mother. Coño. Her *mother*.

Eloise's mother was going to berate her for hours when she found out what had taken place here tonight. Probably with a chancleta or a broom or something equally disturbing.

Eloise started for the door and pulled up short. Unease rippled down her spine.

What about the gringa?

Irritation tugged at the smooth brown skin on her forehead. It wasn't Eloise's fault that the girl had walked through the mirror. If something unfortunate happened to her, Eloise could not be held responsible. She'd warned the gringa. In fact, her last words had been ones of warning.

Eloise stepped toward the mirror, willing it to tell her where Philippa Montrose had gone. At her nearness, it thumped once, as if it could sense the magic in her veins. Then the silver began to deepen, its edges revealing a slow-moving rime, the frost spreading in sharp tendrils.

Eloise's unease spread like blood across bleached linen.

"You're in danger, gringa," she said into the mirror. "Run while you still can."

The mirror pulsed again.

"Coño," Eloise muttered. Oh, well. What more could she do? Only a fool would go after the girl. And Eloise Henri might be many things, but a fool was not one of them. She collected her satchel and made her way to the door, checking once more over her shoulder to make sure neither she nor Philippa Montrose had left anything behind.

"Vaya con Dios," she murmured, a quick prayer for the gringa's safe return. Her heart in her throat, Eloise made her way down the first flight of stairs, her steps soundless, her movements quick.

"Who are you?" a warbly voice demanded near the landing of the floor below, causing Eloise to stifle an oath.

She whirled around to see an elderly woman sporting a judgmental frown, her hooded eyes narrowed as she tried to determine Eloise's identity through the darkness.

Eloise knew who she was. Most people of color in the Quarter did. Mrs. Muriel Buncombe, whose late husband was rumored to have been a founding member of the Knights of the White Camellia. Wealthy slaveowner Colonel Alcibiades DeBlanc of the Confederate Army gathered disgruntled white soldiers, lawyers, editors, and others to oppose Reconstruction. This group of hatemongers had supposedly ceased to exist in recent years, but Eloise believed that just about as much as she believed in the South's so-called surrender, which was not at all. If she were a betting woman, she'd bet their disbandment was nothing more than a tactical retreat. They would be sure to flourish once more in the near future, like weeds fed on nothing but bullshit and braggadocio.

"What are you doing here, girl?" Mrs. Buncombe asked, taking an unsteady step in Eloise's direction. "You here for the wash?"

Anger bubbled in Eloise's chest. It made her hot enough to spit. "I sure am, missus." She held up her parcel, bunching it in her arms to make it seem larger than it was.

"Well, get on with you, then," Mrs. Buncombe drawled. "Be quick about it."

"Of course, ma'am." Eloise ducked away, her blood boiling.

She wanted to argue. To point out how wrong it was for Mrs. Buncombe to assume Eloise was a charwoman. As if she could do no better for herself. Her father, Emmanuel Henri, was a freedman who'd built his own successful import business. Her mother's family had hailed from the Caribbean, and Valeria Henri could read and write and curse her enemies in four different languages.

Eloise was educated and accomplished. But it didn't matter. Her skin was too dark, her hair too unruly. To women like Mrs. Buncombe, a girl like Eloise was nothing more than a workhorse.

Again, that same spark of unease flared around her heart.

She'd left Philippa Montrose behind to fend for herself in a world of unspeakable danger.

Now Eloise was hesitating. Again. She quirked her lips to one side. Perhaps it wasn't hesitation as much as it was guilt. Would the gringa have walked so determinedly through the mirror if Eloise hadn't baited her? The entire time they'd been in the flat, Eloise had spared no effort to convey her disdain for anyone who wavered about like a ninny, uncertain of what to do or how to be.

That was it. Eloise felt guilty. She didn't care for it. It tasted like bitter bile on her tongue. But what could she do about it?

She considered going to the Court of the Lions. Her mother had told her that their new coven was located on the top floor of the Hotel Dumaine. But Eloise couldn't stomach the idea of confessing that she'd broken into Shin Jaehyuk's flat and trespassed on a vampire's domain.

But perhaps . . . *perhaps* . . . , Eloise thought to herself.

If she went to Detective Michael Grimaldi, perhaps he might help her. They'd been close friends as children, and his family hailed from a line of infamous rougarou. Werewolves who'd warred with the likes of Nicodemus Saint Germain and his coven of blood drinkers for generations.

Michael would believe Eloise's story. He might even know of a way to help. And—given that he'd recently caused the accidental death of his cousin Luca and suffered the fate of his family's blood curse for it—he would be the last person to scold Eloise for what she'd done. Once Eloise confessed everything that had happened, she could wash her hands of the entire affair and leave these matters to the young detective, who'd pledged to serve and protect the citizens of the Crescent City. He was much more suited to the task than she was. After all,

Eloise might have baited Philippa Montrose, but she certainly hadn't told the girl to march through the mirror without a care in the world for what might happen.

Yes. Eloise knew what to do.

With that, she pivoted on her heel toward Jackson Square.

Toward the main headquarters of the New Orleans Metropolitan Police, to speak with the Quarter's newest werewolf.

———◆◆◆———

Whenever Pippa Montrose lost sense of herself, the memory of that awful night would return. In moments of disquiet or discomfort—those times when her uncertainty plagued her well into the dawn—the events of that evening would replay in her mind.

"What have you done, Richard?" her mother demanded of her father.

"What needed to be done," he replied, his calm demeanor belying the stench of whiskey on his person. Though Pippa stood around the nearest corner, concealed in shadow, she could smell it on him. It clung to his clothes like desperation to a lost man's soul.

The panic in her mother's words sharpened. "The constable came to speak with us. There is to be a formal inquiry."

"And if there is, nothing will be done, Eugenie. I've already spoken to the Lord Chamberlain. The Crown will not permit such a scandal to take shape on a peer," Pippa's father said. "I am the bloody Duke of Ashmore." His laughter was loud, followed by a hacking cough. "You think they will put me in prison?"

"We will be ruined," her mother wailed. "They will all know

what has become of us. The insurers are demanding a full ac-
counting of what happened. We cannot ignore what this will
mean for our family."

"It will mean nothing," her father said, his voice low. Mocking.
"As always."

"Richard, I beseech you—"

Pippa peered around the corner in time to see her mother rush
at her father and fling her arms around his neck.

"Please!" she said. "I beg you, Richard. No more of this. We
cannot continue as we have."

He untangled her arms, his bearded face—once so distin-
guished—mottled by fury and indolence. "I don't have time for
this nonsense. Bring me something to eat. I'm famished."

"It's the middle of the night." Her mother began to cry, a hand-
kerchief pressed to her lips.

"Then rouse the cook."

"Cook?" her mother said, tears cascading down her cheeks as
she watched her husband stumble toward the sideboard to pour
himself a drink. "What cook? It's been months since she's left our
employ." He drained his glass.

"Damned ungrateful bitch."

"We couldn't afford to keep her. Why would anyone stay?"

Pippa heard her mother's unspoken words. The ones Pippa
knew they were all thinking. Why should *any* of us stay?

"Why do you think I burned the damned thing down in the
first place?" the Duke of Ashmore bellowed. "The insurance
money from its loss will keep us afloat."

The duchess covered her face with her hands. "The insurers won't continue to ignore these illegalities. The jewelry theft was one thing, but now . . . you've turned to arson? Richard, they were already suspicious. They know about our reduced circumstances. We cannot—"

"Enough!" her father shouted, whipping around. "I provide for this family, and you smile and keep quiet. That is the way it's always been and will forever be." A snarl ripped from his throat when he knocked over a candlestick in his attempt to pour himself another drink.

Pippa gripped the corner of the wall. Pieces of chipping paint and plaster—proof of ongoing neglect—flaked from her fingertips.

Again, her mother moved toward the duke, her features pleading. "Richard, I beseech you—" She screamed as he turned on her, causing her to lose her balance and fall to the worn carpeting at her feet.

Rage caught in Pippa's throat. The paint flecks fell like snow, collecting on the oaken floorboards and the intricate paneling. Vestiges of grandeur from a bygone time.

The duke loomed over his wife, the whiskey sloshing in his hand. "I told you not to bother me any longer," he yelled. "If you persist in acting like a nagging fishwife, I'll see to it that Dr. Yardsley recommend a sanitorium so that we may both find the peace we seek."

The sight of her mother cowering was too much for Pippa to bear. Her father had never hit her mother before. At least not as far as Pippa could recollect. But there were many things her father had not done before. With each passing year, it became *clearer there were no limits to what he might do. If her father sent her mother to a sanitorium, Pippa would never see her again. Of that, she was certain. Without a word, Pippa emerged from the darkness and reached for her mother's arm to help her stand.*

"I'm going to take Mother, Lydia, and Henry to Aunt Imogen's," Pippa announced.

Her father laughed, then tossed back the remainder of his drink. "You?" A cough flew from his shining lips. "You will go nowhere without my permission, Philippa." He slammed his empty tumbler back on the sideboard.

"We cannot stay here, Father. Not when you're like this." Though her shoulders shook and her knees knocked, Pippa forced herself to stand tall. To earn each of her sixteen years.

"You will bloody well do what I tell you to do, you spoiled brat." He stepped closer, his hands clenched at his sides. "After all the blunt I've wasted sending you to painting lessons, providing a fencing master and the best governess in the county, you will obey your father, Philippa."

"I will not," Pippa said as she shifted to stand between her mother and father. She felt her mother's fingers tighten on her elbow. A halfhearted attempt to pull her away.

But Pippa did not want her mother to pretend to save her. Not anymore.

Pippa didn't flinch when her father grabbed her by the wrist and hauled her closer, his fetid breath washing over her face, nearly causing her to retch. "You are my daughter. You will do as you are told."

Pippa trembled, forcing the last of her fear to give way to rage. "I am not afraid of you. I'm taking them away so they will be safe. If you want to destroy yourself, I cannot stop you, but I will not let you destroy them."

He bared his teeth. Then, without warning, he slapped Pippa, the sound reverberating through the silence, amplified by the last of the crackling embers in the fireplace.

Pippa covered her cheek with one hand, feeling the burn of her father's touch as it seeped into the roots of her hair. As it pulsed with the beat of her heart. Shame washed over her. A soul-deep shame. The kind Pippa could not shake. Tears welled in her eyes, but she stared her father down. Willed the Duke of Ashmore to turn away first.

He winced. The slightest glimmer of awareness. Then his brow furrowed with anger. Resolute in his path forward. "I'll see this house burn around us all before I allow any of you to defy me." Once more, he gripped Pippa by the wrist, pulling her close so that he could tower over her.

She remained stoic, but terror rippled down her spine. A part of her genuinely believed he would see his family burned alive rather than lose his hold on them.

"Richard," her mother sobbed quietly. "Please. Stop." It was the cry of a wounded animal.

He glowered at Pippa, his throat bobbing. "Defy me, Philippa, and it will be at your own peril." His bloodshot eyes bored into hers.

Pippa inhaled deeply, fighting back her own tears. Demanding that they remain at bay. She wanted to lash out in kind. To strike her father in the face and scream at him for all he'd done. All he'd failed to do. He'd allowed their family to lose everything, while he drank and gambled and whored away the last of their respectability.

And now he was threatening his family with bodily harm.

Muffled footsteps emanated from behind them. Her mother began to weep even louder.

"Pippa?" Henry's soft voice, marred by sleep, cut through their mother's pitiful cries.

"Everything is all right, Henry," Pippa said in an even tone.

Lydia walked toward them, her blond curls loose, her lower lip jutting out. She took hold of the duke's pant leg, and a fresh wave of fear raked over Pippa's body. If the duke lashed out at Lydia, Pippa would never be able to quell her rage. Either she or her father would be taken from their home in chains.

"Father, what's wrong?" Lydia asked. "Are you cross with us?"

Pippa could not stop shaking. She could not control herself much longer. The temper she'd inherited from her father threatened to burst from its cage at any second. She could not allow it to take control of her. No matter how badly she wished to strike out at her father, she could not do such a thing in front of her younger brother and sister. Henry was but nine, and Lydia only six. She'd taken too many pains to conceal this darkness from them.

As calmly as possible, Pippa tried to free her wrist from her father's grasp. Even without looking, she knew there would be bruises on her skin tomorrow. He'd never struck Pippa before. But he didn't have to hit her in order to terrorize her. In order to make her feel unsafe no matter where she was. Pippa had known this from an early age, and she would die before seeing her sib- lings suffer the same fate.

She continued staring at him, her body trembling as his chest heaved, rising and falling with his own barely checked rage. To his credit, he let her go, though his eyes never once left hers. Something cut through to her heart. When she was small, her father would carry her on his shoulders. Let her reach for the crystals in the chandelier above them. He would read to her. The sound of his booming voice had been a source of endless delight, rather than one of constant fear.

But the Duke of Ashmore was not that man anymore.

Pippa took hold of her siblings by the hands. "Off to bed we go, pets," she said. "If you're good, I'll tell you another story." She smiled down at them, her anger simmering below the surface. Continuing to beg for release.

She knew what to do next. This would not be a spontaneous act. This would be one of careful consideration.

It would be wrong. And yet the most righteous choice.

⌒

Once the memory of that awful night faded, she felt as if she were slipping into a warm bath.

The enchanted mirror's surface gave way, welcoming Pippa through it. A silken curtain parting to reveal . . .

A mist-covered forest. The kind reminiscent of northern En- gland or the Scottish Highlands of her mother's youth. Pippa exhaled in relief, her shoulders dropping, her chin tilting toward the overcast sky. It was as Eloise had said. The traveling silver had taken Arjun and Pippa across the Atlantic Ocean in the blink of an eye.

England. Home. Pippa laughed at the miracle of it all, then spun about, her golden curls whipping across her face, her jade-green skirts twirling through the sultry air.

Sultry air?

Pippa stopped short. To be sure, the English countryside had an occasional balmy day, but they were few and far between. This breeze was more in keeping with the shores of southern France. Of the Italian Riviera.

Certainly not of a misty English moor.

Pippa swallowed. Looked around, the fine hairs on the back of her neck standing straight.

As if the forest had heard her thoughts, the warmth gave way to a sudden chill. The sun ducked behind a dark cloud, casting a grey pallor over everything in sight. A gust of icy wind raked through the treetops, the echo of tinkling glass chasing in its wake, as if warning Pippa. As if telling her.

Nothing was as it seemed.

Pippa wrapped her arms around herself, her teeth starting to chatter. The chill faded as she took another step, the temperature warming by degrees. Something glittered in the distance to her left. Pippa whirled around, gnawing at her lower lip.

How odd. The leaves almost appeared as if they were coated with silver dust. As if the breeze bore tiny diamonds on its wings.

A dull whine began to echo in Pippa's mind. The sound sharpened to a hum, as if her ears had been filled with water. In her periphery, an object plummeted from the sky toward her head.

Pippa shouted, falling to her knees, her arms wrapping about her skull. The hum swallowed itself all at once, her hearing returning to normal the next instant. Though her heartbeat raced in her ears, Pippa uncovered her head and looked around.

A pair of birds flitted above, passing through a beam of white-gold sun filtering between the clouds. The snow-white doves wove through ribbons of light, chasing after each other, their harmony sweet.

Inhaling through her nose, Pippa stood. Brushed the dried grass and soil from her skirt. Then she glanced at the doves as they landed in tandem on a branch of fluffy pink flowers. One of the birds cocked its head her way, its dark eyes unblinking. Pippa stepped closer, mesmerized. Moving as if in a stupor.

The pair bobbed closer together. Cooed in unison. Paused to nuzzle each other's breast.

Then the smaller one tore out the throat of its mate.

Pippa shouted as the dead dove toppled from the trembling branch, bright red blood dripping from its snowy feathers like garnets glistening in the sun. When the body of the bird landed on the moss-covered forest floor, the tips of its feathers turned gold. Then black. Then the bird began to shrivel before Pippa's eyes.

She glared up at its murderer, who continued studying her from above, its grey beak stained crimson. Pippa blinked hard. A scent wound through her nostrils, like the bergamot in a cup of tea, the smell of warm citrus causing her eyelids to flutter.

Somewhere in the far reaches of her mind, she heard a voice shouting. It sounded almost like . . . Eloise?

You're in danger, gringa. Run while you still can.

Pippa blinked hard again, her eyelids drooping.

"Stop," she cried out, pinching her cheeks, compelling herself to remain awake.

Some unseen force was trying to make her lose consciousness. She spun in place, intent on returning through the mirror the way she came.

Nothing was there. No sign of a reflective surface, nor any kind of portal. Pippa pivoted on her heel, fear gripping at her heart and scratching at her stomach. The scent of bergamot grew heavier, weightier, as if buoyed by her fear. Stumbling on the thick moss, Pippa groped through the air, hoping the invisible portal was still there, if she knew where to look.

Something zipped beside her ear, like the drone of a buzzing bee. Pippa cried out again in dismay as a thud resounded in a tree behind her. She turned around, her eyes darting to the four corners, only to feel something graze just past her cheek and land in the dirt a stone's throw from where she stood, its feathered fletchings quivering.

An arrow.

Someone was shooting arrows at her.

Good God. *Someone was trying to kill her.*

Where *was* she? Some nightmare version of the English countryside? The lawless Scottish Highlands?

Pippa took off running before her mind had a chance to

reason the obvious. Before panic set in, leaving her immobile, like a doe caught in the crosshairs.

Another arrow whizzed past her shoulder.

In desperation, Pippa almost yelled back. Why were they firing at her? What could she possibly have done in the two minutes since her arrival? Perhaps they thought her a trespasser. If she stopped and tried to reason with them, maybe—

She tripped just as another arrow lodged in a tree to her right.

When she landed on the forest floor, she looked up—

To see bees the size of her corgi, Queen Elizabeth, hovering in the branches above her, their round bodies covered in shimmering striped fur.

"What in God's name?" she cried, panic descending on her in full force.

The scent of bergamot assailed her once more. Pippa felt herself slipping, slipping, slipping out of consciousness, the hum of the buzzing bees drawing her down, down, down into the fathomless deep.

———— ✦ ————

A rjun leaned against the trunk of a birch tree along the fringes of the Great Hall, deep in the Summer Court of the Sylvan Vale. As always, he affected a look of boredom. One cultivated throughout the years.

Ennui. Complete ennui. He'd learned as a boy that anything more would attract unwanted attention. Given the daunting task looming over Arjun, it was important that he remain beyond notice.

Offhand, Arjun could think of three healers in the Vale with the necessary skills to bring Odette Valmont out of her death-like sleep. Just because he believed them to possess the knowledge did not mean that any of the three would be willing to help a vampire, especially the blood offspring of Nicodemus Saint Germain.

One of the healers outright disdained creatures who were not full-blooded fey of the Summer Court. Arjun knew this from personal experience. A story he did not care to recall, as it brought back memories of having fallen from a tree when he was ten years old. Of a broken bone in need of setting. Of stifled tears and his mother's brutal lectures.

He winced, a phantom twinge knifing through his right leg.

The other two healers might be persuaded to help with the right . . . enticement.

Arjun hated to think what that might be. The appetites of the fey never ceased to amaze him. His time studying the law under the tutelage of a progressive member of the British peerage had afforded him a chance to learn the complexities of human nature. A shame these studies did not apply to the fey or to any vampire of his acquaintance.

Not that it mattered. He'd promised his found family he would help Odette. As such, Arjun would do what needed to be done. He had already made inquiries as to the whereabouts of the two remaining fey healers, only to learn that one of them would be present at today's banquet in honor of Lord Vyr's engagement to Liege Sujee. It was the sole reason Arjun was willing to be seen at court, away from the relative safety of his mother's lakeside abode.

Above him, giant bees gathered in a canopy of towering oaks. Their steady hum reverberated through the branches, which had laced together to form a vaulted ceiling reminiscent of a church, the autumn leaves like stained-glass windows. At his feet lay a carpet of clovers, their green scent wafting through the air, mixing with the perfume of the enchanted forest. Of amber and moss. Of cloudberries and wine.

Arjun listened to the lazy gossip of the fey gentry, the whispered words seething with scandal and vice. Who had done what with whom . . . and in what kind of compromising position. Which fey lord had tumbled with which fey lady. Or liege.

Or both. Who had been caught unawares by their mate. Perhaps even prompted to join. Or enraged to the point of demanding satisfaction at dawn.

"His wrist still has not healed from the wound he received at the duel," said a fey lady with bronzed skin, sharply pointed ears, and upturned eyes the shade of purple irises. Ratana was her name, Arjun recalled. Her elder sister, Sinora, had once propositioned Arjun at a party, asking him to meet her for a midnight tryst in the sparkling waters of Lake Lure. She'd punished him for his rejection by turning his skin the same hue as Ratana's eyes.

Through it all, ennui had been Arjun's mantra. No matter how much his heart might ache or his blood might boil. And boil it did, many times over. Arjun Desai never forgot an offense, nor did he fail to recall every detail anytime someone—especially a fey—caused him strife. Never mind that it made him slip now and then into the realm of pettiness. He was, after all, part fey. Petty had become the sugar in his daily cup of tea.

And it was, in a word, delicious.

Ratana paused to sip the mystwine in her gilded goblet, the artfully tattered edges of her dagged sleeves billowing about her. "A pity, for the fool did have such talented fingers."

The suggestion in her words caused a ripple of laughter to flow around her.

Arjun sighed. Another duel. Another day at court.

The Code Duello had recently come into fashion among the gentry of the Sylvan Vale. As was often the case, the fey found themselves fascinated by the happenings in the earthly realm.

Religion especially intrigued them, as they did not believe in such a thing, nor did they understand human notions like racial superiority. Honor and heroism amused them most of all, as did mortal man's often contradictory ideas of morality.

In the Vale, there were members of the gentry who dressed like men but disdained the title "lord." Similarly, some chose to dress as women and eschewed the title "lady." Instead they were known as lieges, and no one gave it a second thought. Such a thing would be scandalous in the halls of London society. In Bombay, Arjun had a cousin who considered themself neither male nor female. Even though society in the East Indies held tight to many conventions—religion among them—not once had Arjun witnessed anyone in his family mistreat his cousin.

The outside world was, of course, another matter entirely.

The English peerage would not be as accepting as his family, even to one of its own. Traditions of the many Western faiths confounded Arjun, for they appeared to function in spaces of black and white, with no room for tolerance of any kind. There was a single god, and a devotee was to worship that one god alone or be branded a heretic. Unless prayer was offered to this god's mortal son, whose flesh and blood were consumed in ritualist fashion before an altar. Bastien was a practicing Catholic. So were Odette and Hortense. To Arjun, this made sense, as it seemed to be the perfect religion for a vampire.

There were innumerable deities in the Hindu faith of Arjun's father, a man who reconciled the existence of fey—whom he called yakshas—alongside his beliefs by saying there were mysteries older than mankind could fathom. As a small child of seven in Bombay, Arjun had tried to abide by his father's faith. He'd failed more often than not. He was too quick to lose patience. Too quick to covet material things. But there was beauty to be had there, if one knew where to look.

Alas, this religion had also been a source of consternation for Arjun as a child, when his father discovered that Arjun's newest playmate, a boy named Saeed, was a follower of Islam. The following day, Arjun was forbidden from associating with Saeed. Arjun never forgot that his father's understanding of faith had robbed him of a friend.

In that respect, the world of the fey was more forgiving.

Perhaps all worlds were filled with contradictions, where one thing mattered greatly to some while another mattered not at all. Arjun couldn't help but think that it might be better if everyone simply minded their own business and allowed people to be who they wished to be and pray how they wished to pray and love whom they wished to love.

"What was the reason for the duel?" an ebon-skinned lord asked Lady Ratana, his tone feigning disinterest.

"Who knows why anymore?" Ratana wrinkled her nose and hooked a length of dark hair behind a pointed ear. "And does it matter? So long as blood or tears are spilt in the process. Even better if death is a possibility."

More laughter.

Arjun's eyes rolled toward the oak branches of the ceiling in the Great Hall.

To an immortal, death was the greatest curiosity. For even

though they *could* live forever, that did not mean they *would*. If they were struck clean through the heart with a weapon of pure iron or if their heads were severed from their bodies with an iron blade, it was a wound even the most skilled of healers could not heal.

It seemed to Arjun that it had taken no more than a fortnight for the members of court to begin issuing duels for the slightest of offenses. A formal challenge would be issued, the duels fought the following dawn in the Glen of the Fey Guild, using pistols armed with iron bullets. Most of the court would dress for the occasion and make it an event, complete with a banquet and a cornucopia and crystal carafes overflowing with enough wine to put Bacchus to shame. More often than not, the bullets missed both duelers entirely. On rare occasions, one or both of the fools would wind up nicked by an iron bullet, their skin singed black from the wound. To Arjun's recollection, a fey had died by duel only once so far, the metal piercing clean through the poor sod's heart, causing him to shrivel within his skin and disintegrate into a husk.

The sexual escapades of the Summer Court were always at the center of the drama. Unlike London or New Orleans or Bombay, in the Vale pleasure was considered pleasure, without limitations. A marriage was not restricted to a male and a female. A union of houses could be with whomever one chose . . . so long as it was not with a member of the Winter Court.

Of course, this put to question the Lady of the Vale's tolerance for Celine's relationship with Bastien. In truth, Arjun could not fathom why Lady Silla would permit her only daughter to carry on with a vampire, but he would wager it was not for a magnanimous reason. The gentry in the Sylvan Vale were rarely generous without cause. Arjun could count on one hand the number of fey he'd encountered with a true sense of decency and kindness.

The last rule of import when it came to romantic entanglements was the cause of most strife at court. Couplings outside of marriage were allowed, so long as written permission was granted from all parties. Needless to say, such permission was rarely granted. These careless displays of infidelity—along with the ensuing drama—had only solidified a belief Arjun had formed from a young age.

Love was for the foolish. And Arjun Desai was no fool.

He caught himself beginning to smirk. To show an emotion beyond boredom.

Ennui, he told himself. *Complete ennui.*

Strange how a fey marriage was treated with such respect. The Rite, as it was called in the Vale, was among the most important occasions in the life of any member of the gentry, for it was one of the few things in an immortal's life that had any lasting sort of permanence.

A member of the gentry was allowed to marry once in their lifetime. Only once. They could take as many lovers as they chose, but a second formal alliance was forbidden, even after a spouse had perished.

"Well, what have we here?" a voice purred through the din to Arjun's left.

Arjun did not even look toward its owner. "You sound like a villain from a poorly written melodrama. Some mustache-twirling moron."

"Mustache?" The figure moved from the shadows into the light, his motions liquid, his long silver hair streaming down his back.

"A kind of facial hair that grows above a gentleman's lips."

Lord Vyr slithered closer, his grey gaze circumspect. "Is it stylish?"

"If you like tasting your dinner well into the night, then yes."

"You are being facetious."

"Me? Never." Arjun offered Vyr a thin smile. His sarcasm was often a source of irritation to the fey, as they could not outright lie. A fact that gave Arjun no small amount of joy, for it was one of the few advantages he possessed as an ethereal.

Vyr's eyes narrowed to slits. "Why are you here, mongrel?" he demanded, the rows of diamonds in his pointed ears flashing. "No one at court misses your presence."

"Believe me, the sentiment is mutual."

"If you've come seeking your friends, they're not here," Vyr continued, the train of his floor-length ivory mantle shimmering, his embroidered slippers reminiscent of those worn by Rajasthani maharajahs. "That foul blood drinker, Sébastien Saint Germain, and Lady Silla's daughter, Lady Celine, are away from court. Don't ask me where they've gone because you know I don't care."

"I'm not looking for them."

"Are they not your friends, halfblood? Are they not members of your little . . . court?"

With a sigh, Arjun faced Vyr. "Why do you care? It's not stylish for you to care."

"Does it seem as if I care? I am merely attempting to converse with a lesser creature. I've concluded that benevolence suits me, on occasion."

Arjun grinned as if he were humoring a precocious child. "And yet . . . all these questions. All this interest. Are you already so bored with your intended?" He scanned the crowd. "Where is the unlucky sod, by the way?"

"Liege Sujee and I are a perfect match," Vyr hissed. "They like the same things I like."

"But do they hate the same things you hate? Because that is truly the stuff of a lasting marriage."

A V formed between Lord Vyr's brows. "And how would you know this? You, who have disdained the Rite since you were a child."

"I don't have to smell shit to know it stinks."

Color rose in Vyr's pale face. "If I could exile you from court, I would. If I could banish you to the Wyld in a fortress of razor-sharp ice, I would. If I could—"

"If I could backhand you with an iron gauntlet, I would. If I could tie you to a post and leave you for the huntresses' hounds, I would." Arjun grinned. "Oh, wait. You already did that to me once when we were nine."

"It is one of my deepest regrets, that the hounds were not allowed to finish their hunt."

Arjun's grin widened. "Let's dispense with the pleasantries,

Vyr. As high as the sky and as deep as the ocean. That's how much I despise you."

Vyr opened his mouth, then caught sight of something over Arjun's shoulder and instead offered nothing in response, his lips pressing into a line.

"And I was so enjoying our repartee." Arjun sighed with mock regret. "Has my mother arrived?" He turned around. "Or is it the Lady of the Vale? I suppose—"

"My intended dislikes when I mistreat those beneath me for sport."

Arjun's jaw dropped, a rare burst of genuine emotion flaring across his face. Then he broke into laughter. "Have you found a match in one of the only members of the gentry with a soul?"

"Liege Sujee is kind and generous."

"You mean, they are easy for you to manipulate."

"No," a soft voice intoned from nearby, the sound like a babbling brook, "I don't see myself as easy to manipulate, Lord Arjun, nor do I think it foolish to believe those we love are capable of being better tomorrow than they were today." Swishing fabric the colors of a sunset sky brushed across the clovers as Liege Sujee, their long blue-black hair falling past their waist in waves, moved to stand beside Lord Vyr. "Over the years, I've come to believe there is no purpose behind unceasing cruelty. I hope that, in time, Lord Vyr will agree with me."

Dubiousness set across Arjun's brow. "I wish you sincere luck, Liege Sujee."

Sujee pursed their lips to the right. "This mortal fascination with luck perplexes me. Hope in those we love is a much more powerful ideal upon which to rely."

A quip threatened to burst from Arjun's mouth. With effort, he remained silent, affecting a look of what he "hoped" was sober agreement.

"Don't concern yourself with the rabble, dearest," Vyr said as he looped an arm around Sujee. "The halfblood has no notion of bettering himself. He is content to live a life alone and apart, for all eternity."

"There is nothing wrong with being alone," Arjun said. "And I do not see myself as apart. In truth, for the first time in many years, I find myself . . . belonging." His mind drifted back to the Court of the Lions. Back to his chosen family in the haunted city of New Orleans.

Contentment warmed through Arjun. Love may not be in his cards, but he mattered to someone. Made a difference in the lives of others. He had a place and a purpose. He would find a healer for Odette and never set foot in the Vale again, unless forced.

A hungry light entered Vyr's grey gaze. The look of a lioness after spotting injured prey. Arjun almost kicked himself at the realization. He'd given away too much. He knew better than to betray himself like that, especially in front of one of the court's cruelest members. A member of the Fey Guild—those of the highest echelon in the Vale—Vyr enjoyed punishing those who sought his praise. As for those who sought to defy him?

They only succeeded in painting targets on their backs.

"What are you doing here, Arjun Desai?" Vyr said. "For once

in your life, tell the truth. You needn't fear any . . . undue judgment." He leaned closer, and Liege Sujee frowned.

"Dearest?" they said. "Perhaps we should attend to our other guests."

"But of course, my love," Vyr replied without turning toward his intended. "I simply wish to know the reason my childhood acquaintance has chosen to attend our engagement celebration at court today."

Instead of responding, Arjun signaled for an unusually tall goblin bearing a tray of tumblers etched with grapevines to come closer. The goblin sneered when Arjun took a drink from the tray and drained its contents without even pausing for breath. Though Arjun nearly choked, he managed to replace the tumbler with a flourish. The taste of oversweet licorice coated his tongue, the emerald-green liquor bracing. Far stronger than its counterpart in the mortal world, a drink known as absinthe. "I'm sure you'll figure out what I'm doing here soon, Vyr. And be quick to use it to your nefarious advantage."

"That is not Lord Vyr's way," Sujee replied. "Not anymore."

Vyr threaded his pale fingers through Sujee's hand. "I seek to help, halfblood. Tell me why you are here, and I will endeavor to be of assistance." His eyes glittered with malice.

It never ceased to amaze Arjun how adept the fey had become at toeing the line of truth. Vyr was not lying when he offered to help. His idea of assistance, however, remained to be seen. Arjun coughed with dark mirth the same instant he caught sight of the healer's arrival, the tall, golden-haired fey's severe countenance unmistakable as it rose above the crowd.

"Whom do you seek?" Vyr demanded.

Sujee placed a comforting palm on Vyr's chest, beneath a brooch sporting the sunburst crest of the Vale. "My beloved, Lord Brehm is waiting to speak with us."

Disregarding his betrothed, Vyr pressed, "Who, halfblood?"

"Where is the Lady of the Vale?" Arjun asked, attempting to throw Vyr off his scent. "I noticed she is not on the Horned Throne, nor have I seen her holding court today. Is she absent from the Ivy Bower as well?"

"She is traveling in the company of her daughter and that loathsome blood drinker. In her absence, Lady Yulin and I were left to hold rank at court."

"A pity," Arjun said. "For the court, you understand."

"Lady Celine and her vampire companion were here this morning," Sujee replied, cutting their eyes at both Arjun and Vyr. "I believe they left to tour the lands of the Summer Court together with Lady Silla. The last I heard was that they were enjoying the sights on the far end of Lake Lure, in the treetops of the Moon Rabbit's Grove."

"Thank you, Liege Sujee." Arjun offered them a dramatic bow, his hand over his heart, his monocle dangling in the afternoon light.

"There is no need to antagonize me, Lord Arjun," Sujee said. "I wish to help you."

"Please don't call me that."

"I told you, my beloved," Vyr interjected. "The halfblood lacks decorum. A complete turnabout from his mother, who is above reproach."

Sujee nodded. "Perhaps her son can be shown a different way."

"I admire how much credit you give to the hopeless, my love." Vyr pulled Sujee close and pressed a kiss to their temple.

Sujee caressed his chin, their polished nails long and glassy. "Forgive us, Lord Arjun, but we should see to Lord Brehm and our other guests." With a nod at Arjun, the two lovers walked in the opposite direction, Vyr's affection for his intended obvious.

Perhaps even a despicable fey lord like Vyr could be changed by love.

Just as Arjun thought it, Vyr shot him an evil smile from over his shoulder, his expression filled with unspoken promise.

"Changed by love, my horse's arse," Arjun muttered. He signaled again for the goblin with the tray of green fairy liquor, and in no time he'd managed to drain two more cups, the spirits lulling the chaos in his mind.

He really should drink less, both here and at home in New Orleans. But he enjoyed the way liquor dulled his senses. The way the world swam before his eyes like a painting he'd stared at far too long. Drinking was something he could do in the company of his fellow members in the Court of the Lions. As a child, Arjun had always despised eating alone.

Calm once more, he chided himself for allowing Vyr to distract him. Straightening his shirtsleeves, Arjun began making his way toward the tall healer. He was halfway there when the din behind him rose in pitch near the vine-covered entrance to the Ivy Bower.

Arjun almost turned toward the sound, the fey part of him

eager. Curious to know its source and take advantage of the information as only a fey would.

Determination furrowed his brow.

He didn't care what kind of nonsense the court managed to drum up today. He had a plan.

Arjun focused on the swarm of overlarge bees hovering in the oak branches above. On the iridescent-green bodies of flies the size of house pets, their eyes enormous and their glazed wings fluttering. Then he resumed striding toward the healer.

"Please!" a female voice choked out from behind Arjun, the cry hoarse.

The sound halted him in his tracks, a strange sensation knifing through his chest.

He recognized that voice.

Laughter rippled through the crowd, followed by the shredding of fabric.

"Please!" the same voice cried, the tone high-pitched, panicked. "Please, I didn't mean to—"

"They never do," another feminine voice intoned, rich with the melody of fey magic. "That is what makes it so delicious. These lovely little mortals with their lovely little excuses."

Arjun fought the urge to turn around. It couldn't be her. It wasn't possible. His ears were playing tricks on him. Or perhaps it was his cursed heart. Ever since he'd met Philippa Montrose, Arjun had been struck by the most inopportune attraction. Perhaps it was her wavering smile or her impossibly long eyelashes. Or that they'd both resided on English shores. Whatever the reason, he'd gone out of his way to help her on more than one occasion, without reason or cause.

Something about her made him act foolish. And Arjun Desai was no fool.

He stretched his neck from side to side. No. It wasn't Philippa. It was some poor unsuspecting mortal who'd fallen into the clutches of the Summer Court of the Sylvan Vale. Even if Arjun felt pity, he would not allow himself to be distracted. He could not save the girl if he tried. Better that it be over soon. He started to take another step toward the healer, but his feet remained rooted to the spot, dread clutching at his throat.

"My name is Philippa, and if you will return me to my home, I can assure you that you will receive—"

Another rending sound, followed by a shriek of outraged terror.

Arjun's heart crashed into his stomach, his eyes going wide.

Philippa. It wasn't possible.

He spun around just in time to see her shove free of her captors.

"Please!" she cried. "I—I'm so sorry for trespassing. I've never— *ahhh!*" Another shriek. More ripping of fabric, chased by a wave of cruel laughter.

Horror flashed through Arjun, hot and fast, his mind churning. She must have been the one to set off the wards at the entrance of his flat. How she'd managed to gain entrance unscathed, he did not know. Nor did it matter.

What could have possessed Philippa Montrose to follow him through the tare?

Arjun forced himself not to react. To remain calm so that he might think. It would be of no help to her if he barreled forward without a plan. He could not do anything that would draw attention to their prior relationship, even in the smallest measure. If that happened, there would be no end to their torment. Arjun could bear it. He'd borne their cruelty for most of his life. If worst came to worst, he could call on his mother for protection. It was true they had not been on speaking terms for some time, but she *was* his mother. Hopefully that still counted for something.

But Philippa had no one. A mortal like her—a good and kind and earnest soul—would not survive long in the Vale. The best she could hope for was a quick death, with as little pain as possible.

The last mortal held in thrall to the Summer Court had been forced to assume the role of temporary executioner. After two years of stabbing errant pixies and back-talking dokkaebi to death with a dull knife, the poor young man had turned the blade on himself.

It had taken him three days to die.

The drama had delighted the fey. That was what they relished most. Toying with a lesser creature, like a cruel boy aiming a beam of sun at an ant through a magnifying glass. One of their favorite pastimes was watching helpless mortals tear themselves apart.

Arjun swallowed. Tried his best to block the sound of the panic in Philippa's voice. To ignore the fear collecting in his stomach. The fury pooling in his chest.

Ennui. Complete ennui.

Arjun dropped his shoulders. Placed his hands in his pockets. Affected an insouciant grin.

What was he going to do? Options flashed through his mind's eye, each more outrageous than the last. He supposed as a last resort he could—

"Please," Philippa shrieked when one of the gentry slashed her arm, causing her sleeve to fall and a thin stream of bright red blood to appear. "Someone help me. *Please!*"

Cool laughter flowed around her like wine. Another member of the gentry hurled an overripe pomum fruit at Philippa, and it exploded against her jade-green skirts, the color of the juice a match for the blood dripping down her arm.

Arjun's fingers flexed at his sides. A muscle rippled along his jaw. He closed his eyes, willing himself to find a solution. Only to be jostled where he stood by a member of the gentry eager for a better view. He whipped around, catching himself, his gaze murderous.

In that instant, his eyes locked on Philippa Montrose.

For a flash of time, Arjun saw nothing but her. The way her hands trembled and her lip quavered. How her dress was ripped along the bodice and shoulder, as well as the hem, as if a murder of crows had pecked at her, exposing her corset and undergarments. She clutched the torn fabric in an attempt to maintain her modesty, a motion that iced the blood in Arjun's veins.

He knew that feeling of helplessness. Knew it all too well.

Her blue eyes went wide with recognition, her expression

asking, beseeching him to come to her aid. Believing he was the only one who could put an end to the court's cruelty.

Arjun shook his head. Ever so slightly.

He still didn't have a plan. Not yet. Without words, he tried to tell her to be patient a while longer.

Philippa bit her lip, her fingers coiling around the shredded pieces of her dress.

Anger blazed through Arjun at the mere thought of how afraid she must be. He recalled a tale from the Mahabharata that his father had told him as a child, when Duryodhana insulted Draupadi by attempting to disrobe her before an audience. Draupadi called out for the god Krishna, who made the length of Draupadi's sari infinite, so that she could never be disrobed.

Many details of the story had been lost to Arjun over the years. But he did remember that it ended on a glorious note of vengeance. All those who witnessed Draupadi's dishonor died horrible deaths on the field of battle. Bhima, one of the heroes of the Mahabharata, was so furious he vowed to break the chest of the man responsible and drink the blood straight from his broken body.

Arjun had always liked Bhima.

"This pretty little flower is just waiting to have her petals plucked," a fey lord named Miraç announced as he tugged a metal pin from the crown of Philippa Montrose's head. A single blond curl tumbled free.

Philippa shuddered as she clutched her ruined dress to her

chest. More laughter followed. A fey lady whose face Arjun could not see pulled free another hairpin.

"No!" Philippa said, a golden tendril falling down her cheek. Tears welled in her eyes.

Arjun moved forward. If she cried again, it would be his undoing.

The fey circling her drew closer, their laughter mounting.

Philippa squeezed her eyes shut. "Mr. Desai!" she screamed. "Please help me!"

Pippa had experienced fear before.

When she was a child, she'd had nightmares. Dark dreams of getting lost in a shadowy wood. Of lying supine on a blanket of moss, a large wooden crate atop her chest, its contents a mystery. As time passed, the chest would shrink in size as it became heavier, until it was a tiny weight threatening to crush her into the earth.

These nightmares had grown worse as her family's situation had deteriorated. Over the years, she'd become well acquainted with the demon of fear, especially when she realized what she must do in order to save her family. Her father had to be stopped, before his threats and vices ruined their lives beyond repair.

Pippa had done what needed to be done to save her little brother and sister.

Her worst fear had come to pass the day she'd concluded she had to leave Lydia and Henry behind in England. That—in order to provide them with a better future—she would have to cause them pain in the present. Nothing in life made Pippa more afraid than abandoning them. That kind of fear was a kind that never died. It ebbed and flowed, but remained constant, serving as an ever-present reminder of what Pippa would lose if she failed.

That fear resided within her. In time, it had become part of her.

But this fear? The fear she was experiencing at this moment?

Pippa had never known fear of this kind in her life. It did not reside within her. It surrounded her, suffocating her, stealing the air and light and warmth from her body.

It was the fear that she might die. And in dying, fail to fulfill not only her promise to Lydia and Henry, but her promise to herself. That she would change her stars. Be in control of her own destiny.

Even when their father had been taken away from them in chains, tossed in the back of a covered wagon with an iron door, Pippa had not felt this afraid. Even when her mother had denounced her. Screamed about betrayal and locked herself in a small room to drown her sorrows in laudanum-spiked tea. Pippa had been left to take care of Lydia and Henry with nothing to their name, but still she had not been this afraid. This fear did not ebb and flow. It only grew, all but consuming her in its wicked jaws.

Inhumanly gorgeous creatures—tall and willowy, with hair and eyes spanning the colors of a rainbow—circled Pippa, their garments like shimmering water, their jewels the size of fruit. Everywhere she looked, she saw eyes that glistened with gleeful malice.

Perhaps this was how a cornered fox felt at the end of a hunt.

It again drove Pippa to recall the advice from her fencing instructor, Mistress Egan:

"If you are ever trapped, do what it is least expected. Be spontaneous."

She'd offered this advice because Pippa's tells were too obvious. As a fencing student, Pippa had often conveyed what she intended to do three strokes before doing it. Her desire to calculate her moves and mitigate risk failed her most in these pivotal moments.

A hand darted toward her in a slicing motion across her arm. A thin stream of crimson trailed after the blade. Pippa yelled, though she did not feel any pain. Now they were drawing blood. Cutting her bare skin. Before she could take stock of her surroundings—of how to begin protecting herself—a large fruit that resembled a bright red apple was heaved in her direction, striking her skirt with a sickening splat. If its aim had been truer, it could have inflicted damage to Pippa's face. To her body.

What did these callous fairies want with her?

Pippa cried out again for help and searched for a weapon.

The circle of cruel captors only tightened, their fingers poking and prodding at Pippa's back. They jabbed her in the stomach. Yanked at her hair. Caressed her cheek. Ran palms down her naked arms.

Touched her without permission, as if she were a helpless creature in a menagerie at the London Zoo. As if Pippa were theirs to do with as they pleased.

The fear became terror. What did they want with her? What were they going to do? She'd made a mistake. Pippa knew that. But did none of these fey possess a heart? A soul? Were they going to *kill* her for this mistake?

Pippa glanced around wildly. Then she spotted a familiar face. Like a light of hope in the yawning darkness. A thread to grasp before drowning in her fear.

Arjun Desai. Of course. The one who'd led her down this fateful path.

Relief flooded through Pippa's body as his hazel eyes fixed on her face. They were like a balm to an open wound. She wanted to fall to the clover carpet and draw her knees to her chest and sob.

Arjun Desai had helped her before. Several times. It was likely the reason Pippa thought of him more than was altogether appropriate for a young woman engaged to another man.

Pippa wanted to say something. To voice her relief and hope their connection might spare her further suffering. To admit how sorry she was for stealing into his flat and following him through the magicked mirror.

But when she opened her mouth to speak, the cad shook his head. Warned her to remain silent.

What? *Why?* And for how long?

Arjun Desai wanted her to trust him. That much was obvious. A part of Pippa wanted to trust him. But when was the last time she'd known what it felt like to trust the word of any man?

Be spontaneous, Philippa Montrose. Stop wavering about and do what they least expect.

Pippa closed her eyes tightly. "Mr. Desai!" she screamed, her voice hoarse. "Please help me!"

Through her tears, Pippa saw Arjun Desai straighten where he stood, his hazel eyes wide.

The next instant, the spark in his gaze turned cold. Almost bleak.

A beardless man in white, his features pointed and narrow and hauntingly beautiful, turned toward Arjun, his pale lips set in a jeer. "You know this pathetic creature, son of Riya?" When Arjun failed to respond, the silver-haired fey's nostrils flared. "You will answer a highborn lord when you are asked a question, halfblood."

Pippa's heart dropped like a stone when she saw the expression of abject boredom on Arjun's face. His hands in his pockets, he sauntered toward her at a leisurely pace. Then he paused to wipe the single lens of his monocle before placing it on his left eye, taking his time, as if he meant to inspect her like a horse at the Drogheda fair.

After studying her through his monocle for a spell, he pursed his lips to one side. Pippa had always thought him handsome, but this was the first occasion she truly noticed the inhuman perfection of his features. The thick arches of his black brows and the honed elegance of his jawline. The cutting edges of his cheekbones and the warm radiance of his copper skin. She wasn't sure how she'd missed it before. Perhaps it was because he'd been in the company of immortal creatures, their beauty unfathomable, even in a city of decadence like New Orleans. Even in a world of light and shadow, where dark things came to life beneath the moon.

If Pippa had a moment to herself, she would laugh at the absurdity. At a time like this, why in Heaven's name was she fixated on the way Arjun Desai looked?

Deep in her thoughts, she started with a sudden realization.

Her heart had ceased pounding in her chest. Now it beat behind her ribs in a steady, unassailable rhythm. As if it believed the worst had passed, now that Arjun Desai was here.

She felt . . . calm.

How absurd. If Pippa could have railed against her foolish heart, she would have. Arjun Desai wasn't a knight on a white horse. He had not leapt to her aid. Why would he protect her from these creatures? What allegiance did he owe her? Pippa averted her gaze, and the fear descended on her again in full force.

What was she to these beautiful creatures, hewn like jewels cut from a nightmare?

The taunting continued around Pippa, long fingers grasping at wayward locks of her hair. At the shredded lace beneath her collarbone. She willed herself to stop crying, for the sight of her tears seemed to delight them further.

Pippa did as she'd done as a child, the night she realized her first hero—her father—had become a villain in truth. She found a way to save herself, if only for an instant.

Whenever the Duke of Ashmore, laden with drink and debt, would stumble home to their dilapidated manor, bellowing for their nonexistent servants, she would retreat into herself. Tuck into a tiny ball deep within her thoughts, to a place no one else could find. To a table with three plates. Three cups. Three smiles.

Pippa. Lydia. Henry.

To a place where they were all safe and warm and loved.

The jeers around Pippa faded to a drone. She began reciting facts to herself, seeking the comfort of truth amid the chaos.

She was in the realm of the fey. Fairies were real, and they were not kind. Her best friend, Celine Rousseau, had been missing for weeks. Pippa was engaged to be married to Phoebus Devereux in less than seventy-two hours.

She needed to find a tare back to New Orleans as soon as possible. Back to that sinisterly beautiful city of vampires and werewolves and otherworldly creatures.

Pippa should have known better than to follow another young man into the unknown. She recalled the night she'd trailed Detective Michael Grimaldi into the swamp and witnessed him change into a wolf beneath the light of the full moon. A full week had passed in disbelief. But she could not deny what she'd seen with her own two eyes. The howls she'd heard with her own two ears. From there, it had not taken long to uncover the identity of the creatures hidden in plain sight in the middle of New Orleans society.

Where werewolves existed, vampires could not be far.

Pippa had suspected what they were even before coming to this conclusion. Victims drained of blood. Skin cool to the touch, as Odette's had been. Incandescent beauty. The kind that did not hail from the mortal world.

She took another deep breath.

Three plates. Three cups. Three smiles.

Pippa. Lydia. Henry.

Her thoughts arranged themselves in neat rows. A renewed sense of calm descended on her, staving off the rising panic. Then something shoved Pippa, startling her from her hard-won peace. Causing the chaos around her to take hold.

She caught herself on her hands just before sprawling across the crushed clovers, her gold cross and the strange necklace of braided iron and silver swinging beneath her chin. Pippa wanted to press into the earth and bury her head like an ostrich, but she refused to give them the satisfaction. Instead she stood once more, her jade skirts stained a deeper hue of green, her fingers smelling of fresh earth.

She looked toward Arjun Desai, her chin pointed high, her heartbeat knocking around in her skull. Again her pulse steadied at the sight of him. As if he were sending her reassurances without words, though he remained apart. Aloof.

Pippa didn't need his silent comfort. She needed him to take action, dash it all. Or at the very least, vouch for her.

"Please, Mr. Desai," Pippa said. "Tell them it was a mistake. I know you don't want them to hurt me. I know you are a good man. Please. Help me."

The same fey woman who had been the first to tear at Pippa's clothes snared her by the elbow and drew her close. "The half-blood can't do anything to save you, little dove." She brandished her right hand, dangling it before Pippa's face. Each of her nails was covered with a bejeweled silver talon, the tip glinting in the light. The fey woman dragged one of the talons along Pippa's cheek. Down her jaw. Pippa's breath caught as she listened to the scratch of metal against her skin.

Quiet laughter swelled around her, its echo sinister. The press of metal continued down her throat until Pippa stopped breathing, worried if she moved, a bejeweled talon would pierce through her flesh.

Pippa looked toward Arjun Desai. Something fired in his expression, though he continued standing there, that same bored look in his gaze, his monocle flashing with the rise and fall of his chest.

The fey woman dug her talons into the thin skin along Pippa's throat.

Pippa gasped, her face turning toward the ceiling of branches. Toward whatever gods might be there to hear her prayers. She waited for the pain, but it did not come. Perhaps her fear had managed to dull her senses.

"Do you think you might die, pretty little mortal?" the fey lady whispered in her ear. "No, no. *It will be much worse.*" Her laughter was like ringing church bells.

Pippa wanted to shudder. To cry out. Warm blood trickled down her neck, soaking through the battered lace along her collar. But she did not flinch, nor did she feel pain. She stared at Arjun Desai. Instead of gripping her skirts in fear, her hands turned into fists, her jaw clenching tightly.

That same something hardened Arjun's features, causing his eyes to flash citrine.

"Her heart is beating like a rabbit in a snare," a male voice said from nearby. The highborn lord with the smooth pale skin and the long silver hair. Everything about him appeared to glow from within. Even the gossamer and gold trimming his garments. "I can hear it from where I stand." He tugged Pippa away from the fey woman and into an embrace, his touch gentle. Belying the chill beneath it. "That's what happens when a mortal feels fear. Their hearts burst from their bodies. But you would know that, wouldn't you, mongrel?"

Pippa realized he was speaking to Arjun Desai. The fey lord's face was angled just so as he continued, "Your mortal father would have taught you that much. Their blood races to their cores to protect their weak little hearts. If I were one of our blood-drinking nemeses, she would look . . . delicious." He breathed in her scent like he could smell her fear, savoring the way she shook in response. Then he smiled wide, as if he enjoyed tormenting Arjun more than he enjoyed tormenting her.

"Do you know this lovely little rabbit, son of Riya?" he asked again in a vicious whisper. "Answer me."

Before Arjun Desai could reply, another set of fingers raked through Pippa's hair, causing the rest of her long blond mane to fall from its careful coif on the crown of her head. The golden curls tumbled over her shoulders and down her back, the blood from the wound along her throat dripping onto the green moss beside her feet.

"What shall we do with you now?" said the fey boy responsible. He looked to be no more than fifteen, despite the pair of ancient silver baldrics crossed on his chest. With a cruel smile, he took hold of Pippa's wrist, tearing her from the grasp of the fey lord with the long white hair. Then he pressed a cool kiss to the underside of her jaw. When he drew back, her blood stained his lips. He reeked of pine needles and something sharp, like smelling salts.

Pippa almost vomited.

Then he shoved her away as if she were poison, a hiss flying from his lips, and a wisp of grey smoke trailing from his neck. He clutched a hand to the side of his throat, anger storming in his luminous eyes.

"A witch's talisman," he said, his voice dripping with rage. "Iron."

Iron? Pippa thought. Was he speaking of the necklace Eloise had made for her?

A fey lady who'd yanked strands of hair from Pippa's head grabbed her by the front of her ripped bodice. "How dare you come to our court wearing that poison?"

"Arjun!" she said, clawing her way free. Staggering backward. It was the first time she'd ever called him by his given name, but standing on propriety at a moment like this seemed ridiculous.

"This little rabbit thinks you might be her hero, son of Riya," repeated the fey lord with the long silver hair. *"Does this mortal mean anything to you?"*

A fey dressed in sunset-colored skirts stepped forward to

place a hand on his shoulder. "Beloved," the fey said to Pippa's silver-haired tormentor. "The girl is frightened. It is enough."

"It is enough when I decide it is enough. If I can't get an answer out of Arjun Desai, then I will do what must be done. She has trespassed on this court, and she will pay the price for it." He caught Pippa's chin. Forced her to look into his inhuman grey eyes. "We will see if that talisman truly does protect you."

"Vyr."

Pippa's breath caught. The fey lord released his grip on her chin.

Arjun Desai took a slow step toward them. As he strode in their direction, the circle around Pippa and the fey lord parted to allow him passage. "While I hate to put a stop to your enjoyment during your own engagement celebration, Lord Vyr," Arjun said in a nonchalant tone, "it might be wise to consult with the Lady of the Vale before you take another plaything under your wing." He offered Pippa a debonair wink, coupled with a grin. "Additionally, I believe this girl is someone of import when it comes to our lady's daughter."

Daughter? About whom was he speaking? Confusion knitted Pippa's brow.

"As I told you before, mongrel, neither Lady Silla nor Lady Celine is at court this afternoon," Lord Vyr retorted. "In their absence, I rule the Ivy Bower."

Celine was a lady of the fey court? And apparently a highborn one, at that. Pippa almost gasped, a spark of anger stirring in her veins. Of course she was. And of course Pippa was the last person to learn this truth.

"Beloved," the fey in the sunset skirts said in a quiet, calm voice. Almost as if the word were a warning. "Please. Let us return to our celebrations. This amusement has gone on long enough. Seek to help, not to hurt."

A half smile curved up one side of Arjun's face. "Listen to your intended, Vyr. And, if memory serves, you are not the only ruler of the court in the absence of the Lady of the Vale." He rubbed the side of his neck while he yawned. "Perhaps you should consult with Lady Yulin before you do something rash."

"Your attempt to seem blithe is all too obvious, Arjun Desai," Lord Vyr demanded. "This pathetic little mortal knows you."

"I told you." The anger in Arjun's words was almost imperceptible. But Pippa could sense it, buried deep beneath the apathy. A strange lilt to his tone. A tinge of violence. "She means something to Lady Celine," Arjun said, "and I would hate to upset Lady Silla by disrespecting her daughter's acquaintance."

Vyr inhaled through his nose. But did not remove his arm from about Pippa's waist. "You lie all too freely. For the time being, I will keep this golden-headed poppet in my care." A grin ghosted across his lips. "And we will wait to see if the little intruder's fate matters to Lady Silla."

Arjun raised a flippant shoulder, though he took another stride forward. "Vyr, I think it best—"

"I lay claim to this human," Lord Vyr said, his tone tyrannical, as if he were making a royal decree. "She is mine."

Indignation collected on Pippa's tongue. A fury tinged by fear, which was, in her experience, among the most dangerous of emotions. She kept quiet, though it was not without effort. Arjun Desai must be playing some sort of game. Pippa wanted to believe he was forming a plan to help her. Perhaps he was slow to react in an effort to buy them some time.

Was she a ninny for thinking that?

An uneasy silence settled on the crowd. Arjun blinked once. Twice, his expression still unreadable. Lord Vyr smiled. Something about the fey reminded Pippa of her fiancé Phoebus' father. The son of political royalty in Louisiana, Remy Devereux had been raised to believe he was entitled to whatever his heart desired. He often took things that were not offered. Fought to hold them at all cost. Ruled over his family with an iron fist.

The fey lord and Arjun Desai exchanged daggered glances.

"No, Vyr," said the fey woman with the jeweled talons, a pout tugging at her lower lip. "You have all the fun. I want this one."

Pippa paled at this woman's notion of fun. "Please, I—"

"You lack the imagination for such a task, Inaya." Vyr grinned. "If you don't dance, do you sing?" he asked Pippa.

She swallowed. Then shook her head.

"Pity," he sighed. "If you can't sing or dance, then we will find something to occupy your time." He laughed. "Take her to my chambers." He gestured for grey-cloaked warriors holding lustrous white spears to follow his orders, his hold on Pippa slackening. "And do away with that iron affront of a talisman."

"No," Pippa said, wrenching free. Before anyone could blink, she tore a dagger from among the many displayed on the nearby fey lord's silver baldrics. "I'm not going anywhere with any of you."

One of the grey-cloaked warriors flourished her spear at Pippa in warning. A slight young woman with a long plait of dark hair and a fearsome countenance. "Put down the blade, mortal whelp."

"No," Pippa replied. "I will not." She brandished the dagger in her right hand like an épée, her feet assuming a fencing stance as she moved in a slow circle, daring any of them to come closer, just as Mistress Egan had taught her many years ago.

"How . . . amusing," Lord Vyr said. "Yuri, I believe this whelp thinks—"

"You ruin everything," Arjun announced with a protracted sigh. He moved toward Pippa, pushing past the grey-cloaked guard. Within striking distance of Pippa's blade. For an instant, she considered burying it deep in his back, a fresh wave of fury unfurling beneath her skin.

"It's truly your greatest talent, Lord Vyr," Arjun said. "To ruin things."

"What are you talking about, mongrel?" Vyr demanded.

"The reason the girl is here is to meet my mother," Arjun said, staring at Pippa without blinking. Speaking to the crowd without any sign of hesitation.

Willing Pippa to play along with his game.

"You've forced our hand, Vyr," Arjun continued. "When all we wanted was to surprise everyone with the news." Then he smiled at Pippa with such unrestrained affection, Pippa could only manage to stare back dumbfounded.

News? What news? Unease trickled down her spine.

Arjun nodded. "She can't be yours. Because she is mine. And I am hers."

What? Pippa stifled an incredulous cry.

"We are to be married," Arjun said. "Philippa Montrose is my bride."

THE COURSE OF TRUE LOVE NEVER
DID RUN SMOOTH.

A MIDSUMMER NIGHT'S DREAM,

WILLIAM SHAKESPEARE

———◆•◆———

S ilence descended around the Ivy Bower in a sudden hush.
Every imaginable oath Arjun could conjure threatened to
burst from his lips. A silent scream echoed within him, the rage
all but choking the air from his chest.

He wanted to rail to the skies. He wanted to wrap Philippa
Montrose in his warmest cloak and carry her far from here . . .
then dump her on the banks of the churning Mississippi and
demand an explanation. How could she be so foolhardy? How
could she have followed him through the tare? Did no sense of
imminent danger occur to her? Did she just wander around the
world with light and love and a crackling fire warming her
heart?

These sodding memsahibs with their sodding breakfast tea.
Unbelievable! Arjun almost shouted.

Arjun wanted to do more than lecture. For the first time in
his life, he understood what his father meant when he'd said
Arjun was due for a good spanking.

Emotion swelled in his chest. He wanted to yell. Break things.
Ennui. Complete ennui.

He straightened. Forced the rising tempest to settle. Once

more Arjun lifted his monocle to his left eye and peered at Philippa Montrose through the magicked lens. Around her swirled the orange color of confusion. The dusky hue of fear, ribboned with the pure white of righteousness. And . . . strangely . . . a flicker of brilliant red anger.

She was angry?

She wasn't the one who'd just pledged her troth to someone she barely knew. His one and only chance to wed, wasted on Phoebus Devereux's meddling fiancée. Well, at least Arjun could not detect any traces of swirling darkness in Philippa Montrose. The staining ink of subterfuge or the murk of deception. He supposed that should make him feel better. Somewhat.

Goddamn it all.

What in hell did she have to be angry about? He was trying to save her lily-white life.

The question remained: would it work?

Arjun knew it was a gamble. Vyr and the rest of the court may not believe him. They may suspect he only wished to protect Pippa, which was true. If Arjun had more time, perhaps he could have devised a better plan. But—as was the case of late—time had become his greatest enemy. To spare her their cruelty, the best he could do was kill her. Or marry her.

Something told him Philippa Montrose would not take kindly to the former suggestion.

Offering to marry her was not without risk. Even if they managed to convince the court they were earnestly in love and intending to wed, there was a strong chance it would make no difference. Arjun's safety alone was a tenuous matter, especially since he'd given up his place at court. To many of the fey present, that meant Arjun was fair game now. He'd renounced his place among them—turned his back on their world—which ranked him barely above a mortal in their eyes.

He supposed his mother's name could put a stop to the worst of their machinations. But would that protection extend to Arjun's mortal bride? Only time, that cursed thing, would tell.

Now, for better or for worse, he was set to wed. Another fool in love.

Arjun wanted to laugh like a madman. Then, as if his innermost thoughts had been shared with everyone present, a burst of laughter exploded from the shadows. It spread like wildfire, until the entire bower echoed with the sounds of unabashed mirth.

"General Riya's only son has fallen in love with a mortal girl," Ratana said with glee, as her sister, Sinora, glared at Arjun, proverbial smoke emitting from her ears. "How rich!"

Another fey lady guffawed. "The general will murder him. Dismember him. Feed his bones to the ice vultures on the borders of the Wyld."

"How delicious." A fey liege cackled. "After all General Riya's patient lectures, her son failed to learn anything from his mother's painful past. A mortal lover? What a delightful pity!"

"Perhaps she will disown him," said Lord Evandyr, his twin silver baldrics flashing. "Then we can show him what it's like to be in the Vale without her protection." His boyish features stretched wide with wicked intent, the iron burn on the side of his throat already turning black.

Evandyr was younger than Arjun. At first glance, he appeared to be no more than a mortal boy of fourteen or fifteen, with sharply pointed ears and sun-kissed skin. He still had yet to reach full maturation, a time when he would cease aging and assume his forever form. Though he looked like a boy, Evandyr considered himself Arjun's superior. His parents were not even members of the Fey Guild.

Arjun's mother was the chief huntress of the Vale. Lady Silla's foremost general, second only to herself. And still this little ignoramus had the nerve to mistreat him.

"Protection?" Arjun said with a grin. "How amusing. I often think of the importance of protection when I look at you, Evandyr. A cundum. A French letter. *Anything.*"

From his periphery, Arjun saw Philippa Montrose's mouth fall agape. He doubted anyone in polite company had ever mentioned anything to do with coitus in her presence.

Evandyr blinked. "What?"

"Lady Evandril should have used protection the night she spawned you," Arjun said.

"Are you . . . insulting my mother?" Evandyr sputtered. "I demand satisfaction."

"No doubt you hear those words often," Arjun continued with a grin. "Alas, I am not going to duel with you. I have bread to bake and a life to live."

"If you are too cowardly to duel, halfblood, then I demand an apology."

"But of course." Arjun bowed, his arms outstretched on either side. "I'm sorry you were born."

Evandyr ripped two daggers from the silver baldric across his chest and lunged at Arjun.

With a knowing grin, Arjun sidestepped the attack and grasped Evandyr by his wrist. The boy's glower smoothed, his eyes widening slowly. Arjun released him with a smirk. Evandyr stood frozen in place, his features immobilized in a mixture of fury and dismay.

"You always forget, don't you?" Arjun whispered. "My mortal father granted me these dastardly good looks. And my fey mother gave me the touch that freezes the blood in your veins." Then he turned to Pippa and held out the same hand.

"Are you *mad*?" Philippa croaked, staring down at his palm, the color draining from her face.

"Oh," Arjun said. "I won't hurt you. I promise." Again he extended his hand.

"A likely story," Philippa cried. "You—you turned him into a statue, with nothing but your bare hand."

"You burned him with an iron talisman, and he's no more the worse for the wear," Arjun said. "He'll be fine. At least he will be . . . in, say, ten minutes." He held out his hand once again, insistent. Damn it all. He was trying to keep her safe. He'd just offered to *marry* her.

Yet Philippa still refused to take his help, her dagger raised in his direction.

"How amusing!" Lady Ratana clapped. "Your bride appears rather reticent, Lord Arjun. Should make for an interesting wedding night. Tell me, *Lady* Philippa"—she paused to snicker behind her hand—"will you be bringing your little sword with you to bed?"

The crowd tittered.

"One of us should," Philippa said through gritted teeth.

Before anyone could say a word in response, Arjun threw back his head and laughed. Philippa Montrose had a sense of humor. He was glad of it. She would need it now, more than ever. Being his wife would demand it of her.

"What is so amusing?" Ratana demanded.

"It doesn't translate," Arjun said. "Suffice to say, I'm pleased with my bride."

"Indeed," Vyr said, a brow crooking into his forehead. "Your . . . bride? How convenient."

Arjun shifted closer to Philippa, his hand itching to pull her against him. To keep her safe. Frustratingly, she shrank away from his touch a fourth time. Again Arjun wanted to scold her. He nearly did, but then the smallest flicker of fear crossed her features.

He understood why Philippa would feel afraid. Of course she would rebuff his pitiful attempts to reassure her. She'd just been manhandled through a crowd of merciless fey. And he thought his own touch would be reassuring? In a pig's eye, perhaps. So instead Arjun looked in her eyes, beseeching her without words to take his lead.

"I can see how this would seem convenient for me," Arjun said to Vyr. "Just as I could see how it would be rather inconvenient for you."

"For as long as I've known you, you've taken no small pains to mock the sacredness of the Rite at every turn." Vyr peered down his nose at Arjun. Then at Philippa. "Why would I believe you to be earnest now?"

Arjun remained straight-faced. "Why should I care whether you believe me or not?"

"You know how we treat this bond," Vyr said.

"I do."

"It is not meant to be tossed aside at the first sign of distress. To be treated as a lark, like it is in the mortal world."

"I know." Arjun nodded, unfazed. In fact, he knew this truth better than most of the fey did. His mother's loyalty to her mortal husband—a man she'd left behind in Bombay, his memories of their life together erased for all time—extended beyond any mere words or promises. To this day, General Riya would not speak directly of Arjun's father, even to her own son. But she still wore his ring on a golden chain around her neck.

And to the knowledge of those at court, she had taken no lovers since.

Arjun and Vyr glared at each other through their smiles, while Philippa bit her lower lip. Arjun did not have to glance down to realize her grasp on the dagger had tightened, the tips of her fingers bloodless.

Vyr quirked his lips to one side, then gazed about at the fey gentry surrounding them as if he were trying to determine his next move. His eyes fell on the lovely face of his intended, Liege Sujee.

Sujee nodded as if to encourage him, a kind smile on their face.

"A marriage bond forged through the Rite is not meant to be broken, even in death," Vyr continued.

Exasperated, Arjun nodded. "I am aware," he repeated through clenched teeth.

"And are you, little mortal?" said the fey lady behind Vyr. "Do you know how precious we hold our vows?" She arched at brow at Philippa.

Arjun turned to his future bride, unflinching. Continuing to will her without words. If she agreed to marry him, he would keep faith, especially if it ensured her safety. Of course he would not hold her to these promises in the mortal world. No human should be forced to honor a vow made under duress. It wasn't an ideal engagement, but—if Arjun *had* to marry one day—the best he could hope was to protect his bride in doing so.

With each thought that unraveled in his mind, Arjun felt more certain of this path forward. Or perhaps he was simply convincing himself that a terrible decision was for the best in that delightfully delusional way of mortals.

"Do you know how sacred our Rite is?" Vyr asked Philippa. "And don't look to the halfblood for cues. Stand on your own two feet."

Something flashed across her features. A mixture of anger and fear. Philippa nodded once. Chewed at the inside of her cheek. "I do."

"You willingly enter this union?" the fey lady behind Vyr pressed.

Another breath of silence. Philippa nodded again. Once more, Vyr looked to Liege Sujee.

"Seek to help," Vyr murmured as if in thought. "Not to hurt."

What happened next made Arjun want to deck Vyr in the face. A sense of serenity took shape on Vyr's features. His entire demeanor shifted, reminding Arjun of a chameleon changing color, donning the darkest of intentions. "How fortuitous. Come now, let us all rejoice together." Vyr turned toward his betrothed. "This gathering is no longer merely a toast to my engagement to Liege Sujee. We will raise our glasses to *two* engagements this night! A double celebration." His smile was wide and brilliant.

Liege Sujee beamed, their hands clapping together with unrestrained pride.

It wasn't possible for love to change a fey for the better. Arjun's father had tried for years. Begged his wife to forgo her ambitions for their son in the Summer Court and be content with their life together. For a while, it had worked. For seven years, they'd lived in Bombay, and Arjun had known nothing of his mother's origins. To him, she was simply Amma. His mother, who sang to him in a voice that could charm Ravana himself. It was true she didn't smile often, but she read to Arjun every night and told him stories of fantastic beasts and fearsome demons and creatures who dwelled in the deep. For seven years, she seemed at peace. She'd looked at Arjun's father the way Sujee looked at Vyr. Sang to herself when she thought no one was listening.

Alas, Arjun soon learned that it was difficult to shake an ambitious spirit.

As these memories swirled through Arjun's mind, his

attention fixed on Philippa Montrose. He wondered what she might be thinking. Though she appeared disheveled—her clothing torn and her face smudged—it was impossible to ignore her beauty. The quintessential English rose, Philippa's skin shone luminous, her lashes long and dark, the faintest sprinkle of freckles dusting her nose. She was like a nymph from a Welsh fairy tale.

Though she'd always struck Arjun as mild-mannered, there had been several occasions in which he'd detected a hint of something else. A kind of burning righteousness. After witnessing her tireless efforts to watch over those she loved, Arjun suspected Philippa to be the sort of person who unfailingly honored her commitments. A girl who refused to abandon her ideals.

It would not be easy to convince a young woman like her that their engagement in the Vale should have no bearing on her plans to wed Phoebus once they returned to New Orleans.

It did not matter. What was done was done. An engagement was not a wedding, after all. In fact, if Arjun played his cards well, there was a chance they might not need to marry for quite some time. After their engagement was formalized, perhaps decades could pass in the mortal realm before the court remembered. The most important thing was Philippa's safety. Once they were engaged, the gentry would hopefully allow her to leave, and Arjun could deposit her through the first tare into New Orleans.

If memory served, there was a tare in an oak tree a league west from his mother's lakeside abode. He might have to chase away the lizardlike ryu guarding it or offer a gumiho one of his mother's prized pearls, which were candy to the deceptively sweet fox spirits. But those were small prices to pay.

He hoped the ryu didn't spew acid. The last one he'd encountered nearly melted off his toes.

Arjun smiled wide. Raised his empty glass. And toasted his impending engagement.

A strange pang cut through his stomach.

He'd never believed he would get married, so why should it matter? It would be trouble enough to convince Philippa that their engagement did not mean anything. Arjun hoped he wouldn't have to convince himself. She should return to New Orleans and live a long mortal life as Phoebus Devereux's wife, with a passel of kids at her feet. This would not bother Arjun in the least. Long ago, he'd sworn never to have children of his own.

Another strange twinge sliced through his gut.

Once the cheers died down—the crystal glasses continuing to shimmer in the rays of filtered light—Vyr turned to Arjun with another slow grin, his lips stretched over his teeth.

Bleeding gods. This was not good. Arjun's heart began to pound, its beat sonorous.

Again Vyr raised his glass. "I have taken a moment to confer with my beloved, and we wish to extend these celebrations further. Since we are all in such a jubilant mood, I thought it prudent to suggest to my intended that we move the date of our wedding forward . . . to tomorrow afternoon."

Another round of cheers followed this announcement.

Thump. Thump. Thump.

Arjun's pulse throbbed in his temples. *This madarchod.*

Vyr directed his gaze to Arjun and Pippa. "My beloved has brought it to my attention that I have not always been kind to my ethereal brother, Arjun Desai."

No. No. No.

"I wish to make amends," Vyr announced, his delight shining like stars in the firmament.

Arjun lifted his glass and returned the fey lord's shit-eating grin. "That is not necessary, my brother."

"Nonetheless, I insist. Liege Sujee and I wish to make a gift of hosting your wedding celebration to the mortal, Philippa Montrose," Vyr announced. "My esteemed brethren, tomorrow we shall have a double wedding. No expense will be spared! The food, the libations, the décor, and—of course—the wedding garments will be the finest in the history of the Vale. Send word far and wide, for it shall be the event of the season!"

"No," Philippa gasped, the newest round of cheers drowning out her dismay. She reached for Arjun's forearm and squeezed, her pale fingers blanching.

Fuck. Fuck. Fuck.

Though Arjun clung to his smile, the blood rose hot and fast in his face. For an instant, he saw red. He dreamed red. He thought about cleaning the revolver he'd left at his mother's home. Of fitting an iron bullet into each of its six chambers. Of taking aim at Vyr's smug face. And firing round after round after round.

Instead Arjun ignored Philippa's panicked entreaty and cheered alongside them. It would do no good to protest. That was exactly what Vyr wanted him to do. So Arjun raised his glass even higher. "Our gratitude knows no bounds, Lord Vyr. Your and Liege Sujee's generosity will not soon be forgotten." He clasped Philippa's hand, conveying without words for her to rest assured. It did not matter what Vyr said. As soon as possible, they would take their leave of court and make their way to the tare on the outskirts of his mother's land. Philippa Montrose would be gone from the Vale within the hour. Arjun vowed it. He made a silent promise that he would do whatever he must to en—

She tore her hand from his. "I . . ." Philippa cleared her throat, her voice rising above the clamor. "While I thank you for your generosity, Lord Vyr, I truly do not feel right agreeing to marry Arjun Desai without his mother's blessing."

Arjun had to admit it was an admirable attempt, by any mortal's standards.

"It is unnecessary." Vyr waved his hand. "We do not follow such mortal protocols in the Vale."

She continued, "But I—"

"If I promise to send a missive that will reach General Riya by this evening, will you grant me a promise of your own in return?" Vyr's tone was eager. Too eager.

Alarm coursed through Arjun's body. Vyr was baiting Philippa. She had no idea that the fey in the Vale considered promises to be bound in blood. He had to put a stop to this. Again Arjun tried to tug Philippa close, to beseech her not to say another word. With a glare, she batted away his hand, her irritation palpable. As if he were a bee buzzing around her head.

"Philippa," he said under his breath, "darling, I—"

"I promise to grant your request, so long as no harm comes to me or anyone else," she said, her tone firm. "And in return, you must promise to send word to General Riya with all haste."

Arjun pursed his lips, swallowing back another round of colorful oaths.

"But of course!" Vyr announced like a rooster crowing to the dawn. "I promise I will send our fastest messenger to the Moon Rabbit's Grove with a letter for General Riya tonight, informing her of our joint wedding celebration tomorrow, and in return, Philippa and Arjun Desai will remain in the Ivy Bower until the ceremony, as the court's esteemed guests."

"Wh-what?" Philippa blinked.

"You simply must," Vyr continued without missing a beat. "That way our most illustrious tailors have enough time to fit you both for your wedding garments."

"The Tylwyth Tegge are our best." Sujee beamed.

Arjun held up a hand. "Though we are honored by your generosity, I'm afraid we must decline."

"You'd prefer the Menehunes?" Sujee mused, their elegant fingers resting on their pointed chin. "I'm told their star is on the rise."

"No," Arjun said, his jaw clenching. "I fear we must decline to celebrate our wedding jointly with yours."

A knowing gleam flashed in Vyr's gaze. "Why? As I stated earlier, your mother's permission is unnecessary."

"As *I* stated earlier, I would like General Riya to meet Philippa before our Rite takes place."

"Interesting. I never thought you cared about your mother's wishes before."

"Before, I wasn't choosing a bride." Arjun grinned.

"I see." Vyr swirled the mystwine in his gilded goblet, his features thoughtful.

Philippa cleared her throat. "If I may, I would also like to see Lady Celine. It would be nice to have her standing by my side for my wedding. It wouldn't seem right for me to marry without anyone I consider family present to mark the occasion."

Vyr canted his head as he considered Philippa.

Another admirable attempt to delay the inevitable. Arjun knew without having to consult his monocle that Philippa was confused. Bewildered. Angry and afraid. Yet she continued to keep her wits about her. Refused to be a pawn. She would make a perfect bride for Phoebus Devereux, though her wits would likely be wasted on the poor sod. Maybe one day Remy Devereux would come to appreciate them, though Arjun doubted it.

"There you have it," Arjun said. "Our marriage rite can wait until their return."

Vyr nodded slowly. "I suppose you are correct."

Arjun's eyes narrowed. "I beg pardon?" He hadn't expected Vyr to capitulate so soon.

"Under normal circumstances," Vyr continued, "I'd be inclined to agree. But . . . your bride did make a promise to me, and I cannot forswear my own vow. I am bound by blood to send word to General Riya about our joint marriage celebrations by this evening. And you are bound to remain in the Ivy Bower as our guests until the ceremony." The gleam in his gaze shone with an evil light. "So, you see, I'm afraid we are all bound by our promises. I'm sure you understand, Lord Arjun." He turned again to the crowd, the corners of his eyes crinkling. "Let us toast once more to the greatest nuptial celebration this court has seen in an age!"

Amid the renewed cheers, Arjun groaned inwardly. Pressed his hands to his temples. Ignored the look of horror on his bride's face.

What was it Lord Asterly of Wetherbourne used to say?

Oh yes. *Checkmate, mate.*

———◆●◆———

A wave of panic threatened to swallow Pippa whole. Silently she counted her footsteps in an absurd attempt to maintain her bearings. Her eyes flitted overhead to study a corridor formed of neatly packed earth, its arched ceiling supported by columns of twisted tree roots. Every so often, a globe of light would wink from behind a column, as if it were a candle flame dancing in a passing breeze.

Ahead of her, Arjun Desai walked with assured strides, leading her toward . . . where exactly?

She hoped he'd devised a way to return her to New Orleans with all haste. Obviously her foolish promise to Lord Vyr prevented them from leaving immediately, when eyes could be upon them. But once the fey court returned to their respective chambers for the evening, she and Arjun could take cover under darkness and return to New Orleans. There was simply no possible way Arjun Desai would actually marry Pippa. If they wed in the land of the fey, would they be forced to remain here? He had a life back home, just as she did. Surely he would never agree to such a thing. Besides that, Pippa was already promised in marriage to Phoebus. She had no intention of being forced to wed anyone else.

This was all a ruse. An elegant ruse to throw the fey court off their scent, so Pippa and Arjun could make their way back where they belonged.

Pippa swallowed the bile. Ignored the acidic taste of her unquenched anger. Anger she held at all that had transpired. At each of the fey who had tormented her. But most of all, anger she felt toward herself.

What had she done? What had she allowed Arjun Desai to do?

What would become of her? It had taken a great deal of effort for Pippa to persuade Aunt Imogen to care for Lydia and Henry until the next holiday season, let alone for the rest of their lives. Pippa had promised to return by winter to take her brother and sister to their new home in America. One where they would be safe and wanted.

If Pippa failed, would Aunt Imogen return Lydia and Henry to their mother, a woman who could barely care for herself?

She swallowed again, her fingers clutching her torn skirts, nausea raking through her stomach. For the hundredth time, Pippa wondered what could have possessed her to walk through that confounded mirror. Pippa could blame Eloise Henri, but she knew it wasn't Eloise's fault. The girl may have struck the match, but Pippa had offered up the kindling.

As a child, Pippa had watched her father blame others for his own misdeeds, as if he were perpetually the victim of his own life story. He drank because his wife drove him to it, the nasty creature. He gambled because he had to find a way to provide for the endless needs of his children, since his own father had failed to afford their estate an adequate living. He chased lightskirts because all the women in his life were cold shrews. And didn't he deserve a measure of love after all his suffering?

On and on it went. Never once did His Grace Richard Montrose, Duke of Ashmore, accept responsibility for any of it.

It had taught Pippa a valuable lesson. If she saw herself as a victim, she would forever be trapped in a cage of her own making. She and she alone must be responsible for the course of her life. Her well-being and the safety of her siblings hung in the balance. As such, Pippa could not afford to be anything less than perfect. The perfect young woman. The perfect sister. The perfect friend. The perfect future wife.

Some days the burden was heavier than others.

Pippa stopped midstride. Her eyes squeezed shut, her hands continuing to shake, the fury and fear at constant war in her mind.

"Don't give in to it," Arjun said. His words were harsh, but his tone was kind. "It will do you no good." He shifted closer. Pippa could sense his nearness. Alas, it failed to calm her as it had before. "Focus instead on the next step," he continued in a whisper, "and believe that you will survive the one after that and the one after—"

"Stop," Pippa said, the trembling reaching her jaw. "Please. Don't speak."

"I'm only trying to—"

"Stop!" Pippa covered her ears, her teeth chattering. "If you keep speaking, I will scream."

"That's an irrational reaction." His brow furrowed. "I'm sure you have questions, and rest assured that I have a few of my own, first and foremost is how in hell you managed to—"

Pippa launched herself at Arjun Desai, her small fists raised. All she wanted was for him to stop talking. If he would just keep quiet, she could grant her mind the time it needed to determine a path forward. But he hadn't listened.

She caught sight of Arjun Desai's shock, even through her fury. Whatever he'd been expecting, it wasn't this. Before she managed to land more than a single blow, he caught her wrists in either hand.

"I warned you," she raged, allowing the full breadth of her temper to find purchase for the first time since she'd wandered into this horrorland. "I told you not to continue speaking." She tried to pull free of his grasp, but he held firm. "You wouldn't listen. Why is it that men never listen?" Her elbow caught him in the ribs. His grip only tightened, despite his sharp intake of breath.

Pippa stomped on his foot.

"Bloody hell," he shouted, shock causing his jaw to drop and his hold to slacken. "You're—"

"Furious," Pippa finished, her voice low. She shoved him away.

"Why in God's name would you be angry with me? I've done nothing but try to help."

"*Nothing* is the perfect word for what you've done." She pointed at the cuts along her neck. "Is this your idea of help?"

"That is nothing. Believe me. They've done far worse to mortals they care not a whit about."

Alarm flared around Pippa's heart, yet she persisted. "You let them peck at me and frighten me and threaten me, and still you don't think I have reason to be angry?"

"You didn't exactly grant me time to devise a plan," he ground out. "Thank you very much, by the way, for breaking into my flat and coming here. *Uninvited.*"

"How was I to know where you were going? I thought you might be meeting Celine and Bastien. She's been missing for so long, and I wanted to make sure she was safe. Is that so difficult to understand?"

"Do you have a habit of going God-knows-where on naught but a whim?"

"Do *you* have a habit of promising yourself in marriage to a girl you barely—"

Arjun covered her mouth with one hand and drew her close. He glared at her, his body pressed against hers in a rather shocking manner. He smelled clean. Like freshly washed linen and something warm. A winter spice. Pippa's pulse started to race when she realized she'd never been held by a man while in such a state. Her dress was torn, and her undergarments were visible. The bare skin of her collarbone brushed the cool jacquard of his waistcoat. When he took in a breath, Pippa inhaled as well. The sensation was of their bodies pressed together . . . most unnerving.

Completely inappropriate.

Pippa nearly bit his palm until she saw his eyes. They flashed with emotion, then slid slowly from side to side, as if to remind her.

Anyone—or anything—might be listening.

Pippa exhaled through her nose. Forced her shoulders to relax. Then nodded.

"You promise?" he whispered.

Her eyes narrowed, but she nodded again.

He drew back. Her trembling began to abate. Arjun Desai paused to clean the lens of his monocle, a motion Pippa recognized as a means to pass time when he was uncomfortable. He perched the lens on his right eye, and Pippa caught herself in its reflection. She looked like a maiden warrior from the Scottish Highlands, her unbound hair in disarray, the blue of her irises sharp. The color deepened when Arjun tilted his head to one side. His lips parted as if he wished to say something. Then he pressed them shut, cleared his throat, and offered her a single nod.

"Shall we?" he said, extending her his arm.

"How polite," Pippa muttered. She took his proffered arm. "Thank you."

"Don't thank me, pet. Not yet."

That tinge of threat lingered in the air as she walked alongside Arjun through the earthen structure he'd referred to as the Ivy Bower. The deeper they roamed through the labyrinth, the more Pippa began to notice the twinkling orbs around them. They seemed to gather in groups, their size ranging from that of a chicken egg to a grown man's fist. The baubles of golden light floated as if they were beneath the water, bobbing slowly above her head. On occasion, one would drift downward, hovering beside her hand, but always beyond reach.

"Wisps," Arjun said grimly. "Don't ask them any questions. Don't even acknowledge their presence. They're eager to help, though their idea of help remains to be seen."

A wisp floated closer. If Pippa stretched out her fingers, she could touch it. A part of her felt drawn to its warmth; nevertheless, she eased away. "They won't burn me, will they?" she whispered. "Or . . . eat me?"

He snorted. "No. But they will follow you around for days, like puppies starved for attention."

Puppies! Pippa stopped short with a gasp. "Queen Elizabeth!"

Arjun pivoted in place, his expression bemused. "What?" He quirked a brow. "Is that supposed to be some kind of newfangled oath?"

"No," Pippa said. "I'm speaking of *my* Queen Elizabeth."

"*Your* Queen Elizabeth?" He cast her an arched glance. "Does the Virgin Queen have designs on returning from the dead?"

"I have a corgi puppy at home."

"Of course you do." He frowned, then resumed walking, his strides purposeful.

"I need to feed her."

Arjun groaned. "By all means, add it to our list of most-pressing concerns."

"You employ sarcasm when you're vexed," Pippa said. "I don't care for it."

"Forgive me while I change my tone," he retorted before continuing down the dimly lit corridor.

"Queen Elizabeth is in my charge, and I don't wish to cause her any undue stress."

"Of course you would be the one to put the needs of your dog above your own."

"You speak as if that is the wrong thing to do. Selflessness is a virtue, is it not?"

"A virtue of fools," he said with a sigh. "Have some sense of self-preservation, Philippa Montrose."

"Pippa. I've asked you before to call me Pippa." She raced to match his strides. "And my self-preservation is well intact, I assure you." She dropped her voice until it was barely audible. "You do have plans to leave once everyone is asleep, do you not?"

He pursed his lips and said nothing.

She blinked. "I was under the impression we were guests here," she whispered. "Are guests not allowed to leave?"

Arjun laughed. "You made a promise. Remember?"

She blinked again. "But I thought we were—"

"You heard Lord Vyr. Promises are blood-bound in the Vale."

Fear struck a cold chord beside Pippa's heart. "Does that mean we must—"

"I'm working on a solution," Arjun interjected in a voice more breath than sound. His gaze flicked upward, toward the wisps, his expression filled with warning.

Pippa understood what he meant. The wisps answered questions. Which meant they gave information to anyone who asked for it. Which *then* meant that the corridors of the Ivy Bower were patrolled at all times by these glowing spies.

Pippa hurried in his footsteps, causing the drifting wisps to scatter toward the arched ceiling. Was she actually going to have to marry Arjun Desai? But what about Phoebus? Not to mention Henry and Lydia! Of all the things she'd considered about being trapped here, not once had she believed her engagement to Arjun Desai to be serious, for he couldn't possibly wish to be attached to her in such an enduring fashion.

What would happen to Pippa if she were to break her promise to remain here until the wedding celebration? What would the fey court do? Would the penalty fall on her shoulders alone, or would Arjun be forced to bear it as well? How would they find her if she were to return to New Orleans? Surely their reach could not extend that far.

Pippa allowed her shoulders to relax. This marriage would never take place. Arjun said he was working on a solution. She should have faith that he, at the very least, was invested in not tying himself to her for the rest of their foreseeable lives.

She lifted her chin.

Tomorrow morning she would be back in the Crescent City in time for her wedding the following day to Phoebus Devereux. His father might have questions about her whereabouts, but from their perspective, she'd only been missing a single evening. Pippa could say she'd gone to visit a friend. While on her journey, perhaps she'd been waylaid by . . . pirates?

Pippa took another deep breath. "Did you know," she said, "that the most successful pirate in history was a woman from the Guangdong Province?"

Arjun stopped dead in his tracks. Pivoted in place, his mouth set into a thin line, a groove etched between his brows.

He said nothing.

"It's in China," Pippa continued without flinching. "Her name was Ching Shih." When he did not avert his gaze from hers, Pippa set her jaw.

His lips twitched. He opened his mouth to reply.

Pippa's stomach growled, the sound echoing into the tree branches above. "Botheration," she muttered while covering her midsection with both hands, as if that would quell her hunger.

Arjun's stare turned thoughtful as he batted away a hovering wisp.

"I'm sorry?" Exasperation punctuated Pippa's apology. "It's not as though I can control it."

"When was the last time you ate?"

She held up her hands. "I don't need to eat anything. Contrary to what you might think, I don't enjoy being a nuisance, and I'll be fine without food for a single evening. It wouldn't be the first time."

"You've gone to bed hungry before?"

"Yes."

A pause. "Have you done that often?" he asked softly.

"That's none of your concern," she said, her tone clipped. "In any case, I refuse to be more of a nuisance."

Arjun mussed the black hair on top of his head. "You will be much more of a nuisance if you wait until you're famished and eat or drink the first thing you see." With that, he began backtracking down the maze of hallways at a rapid pace, causing a quartet of wisps to retreat to the eaves in a scurry. He marched without stopping, Pippa chasing his heels, until he halted before a set of double doors constructed of what appeared to be solid silver vines, their large leaves overlapping like the feathers on the wings of a bird.

Arjun turned toward Pippa and said, "I suppose now is as good a time as any to tell you there are rules by which you must abide while here in the Sylvan Vale."

"Of course." She straightened like a soldier and smoothed the front of her ruined green dress. "You needn't worry. Under normal circumstances, I'm not one for breaking rules."

His laughter was sharp and loud.

"I didn't realize Eloise planned to steal into your flat," Pippa protested. "I only went with her because I wished to learn what became of Celine."

"Eloise Henri!" Arjun choked, his thick brows shadowing his features. "I should have known. I suppose she's the one who fashioned that protection talisman around your neck?" He exhaled. "She did at least one thing right, then," he grumbled.

From his tone, it was clear Arjun had more to say on the matter. Perhaps when they were afforded some privacy. Pippa would be glad of it. She, too, had much she wished to say. She desperately wanted to speak with Celine. To make sure her dear friend was all right and to understand why Celine had left with Bastien in such a hurry, without giving word to anyone who cared.

But none of this could be said now. Not with so many . . . ears so close by.

Did wisps have ears? Voices? How did they speak?

Pippa and Arjun exchanged glances. "You mentioned rules?" she said.

"Right." He nodded. "The first and most important one is this: when in doubt, the answer is no."

"Pardon me?"

Arjun stepped toward Pippa and tucked his hands into his pockets. "If you're wondering, should I touch that prickly flower with the most intoxicating scent I've ever smelled, the answer is no. If you see a glistening piece of fruit hanging from the branches of an overladen tree, and you think, 'My, wouldn't that be a delicious treat?' The answer is no." He bent closer, his voice becoming softer with each sentence. "And lastly, if any fey offers you *anything*—a word of praise, a crust of bread, a golden lyre for you to play—no matter how innocuous it might seem, the answer is what?" He raised a single brow.

Pippa's stomach tightened, bristling at his pomposity. "Perhaps, if you could grant me a moment to consider . . . is it possible the correct answer is . . . no?"

Again his lips twitched. "Sarcasm doesn't suit you."

"No. It doesn't," she agreed. "I'm not a blackguard."

"Forgive me, meri pyaari." He pressed both his hands together as if in prayer. "I wish only to keep you safe and happy, for all eternity."

Eternity? Pippa knew he was mocking her, but it nonetheless caused a twinge to knife beside her heart. She was supposed to be marrying Phoebus in two days' time. Before God, she would pledge her undying fidelity. For a love that was meant to last beyond time.

Eternity.

"Did you know that penguins mate for life?" Pippa said.

He cut his hazel eyes. "That's the third time you've altered the course of our conversation in a rather ham-fisted way. Is your knowledge of useless facts meant to impress me?"

Another pang slashed through Pippa's stomach. Her father had said something similar. He'd told Pippa time and again how young men would not want to marry a girl like her. That young women with minds of their own were as desirable as a wet cloak on a winter's eve.

"Would it hurt you to be a little kind, *dear fiancé*?" Pippa asked. "I've had a rather trying day."

He offered her a noncommittal tilt of his head, first to one side and then to the other.

"What is that supposed to mean?" she pressed.

"It means . . . whatever you think it means." He mussed his hair again. "Apologies for trying your patience, *my love*. I'm only trying to keep you safe."

Guilt warmed through Pippa's stomach. Despite the sarcasm in his tone, Arjun's admission shamed her, for it rang true. Almost everything Arjun Desai had done in the last hour, he'd done to protect her. There could be no doubt of that now. Especially after he'd hinted that the court's earlier torments were a trifling of what they could do. Pippa wondered about the cost of his actions. If their marriage rite was so sacred, would Arjun be punished for lying to everyone at court about his intention to marry her?

What might happen to them both even now? How much danger were they in?

"If we are to be married, why would anyone wish me harm?" Pippa asked quietly. "I thought introducing me as your bride would serve as its own sort of protection."

"It does. My hope is that it prevents them from hurting you outright." Arjun took in a careful breath. "But that's not all they are capable of doing. They can make you hurt yourself. The wounds with the most lasting effect are not skin-deep."

Pippa's breath caught at his expression. In all the months she'd been acquainted with Arjun Desai, she'd never seen him look sad. "Have they wounded you in such a fashion?"

"Not in recent years." His grin was pointed. "I don't allow anyone to make a fool of me twice."

"I . . . understand," Pippa said, though she did not. "What kind of creature wishes another creature harm?"

"Humans. Throughout all of recorded history," Arjun replied.

She thought of her father. Of the things he'd done. Of the threats that continued to ring in her ears well into the night. "I know you're right. Is it foolish of me to wish it weren't so?"

Arjun did not answer immediately. "No," he said. "I suppose it's not foolish to have hope."

Pippa's stomach growled again. Annoyed, she tried once more to muffle the sound. "Are there any more rules?"

He nodded. "Three more, and then we shall find you something safe to eat. I want you to promise you will not eat anything I do not directly provide, and that you will never, under any circumstances, remove that talisman necklace." He took hold of one of the large thorns dangling from the twisted chains of silver and iron and rolled it between his thumb and forefinger. "I don't understand the magic in it, but I believe it might be the only reason you're still alive."

"Why doesn't it burn you like it did that other fey lord?"

Arjun released the thorn. "An ethereal like me—a child of a mortal and fey coupling—possesses very few advantages over full-blooded fey. This is one of them."

Pippa nodded, her palm covering the talisman and the golden cross she always wore. It had belonged to her grandmother, and it was the only thing of value she'd brought across the Atlantic.

"Lastly," Arjun said, "if you're struck with the sudden fancy to venture off on your own without telling me, what is the correct answer?"

"I'm not a child, Mr. Desai." Pippa bristled.

"I didn't say you were a child." A muscle twitched below his left eye. "Do you wish to grow a tail or have your nose resemble that of a pig? Or perhaps find devil's horns protruding from your skull or discover cloven hooves where your feet used to be when you wake tomorrow morning?" His gaze narrowed as he stepped even closer, causing Pippa to fall in his shadow. "Or worse, do you war t to know what it's like to drink from a goblet filled with the dying tears of a poisoned nymph?"

Pippa shook her head, her eyes wide. Bewildered.

With a nod of satisfaction, Arjun pressed his palms against

the solid silver double doors. The leaves etched on its surface folded into themselves like a shuttered fan. A series of locks clicked open, the doors swinging wide without a sound.

Pausing to steel herself for a moment, Pippa followed Arjun into a cavernous room with a domed ceiling and countless shelves illumined by white-flamed torches, along with a massive fireplace filled with glowing embers and pots of fired porcelain.

At first glance, the space resembled a larder of sorts. Hanging above a long worktable spanning the center of the dimly lit chamber were trellises laden with dried herbs. Stoneware bowls, glazed cups, solid silver plates, and golden goblets lined row after row of oaken shelves. Wooden spoons and glass jars with sealed lids containing strange-looking liquids and glimmering powders covered the worktable's surface. If Pippa allowed her sight to go hazy, she supposed she could be in the kitchen of a grand old English manor home.

Arjun moved toward a locked metal cabinet in the back corner. It appeared to be a small vault with a keyhole, held in place by crisscrossing chains of iron and silver. He knelt to open it and began removing small glass vials of colorful spices, burlap bags of dried beans, a sack of what looked like wheat flour, and a jar of something that looked like oil. When it became clear to Pippa that he intended to prepare a meal for her, she stepped toward him, her hands raised in protest.

"Please don't trouble yourself," Pippa said. "If you have a small round of cheese and perhaps some ham or dried meat, that should be more than enough."

"Alas, I cannot oblige you on that score. No one in the Vale eats meat."

"Oh?" Pippa's eyes widened. "Why not?"

Arjun continued assembling ingredients, which he then proceeded to decant into a large wooden bowl before pausing to wash his hands. "Several hundred years ago—when the Otherworld was divided into the Sylvan Vale and its shadowy counterpart, the Sylvan Wyld—those with a taste for meat were thought to be sympathetic to the blood drinkers, so they were forced to leave or asked to change their ways. No one here consumes flesh of any kind, lest they be accused of being sympathizers. Or worse, of being dark fey themselves."

Pippa nodded as if that made perfect sense. "Of course."

Once Arjun had finished mixing a pale pink powder into the flour, he proceeded toward the fireplace, where he stoked the dying embers before placing a large griddle among the flames.

Without a word, he poured water and oil onto the flour mixture and began kneading it into a dough as if he'd done this a hundred times before.

"May I ask what you're preparing?" Pippa leaned closer.

"Roti."

Pippa stared at him quizzically.

"Rounds of flatbread," he clarified. "They can be made quickly because they don't require any leavening."

Leavening? Did wonders never cease? Arjun Desai did not seem at all the type to know how to bake bread, let alone do so with such a startling display of proficiency. Most of the men in Pippa's life were disinclined to work in a kitchen, which had been labeled the purview of women for as long as she could remember.

"You know how to cook?" Pippa asked.

"I learned early to fend for myself in the Vale," he said as he began shaping the dough into individual rounds. "And the best way for me to know beyond a shadow of a doubt that what I am consuming will not harm me is to prepare it myself, down to every crumb of bread and every drop of drink and every speck of seasoning."

"Were they really so cruel to you?" Pippa asked. "To one of their own?"

His eyes flashed, though one side of his mouth kicked up. "I'm not one of them. Make no mistake. Only one of my parents is fey."

"Your mother?"

He nodded. "But my father isn't. Which makes me a 'cursed halfblood,' despite my mother's place at court. My blood is tainted, and—as you've no doubt realized by now—anything to do with blood matters a great deal to the gentry."

Pippa nodded. "The peerage in London treats illegitimate children in a similar fashion. It's always troubled me greatly. A friend of mine runs a home for a few of these unfortunate souls. The ones discarded by their wealthy fathers and forced to forge their own path."

"Do all their fathers deny them, or are there any lords in possession of a heart?"

"Most of the time they deny them. But on rare occasions— especially if one of the children shows aptitude or perhaps if their fathers are unable to sire legitimate male heirs—the boys are brought into the fold."

"How English."

Pippa nodded. "If they are girls, they are more often left to molder."

"Not solely a fault of the English, but I enjoy blaming you colonizers whenever possible."

"I beg pardon, but are you not an English citizen?" Pippa blinked. "You speak the Queen's English like a Londoner, and it's clear you were trained to be a solicitor in an English court. The East Indies are, after all, part of the Queen's emp—"

"No," he cut her off, his nostrils flaring. "I will *never* be English. And you would do well to remember that. Conquering a man's country does not mean you have conquered his soul."

"I—I'm sorry. I did not mean to offend."

He paused in his bread preparation. "And yet you English so often do."

Pippa felt her skin flash hot, then cold, her cheeks aflame. "I'm sorry."

"You apologize a lot."

"Erm . . . I'm sorry?" She chewed on her lower lip.

Arjun's laughter was dry, but not unkind. With deft hands, he took the four rounds of dough and flattened each of them with a small rolling pin, until he had four discs of almost equal size and thickness. He shifted toward the fireplace and poured oil onto the surface of the heated griddle. Once the oil started smoking, he transferred the dough onto the dark metal. Arjun worked quickly, waiting less than a minute to flip the thin flatbread with his bare fingers, his motions smooth. Unflinching. Eloise would have liked to see Arjun cook. He was the furthest thing from a hesitater. Watching him work was like watching one of the painters in Hyde Park. It reminded Pippa of all she did not know. How Arjun Desai was as much a mystery to her as she was to him. Twice she caught herself staring at his hands. They were beautiful. His fingers were long and graceful, his nails trimmed. Meticulous. Just like the way he cooked.

Pippa cleared her throat. "Mr. Desai—"

"Arjun. As much as I have enjoyed you calling me that over the last few months, we *are* about to be married, Philippa." He glanced at a wisp nestled in the corner of the domed ceiling. Its light was dull, which suggested to Pippa that it was resting, but Arjun's warning did not go unheeded. A reminder that they were never alone.

She cleared her throat. "Pippa. I've asked you several times now to call me Pippa, for the same reason."

"Ah, yes, if I recall, your mother called you Philippa, and you dislike the name for this reason."

"I'm surprised you remember."

"I remember every word you say, *my darling.*"

Pippa frowned. "Will there be a time when we might speak . . . privately, *my love.*"

He glanced her way and laughed. Then he turned back toward the fireplace. Quick as lightning, he smeared butter onto each roti and presented the stack to Pippa. After wiping his hands on a clean length of linen, he offered her a small terra-cotta bowl of what appeared to be thickened cream.

"This is dahi," he explained. "Curd prepared from the milk of a goat. If you'd like honey as well, I have a small jar from New Orleans. It's safe for you to eat. Everything in my own personal store is spelled to prevent rot." He retrieved the honey from his vault, pausing to place the glazed porcelain vessel beside the bowl of dahi. "Cheers." With that, Arjun began collecting his cooking accoutrements and restoring them to the shelves of the small metal chest.

"Are you not going to eat anything?" Pippa asked.

He looked at her over his shoulder. "No."

"Oh." Pippa averted her gaze.

"Is something wrong?"

"I would prefer not to eat alone." It pained her greatly to admit it.

"What?" Arjun stood.

"I . . . dislike eating alone."

For a moment, he appeared startled. Then he recovered, a knowing smirk tugging at one side of his lips. "I believe you'll manage this one time."

With a frown, Pippa tore at the piece of warm bread in her hands, trying in vain to ignore a dangling thread of disappointment. "You never answered my question. Will there be a chance for us to speak privately?"

"Most assuredly." Arjun came to stand before her. "For I would still very much like to know how you and Miss Henri managed to gain entry into my flat this evening."

Pippa winced.

"We will definitely speak," he continued. "Later. In our chamber."

"Our?" Dismay colored the word, Pippa's thoughts in a flurry. "Would it be possible for me to have my own chamber?" She bit her lip. "After all, we aren't exactly married as yet, and—" She stopped talking when she saw the expression on his face. "When in doubt . . . ," she murmured.

"The answer is no," he finished.

Good Lord. Tonight, Pippa would be sharing a bedchamber with Arjun Desai.

———◆◆◆———

Ever since childhood, Michael Grimaldi had possessed a fascination for lost causes.

It began when he was a boy with a fish. She was his first pet. He named her Goldie, much to his cousin Luca's amusement. Michael had rescued Goldie from what he believed to be an uncertain fate. When he'd asked why Luca was returning her to the pond, Luca had told him Goldie was old. That she'd stopped swimming around in her bowl and had grown listless. She wouldn't live much longer, so it seemed better to return her to the pond than watch her perish.

Despite his cousin's warning, Michael had taken Goldie home. He'd fed Goldie and talked to her and nursed her. His family had been gentle with him when eight-year-old Michael had said he thought she was getting better. But they'd known.

When Goldie died a week later, Michael had been inconsolable. He held a proper New Orleans funeral for her, complete with a jubilant processional. Luca helped him build a small carriage to bear Goldie's body to her final resting place. His best friend, Bastien, constructed a small box for Goldie to use as a coffin. As usual, Bastien's work was beautiful. He used gilded paint and brass fasteners to make it look grand.

"Gold for Goldie," Bastien said, with a sad smile.

Even at that age, Michael realized Bastien knew a great deal about death. For the first time, Michael felt like they could share in that loss. It had been a pivotal moment in his young life, the idea that he could do his best—try his hardest—and it might not make a difference.

Still he refused to learn his lesson.

As time passed, Michael continued to take on causes others deemed lost. Even when his own family told him to stay away from Bastien—that a friendship with the heir to the Saint Germain fortune would cause him nothing but undue grief—Michael persisted in defending Bastien.

He'd known their families were supposed to be mortal enemies. It wasn't merely because Bastien hailed from a family of vampires and Michael's veins ran wild with the magic of werewolves. It ran deeper than that. To a realm of curses and blood oaths. To centuries of warfare and broken promises.

They were Grimaldis and Saint Germains. Montagues and Capulets.

And even though his nonna demanded that Michael no longer associate with Bastien, he believed there could be another path. After all, centuries ago, vampires and werewolves worked together. They'd been exiled from their homeland as one.

Should they not join forces now for the common good?

It had taken Michael too long to realize that the only common good that existed for Sébastien Saint Germain was the common good that benefited his kind and his kind alone. Michael failed to see this truth, for Bastien wielded his charm like a master illusionist, and Michael believed in his friend's goodness even when faced with mounting proof to the contrary.

Michael first noticed it in the way their schoolmates clamored for Bastien's attention, as if the favor of the wealthiest boy in their class would rain gold upon them as well. How Bastien won over anyone who strolled into his path. Then, quick as lightning, he would use his charm to influence their hearts and minds, bending them to his will. As a boy, Michael thought if he spent enough time in Bastien's presence, he would learn to master this skill. Perhaps then he would have the standing and influence he desired so greatly. To walk into a room and have people respect him on reputation alone.

But all his illusions had well and truly been shattered the spring of their first cotillion season, when Michael found Bastien canoodling with the young lady Michael had been admiring from afar.

Bastien had been . . . unapologetic.

And now? Bastien had done far more than canoodle with the young lady Michael admired. He'd stolen away with the girl to whom Michael had pledged his heart. His future. His happiness.

The girl he wanted to marry. Celine Rousseau.

In a sea of unforgivable acts perpetrated upon Grimaldis by Saint Germains, this was the one that Michael could not forgive or forget. Whenever he thought of Celine—of losing the future he'd dreamed of building with her—something hardened around his heart. A pain that reached bone deep, making it difficult to find joy around him. He could not laugh, nor could he cry. Not even at Luca's funeral.

He was numb to anything except this pain.

Bastien could have chosen any of the Crescent City's most desirable belles. They would have fallen over themselves to catch his attention. Michael had loved only one girl his entire life. And Bastien had taken her from him. Had used his power and charm and influence to have the one thing Michael had ever truly wanted. Ever truly dreamed of having. Bastien had stolen Michael's future.

Michael intended to return the favor.

The only good Saint Germain was a dead one. Well and truly dead.

His hands clenched tight at his sides as the pain coiled like a snake through his body, Michael Grimaldi stood in the darkness before the immense mirror along the far wall of the flat shared by Shin Jaehyuk and Arjun Desai. He'd expected to feel some trepidation. He would be the first in his family for more than two centuries to set foot in the land of the fey.

"Did you bring everything as instructed?" Valeria Henri said from beside him. At her back stood her daughter, Eloise, who wore a murderous look, her lips pressed into a pout.

He nodded. Michael had strapped a blade of iron to his left side, and a solid silver dirk to his right thigh, the sheath fashioned of sturdy leather, for if it cut Michael, it would cause him a great deal of pain. Creatures who were once dark fey—werewolves like him and vampires like Bastien—could be rendered immobile by such a wound, perhaps even made to suffer the final death. The revolver tucked into his holster was filled with bullets of alternating metals. Three shots apiece. Across his shoulder was a rucksack with food and a canteen of fresh water.

Valeria Henri fastened a thin chain around his neck. "This will protect you from the worst of their glamours. It will also dull most physical pain. But should you eat or drink enough of anything spelled, I cannot promise you the talisman will continue working. Its effectiveness will also lessen the longer you linger in the fey realm."

Michael nodded. "Thank you for your help." His words were terse. Terser than he meant them to be. After all, the Henris—a family of ancient sibyls, enchantresses, and necromancers—had aligned themselves with the wealthy vampires during the great schism.

Valeria made a face, her expression one of exasperation. "I'm not helping you so much as protecting my damned fool of a daughter." She glared over one shoulder at Eloise, who sniffed loudly, but nevertheless took a careful step backward. "If the vampires find out what she did, they might enact their own form of justice on her, and I will not allow that to happen." Valeria's lip curled. "I will be certain to deal with Eloise in my own way."

Eloise spluttered. "Why should I be blamed for—"

"¡Cállate!" Valeria said, the word a harsh whisper. "If you had any sense, you wouldn't speak until the next full moon." She turned toward Michael, the fire still smoldering in her gaze.

"I . . . am indebted to you," Michael admitted. "Had you not come to my aid tonight, I would undoubtedly be less prepared for this ordeal than I am now."

"Just bring Miss Montrose home as soon as possible," Valeria said. "She is not meant to exist in that unforgiving place. Nor are you."

He nodded, his features determined.

Valeria cut her eyes. "I chose to help you because I've always believed you to be sensible. Don't prove me wrong by acting lovelorn and reckless, Detective Grimaldi."

"Excuse me?"

"I suspect your motivations for going to the Vale to be more than a desire to find the foolhardy Miss Montrose."

"You're speaking of Celine Rousseau."

She didn't mince words. Neither would he.

Valeria nodded. "All the magic folk in the Quarter are aware of the love you hold for her. And the animosity you hold for Sébastien Saint Germain."

With a snort, Eloise started to speak. Her mother silenced her with a glance.

Something flared beside Michael's heart. Despite his efforts and the efforts of his family, this feud had managed to seep into every aspect of his life. "It's true my feelings for Celine are no secret. But after what happened to my cousin Luca and to Bastien's uncle, I have no intention of stirring up further trouble. For either me or Bastien." He gripped the leather sheath in his fist, a familiar ache coursing through his veins at the memory of Luca. At the way his cousin had looked at Michael in the moment of his death, staring down the barrel of a revolver Michael held in his own hand. "If Celine was foolish enough to choose Bastien, then she has sealed her own fate." He fought to convey a look of indifference.

Michael needed to harden his resolve. If he allowed this pain to get the better of him, he would lose his focus. He had not meant to kill his cousin. It was an accident. One Michael had already paid for, in blood curses met beneath a full moon. In each of his excruciating transformations from man to beast.

"A convincing effort. Unfortunately I am not entirely convinced," Valeria said. "If I may offer a final word of warning, do not become entangled in fey affairs. Celine is the daughter of the Lady of the Vale. From what I understand, her mother rules the Summer Court. If you anger Lady Silla or cause trouble while you are in her domain, nothing and no one will save you from her ire."

"I understand. Use the tare to get in. Find Philippa Montrose. Use the tare to get out."

Again Valeria nodded. "I have spelled this ring to help you locate the talisman necklace my irresponsible daughter made for Miss Montrose." She handed Michael a gold ring with a black stone in the center. He placed it on the smallest finger of his left hand.

"There is a small needle in the center of the stone," Valeria continued. "It works like a compass, with the young woman's location pointing north."

Michael studied the stone. When he focused on its center, he noticed the thin white arrow spinning in a lazy clockwise circle. Likely because Pippa was no longer present in the earthly realm. "I thank you again for your assistance, Madame Henri. I will not forget it."

Valeria threaded her hands together and straightened. The crown of folded cloth on her head cast angular shadows on the darkened walls of the flat. "I pray you heed my advice," she said. "Do not make matters worse between the Brotherhood and the Fallen. You are too young to remember what happened last time. Too much blood was spilled; too many beloved members of both families were lost."

"I can promise I will do my best to avoid an altercation with any fey, light or dark." Michael's cheeks hollowed as he stared at his reflection in the tare, its silver surface undulating at his nearness. "But I will not hesitate to defend myself if I—or any-one in my charge—is attacked."

"Aren't we all just trying to protect the ones we love? That's how it usually begins." Valeria sighed to herself and gazed at her daughter sidelong. "Go with haste, Michael Grimaldi, and may your better angels guide you."

———◆◆◆———

Pippa still felt cold, even though the fireplace in the cavernous chamber roared with flames of sizzling gold. Perhaps it was a result of the room's size. The candlelit chamber she and Arjun were meant to share as the Summer Court's guests reminded Pippa of the ballroom at Ashmore Hall. Its coved ceiling of packed earth had to be at least fifteen feet high in its center. There were no windows anywhere to be found, which confirmed a suspicion Pippa had held for the last hour; most of the Ivy Bower actually lay underground, like a cleverly devised abode tunneled by an industrious mole. An ingenious design, for it made it a fortress difficult to breach.

The rounded wall to Pippa's left was carved in a depiction she could not distinguish from a distance. An immense mural of a forest at dusk filled the wall to her right. A single chaise and stool of light ash were positioned near the stone fireplace, alongside a woven rug with threads of gold and silver braided through its center to form a sunburst. To her back was a huge bed on a low dais with a headboard in the shape of creeping vines of ivy. Its surface was littered with blankets of fur and pillows of shimmering pale silk.

Pippa intended to ignore the bed for as long as possible.

"Where is Arjun?" she asked with another shiver.

"How should I know?" spat a fairy with wings that greatly resembled those of an emerald dragonfly. She held up the tattered remnants of Pippa's green gown. "Toss this with the rest of the refuse," she instructed another winged fey, who was applying a healing salve to the cuts on Pippa's skin.

"What?" Pippa reached for the dress. "You can't throw that away, it's my—"

"Out with the trash it goes!" the fey interrupted with a snap of her fingers. The garment and the smaller fairy vanished in the blink of an eye.

Unease dripped down Pippa's spine like cold water. She grasped her underclothes tightly, wrapping her arms around her bodice. If they tried to take what remained of her garments, Pippa would scream.

She breathed carefully as she stood on a low stool with no less than a dozen fairies the size of her fist flitting around her, measuring and muttering and snipping all the while, their tiny shears honed from solid gemstones. Ordinarily Pippa would find the sound soothing. Some of her most cherished memories as a child were the ones she'd spent in the garden of her family's county seat at Ashmore Hall, bees buzzing in her ears and the perfume of flowers and earth filling her head.

"Stop moving!" a fairy shouted in her left ear, its voice tinny and raspy all at once.

"I'm not," Pippa said through gritted teeth. "I'm only breathing." She gripped her forearms.

"Then stop doing that, too."

Pippa frowned.

Another tiny fairy—Pippa believed it was called a nixie—buzzed to a stop before her face, her hands on her full hips. For the first time since they'd arrived, Pippa could see one of the creatures up close, in full detail. The nixie was the size of Pippa's hand, her skin the hue of an orange, her figure like that of a shapely young woman, her wings diaphanous and multicolored, like an oil slick across a puddle of water. She wore a thin garment of sparkling white. In fact, the fabric was so thin, Pippa's eyes went wide. As round as saucers.

She could see . . . everything underneath.

"What are you staring at?" the nixie demanded.

"I'm sorry." She averted her gaze.

The female fairy's shining black eyes narrowed. "Yes, you are, little mortal." She glared at the silver-and-iron talisman around Pippa's neck. "But not as sorry as you should be."

"Twygge, that's enough," another nixie said.

This nixie was a bit bigger than the others. Perhaps the length of Pippa's forearm. His hair was black as pitch and spiked all across his scalp, his skin pea green.

"Pardon their rudeness, Lady Philippa," the green nixie said, waving a hand about in the air, as if to cast aside an errant thought. "I'm Twylle, chief designer of the Tylwyth Tegge." The nixie wore a simple crimson garment styled in a manner that reminded Pippa of the togas worn by Romans in the empire's heyday. It, too, left little to the imagination. Pippa glanced away just as she noted how . . . well-endowed Twylle was.

Twylle continued. "Twygge is rather spiteful on a good day, but it's only because she is new to the task and lacks the experience. The pressure to be perfect can be a chore for some." His hand rested across his exposed chest. "Not for me, of course. I have dressed the gentry in preparation for the Rite for over five hundred years now."

Pippa offered Twylle a nod. She remembered Arjun's warning not to trust any of the fey. But something about Twylle was . . . reassuring. "I understand the pressure to be perfect," Pippa said with a tentative smile. "More than you know."

"Hmm." Twylle's wings buzzed. "But aren't mortals so dreadfully imperfect?"

Normally Pippa would find the question impertinent. But it was the first time a fey in the Vale had engaged her in seemingly normal conversation. Twylle made the effort to look her in the eye and treat her as more than an insect beneath his boot.

"We are," Pippa agreed. "I rather think it's what makes us interesting. My mother strove for perfection all her life. In fact, I think her desire for perfection actually *made* her imperfect, for she was never happy, even though she is a duchess."

Twylle drew back, his purple eyes wide. "Upon the Vale, what is a . . . dew-chaise?"

"Not dew-chaise. DUH-chess. Erm, I suppose you could say it is something like royalty?"

"You're a *royal* mortal?" the spiteful Twygge announced from behind Pippa. For an instant, Pippa swore she felt something tug on a lock of her hair.

She winced. "My parents are, more or less."

"Which means you are as well, does it not?" Twylle buzzed again, his arms crossing. Then he whistled once, and all the other fairies ceased with their flitting and hovered in midair, awaiting his orders.

"I suppose so," Pippa said. "In a fashion. But I—"

"Well, then, you simply must have a crown." Twylle took off, clapping his hands, directing the other nixies, who resumed twittering about. "My little lieges, lords, and ladies, our task is no longer to clothe Lord Arjun's mortal stick of a bride, but to clothe a royal dew-chaise."

"Dew-chaise?" a purple nixie said, its voice high-pitched.

"Yes, dearie," Twylle replied. "It's a mortal royal."

The chirruping began anew.

Pippa held up both hands to a fresh wave of objections. "Twylle, I—"

All at once, the double doors to the chamber burst open, causing the fairies to shriek and brandish their tiny scissors and bare their glistening fangs. Pippa started where she stood and nearly fell from the low stool but managed to catch herself in time.

At the door stood Arjun Desai, his features determined. Another cloud of nixies surrounded him, their protests loud and high-pitched. He was barefoot and half dressed, his jacquard waistcoat nowhere to be found and his white linen shirt unbuttoned and uncuffed.

Pippa's face turned hot. The anger in his hazel eyes was

palpable. He studied her from stem to stern, as if trying to form a mental picture . . .

Of Pippa, who was half dressed as well.

Too late, Pippa remembered she should feel outraged. Not strangely flushed and uncomfortable. "I'm—not dressed!" she sputtered, then hated herself for saying something so ridiculous.

"Neither am I," Arjun replied without missing a beat. "But they wouldn't tell me what they were doing, so I wanted to see for myself. In my experience, the littlest ones have the sharpest teeth." He grinned, his shoulders dropping, his attitude of amused boredom returning in the blink of an eye.

But the Tylwyth Tegge had witnessed him barge through the door like a knight storming a castle, and despite his cavalier attitude, it was clear to all those present that Philippa Montrose mattered to Arjun Desai.

Even though Pippa knew their engagement to be no more than a ruse, she could not help the warmth that blossomed in her stomach at the thought.

Good Lord. Was she this starved for a chance to feel important to someone? Feelings were such ridiculous, illogical things.

Arjun strolled toward her, batting away the continued protestations of the nixies chasing after him. "I believe we can both be measured for our wedding fripperies in the same room."

"You're not supposed to see her dress," Twylle said, his tone testy. "That's the mortal way, is it not?"

"I won't see her dress, as it's not yet ready," Arjun replied. "And I'm only half mortal, so does it really matter?"

"If it matters to the dew-chaise, it matters to me," Twylle said, hovering in front of Arjun so that he might glower at him face-to-face.

"A what?" Arjun asked Pippa.

Pippa grimaced. She'd kept her family's name a secret ever since coming to New Orleans. Not for a nefarious reason. But simply because the truth of it embarrassed her. The Duke of Ashmore was ruined. Locked away in prison for the next twenty years after committing arson and insurance fraud. So brazen were his criminal acts that even the Crown had refused to intervene.

If people in England knew who Pippa's family was, they would stare at her like she'd grown a second head. On the long journey across the Atlantic, Pippa had decided it was far easier to move about the world under a cloak of anonymity.

"They think I'm a duchess," Pippa said with an apologetic look.

Twygge yanked again on Pippa's hair, eliciting a stifled shriek. "You said your mother was a dew-chaise, mortal," the orange fairy yelled. "Did you lie to us?"

Pippa thought about lying even then. But why? What did it matter? It had taken months for her to accept it, but her father could not hurt her now any more than he could help her.

She'd made certain of that the night she'd set fire to his office and sealed his fate.

"No," Pippa said. "I didn't lie. My mother is a duchess. My father is a duke."

Arjun's eyes narrowed almost imperceptibly. Pippa expected him to press her for information. Since he lived in England for a time, he must know about the ton and the way the English peerage conducted their affairs. For the daughter of a duke to travel across the Atlantic and agree to marry someone without her father's permission, there had to be a story of note.

But blessedly Arjun did not ask any further questions.

Twylle clapped even louder, his features stern. "Whatever plans we had for the dew princess' wedding garments must be discarded. The gown must be something far grander."

"But, Twylle, we only have a single evening to complete the—"

"Bah, bah, bah," Twylle interjected. "We are the Tylwyth Tegge! We will not allow such a paltry thing as time to prevent us from achieving excellence." With a flourish, he unrolled a skein of sparkling, translucent fabric and held it against Pippa's cheek, his wings beating in a pulse of frenetic energy. "This would look perfect against your bare skin. I'm envisioning a gown with a train the length of a mortal man. A sizable one, at that." He winked. "It will be the talk of—"

"Surely not with this fabric," Pippa interrupted. Though it felt like cool water on her cheek and shimmered like a lake at sunset, she hoped the winged fairy did not intend to do what she suspected him of wanting to do.

Twylle sucked in his cheeks. "And why not? It is among the finest in the Vale. Only the best silk shrives are able to weave this kind of tussore. The larvae are fed pure gold, iced sapphires, and sweetwater for months. And—"

"But it's completely translucent! It conceals *nothing.*"

"And why should that matter?" Twylle rolled his eyes.

Pippa swore she heard Arjun's soft laughter behind her.

"I'm—I'm a bride," Pippa said, her expression incredulous. "I can't have my bosom or my . . . my bits exposed at my wedding!"

Arjun snorted. Loudly. Pippa felt color creep up her neck. She'd mentioned her nether regions in front of a young man. A proper young lady should be appalled. And yet it wasn't even close to the worst thing that had happened to her today.

If Pippa intended to show courage while in the Vale, she could not allow the mention of a woman's intimate parts to throw her into a tizzy.

"Bits?" Twylle buzzed before Pippa's face, his arms akimbo. "Upon the Vale, I have no idea what 'bits' are." He scoffed. "And your breasts are beautiful. Small, but shapely and firm. A lovely color, too. Just look at how they're blushing. Quite becoming." He studied her a moment. "You are rather striking, my little dew-chaise, despite the disadvantage of being a mortal. If you'd cease with the silly questions and wear something besides rags, I might even start to believe you belonged here."

"Stop," Pippa begged. This was without a doubt the most improper conversation she had ever held in public with anyone, including her own mother. Which was a feat in itself.

"No, please, Twylle," Arjun said, laughter in his voice. "Do continue."

"What precisely do you find to be a laughing matter, *dear fiancé?*" Pippa asked quietly, her cheeks still flaming.

"Nothing of note," he replied. "But I learned as a child that laughter is often the only thing that can save you in the Vale, *my love.* It says so, right in your Bible. Proverbs, I believe."

"The latter part of that passage mentions dried bones," Pippa muttered.

"Is that a threat?"

Pippa turned toward him to cast Arjun an arched glance and found herself at a loss for words.

The Tylwyth Tegge had finished removing Arjun's shirt so they could drape richly colored fabrics replete with embroidery across his bare shoulders. The chiseled planes of his bronzed stomach and chest flexed with even the smallest movement. Pippa looked away before he caught her staring. Not that it would matter. Apparently nothing embarrassed Arjun Desai, while by all rights, Pippa should be sinking to the ground, wallowing in shame.

She wondered what might embarrass him. And what she would do if she were ever afforded such information.

At that precise moment, Pippa felt the lacing on her stays slacken. The snipping of shears cut through the silence. With a gasp, she pressed her hands to the front of her bodice.

"Leave me my undergarments, please," she said, panic starting to build in her stomach. A line needed to be drawn, no matter how ridiculous it seemed. She would not disrobe in front of Arjun Desai and a passel of tiny fey creatures. She refused.

"Please, Twylle," she said. "This"—she took a deep breath—"this isn't proper, nor is it right."

"Twylle, the dew-princess is unhappy," Twygge said as she hovered into view, her tone acerbic. "She won't look beautiful if she's unhappy."

Twylle flitted beside Pippa's shoulder. "And what would make you happy?" the green nixie asked, his purple eyes wide. "In the mortal world, what would you wear for your wedding?"

Pippa thought of the dress waiting for her back in New Orleans. Her future mother-in-law, Marguerite, had worn it to wed Remy Devereux twenty-two years ago. It was not crafted in Pippa's style or taste, but it was proper. If Pippa had her way, she would have asked Celine to design her wedding gown. Something simple, hearkening to the Georgian era, long and flowing, with a high waist and delicate needlework, like the dress her grandmother had worn. "White is the most common color for a wedding," Pippa said, "but I suppose it doesn't matter so long as the fabric is opaque and—"

Gasps rippled around them. "White," one nixie announced. "It would look grand!"

"And silver!" said another.

"Gold, too."

"Yes, gold!" shrieked another, to a chorus of agreement.

"No gold!" Twylle shouted with a slash of his right hand. "No gold."

"But it would be—"

Twylle clenched his jaw. "No. Gold."

An argument began to ensue between the Tylwyth Tegge in a language Pippa could not understand.

She glanced toward Arjun with a helpless expression and was met—yet again—with his amusement, which only succeeded in unsettling her further. He appeared unconcerned with their shared predicament, which made Pippa wonder whether he was simply quite gifted at concealing his thoughts or if he was truly as indifferent as he seemed.

Neither possibility comforted her in the slightest. There was so much Pippa wanted to say. She wanted to ask if his mother would put a stop to their wedding. How she might get word to Celine. What his true thoughts might be.

If Pippa could only learn what Arjun were truly thinking, at the very least it would aid her in determining a path forward. A way home.

A thought struck her cold. What if Arjun never devised a plan? Lord Vyr had mentioned that Arjun Desai did not consider marriage to be a matter of import. Arjun had been quick to offer it as a solution. Maybe it didn't matter to him if they were forced to marry.

Perhaps it was merely another lark.

But marriage meant a great deal to Pippa. She'd hinged the fate of her family on her future union. To her, it was a vow given before God. How could she wed Arjun Desai one afternoon and Phoebus Devereux the next? Besides that, Pippa knew Phoebus was the sort of man who would not shy away from taking charge of Lydia and Henry once they became part of his family. To

Phoebus, honor and family mattered a great deal. Did they matter to Arjun Desai?

What, if anything, mattered to him in truth?

Another flitting fairy clipped away a shred of torn lace from Pippa's chemise sleeve.

"She asked to keep the rest of her garments," Arjun said at once, cutting through the chatter, his tone firm. "Listen to her."

A moment of silence followed his admonishment. Then Twygge fluffed the translucent fabric draped across her orange chest and tossed her pale pink curls. "Let us speak frankly, Twylle. You object to using gold not because you think it overdone, but rather because the Menehunes have been using white and gold for—"

"I told you not to mention that name to me again," Twylle said through his teeth, the tips of the black spikes on his head trembling. "Those cursedly cheerful island-dwelling fiends will not be the cause of any more grief."

"Very well," Twygge said with a sniff. "But if I might make a suggestion, perhaps we could use a touch of pink in the dew princess' gown? Would that not offset the comparison, were we to use gold as well?"

"Yes, pink!" another cry of exuberance rose among the buzzing nixies. Soon the sound echoed throughout the cavernous room. "Pink would look divine against her skin and those little peri bites."

"Peri bites?" Pippa asked.

"Those tiny marks across your nose," replied a nixie with butter-yellow skin.

"My freckles?"

Laughter rippled around her. "Frek-elles?" Twygge said. "You say the silliest things, mortal." She glanced at Arjun, then back at Pippa. "I wonder if your offspring will have these peri bites, too."

Offspring? Pippa paled. She waited for Arjun to offer another cutting remark.

Instead he laughed. "Any of our offspring will be handsome, without a doubt. With her eyes and my hair, as well as her wits and my humor, they shall be a force to be reckoned with."

"If the children are beautiful, it would make Lord Vyr angry," another nixie said, their glee obvious.

"The best reason I've heard yet for having children," Arjun replied. "If it won't upset Lord Vyr, then why bother going to all the trouble?"

Pippa refrained from frowning. It worried her that she could not tell if he was in jest. If this was what Arjun thought of children—that they were nothing but trouble—then it was even more important for Pippa to return to New Orleans with all haste so that she could marry Phoebus. Lydia and Henry's future depended on it.

All around her, fairies twittered, conversation resuming in multiple languages. Two more of the Tylwyth Tegge unrolled a new skein of snow-white fabric, its surface as soft as a cloud of feathers.

Twylle clapped his hands again. "Bah, bah, bah! Enough of this nonsense. To work, all!" He flourished the length of sparkling fabric he'd cast aside only a moment before. "And I will still find a place for this beauty. Somewhere." His grin was mischievous. "Call for the silversmith! We've a crown to make." He buzzed closer to Pippa. "Now, my dewdrop. Do we like diamonds?"

⁓ఌ—

Pippa stared at the coved ceiling of the bedchamber she'd been forced to share with Arjun Desai. Two wisps had taken refuge in opposite corners, their light faint and warm. Glowing steadily, which meant they too were sleeping, as Arjun had explained before blessedly choosing to repose on the chaise beside the stone fireplace.

Frustratingly, Arjun and Pippa had not been afforded an opportunity to speak in private. The two confounded wisps had refused to leave the chamber, despite Arjun's gentle cajoling.

Pippa did not want to consider what would happen if either wisp reported their unfiltered conversations to Lord Vyr or to any other member of the fey gentry.

From the depths of the chaise, Pippa heard a soft intake of breath. The gentlest snore.

How in God's name had Arjun Desai managed to fall into a deep sleep with no more effort than a newborn babe? Even in repose, Pippa could bet he was smirking. All while she lay restless in the shadows, her thoughts roiling through her mind like a kettle at full boil. No matter what she did, she could not coax herself to rest. She turned to one side and studied Arjun's silhouette through the layers of firelit darkness.

It was a small chaise. He looked cramped, his legs folded at an odd angle, and his neck twisted to one side. Undoubtedly it was uncomfortable for him. But Pippa refused to ask Arjun to share the bed with her, even if there was more than enough room for them both. There was something about sleeping beside another human that lent itself to a deep kind of intimacy. A trust Pippa did not yet hold for Arjun. Yes, he'd fought to keep her safe, and she felt gratitude for it. But still she did not know his heart. And in order for Pippa to trust in anyone, she needed to know their heart.

Even before Celine had confided in her and told Pippa about the horrific circumstances that had caused Celine to flee Paris under cover of night, Pippa had seen a kindred spirit in Celine. She'd known her heart. Beneath a story of murder and heartbreak, Pippa had recognized a fierce kind of love. That was Celine. Brazen and bold. Uncompromising and unafraid.

The furthest thing from a hesitater.

Pippa sighed to herself. Her best friend had vanished with her vampire love to a fairy realm, fearless at all turns. And here Pippa was, staring at the ceiling, hemming and hawing, uncertain of what to do or where to go. For the tenth time in as many minutes, she considered waking Arjun so that they might speak. She glanced at the two glowing spies resting in opposite corners of the ceiling. Then she listened again for Arjun. His breathing was slow and constant. When she sat up to see if he was in true repose, nothing stirred in the shadows.

Pippa could not afford to hesitate. To lie here in the dark with her thoughts, unsure of the correct path forward. Arjun had vowed they would speak in earnest tonight, just as he'd sworn to devise a plan for them to leave the Sylvan Vale.

Neither vow had come to fruition, and Pippa refused to wait on the unfulfilled promises of any man.

She drew aside the covers and exhaled a shaky breath. For an instant, Pippa toyed with the handle of the lone taper positioned on a low table resembling an overgrown mushroom, its cap hard and polished, as if it were made of ivory, its base hewn from glossy mahogany. It shouldn't look beautiful, but as many things did in this strange world, something about it caught Pippa's eye.

She took another deep breath and left the candle on the mushroom nightstand. Its light might draw unwanted attention. Her knees knocking, she donned her boots and padded toward Arjun's open rucksack, which was strewn beside the chaise. From its contents, she withdrew the heavy cloak she'd noticed earlier and wrapped it around her shoulders. Arjun stirred, his bare arm shifting over his face, sending the scent of fresh linen and cinnamon her way. Pippa bit her lower lip. She waited until she was certain Arjun had not awoken, her heartbeat echoing in her skull. Then she shuffled toward the double doors and into the darkened corridors.

Five feet past the door, she hesitated once more, wishing that Celine were with her. Or even Eloise. Both young women would push Pippa to act rather than waste time deliberating. And yet Pippa could not ignore the whispers of warning in both her ears. Arjun had said it wasn't safe for her to wander around alone. He'd made her promise not to go anywhere without him.

Pippa harrumphed. He'd also promised they would speak in private. That he would share his plan to spare them from having to marry in a joint ceremony with Lord Vyr and Liege Sujee.

If he did not mean to keep his promises, then neither would she.

Pippa waited until she caught sight of a smaller wisp just around the bend emitting a faint blue glow. Arjun had said the wisps enjoyed being helpful and providing answers. Perhaps it was foolish, but Pippa thought the smaller ones might be a bit younger. Maybe they were more impressionable as well? Could she cajole this one into answering a few questions? With great care, Pippa approached the sleeping wisp.

"Hello?" she whispered quietly.

The wisp started, its glow brightening. Flickering as it woke from its respite.

"I don't mean to be a bother," Pippa said, her voice almost too soft to hear, "but I was wondering if you knew of the tare near the lake close to Lord Arjun's family home?"

The wisp flickered as if in thought. Then brightened all at once before rising into the air, its movements quick. Eager.

"You do?" Pippa said with a smile. "I would be ever so grateful if you wouldn't mind taking me there." She bit her lip. "With all the excitement of the wedding celebration tomorrow, I'm having a difficult time sleeping, so I thought about taking a walk. I'd like to see the tare, so that I might know where it is in the future."

The wisp seemed to hesitate, then a series of bell-like chimes emitted from its center, the sounds low and resonant. Softly beautiful. Almost as if it were speaking to her.

When Pippa failed to respond, the wisp appeared to repeat itself.

"I'm sorry," Pippa said. "I don't understand what you're saying."

It floated down a bit as if it were deflated.

Pippa thought quickly. Promises meant something in the Vale. "I understand your hesitance. You can trust me. If I promise not to do anything besides look, will you take me to see the tare?"

A part of her felt wrong for misleading the little wisp. But Pippa knew this particular part of her would not come to her rescue when it came time to flee. If she listened to it, she would still be staring at the ceiling, quibbling until dawn.

Pursing her lips, Pippa said, "I'd be ever so grateful for your help." She offered the wisp her most winning smile. Never mind that her mouth wavered just so. "I would be in your debt."

The wisp drifted to the side for a spell, in obvious deliberation. Then it shook off its uncertainty in a sudden burst of energy. Chiming like church bells on a Sunday morning, the wisp began gliding through the corridor, pausing to grant Pippa a moment to follow. They traveled down the length of another hallway, the ceiling of woven branches drawing closer together. Yet another corridor narrowed even further until Pippa could almost touch the walls and ceilings from all sides. She stopped before following the wisp down a final slender hallway that appeared to dead-end.

"Are you sure it's this way?" she whispered, feeling cornered, the tiny hairs on the back of her neck standing straight.

The wisp bobbed up and down as if to nod, chiming all the while.

Pippa drew her borrowed cloak closer and resolved to cease with her dithering. She could not wait for Arjun Desai to help her return home.

At the end of this narrow corridor was a solid door of what appeared to be oak. The hinges and the handle were solid silver. Around the frame itself were stones embossed with glowing symbols that reminded Pippa of the wards Eloise Henri had brought to life outside the entrance to Arjun Desai's flat in the Quarter.

The wisp waited by the silver handle, a low toll emitting from its center, its echo distinctly inquisitive.

"One moment," Pippa whispered.

The last doorway like this had tried to burn Pippa from the inside out. This world of fey creatures had shown her time and again, even in her short visit, that it was a world of danger and malice, its beauty nothing more than a smokescreen for something far more sinister. Already in less than a single evening, she'd been threatened with all kinds of violence, had her throat sliced by bejeweled talons, and had the clothing torn from her body like a wretched soul in a sanitorium.

Would this little wisp cause her harm or lead her down the wrong path?

Pippa stared at the glowing orb. Something about it struck her as . . . cheerful.

She'd already asked Arjun if wisps would burn her or eat her. If they were truly dangerous, would he not have said as much?

Pippa reached for the handle, and a trill of excitement emanated from the wisp.

She would not wait for Arjun Desai to save her. She would be in control of her own fate. Like the day she set sail for America, she would be the one to determine the course of her life.

The wisp soared soundlessly into the misty darkness beyond the Ivy Bower.

Pippa followed its lead, a shudder passing over her as a familiar burning sensation tried to take root around her heart. This time she knew to expect it, but it nevertheless took her breath away. It tingled at her fingertips. In response, Pippa flexed her hands. The feeling felt . . . sharper than before. Not necessarily more painful. Just more distinct.

She paused to look back at what she expected to be an immense mound of earth, covered in ivy and winding branches. A gasp flew from her lips.

Nothing was there. It seemed like a commonplace grove of immense oak trees, forming a circle with a stone dolmen in its center, like the famous one at Stonehenge in Wiltshire.

"Where is the Ivy Bower?" Pippa asked.

The wisp seemed to sigh. Then it flickered with impatience.

Pippa had lost consciousness the first time she was in the forest. She'd only regained awareness once her bow-and-arrow-wielding captors had brought her to the Ivy Bower.

"It must be spelled to keep its location a secret," Pippa murmured to herself. The magic of this place continued to astound her, reminding her at all turns that nothing was as it seemed.

Fretting all the while, Pippa followed the wisp into the shadowy mist.

Through the forest have I gone.

A Midsummer Night's Dream,

William Shakespeare

———◆•◆———

It had been years since Arjun Desai last experienced a troubled dream.

He didn't like calling them nightmares. It was a habit he'd learned from his father, who said even the darkest visions served a purpose. That a body tensing was a body preparing to defend itself.

If this dream was meant to serve as a warning, it was indeed a distressing one.

As soon as Arjun fell asleep, his dreams rose in a swirl of colors surrounding Philippa Montrose's lovely face. No matter how much he tried to ignore it, the hue that caught his eye—the one that seemed to swallow the anger, the fear, the uncertainty, and the anguish—was a pale shade of pink. The color of clouds on a late-summer afternoon.

The color of desire. He'd seen it through the monocle. It had caught him unawares.

Philippa Montrose desired him. In that moment, it was as if the lens had become a mirror, for Arjun could not remember the last time he'd felt so drawn to a mortal. In fact, he avoided developing romantic feelings for humans, as the idea of falling in love with something so fragile—so close to death, even in their prime—made him uncomfortable. He'd already lost his father to stolen memories, and the loss at such a young age had been a profound one. The idea of loving another person only to lose them in a few short decades seemed foolish.

As with many things, the benefit did not outweigh the cost.

And yet, the longer Arjun spent time in Pippa's presence—the more he baited her just to see her frown or watch her wavering smile—the more the shade of desire thickened around them both, until it was on its way to becoming a fog, obscuring all else from view.

"Wake up, you fool."

The tinny voice echoing in Arjun's ear caused him to bolt upright and swipe the side of his face. His fingertips grazed a pair of flitting wings.

A set of tiny, razor-sharp teeth bit into his thumb.

"What in Hades' name?" he shouted, flinging his hand through the air.

A screech of outrage echoed into the darkness. The next instant, something flew straight at Arjun's face, and a tiny hand tweaked him on his nose. "I'm here to help, and you nearly killed me, you halfblood swine!" At the sound of the nixie's outrage, the two sleeping wisps flashed awake in a chorus of trills.

"Twylle?" Arjun groaned. "What are you doing here?"

The nixie tsked. "You absolute waste of fresh air." He spoke directly in Arjun's ear to prevent his words from being overheard. "Your bride has fled this place."

"What?" Arjun kicked away the blanket strewn across his legs. He stood in a fluid motion, his gaze trained on the absurdly large bed.

A string of curses sailed from his lips.

"When?" he demanded as he grabbed his shirt and reached for his shoes.

Twylle crossed his arms. "It's sheer dumb luck that I overheard a pair of wisps gossiping in the corner outside our workshop," he whispered. "They said they saw one of the youngest members of their tribe leading the dew princess out of the Ivy Bower on an evening stroll . . . to her certain death."

"Which direction?" Arjun raked his hands through his hair.

"How should I know?"

Arjun thought quickly. Just before retiring for the night, he'd casually mentioned the tare a league west of his mother's lakeside abode. A seemingly errant comment meant to mollify Pippa's worries. If he had to guess, that was where she was headed. He said a quick prayer to all the gods who might hear him that he would find her in time. He would deal with the eavesdropping wisps later. They had always been among the easiest fey to deceive.

With that final thought, Arjun grabbed the revolver from under his pillow and raced through the door.

WOULD YOU TELL ME, PLEASE,
WHICH WAY I OUGHT TO GO FROM HERE?

ALICE'S ADVENTURES IN WONDERLAND,

LEWIS CARROLL

———◆●◆———

When Pippa saw the lake glistening beneath the stars of the twilit sky, her shoulders fell with relief.

Obviously the wisp was leading her in the right direction, toward the tare near Arjun's family home.

Her smirking fiancé would not be pleased with her for wandering off on her own and leaving him to deal with the aftermath of her disappearance, but Pippa was sure he could weather the ensuing storm. After all, she was a mortal, and the fey of the Summer Court held no illusions as to her inferiority. Besides, Arjun Desai seemed well versed at navigating the intricacies of the gentry.

"Is it much farther?" Pippa asked the wisp.

The wisp paused to bob from side to side, shaking its . . . head.

In that moment, it dawned on Pippa that it was possible the wisp might be reprimanded for its role in her departure. "I want to thank you for your help." She chewed at the inside of her cheek. "Your guidance has been invaluable."

The wisp turned in place and offered Pippa a cheerful chime in response.

Pippa took a deep breath. If she were truly selfless, she would not risk the wisp's fate to save her own. But as much as she wished to deny it, Arjun was right when he'd told her she needed to have some sense of self-preservation.

He would be proud if he knew what Pippa had done to spare herself—and her brother and sister—from their father's wrath. Pippa had yet to feel anything for her actions that night. Not fear or shame or regret or even exuberance. She'd been careful. Cold. Methodical in her planning. Using the Duke of Ashmore's seal, she'd even sent word to the custodian of her father's office to ensure no one would be present the night she set fire to the building. So that no one would be hurt. There had been no room for emotion in her actions. Only the silence of awareness. The need to protect.

It had been quite simple, in the end. Because her father had already perpetrated insurance fraud and arson, it was the work of a moment to place one final nail in his proverbial coffin. One that ensured Richard Montrose, Duke of Ashmore, would no longer be free to harm their family.

Pippa grimaced. Any lingering pain she felt now was the pain of losing the last shreds of affection she held for her mother. It was the kind of hurt she could not swallow, much less discuss.

She continued trudging after the little blue wisp. "I don't suppose you know why the members of your court seem to disdain mortals so much."

The wisp floated up and down, as if raising a shoulder.

"It is nice to know there are those willing to offer a measure of kindness," Pippa said. "I won't forget it . . . erm . . . I wish I knew your name."

The wisp paused midair. Looked left. Looked right. Then rose all at once. Pippa looked up. It floated just beneath the stars, which glimmered in the warmth of a glowing half-moon. Strangely—though it must be well past midnight—the sky clung steadfastly to the light, the way it did in the summers of northern Scotland. As if it would never allow darkness to settle upon the land. The wisp chimed as if it were speaking rapidly, gesturing to the silver stars.

"Is that your name?" Pippa asked.

The wisp brightened all at once.

"Star?"

It shook its head and brightened once more, like a flash of starlight.

"Starlight?" Pippa asked.

The wisp cheered, spinning in a circle.

"Starlight!" Pippa grinned. "If there is anything I might do to show you my appreciation, please don't hesitate to tell me." She paused. "Is there something you might like from the mortal world?"

The wisp paused in thought. Shook its head. Then resumed its trek beside the lake before stopping mid-glide, as if a thought had suddenly occurred. It moved higher, almost eye level with Pippa.

"Is there something you would like?" Pippa repeated.

It paced, then began swiveling around. Pippa followed the

wisp as it blurred past the gnarled trunk of an immense tree she did not recognize.

Her foot caught on a root as she struggled to keep up with the glowing sphere.

"Blast!" She braced her palm on the bole of the gnarled tree, catching herself before she could fall.

The wisp glided to a halt with a sound Pippa could only guess to be a shriek.

She tried to push away from the tree trunk. "Is everything all ri—"

Her hand. Her hand was stuck to the tree, as if she'd pressed her palm into glue.

Pippa turned toward the trunk, her eyes wide. She tried to pull back again.

And the trunk grew around her fingers, swallowing them.

"Oh!" Pippa cried out, fending off a fresh wave of panic. "It's . . . it's *eating* me!"

The wisp bobbed closer, making more shrieking sounds.

Pippa almost pressed her boot into the tree trunk to get better leverage, then stopped herself at the last instant.

"Help!" she yelled. "Dear God, please *help me*."

As soon as she raised her voice a third time, the root that had tripped her in the first place came to life, wrapping around her ankle. It tugged her toward the tree trunk, and Pippa screamed louder, holding out her free hand to stop her face from being pressed into the bark.

Before she could blink, her other hand was swallowed by the

bubbling surface of the tree. The ground emitted a strange swallowing sound. Pippa struggled to wiggle her fingers within the wood, but they felt frozen, as if they'd been turned to stone.

Behind her, she could hear the wisp going mad, its chime loud and sonorous. Then she heard something in the branches above. Something chittering.

Her heart leapt into her throat, her cries dying on her lips.

Of course her shouts would draw the attention of even more danger. It appeared to be her lot in the world of the fey. Pippa wanted to bury herself in the shadows of the tree trunk and pray to the Holy Mother above that whatever this creature was, it would leave her be.

What would kill her first, the tree or the monster?

Something that sounded remarkably like the croaking of a frog was above her head. Steeling herself, Pippa looked up to find a lizardlike creature clinging to the tree trunk less than an arm's length away from her trapped right hand.

She swallowed. It tilted its head. It was the brilliant green of chalcedony, with shifts of blue in the shadows. Similar to the color of her best friend Celine's eyes. The lizard creature smiled at her, its pink tongue flicking from its mouth to lick one of its black eyeballs, the bright half-moon mirrored in its cool gaze.

Strangely it did not appear threatening. Yet.

Pippa swallowed again. She'd stopped moving, and the tree appeared to have ceased consuming her hands and her left foot. Perhaps if she kept still long enough, someone would rescue her.

Another croak resounded, this time louder. Closer.

With great care, Pippa angled her head toward the odd blue-green lizard. The spikes along its back were tipped in brilliant yellow, its long nails black and shining.

It peered at her once more before opening its mouth . . . and spewing a green substance that hissed against the trunk of the tree. A small fleck splashed onto Pippa's cloak, and the fabric started smoking, disintegrating before her eyes, as if it had been burned with acid.

Pippa swallowed another scream. As the acid seared through the trunk of the tree, the bark began spreading up her arms and wrapping around her boots, bubbling beside her skirts. Panic gripped her from the inside. She tried not to struggle, but the lizard creature crawled closer to her head, another ominous croak emitting from its terrifying mouth.

Her limbs began to shake of their own volition. Pippa could no longer hear the chiming of the wisp, and she dared not risk turning her head again. It appeared her floating companion had abandoned her, just as her last dregs of hope had started to fade.

The acid-spewing lizard was less than half an arm's length from her now. How was it that the tree did not want to consume it? Pippa shuddered when she heard its long, glossy nails tap against the tree bark. *Tap. Tap, tap, tap. Tap, Tap.*

The tree had swallowed Pippa up to her elbows. Then it tugged her left leg from underneath her, causing her to lose her footing. Her left cheek slammed into the trunk, sticking hot and fast, like an insect trapped in amber. Pippa screamed as the bubbling bark swelled around half her face. She flailed and twisted, even though she knew it would cause the tree to consume her quicker. Fought for every gasp of air, not knowing if it would be her last.

Her left ear was swallowed, her screams turning into lasting wails. Tears coursed down her cheeks.

"Philippa," a deep voice said from behind her. "Stop moving. Stop screaming."

"Arjun?" Pippa rasped.

"And definitely stop talking." He came to the trunk and rested both his hands on its surface. The bubbling stopped the following instant. Pippa's breathing turned shallow. She still did not trust that all would be well, despite Arjun's heroic appearance in her hour of need. Later she would remember to feel grateful. At this moment, all she felt was resentment. Being rescued was not nearly as romantic as the stories had made it out to be. Pippa felt far too foolish to swoon. The fear was still too sharp, her panic too raw, especially since half her face was still encased in the bark of an evil, flesh-eating tree.

Arjun shifted into view, his features stern. His clothes were disheveled—the buttons fastened at random—and his black hair in disarray. Over his shoulder, the wisp hovered, its motions erratic. Almost nervous.

Though he crossed his arms as he regarded her, his expression was not unkind. "Of all the confounding women I've ever met, you are the most confounding," he said quietly.

"Say whatever you will," Pippa said, her voice hoarse from screaming, "but please get me out of this damnable tree."

"Why did you touch it? I told you not to touch anything."

"I didn't plan to touch it. It was an accident." Anger began to build in her throat. Why was he lecturing her? Did she appear in need of a lecture? "There will be plenty of time later to chastise me. I—I have words for you as well, *beloved fiancé*."

Arjun canted his head. "You're lucky this little wisp managed to find me. Another minute more, and you might not have broken free in time."

"I don't"—Pippa stammered—"I'm not free yet. Why are you waiting to help me?" She shuddered, her fear mingling with the anger. "Are you—are you trying to teach me a lesson?" Her voice turned small. She would not cry. She refused to cry any more in front of him.

"We have to wait for it to harden," Arjun explained.

"How—how did you make it stop?"

"I froze the water inside it." Arjun moved closer, then tapped a raised fist on the bark wrapped around Pippa's right wrist. "Which is what I did earlier with Lord Evandyr." As he spoke, he untied the cloak from around her throat—which was half encased in the bubbled bark—and let the rest of the fabric fall to the forest floor.

Pippa tried to stem the tide of emotions swelling within her. "Can all fey do this?"

"No. Certain members of the gentry possess elemental magic. It's what separates them from the rest of the fey who reside in the Sylvan Vale." With his knuckles, he rapped on the bark encasing her other hand, then stepped back once more. "I'm going to use the handle of my revolver to break through, so don't be alarmed when you see a weapon." He grinned. "I've no plans to shoot you. Yet."

"You brought a revolver?"

He quirked his lips to one side of his face. "Answers help calm your nerves, don't they?"

"Information . . . soothes me."

"I've noticed. Do penguins do anything else of note?" As he spoke, Arjun withdrew a revolver he'd tucked in the back of his trousers. With care, he removed the bullets in the chamber and turned the barrel around to wield the weapon like a hammer.

"Not—not that I can recollect," Pippa murmured. "Not now, at least." She couldn't seem to stop herself from shaking.

Arjun nodded, then began working. "Only a few members of the fey gentry are able to access elemental magic. Long ago, everyone among the highest ranks could control one element, be it fire, water, earth, or air." He chipped away at the bark, which began flaking around them. "On rare occasions, a gifted fey might be able to control two or three, but never all four. The fey blame intermingling with lesser beings—including mortals— for why their powers diminished over the years. It's why they're so concerned with the purity of their bloodlines." He raised his voice to combat the sound of metal striking wood. "The irony of ironies is that their incestual predilections over the centuries have made those in the gentry largely barren." Arjun rolled his eyes. "It infuriated them to no end that a halfblood like me inherited my mother's ability to manipulate water, though I never understood why. The most I can do is freeze the water in something for ten or fifteen minutes. Even less if the other creature is a vampire or a werewolf or some kind of fey, dark or light." He shifted to Pippa's other hand and carefully began cracking through the bark, which fell apart like a layer of clay or a shattered plate. "Mind where you step. These shards can be very sharp."

As soon as her hands were free, Arjun bent on one knee to extricate her ankle from the tangled roots.

"I'll do that," Pippa said, color flooding her cheeks when his hand touched her bare skin. It unsettled her to have him kneeling at her feet, touching her leg. It was ridiculous, to be sure, but Pippa's nerves were already close to unraveling. The last thing she needed was to feel the warmth of his skin on hers. She already felt too much like a loose knot about to come undone.

"Are you really concerned with propriety at a moment like this?" he mocked.

"No. I . . . don't like being touched."

"Liar."

"Pardon me?"

"It's all right," Arjun said while he worked. "I'll keep your secret if you keep mine."

"And what is your secret?" She swallowed.

"I like touching you as much as you like being touched by me."

"Preposterous," Pippa spluttered. "What makes you think I— *oof*!"

He stood at once, catching her as the tree relinquished its

hold and Pippa fell from its grasp. His arms encircled her waist, her hands pressed against his chest for a heart-stopping beat.

Pippa looked up. The half-moon was mirrored in Arjun's eyes. He held her gaze in his, as if he'd reached for her hand. As if he might never look away. His arms tightened the same instant Pippa gripped the front of his loosely buttoned shirt. They were like the roots at their feet, reaching and twining, searching for something to grasp. Seeking a mooring along a deserted coast.

His warmth seeped through her thin undergarments onto her skin, the scent of winter spices suffusing the air. Pippa's throat went dry, and her senses sharpened until she swore she could hear the leaves rustling in the wicked tree and the enchanted wind riffling through her curls.

She did the only thing she could do.

Pippa kissed Arjun. It was heedless. Thoughtless. Breathless.

Her lips were on his. Pippa slanted her head, her fingers curling through his thick hair. He lifted her until she was a cloud floating above a restless sea. In that instant, nothing else mattered. No lies. No promises. No past or future.

Only now.

With a sigh, Arjun deepened the kiss, his tongue touching hers in a wordless reply. Pippa's heart careened through her chest like a caged bird. She squeezed her eyes shut, unwilling to wake from this peculiar dream of danger and delight. It was the first time Pippa had ever been truly kissed. She knew without being told that this was the kind of kiss destined to linger in her memory. To become a tale all its own.

His lips grazed beneath her chin. With a brush of his thumb, he tilted her head up to whisper her name against her skin. "Philippa." A shiver chased down her spine.

Pippa opened her eyes to a sky full of stars. She gasped, awareness tingling through to the tips of her toes.

Arjun's laughter was a gentle caress. "I won't tell if you won't tell."

ON WHOSE EYES I MIGHT APPROVE
THIS FLOWER'S FORCE IN STIRRING LOVE.

A MIDSUMMER NIGHT'S DREAM,

WILLIAM SHAKESPEARE

———◆◆◆———

Arjun Desai was not often at a loss for words. Now he found himself searching the shadows for the right thing to say. Mulling over how to start a simple conversation while failing to silence his mind.

"Are you awake?" he spoke into the cavernous chamber, his gaze focused on the packed-earth ceiling. If he peered through the darkness, he could see the mica and the shimmering rocks imbedded in its depths. The way the firelight flickered across the space as if it were catching the facets of a diamond.

"Yes," Pippa replied after almost a full minute of silence.

"Were you deciding if you were awake?"

"No. I was deciding whether or not to speak."

Arjun paused. "It appears our wisp friends have left us alone for the time being."

"What do you think they will report?"

"The simple truth, as always. We did not share the bed. That you disappeared on an evening stroll, only to return with me. Hopefully nothing more in the way of details." He would make certain of it, even if he had to bribe the little interlopers. They were absolutely mad for mortal spun sugar.

Pippa sighed. "Is it finally safe to speak frankly?"

Arjun propped an arm beneath his head. "It is never safe to speak frankly in the Vale. But there are no spies in this room at present. Nevertheless, I would keep our voices down."

"I suppose . . . I suppose you should come here, then."

Arjun almost laughed. In fact, he would have done so, had he not been alarmed by how his pulse jumped at Philippa Montrose's request. Like an eager lad instead of a suave young man. He stood and made his way—casually of course—to the immense bed set upon the low dais. It was a ridiculous affair, its headboard comprised of twisted branches that undulated when touched. Some fey contrivance meant to improve the lovemaking experience, no doubt. He was certain Pippa had yet to notice it, or she would have screamed.

Arjun supposed it was in fact terrifying to have a headboard that writhed at your caress.

Everything about this chamber was suggestive, down to the sheer expanse of the counterpane. A bed with a surface meant to accommodate . . . more than two people. A thought Arjun found rather exhausting. It was difficult enough to manage one member of the gentry in polite conversation, let alone several at once in flagrante delicto. The idea of dying naked in an overlarge bed, his hands and feet bound by enchanted vines, did not entice him at all.

Well . . . perhaps if he were the one to do the tying . . .

Arjun cleared his throat as he lowered himself onto the side of the dais farthest from Pippa, like some kind of chaste monk.

She stirred in place and faced him, her cheeks rosy, her blue eyes brilliant.

"I wanted to apologize," she said softly, her lips moving with care, drawing to mind an image of their shared kiss in the shadow of a killer tree. A regular Thursday evening, really. "What I did in the forest was—"

"We don't need to discuss what happened. It was nothing of import." Arjun snorted, his expression easy, despite the heat of the memory on his skin. Of the way she smelled, like an English garden in springtime. Of the way she'd felt in his arms. "There are much more pressing matters." *Such as living to see the next day,* he added in his head.

"I—" She hesitated, her furrowed brow accentuating her heart-shaped face. "That was a rather unkind thing to say."

Arjun straightened, not even bothering to conceal his dismay. "That was not my intention, Pippa."

"I don't know that your intentions should matter if you've hurt someone. And even if it doesn't matter to you, I—I kissed you, which matters to me." She paused. "I've only ever kissed one other man."

Though Pippa had not mentioned Phoebus by name, a hot streak of jealousy cut through Arjun's stomach at the thought of her milksop of a future husband, which only served to unseat him further. Arjun Desai had lived nineteen years without playing the jealous lover. He would not start now. Perish the thought.

"I—" Arjun ruffled his hair and averted his gaze. He fought the urge to do as he usually did when it came to delicate matters of the heart. To gloss over details. To lie rather than appear vulnerable in any way. "It's . . . not as though I have a great deal of experience with that sort of thing either."

Pippa sat up, the fur counterpane sliding down her bodice with maddening slowness. "I would have thought otherwise."

"Because I did it so well?" he teased.

She shook her head. "Because you are a man."

He laughed. "Jokes about my prowess aside . . . you are the first mortal I've ever kissed," he confessed. Pippa was also the first kiss Arjun had ever experienced without having consumed copious amounts of fairy liquor beforehand.

"The first mortal?" She tucked a blond curl behind her ear, her lips pressing into a thin line. "I see."

"Are you jealous of the fey girls I've kissed, Philippa Montrose?"

Her skin flushed, her jaw dropping. "No. No, of course not." She wrapped her arms around her knees and let her curls fall forward like a cloak.

Arjun hated that he found her jealousy becoming. Or, at the very least, the fey part of him appreciated it. "A pity. Jealousy is a powerful weapon to wield in the Vale."

"If I wielded it well, could I persuade you to take me home?"

"You wouldn't need to wield a weapon to persuade me of that, Pippa," Arjun said, the words barely above a whisper. "But for our promises, I would whisk you back this very minute."

"I see," she said quietly.

"Don't fret," he continued. "All is not lost. Trust me. And my mother."

Pippa nodded.

The conversation faded to silence. Arjun waited for the discomfort that was sure to follow. The inexplicable need he'd felt since he was a child, to fill any silence with words or laughter or something trite.

Yet there was no discomfort. How strange. Was it her or was it the circumstances?

Arjun refused to believe it was Pippa. It was enough for him to have found a family in a coven of vampires. Losing anyone who mattered was a wound that took forever to heal. At least those in the Court of the Lions were lethal, immortal creatures in their own right. Arjun could not—would not—come to care for a fragile mortal girl. Caring for Pippa Montrose was like holding a glass of delicate crystal aloft in a hurricane.

"I should thank you for coming to my aid again tonight," Pippa murmured. "And then I really should apologize."

"You're welcome," Arjun replied, his voice unforgivably husky. "And you *should* apologize."

"I will if you would let me!" She frowned.

"Why did you follow me through the tare?"

"I . . . thought you might be going to see Celine and Bastien."

"Is it so important to know where they went?"

"It's not about knowing where they went. I want to know that Celine is safe. That—wherever she is—she is happy and free."

"You care for your friend enough to risk your life and limb?"

"She isn't just a friend." Pippa paused. "On the long journey across the Atlantic, when we thought we were alone, we found safe havens in each other. She became my family. Have you ever had a friend who was like family?"

His expression turned thoughtful. Arjun considered how each of the immortals in the Court of the Lions had wormed their way into his heart. The pain he'd felt at Nigel's betrayal. The ache that echoed through his soul when he thought of Odette lying in her deathlike sleep.

Odette. Arjun raked both his hands through his hair and squeezed his eyes shut.

"What would you do if you thought your family was in trouble?" Pippa asked. "For me, there is no stone I would leave unturned. I would do anything and everything to protect them."

Arjun understood her well. His whole reason for coming to the Vale in the first place was to find a healer for Odette, a task that had been derailed by this confounding mortal girl. "Fuck," he said. This was no time for a romantic interlude in the forest or a blasted joint-wedding celebration with one of his archenemies.

"That's the second time in my life I've heard that word spoken aloud," Pippa mused, her tone circumspect.

"When was the first time?"

"When Bastien said it the night we all met."

"I remember now. Were you frightened?"

Pippa frowned. "Bastien has always frightened me. He's . . . too much of everything all at once. He's a lot like Celine. If she does or says anything, it's bold and brash."

"You're not wrong on that score." Arjun almost laughed when

he thought of Celine Rousseau's ability to find danger and waltz in its face with the Devil himself.

"Most days, I'd prefer to be at home with a blanket and a cup of tea," Pippa continued. "I've never minded being a wallflower." She grinned to herself. "It's far easier to overhear the gossip that way."

The similarities between them unnerved Arjun, just as they had when Pippa admitted how much she disliked eating alone. "I prefer the fringes as well," he said. "It's safer to remain unseen."

Pippa smiled her wavering smile, her bare feet toying with the fur counterpane and her delicate hands folded across the torn lace of her underpinnings. When she blinked, her thick lashes fanned across her high cheekbones in a gentle caress.

Arjun took a slow, steadying breath.

If Philippa Montrose thought herself relegated to the shadows, it was most definitely by choice, for she was the furthest thing from a wallflower. Even without the monocle, Arjun could sense the color of desire thickening around him, swirling like a pale pink thundercloud. He cleared his throat again. "I wrote my mother about our wedding while Twylle finished designing your gown. I hope to hear from her no later than early tomorrow afternoon." *Plenty of time to put an end to this farce of an engagement,* he thought to himself, aware that eavesdroppers might still be lurking nearby.

"Where is she?"

"I'm told she's leading a patrol along the westernmost shores of the Sylvan Vale. Apparently there have been some recent altercations with the water nymphs there. They've always tried to challenge the Lady of the Vale's authority. Some gripe about the absurdity of land dwellers holding dominion over those who reside in the water."

"What do you think your mother will do?"

He propped his head on an elbow. "One of my mother's steadfast rules is with respect to falling in love with a mortal." Though he did not elaborate, Arjun was certain Pippa understood his meaning.

"My mother would likely share the sentiment," Pippa said.

"I gathered as much." He laughed. "The duchess, as I recall?"

Pippa nodded.

"One day you will have to tell me that story."

A pained expression crossed Pippa's face. "There's not much to tell."

"I doubt that." Arjun studied her profile. Admired the halo of blond fringe that refused to be tamed along her forehead. But more than that, he appreciated the ease he felt in her presence. As if they'd known each other for years, rather than a few months. A thought took shape in his mind. A request he rarely made, for it would be near impossible for him to return the gesture. "If I may, I'd like for us to continue being honest with each other. Truly honest. It's been . . . refreshing not to play games in the Vale."

Pippa met his steady gaze, her blue eyes piercing. "You play them well, though."

"Out of necessity."

"Liar," she echoed his earlier admonition. "I rather think you enjoy them."

"Just as I enjoy lying on occasion."

"Not even a moment after you asked for honesty," Pippa scolded, only to sober the next instant. "I don't know how I'm going to lie to Phoebus about where I've been."

"It shouldn't be too difficult." Arjun grinned, despite a fresh (and infuriating) wave of jealousy. Damn it. He had no right to be jealous. And of Phoebus Devereux, of all people?

Bastien and Boone would not stop laughing at him if they knew.

Pippa's cheeks warmed. "That's unkind and unwarranted."

"But fitting."

"You object to Phoebus?" she demanded, her cheeks hollowing. As if her hackles were raised in an effort to spare her addlepated intended any of Arjun's judgment.

Damn it again. Phoebus didn't deserve her.

"On the contrary," Arjun said. "He's a fine young man, if a bit . . . uncomplicated. I object to the tyrant he calls a father. Remy Devereux is more than any young woman should bargain for in a future father-in-law."

Arjun did not fail to note how Pippa flinched at the name. "He may be a bit overbearing, but Mr. Devereux loves his son," she said. "Of that I have no doubt."

"Love is not enough, *my darling.* Of that I have no doubt." Irritation flared in his chest as Arjun considered what Remy Devereux might have done to prompt Pippa's reaction. But he said nothing. After all, it was none of his affair how Remy Devereux dealt with his son and his future daughter-in-law.

Pippa remained silent for a time. "Why does your mother object to mortals?"

"Because she married my father and has made no effort to hide the fact that she considers it her greatest mistake." He glanced her way. "The fey gentry are not permitted to marry and divorce at will like Henry the Eighth. A spouse, once chosen, is chosen for all time, which is why it must be done with care and consideration."

"So marrying has a true sense of permanence for you."

"It does," he said. "But I would never expect a mortal to obey the laws of the Vale."

"Nonetheless, marriage has a sense of permanence for me as well, which is why I appreciate your mother's perspective." Her eyes gleamed in the waning candlelight. "I didn't realize until this moment how much you risked by agreeing to marry me," Pippa said, turning toward him once more with a look that sent a frisson of warmth into his stomach. "Thank you, Arjun. I hope, after all this, you might consider me a friend in truth."

"Wouldn't that be nice?" Arjun agreed. "To be friends with one's wife." Though his words sounded teasing, he didn't mean for them to be. Pippa's kindness—her openness and generosity—didn't deserve to be met with his derision.

He was struck by a sudden awareness. It was far too easy to spend time with Philippa Montrose. Arjun . . . *liked* her. Beyond the way she looked in the firelight, like a fairy maiden from a Tennyson poem, her hair in disarray and her clothing torn asunder. She was kind and warm, her humor a quiet delight.

She reminded Arjun of coming home. Of feeling safe and at ease in his own skin.

Arjun cleared his throat. "We should rest," he said. "Tomorrow is certain to be eventful, though I swear you can put your faith in my mother's affections. Or lack thereof."

Though her smile wavered most becomingly, Pippa did not look away. "Thank you again, Arjun. I appreciate you—your help—more than words."

"You're welcome, Pippa."

FOR NEVER WAS A STORY OF MORE WOE.

ROMEO AND JULIET,

WILLIAM SHAKESPEARE

———◆◆◆———

S ébastien Saint Germain stood over the body of the monstrous wildcat and sighed.

He hoped the creature would live. It had been a risk to hunt it, for though it resembled a cougar, it was much larger and stronger in truth. Unpredictable, with a keen sense of intelligence Bastien had yet to encounter in the swamps beyond New Orleans, where he preferred to feast on unsuspecting gators. Something about the coolness of their blood tasted most refreshing.

This beast's whiskers were long, its fangs nearly the width of his palm. Scraps of fabric hung from Bastien's shoulder where it had clawed at him with frightening tenacity.

Another minute or so, and the beast might have bested him.

He supposed it made sense. For one, the fey wildcat was nearly the size of pony, its musculature thick and broad, with a ridge of sharpened bone running down its spine.

Bastien grunted as he massaged his collarbone, waiting for the jagged wound there to heal beneath the light of the halfmoon set high in a pale sky. He forced his sharpened senses to drown out the sounds of the forest so that he might listen for the low thud of the beast's heart.

He heard nothing. He crouched down and studied its massive chest.

Remorse bloomed around Bastien's heart. It had been a point of pride that he'd only killed one of the creatures residing in the Sylvan Vale's enchanted forest, and that had been an accident.

He hated the idea of striking down a magnificent beast like this one. It had proven a worthy foe. What remained of Bastien's ivory silk shirt was stained with both of their blood. Crimson mud caked his bare hands and feet. Usually he did not make such a mess when he ate. Of all the vampires in the Court of the Lions, Jae was the one to feast with the sort of abandon that ran counter to how he comported himself in public. But that was often the way of it. The most proper blood drinker was usually the first one lost to insatiable hunger.

Bastien ran a hand along the back of his neck, his fingertips brushing across the scruff at his jaw and the short black hair on his scalp. He didn't need to consult a mirror to know he was a frightful mess.

He wanted to return home. In more ways than one.

With another sigh, Bastien looked toward the Sylvan Vale's odd excuse for a night sky. A land of perpetual sun even past twilight, the world of the summer fey boasted a blue half-moon, one of three in existence. The other two spanned opposite ends of the Sylvan Wyld, the wintry counterpart to the Sylvan Vale.

The glowing half-moon above should have been glorious to behold, but it only cast Bastien's worries into sharper relief.

He was not where he was supposed to be. Far from the world he'd known his entire life. A part of him had wondered if, with time, he might feel more at home here. After all, his blood-drinking forebears had hailed from this realm. But it remained as foreign to him as the smoke-laden cities of Boston and Philadelphia. Worlds without the vibrant music or color of home.

Bastien knew he should not have followed Celine to the Sylvan Vale. The second she asked him to go with her, he realized it was a mistake. Yet he'd gone anyway. He'd looked into the eyes of the girl he loved and known with unshakable certainty that he would follow her to the ends of the earth and beyond.

The Sylvan Vale offered Celine a chance to escape her fate, which had finally managed to find her from far across the Atlantic. Bastien still regretted not killing the French detective who tracked Celine down at the behest of a wealthy Parisian nobleman. In Bastien's estimation, the nobleman's son—the young man Celine had killed for trying to rape her—deserved everything that happened to him and more.

But Bastien knew leaving New Orleans with Celine was not merely about accompanying her to the Vale so she might flee French justice for a time.

He wanted to escape his fate every bit as much as she did.

Bastien failed his family that night on the riverboat. He failed his uncle Nicodemus and his blood sister Odette. He failed them all.

His mind clouded over at the memory of his uncle's final

moments. As the fire of the rising sun consumed Nicodemus in less time than it took for a child to count to ten. As his true sister—maddened by a life of loss and strife—drew a silver blade across Odette Valmont's throat with stunning finality.

He hadn't been able to save them. And Bastien could not face the rest of his family, who'd taken away Odette's lifeless body in the vain hope that they might undo what could not be undone.

Perhaps if he gave himself enough time away from the mess in New Orleans, the pain in his chest would not be as sharp. His shame would not be as all-consuming. Maybe—one day— he would be able to look the rest of his family members in the eye again. Bastien was so tired. So wearied by all this death and destruction. These constant decisions that held such precious life in their balance.

Alas, the world of the fey had not provided a reprieve from these worries.

Bastien took his time crossing the densest part of the forest beside the shimmering waters of Lake Lure. He walked at the pace of a mortal man as he took in his surroundings.

The land of the Sylvan Vale was lovely. The more Bastien sur-veyed it, the more he was forced to acknowledge that it resem-bled an actual, Eden-like paradise. The pristine beaches along its westernmost shores were comprised of crystalline sand and sparkling azure waters. Its moss-covered woodlands beckoned travelers to settle beneath a canopy of trees while colorful leaves and soft petals rained down upon them like gently falling snow. The air itself was perfumed with intoxicating scents Bas-tien could not readily identify. Like night-blooming jasmine and melting sugar, mixed with something sharp. The green of crushed mint, perhaps.

The lake in the center of the domain was this region's shining jewel.

Lake Lure. He squinted into the distance, studying the surface of the water. From here, perhaps he could fool himself into believing he was still in the mortal world. Then he breathed in the crisp night air. Let the magic take over, reminding him he was nowhere close to home.

Bastien could smell the enchantment in the water. Beneath the lulling waves of Lake Lure swam creatures Bastien recognized from storybooks. Earlier today, he'd watched Celine's mother speak to an actual nymph, its pointed ears frosted with blue gemstones. A creature that resembled the mermaids in fairy tales, but with large eyes like those of a fish and skin the color of a clouded sky. Woven through the nymph's deep green hair were leaves and shining bits of dark metal. Its nails looked as sharp as talons, and its teeth were ivory points. At a distance, the nymph was beautiful. But up close, only a fool would fail to recognize the danger. The malice embedded in the creature's icy stare.

Bastien took another breath.

The nymph's blood did not smell the same either, at least from afar. He had yet to taste it, of course. Celine's mother had assured him she did not mind if Bastien hunted the creatures in her domain, provided they could not speak to him directly. As if that were the lone trait that separated those who mattered from those who didn't. But Bastien had seen the way her court had bristled. The daggered stares they'd aimed in his direction.

They despised the thought of him feeding on any fey creature, highborn or lowborn. Which meant they saw Bastien as the lowest of all.

If they knew how hungry he was now—how hungry he'd become ever since he crossed into their world a few short days ago—they would not allow a monster like him to roam their woods freely.

No matter how careful Bastien was or how often he hunted, he could not keep his bloodlust in check. He felt hungry all the time. Only today, he'd wondered what the blood of a member of the gentry—a summer fey male who persisted in saying cruel things to any creature unlucky enough to serve him—would taste like and found his mouth watering at the thought. If it was anything like how he smelled, it would be like the finest filet mignon served to a starving man.

He knew why his hunger had become so insatiable.

A vampire like Bastien was not meant to subsist on the blood of woodland creatures, even enchanted ones. It was not about the hunt. It was more than that. At home in New Orleans, Bastien relished selecting his prey from the dregs of the Crescent City's underworld. The men and women who moved through life without remorse, their humanity a mutable thing on any given day. The ones who were a law unto themselves.

Bastien had especially enjoyed hunting men who harmed women. When he peered into their thoughts and bore witness to their most violent memories—their hot blood flowing into his mouth, warming his veins—he'd relished that small sliver of justice. Perhaps it was wrong for him to turn to violence as a solution, but Bastien rather thought it was him speaking a language his victims would understand.

It was more than sating his physical hunger. It was the hunger he felt in his bones for something more. Something the paradise of the Sylvan Vale refused to grant him. A refuge for his darkest thoughts and wickedest deeds. A place for him to doff his crown of devil horns and rest his weary head.

As Bastien walked, he marveled at how he and Celine had only been in the Sylvan Vale for three days and three nights. Given his experience the last time he traveled to the land of the fey, he was certain weeks had passed in New Orleans. In a month it would be nearing fall. Fall in the Crescent City was his favorite time of year. It wasn't cold, but the air seemed to change like the turn of the breeze, filling with the scent of spice and smoke. All Hallows Eve would follow soon after. For Bastien, his city came alive that night, when the veil between worlds was supposedly its thinnest.

Behind him, a twig snapped underfoot.

Bastien spun in place, his fangs bared, his hands forming claws. Like a bolt of lightning cutting through the clouds, he blurred into the tree branches to give himself the advantage of higher ground.

Soft feminine laughter echoed through the darkness.

"I did not mean to alarm you, Sébastien," Lady Silla said as she wandered into the moonlight, her bare feet padding across a bed of moss, and her pale blue gown of starlit fabric trailing after her like flowing water. She smiled at him, her expression kind.

Bastien dropped from the trees in a soundless motion. He returned her smile, though he remained wary. If there was one thing he'd learned about Celine's mother, it was that everything she did, she did with intention. Lady Silla meant to follow him unawares through the forest, just as she meant to reveal herself at that exact moment.

It unsettled Bastien that she could approach him without warning like that. But Lady Silla was not the ruler of the Vale by mere happenstance. She was a powerful enchantress in her own right. From what Bastien had observed thus far, she could control air and perhaps earth as well.

She studied his appearance with open curiosity. The way his fey garments did not fit him well. How his silk shirt was shredded along one shoulder. The way the mud and gore clung to his body.

Bastien looked like a feral beast, while Lady Silla resembled a princess from a fairy tale, her black hair long and dark, a circlet of pearls and diamonds gracing her brow, and powdered gold dusting her forehead and cheekbones, her lips gilded with gloss.

Again, she sent him a disarming smile. "Have you enjoyed your hunt?"

"I have. I thank you again for granting me leave to tour the lands of the Sylvan Vale." He wanted to ask her if she had enjoyed watching him hunt, but it was an inappropriate question, in more ways than one. For the fifth time today, Bastien wished he could tell Celine how uncomfortable he felt in her mother's presence. But Celine had only just found Lady Silla after years of believing her dead. She was not yet ready to hear Bastien's unfiltered thoughts.

"You are quite welcome," Lady Silla replied. "My most fervent wish is for you to feel at home here among my people." Again she smiled, her features serene.

He returned the gesture, though his jaw remained tight.

Her dark eyes narrowed along the edges. "As you likely suspect, I did not stumble upon you by chance. I followed you here so we might speak plainly."

Gesturing with his hand, Bastien gave her leave to continue.

"I fear you do not trust me." She laced her fingers together as she spoke.

"If we are to speak plainly, I don't trust many people."

"Under normal circumstances, I would approve." Lady Silla took a step toward him. "But I'm not certain what I might have done to earn your particular mistrust. We both love my daughter, do we not?"

"I love her, if that is what you wish to know. She is my constant, in this life and the next."

She canted her head. "Do you believe I love my daughter, Sébastien Saint Germain?"

"Yes." His fingers flexed at his sides, the muscles in his arms tensing, ready to take on a defensive stance. He hated how he could not seem to control it. As if his body knew a truth his mind continued to deny.

The Lady of the Vale did not miss his hesitation. She took another step closer, and the moss at her feet burst to life, forming a carpet of green clovers. "Do you believe I want what is best for her?"

"Yes." Bastien took a step closer as well. If he lowered his guard, he alone would suffer.

She tilted her head to the other side in response, as if she were mildly amused.

Bastien continued. "And I believe you do not think I am what is best for her."

"Don't take it to heart. I think no man—mortal or fey—will ever be appropriate for Celine. But perhaps . . . perhaps there might be someone more fitting than the blood-drinking descendant of Nicodemus Saint Germain." Her expression was cruelly kind. "You see, I don't object to you directly. There are many admirable attributes in you. But my plans for my daughter are for far greater things. Greater than I could even hope to achieve."

"And if Celine disagrees with you?"

"I am hopeful my daughter and I will come to understand each other better in time."

Bastien was accustomed to Lady Silla's perfect responses. The sort no one could find fault with offhand. But once he peeled away a layer, it was impossible to ignore what lurked beneath her words. Lady Silla never said she disapproved of his relationship with Celine or that she would stand in their way. Rather that she was "hopeful" these circumstances would one day change.

Underneath her civility skulked a tacit threat. And Bastien's nature—for better or for worse—refused to dismiss it.

"Enjoy your stroll back to the Moon Rabbit's Grove," Lady Silla said with an elegant nod of her bejeweled head. "Perhaps I will return later, and we might all share a pot of tea."

Bastien waited for her to take leave, for he had yet to turn his back on a single fey in the Vale. His instincts would not permit him such latitude.

Lady Silla laughed softly, as if she could hear his innermost thoughts. Then she spun in a slow circle and vanished into the shadows.

◦✵◦

Bastien nodded at the two Grey Cloaks stationed by the entrance of the main dwelling high above him, the spiraling stairs leading upward lit by enchanted silver flames and the occasional wisp, which hid as soon as it caught sight of him.

The Lady of the Vale's abode in the Moon Rabbit's Grove beside Lake Lure was the most interesting structure Bastien had ever seen, which was a feat in itself, given that he'd spent most of his life in New Orleans. An ordinary house in the Crescent City was haunted. The better ones were cursed. And the most beautiful home concealed maiming spikes in its intricate scrollwork. Each one told a fraught, delicious story.

Bastien wondered what the story of this home hidden in these soughing branches might be.

The trees in the Moon Rabbit's Grove were tall and wide. Immense, like the sequoias Odette had described out West.

Perhaps a hundred feet high, with trunks as thick as a building, these trees provided the perfect support for a grand treetop residence. The largest structure in the grove boasted a space that shared sides with three of the widest tree trunks. Within its rounded walls of carved redwood was a receiving chamber, along with a room containing a crescent-shaped dining table, and a library complete with curved bookshelves. One entire section was open to a view of Lake Lure, long linen curtains billowing at either end, meant to keep out the elements.

Though Bastien would only admit it under extreme duress, he found the Moon Rabbit's Grove the most enchanting place in the Sylvan Vale. As a vampire, he supposed no one would begrudge him his general disdain for anything related to this land of perpetual sun. But here, deep beneath this canopy of immense trees, every ribbon of light that touched the forest floor seemed like a tiny miracle.

As Bastien made his way up the staircase, which spiraled around the perimeter of the immense trunk, he moved aside to let two winged servants pass by. They twittered in a language he did not understand, their wings catching flickers of moonlight. He swore he heard one of them squeal with discomfort at his proximity. It did not surprise him. No one in the Vale took effort to hide the fact that a blood drinker living in close quarters with them was problematic, to say the least. Only yesterday, Bastien swore he saw three glowing wisps shudder at the sight of him.

It made no sense. Did they have blood he could drink? Did they glow with the light of a star? How would they taste? Bright and . . . sparkling? Bastien missed the taste of champagne.

Maybe he should pour one of the wisps into a crystal goblet and drink to his heart's content.

He smothered a smile as he pushed open the arched double doors carved like the wings of a bird in flight. If he had to surmise where Celine might be, Bastien knew the dining space and the library were among the safest guesses. There were few things in life that Celine enjoyed more than a delectable meal followed by a good book.

Their bedchamber—high in the treetops on the other side of the grove—was reserved for them alone. No books or food or intruders were allowed. Even the light of the sun or the glow of the moon had no place within those walls. It was the one space in which Bastien did not have to remain vigilant at all times.

As he rounded the corridor just beyond the library, a new scent wound through his nostrils, stopping him short. He frowned, then quickened his footsteps.

New blood was here. A scent he did not recognize.

The door to the library was slightly ajar, a ribbon of warm lantern light wavering within. He reached for the handle, and a peal of rich laughter echoed from inside the curved walls.

Celine.

"How absurd," she said, her voice delighted. "This is the most wonderfully absurd thing I've heard in a long while. It's just not possible."

"I'm afraid it is," a male voice echoed from the far corner. "I am proof positive of that fact."

Bastien's hands balled into fists at the sight of a debonair young man, no more than twenty years of age, with tanned skin, thick black hair, and eyes like a desert cat's, perched on the back of a mushroom chair, his features unforgivably all-knowing.

It took less than five seconds for Bastien to dislike him. Immensely. Perhaps it was nonsensical, but the boy smiled at him so slowly—so perceptively—that Bastien's only rational reaction was to respond with intense hatred.

Who in hell was this boy? And what was he doing here with Celine?

"Who are you?" Bastien demanded in a guttural whisper. Though it was clear Celine had not been threatened, he refused to relax his vigilance, even for a moment.

This world—and its many underlying threats—would not allow him such comfort.

The young man snapped shut the book in his hands and stood in a fluid motion, as if he were a dancer or—given the curved blade hanging at his left hip—a master swordsman. "I didn't mean to alarm you." He offered Bastien another reticent grin, as if the gesture did not come to him naturally. As if Bastien had yet to earn a real smile. Though the young man had the appearance of a rake, a quiet intelligence lurked in his eyes. He held fast to Bastien's stare, his hand shifting to the bejeweled hilt of his sword as if on instinct.

Irritation blossomed in Bastien's chest. For a wild instant, he considered drinking the boy dry. He blurred closer, intent on startling him. Focused on making certain the young man knew who the true threat was.

The boy did not flinch.

Bastien's eyes narrowed. He took in a slow breath, trying to determine if the boy was mortal or fey. Friend or foe. Or perhaps a mixture of both.

"My name is Ali," the young man said. He straightened and waited while Bastien measured and weighed him. "I'm mortal . . . mostly," he added. "A guest of Lady Silla."

Another mark against the young man. Bastien continued to take stock. The boy was almost the same height as he was. His black hair was longer than it should be, as if he'd delayed having a proper haircut for several months. His eyes were like those of a predator. And why did he insist on keeping his weapon so close at hand? Upon closer examination, it was quite a work of art. The sort of curved sword Bastien recognized from Moorish art.

"Why are you here?" Bastien asked, his voice low. Menacing.

Celine frowned and took hold of his arm. "What's bothering you so?"

Ali remained unfazed. "Lady Silla said you would not trust me offhand."

"What else did she say?" Bastien replied.

"That you're quite different from Lady Celine." Ali sat down once more, his expression unperturbed. "Not nearly as likable."

Celine huffed. "Bastien is incredibly likable when he wants to be. Dare I say, he can be quite charming when it strikes his fancy. Don't worry, Ali. As soon as he hears your story, he will be as enchanted as I am, both by you and the possibilities."

"If I may," Ali said with a look of admiration at Celine, "please know the sentiment is returned on all accounts."

This was not to be borne. This unwanted guest had availed himself of Celine's hospitality—and Bastien's patience—far too long. And Bastien was loath to admit it, but a flash of possessiveness cut through his core. An air of unmistakable nobility surrounded the boy, down to the drape of his embroidered jacket, which he wore with a great deal more ease than Bastien ever did. As if the style suited him well.

There could be no question that Lady Silla had invited Ali to the Moon Rabbit's Grove with a clear purpose. Bastien recalled the way Celine's mother had studied him, her head tilted appraisingly, the last time they spoke less than half an hour ago. The way she'd suggested there might be a young man more suited to court her daughter than the blood heir of Nicodemus Saint Germain.

When he was mortal, Bastien had prided his ability to hold his true thoughts in check. But with each day in the Sylvan Vale, that skill seemed to diminish by degrees. His hunger was too great, his irritation too palpable. He was not among his own people. These fairy paths were unfamiliar to him.

He was not himself. He was being reduced to his basest element. To kill or be killed.

Now Bastien was quite certain that Lady Silla had introduced a rival for Celine's affection. Of course it would never work. The love Bastien and Celine shared was not easily torn asunder, like the fragile young love of lore. Celine had watched Bastien die. It may not have been his choice, but Bastien had forfeited his soul to keep her safe. Beyond that, they both saw in each other what they had been searching for their entire lives. Their match. The one who made them better today than they were before.

Theirs was a true love story. He knew the curve of her body in the dark. She felt his anger, his sadness, his joy even before he uttered a word. True love stories like theirs never had an ending.

So be it. Bastien was well-versed in playing games. He had been raised in the Court of the Lions. A witness to the endless spectacles his uncle engaged in with dark delight.

If the Summer Court wished to offer Bastien an enemy, he would be glad to oblige it.

"I hope you don't mind that Lady Celine has been assisting me," Ali continued, something hardening in his gaze. Likely an appropriate response, given Bastien's steely demeanor.

"It's not my place to mind what Lady Celine does with her time," Bastien said.

A flicker of surprise flashed across Ali's face. "I would have thought otherwise."

"Because you believe I am the kind of man who controls his woman with an iron fist?"

"Bastien!" Celine said, distaste flashing in her green eyes. "If you insist on behaving so boorishly, you can see yourself out for the evening."

"Not at all," Ali said. "You just seem to be the sort of young man to keep a watchful eye on anything and everything you hold dear." He returned Bastien's cool gaze.

"Whether I keep a watchful eye over anyone or anything is irrelevant. Celine will not tolerate tyranny from a man, especially from a lover."

Ali cast Celine an appreciative glance. "It's why I liked her immensely, from the moment we met."

Bastien sucked in his cheeks in an effort to cool his head.

Celine frowned at Bastien, then offered her warmest smile to Ali. "The last few days have been rather . . . difficult for us. But the last hour has definitely been a highlight. Your story has opened up so many possibilities!" She turned toward Bastien, her expression brightening. Determination furrowing her brow, she took Bastien by the arm and brought him closer to Ali. "Ali is the first mortal I've encountered since coming to the Vale who is not in thrall to another fey. It is so rare for someone like him to be invited as a guest of the fey court without any demands being made upon his presence." She paused, her lips pursing to one side. "I've spoken at length about this with my mother, and I am hopeful this will change in the future. How wonderful would it be if mortals could journey to the world of the fey without fearing for their lives or being tricked into servitude?"

Ali nodded, his features enthusiastic. "Or if the fey were not relegated to using glamour to control mortals but could be as they are and travel to the mortal world, without fear of reprisal?" he continued. "If mortals and fey could exist in each other's worlds in an open, honest way, what might that do for trade? What might that do for the exchange of information?"

Bastien could think of nothing worse than allowing such petty creatures as the fey to roam free on the mortal plane. "Forgive me, Ali, but how do we know you are not in thrall to a fey?"

"Because my mother told me so." Celine's voice turned cross. "Do you believe my own mother would lie to me? We've been informed countless times that the fey cannot lie."

Bastien sighed to himself. "I don't think she would lie to you,

Celine." The strain of keeping his thoughts to himself was quickly wearing thin. "But Lady Silla did stay in hiding for so long, allowing you to believe her dead."

"Because my father made her promise to do just that, until my eighteenth birthday. You know that!" Celine spoke as if she were talking to a petulant child. "My mother has done nothing but be welcoming and warm to us both. I'm not sure why you continue to mistrust her. It's . . . frustrating."

Bastien said nothing. As with her mother, nothing Celine said was wrong or untrue. But it troubled him that the girl he'd known since the beginning of the year—the girl with such an inquisitive spirit—was so willing to trust the woman who had abandoned her without hesitation.

"Forgive me, Lord Bastien," Ali said, his tone apologetic. "I do not wish to be the cause of strife between you." He put out his hand and offered Bastien a measured smile. "Lady Celine has told me people in your world 'shake hands' when they first meet. I imagine it has a lot to do with showing a new acquaintance that they have nothing to fear. Our introduction has not gone as I would have hoped. Perhaps we may start anew?" His stare was piercing. Direct.

The kind of stare Bastien ordinarily liked to see. Fearless above all.

Bastien took Ali's hand and shook it.

"I hope I can trespass upon your hospitality a moment more," Ali continued. "I've been trying to find the solution to a rather confounding problem, and Lady Celine was kind enough to offer her assistance. In our excitement, my manners have escaped me. But I would be grateful for your input, as a man living in these modern times."

Bastien turned to Celine. It was past time for him to change tack. He could not continue to behave like a grumpy old man. Angering the girl he loved would not serve him well, nor would it enable them to make their way back to New Orleans together soon. "I owe you an apology as well. I"—he took a deep breath—"miss my home, and it's wearing on me in a most unbecoming way." He offered the young man a tight-lipped grin.

"Finally some sense." Celine rolled her eyes, and then said in an excited voice, "I've been waiting to tell you something beyond exciting. Bastien, did you know that, despite what you may think, not everyone in the Vale is speaking English? Ali told me the magic of the Vale makes it so that you hear everything spoken in the tongue with which you are most comfortable conversing. The fey in the Sylvan Vale have an entirely different language, and yet we can communicate all the same!" she continued, her lovely features animated. "Ali isn't actually speaking English to us, and when he hears me speak, he hears what I'm saying in his native tongue, a language called Farsi."

"Unless of course there is no translation in Farsi for what you are saying," Ali added.

"Ali has been invited by my mother to stay with us so he can avail himself of the library here," Celine finished. "I know you enjoy research, so I thought we might help him in his endeavor."

Bastien sent her a wry glance. Celine preferred books with

stories and tales of derring-do. Magical worlds filled with sinister shadows and resplendent jewels. But his greatest love knew him well. It could not have escaped her notice that Bastien was becoming increasingly removed from everything around him. He said little and spent more time alone than he ever had in the past.

For most of Bastien's life, he'd never been granted much time to himself. Though he hadn't realized it when he was a child, it was because the members of his immortal family were occupied with trying to keep him safe. As such, they knew where he was and what he was doing at any given moment of the day. More often than not, one or two of them would accompany him on even the most mundane outing. It hadn't bothered Bastien in the past. But now, he recognized how . . . revived he felt after spending some time in the company of no one but himself.

"Bastien?" Celine asked, a single dark brow arched into the smooth skin of her forehead. "Have we lost you entirely?"

He shook his head, a smile ghosting across his lips. Bastien didn't know what the best course of action was. It was a strange feeling for him, this uncertainty. But he knew he loved Celine Rousseau more than anything in the world. Her courage and her brazenness. The stubborn way she refused to back down. The way she loved just as she lived, without reservation.

Bastien relished the dark beauty inside her. Just as she relished the darkness he wore as a vampire, like a cloak of blood and stars. For most of his mortal life, he'd been protected. Now he was a protector.

And he would do whatever needed to be done to keep Celine safe and happy.

"I'm here," Bastien said with a tentative smile. "What do you need from me?"

She brightened. "Ali is trying to find a mirror."

"What?" Bastien cast the young man a quizzical look.

"It's a mirror that defies the notion of time," Ali said.

"He said that, with it, one could travel to another period in history," Celine said. "Perhaps even change an event in the past." Her words were eager. He knew what event in particular she yearned to change.

Bastien's heart quickened at the thought. He, too, had a night he would like nothing more than to undo. Perhaps more than one night. "Why are you searching for this mirror?" he asked Ali.

"Because I am lost in time," Ali said. "I . . . don't know how I came to be in the Sylvan Vale in the mortal year of . . . what was it?" he asked Celine.

"1872."

Ali sighed. "I think the mortal years are passing by quickly here. The last mortal who came to the Vale said it was 1813. To my recollection, that cannot have been more than a few months ago."

"How long have you been here?" Celine said.

Ali mused for a moment. "No more than a year."

"My mother says time moves differently in the world of the fey," Celine replied. "In the span of a single day in the Vale, an entire week or more may pass in the mortal realm. There are stories of humans who ventured here for a few short weeks and found that a year of their lives had passed on earth."

"And I become farther and farther removed from my family and my place in time," Ali said quietly, his expression grave.

Bastien nodded. "Your reason for wanting to travel back in time is to be reunited with your family?"

"Yes," Ali said. "I want nothing else in the world."

"And I want to help Ali," Celine said, her tone firm. "In doing so, perhaps we might even help ourselves."

"Do you suppose . . ." Bastien paused in thought. "As Celine suggested, would it be possible to change something that happened in the past if we were able to find this mirror of time?"

"It's possible." Ali frowned. "But I worry that it could change the course of everything that happened after."

Bastien took a seat on the lounge beside Celine. For the first time since meeting Ali, he allowed his body to relax. "Ah, I see. So if I were to change the events of the day I first met Celine, there is a strong possibility I would not meet her at all."

Ali nodded. "It's a fascinating and frightening prospect all at once."

"Where is this mirror now? And why can't you simply return through it?" Bastien asked.

"The answer to both those questions," Ali said, "might require much of you to believe."

Celine laughed. "We are living in the treetops of a fairy abode. My mother is a fairy queen, and my lover is a vampire. I believe we are up to the task."

"It was a . . . mistake," Ali said, his features drawn. Grave in their sadness. "In the land where I come from, we have magic as well. After I arrived in the Sylvan Vale, I realized that such magic must exist in all parts of the human world, and that much of it likely comes from different realms like this one. My mother retained a bit of this magic, and it allowed her to control air. With it, she could make certain things—certain odd things—fly. I have some of this power, but it is erratic, and I do not know how to control it. I took one of her . . . flying contraptions and used it to travel to a place I should not have gone." He drifted for a minute, lost in a memory. "While there, I found a mirror, and when I touched it, it swallowed my hand like the surface of a pool. My curiosity got the better of me, and I pushed through to the other side and found myself in a room filled with similar mirrors. Walls of them, like some kind of labyrinth. Soon I lost my way, and when I tried to return through the silver I first used, I stepped into another one that brought me to the woods just beyond the Ivy Bower."

"Luckily my mother was present at court that day," Celine interjected. "It's possible Lord Vyr would have ordered him to turn into a singing dog or something of the like."

"They did in fact make me sing," Ali said with a half smile. "Fortunately I have a fine singing voice and a gift for poetry. This caught the attention of your mother, and she spoke with me at length, as the labyrinth of mirrors has been something she's hoped to find for many centuries. I've been at the Summer Court for a year now, trying to determine how I might return to the mirrors and make my way home."

Despite his initial mistrust, Bastien realized they shared a common goal. Both he and Ali wanted to return home. He still did not trust the boy—and most definitely did not trust Lady Silla's reason for introducing Ali to Celine—but the time-traveling young man's story was indeed a compelling one. And it tantalized Bastien that uncovering the truth behind Ali's search unsealed worlds of possibility.

Ali opened the book in his hands. "You see, there have been documents throughout the history of mankind suggesting that certain individuals were able to travel through portals to a different time and place. The most likely gateway is some kind of mirror or some kind of enchanted monolith."

"Like the sarsen standing stones in the English countryside," Celine said. "Ali and I were discussing some of these dolmens throughout the world, and he recently learned that the British Isles are second only to Korea for having the most of these gates still intact."

"Lady Silla has been providing assistance to me for quite some time," Ali said. "And I am honored that Celine has taken such an interest."

Bastien studied Ali for signs of subterfuge. He still felt as though Ali had yet to share the entire story, and he knew better than to trust that the boy's motivations might be as pure as the simple wish to go home.

But if Bastien could change the events of that night—to prevent Odette's final death at the hands of his sister, Émilie—he could return home. If Celine could find a way to alter the facts of the evening she'd killed the French nobleman's son, perhaps the detective would not be able to find her.

Then she, too, could return to New Orleans without fearing the reach of Parisian justice. Of even the slightest chance she might face the dreaded guillotine.

Not that Bastien would ever allow that to happen. He would tear apart anyone who tried.

"How might I be of assistance?" Bastien asked Ali. He offered the newcomer the first true smile he'd shared with anyone since sunset and was met with Ali's first earnest smile in return.

"Well," Ali began, "when I was in the maze of mirrors, I noticed . . ."

———————◆◆◆———————

Pippa stood before the entrance to the Summer Court just before sunset, a ball of nerves gathering in her stomach. Her fingers smoothed across her snow-white skirts, the hem and sleeves fading to a dusky-rose hue. It was a gown unlike any she had ever worn in her life, the silhouette far more fitted to her natural form than the dresses she was accustomed to wearing. Of late, her corset and undergarments were intended to create the fetching shape of an hourglass. Instead, this gown clung to Pippa's slender body, her figure appearing almost willowy. As if she belonged in the fey world.

Just as Twylle had promised, this was the finest garment Pippa had ever worn. The white was so bright it glowed from within, the silk overlaid by the translucent fabric the green nixie had first suggested, which shimmered with each of Pippa's movements. Tiny diamonds and seed pearls formed a fitted bodice across her chest. An occasional rosy tourmaline was stitched among the other gems at random, meant to accent the fading pink dyed along her sleeves and hem.

Despite that this was the most beautiful gown Pippa had ever worn, the only sentiment that clung to her was one of supreme discomfort.

She'd been gone from New Orleans for nearly twenty-four hours. By now, Phoebus would have informed his father that she was missing. Undoubtedly Remy Devereux had contacted the police, which meant that Michael Grimaldi knew of her disappearance.

The first place he would go would be to the Court of the Lions.

Unease unfurled down Pippa's spine.

She was to be married in less than two days. She did not have time for this nonsense.

Pippa glanced toward Arjun Desai, who'd moved into position beside her, a look of affected boredom on his brow. She wasn't fooled by his appearance. Not anymore at least. Following the events of last night, Pippa had decided Arjun was not as world-weary as his features suggested. If anything, she suspected him to be harboring a well of emotion. How deep this well was, Pippa could only guess.

"Don't fret," he murmured. "As soon as my mother puts an end to this farce, you will be on your way."

She nodded. He took her hand. "To keep up appearances," he reassured her, his touch warm. Only a day before, it had been oddly comforting. Now Pippa came to realize she found it simply . . . comforting. Strange, that. She nodded again. Together they walked toward the curtain of vines before them. Pippa gasped when the waxen leaves parted of their own volition, as if the vines sensed their nearness.

Hand in hand, Pippa and Arjun stepped through the curtain

into a tunnel of undulating ivy. Pippa shrank back in discomfort when the leaves reached for her. When they moved to caress her skin with the gentleness of a lover. She looked at Arjun, but she did not notice the vines grasping for him.

"They're meant to deter unwanted intruders," he murmured, squeezing her palm and threading his fingers through hers, his touch warming through her skin.

All at once, Pippa found herself recalling Phoebus' touch. How he had trembled the first time he took her hand. How his palm felt clammy. She'd been endeared by it at first. Phoebus had been so nervous—so out of sorts—that he'd fumbled, both in words and in gestures. It did not bother Pippa that he was a bit blathering, nor that his spectacles were unendingly smudged. He was kind and gentle. After living under her father's roof, Pippa had wanted nothing more.

Arjun Desai did not tremble. His touch was warm. Firm. Unflinching. He moved with surety and precision, as if daring the world to toy with him.

It had been so long since Pippa found herself thinking she could lean on someone fully. Even with Celine, their friendship had felt like one of shared strife. They supported each other. Loved each other. Pippa had wanted Celine to lean on her when her friend experienced difficulty.

And yet . . . Pippa had not truly leaned on Celine. Not once had she told Celine about her little brother and sister. It had just felt wrong. Especially when Pippa could see how troubled she was. How the circumstances surrounding Celine's decision to leave her home in Paris had worn away at her.

Pippa had wanted Celine to confide in her. But Pippa had failed to share her troubles just as much as Celine had. Perhaps if they had been more earnest—if Pippa had relinquished her pride—they could have helped each other. Spared each other a measure of the pain they'd both experienced of late.

Regret was a strange emotion. And if—

"What in the nine hells?" Arjun said the instant they cleared the tunnel of shifting vines to enter the Great Hall of the Ivy Bower. Birch trees lined the walls, their branches joining with the mighty oaks above to form a vaulted ceiling. Beams of amber light filtered through the autumn leaves.

Alarm coursed through Pippa's veins. "What's wrong?"

"My mother," Arjun replied under his breath. "My mother is already here."

"Where?" Pippa craned her neck.

"Standing with Lord Vyr on the dais at the opposite end of the room, beneath the arch of silver vines." His grip on her hand tightened. "She's wearing a white cloak with shining trim."

Pippa's alarm rose into a flush of panic. "Should she not have come to speak with you first, as you requested in your—"

"Don't worry," Arjun said with a wide smile, nodding at another member of the gentry close by. "It will be fine. All will be well."

Despite his assurance—all his calm precision—Pippa could not silence the dread building in her stomach, which begged to disagree.

———◆◆◆———

Arjun always hated when people said they needed to pause and take a deep breath first. What purpose would that serve? To provide more air to your lungs for a better scream? Or perhaps a final chance to tuck tail and run?

Why didn't they just say they needed a moment? What did air have to do with it?

For the first time in his life, Arjun understood the sentiment. At this minute, he needed one last breath of fresh, unencumbered air . . . in the vain hope that it would fill his body and carry him high into the clouds, far away from this place.

Beside him, a beam of light struck Pippa's brow, momentarily blinding her. She winced away from it, her long eyelashes fluttering. Arjun squeezed her hand again, but he knew it was no longer reassuring. His grip was too tight, his touch too filled with worry.

What the bloody hell was his mother doing with Lord Vyr? She was standing on the dais as if she were condoning this whole affair. When had she arrived to the Ivy Bower?

And why in God's name had she not come to speak with Arjun—*her only son*—yet?

She wouldn't fail him. She couldn't fail Arjun in this. The one truth his mother had held fast to from his childhood regarded the perils of marrying a mortal. Joining hands with a human for all eternity would be the biggest mistake of his life.

He took another deep breath. Tried to root out the truth. If the past was any indication, his mother was undoubtedly delaying the inevitable to teach Arjun a lesson. She'd done this in the past, like the time he'd fallen from the tree and broken his leg after refusing to heed her advice. Climbing trees was a dangerous affair, after all.

Arjun stood straighter. Affected a nonchalant grin. If she was going to toy with his fate like this, he saw no reason to stand in her way. Perhaps he would wait to see who flinched first. It would be like when he'd witnessed two phaetons race on a track outside Cambridge. How the two drivers had angled their carriages toward each other on a collision course. How everyone had cheered and jostled for a better view, waiting to see which driver would succumb to his fear first.

Hang it all, Arjun refused to swerve before his mother did.

He looped his arm through Pippa's and glanced at the collection of elegantly attired fey milling about the space, their finery even more ridiculous than it had been the day prior, the fabrics reflecting gold and silver thread, their headdresses unforgivably elaborate: antlers and horns, coiled loops of hair dyed every color of the rainbow, coronets with dazzling stones the size of Arjun's fist, tiaras fashioned from glittering diamonds and glowing emeralds. Low-slung sashes and bandoliers of shining silver. One young woman wore an immense dress with a skirt that changed colors as she walked, the hem flaring out like the fins of a mermaid around her feet.

"Arjun." Pippa's voice shook.

"All will be well, my love," Arjun murmured. "Trust me. My mother is as inevitable as death and taxes."

"Do they have taxes in Fairyland?"

Arjun nodded. "That throne—like so many things in life—isn't free." He scanned the crowd, watching as the gentry laughed and carried on, their goblets catching on rays of filtered light, their jewels flashing as if in warning. Irritation gathered at the bridge of his nose. Pippa pressed closer to him, her shallow breaths washing across the side of his neck in an unsettling fashion. If Arjun didn't know better, he would think she was trying to entice him. And though he appreciated her nearness—for it shrouded the content of their conversation under a cover of affection—he did not care for the way it caused his stomach to clench or his jaw to ripple.

A flitting fairy buzzed into sight an arm's length from Pippa's face. "Lady Philippa?" the two-foot-tall winged fey asked, his voice raspy and high-pitched.

"Yes?" Dread pulled at every feature of Pippa's beautiful face. She would make a frightful card player, that was for certain.

"You are to come with me," the purple-skinned fey continued. "Now."

Pippa blinked. "Why?"

"The ceremony will start presently." The winged fey blinked his black eyes, mocking her. "Lord Arjun is to be led to the dais by his mother. It wouldn't do for you to walk with them, now would it? You're not quite a member of the chief huntress' family, after all."

Pippa sent Arjun a questioning glance. In response, Arjun studied the purple fairy for a moment. Then, without warning, he grabbed the fey by one of his clawed hands. The outraged creature gnashed his teeth and hissed, spittle flying from his lips.

"Who is leading her to the dais?" Arjun demanded.

"No one, halfblood," the fey screeched, the sound like nails on slate. "She has no kith or kin at court, as you well know."

"Then who is responsible for her?" Arjun arched a brow. "You?"

"What of it?" The winged fairy squinched his nose and bared his fangs.

"Good," Arjun mused. "If something untoward happens to Lady Philippa, it's good to know whose wings I'll be collecting. Yours would make a fine addition to my trophy wall in the earthly realm. They're ever so dainty. Ever so . . . fragile."

The little fairy gasped, his black eyes rounded in outrage. "I hope she snaps your tiny spindle in half tonight, you miserable mongrel! Release me." The fey struggled to pull free of Arjun's grasp.

"What anyone does with my *sizable* spindle is none of your affair. Promise no harm will come to Lady Philippa on your watch, and I'll let you go."

"I promise, I promise," the fey yelled, his burgundy jacket straining from his effort to free himself. "No harm will come to Lady Philippa while she is in my care."

Nodding, Arjun released the fey's hand. The fairy lifted up the back of his jacket, yanked down his trousers, and flashed

Arjun his purple backside. Then he gestured for Pippa to follow him.

Pippa snared Arjun by the elbow. "What if—what if—" she whispered, her words soundless. "I have to get home. I have to keep them safe."

Though he was puzzled by this, Arjun gripped her hand in his. Now was not the time to indulge his curiosity. "Keep close. Remember the rules. All will be well." He tightened his grasp as a reminder. As long as they were together—as long as he held her palm in his—all would go as planned. All would be well.

"Do you promise?" Pippa squeezed his hand.

Arjun caught himself before replying. If a fey broke their promise, they risked being banished from the Otherworld. Ethereals like Arjun were not held to the same standard, but it had been a point of pride to him that he'd never broken a promise once in his life. If there was any chance he might break it, Arjun would not offer it in the first place.

He wavered for an instant.

Pippa's eyes widened. "Do you promise?"

Arjun thought of the two racers set on a collision course. Of how his mother would never—under pain of death—yield in her convictions. "I promise."

———◆◆◆———

Pippa stood at one end of a long aisle carpeted with thick clover. A shower of white petals drifted through the air. Nueyyla, her winged pixie guardian, hovered beside Pippa's left ear, his anger still evident in the splotches marring his purple cheeks.

"You have something prepared," Nueyyla said in a scratchy voice. "Do you not?"

"What? What are you talking about?"

Nueyyla tsked. "If you don't have something prepared to offer as tribute to your impending union, you will be asked to spill blood." The two-foot-tall fey practically vibrated with glee at the thought.

"What?" A mixture of panic and fury swirled in Pippa's stomach. "What is wrong with everyone here? *Blood?*"

"There is magic involved in the marriage rite," Nueyyla said. "It isn't just words. It's a promise. Powerful magic—binding magic—like this has a price."

"I will not pay for a promise with my blood. It's barbaric," she whispered hotly. *"And why did no one tell me this until now?"*

Nueyyla sniffed. "A union of this import demands some kind

of sacrifice. Paying for magic in blood is an old custom and hasn't been required for some time during the Rite, but Lord Vyr insisted on honoring our past in celebration of his future." He nodded toward the enchanted silver fire sparking near the opposite end of the clover aisle, the center of its flames flashing a white-hot light. "A few drops of your heart's blood fed to the Mystflame should be more than sufficient." Nueyyla turned his head and offered her a slow, wicked grin. "Are you handy with a blade?"

Pippa knew the little fey relished the idea of her having to search for an instrument to pierce her skin. "You asked if I had something prepared," she asked, her voice hurried. "Is there something else I can offer to the flames in tribute?"

The pixie snarled, his nostrils flaring. He said nothing.

"I know you can't lie," Pippa continued. She bent her head so she could stare the hovering fairy in the eye. "Now answer my question. Please."

Begrudgingly, Nueyyla crossed his arms. "If you have nothing prepared, you may sing a tune or dance a jig, so long as you freely give these things of yourself." He paused. "Years ago a mortal offered poetry. Another threw his painting into the fire." He coughed, amusement once again shining in his eyes. "Do you possess any real talent, mortal?"

"I can . . . sing."

"Very well," Nueyyla said with a pout. "You may offer the fire a song . . . or your heart's blood. The choice is yours."

Pippa chewed on her lower lip. She hadn't sung in public since her grandmother's death. The songs she knew how to perform well were in Gaelic, the language of her mother's family. Her hands curled into fists. Singing had long since ceased to provide Pippa with a refuge. Now it brought with it only the pain of memory.

What did a mortal song mean to these capricious fey? If Pippa sang in their presence, they wouldn't know what it cost her. What it meant to her.

Arjun had sworn this marriage would never take place. He'd promised, after all. It wouldn't come to that. She wouldn't have to sing. Pippa had to believe it wouldn't come to that.

"My lieges and lords and ladies," Vyr announced from beside the Mystflame roaring at the opposite end of the Great Hall.

A hundred heads turned in his direction, the noise from the milling crowd fading to a din.

"Welcome to the celebration of my marriage to Liege Sujee, as well as Lord Arjun's marriage to the mortal, Philippa Montrose." His grin widened. "It is a pleasure to share in the joyous celebration of the Rite with those we hold near and dear."

A smattering of applause followed this announcement.

Pippa's eyes searched the crowd for Arjun Desai. She expected to see him standing on the dais beside Lord Vyr. A ball formed at the base of her throat when she realized Arjun Desai was nowhere to be found. The time she'd spent bickering with Nueyyla had cost Pippa her bearings. Panic began to take root in her chest.

"You are Philippa Montrose?" a soft voice said from behind her.

Pippa whirled where she stood, her arms tangling in the diaphanous cloud of her veil, the small pink tourmaline stones glittering as she struggled to free herself. "Yes," she said. "I am Philippa."

The woman who stood before her was small. Slight. She appeared no more than twenty-five years of age, though her hazel eyes were wise. Sharp. Attuned to every detail. She wore ivory fitted trousers and a matching doublet made from a fabric that greatly resembled raw silk. A matching ivory cloak with a silver insignia was thrown over one shoulder. Her black hair was collected in an intricate bun at the crown of her head, held in place by several diamond-studded pins.

The fey woman studied Pippa in silence, her eyes scanning slowly from the top of Pippa's head to the tips of her silver-slippered toes.

"You wish to marry my son," the woman said in a grave tone. "Why?"

"I—" Pippa gasped once. Then straightened as Nueyyla flitted closer, his face fixed in delighted horror. Pippa's mind churned through possibilities, searching for the right answer. Should she tell the truth? Should she lie? What answer would best serve her purpose to take leave of the Sylvan Vale as soon as possible? Could she tell the truth, with Nueyyla standing near, listening to every word she uttered?

And where in God's name was Arjun?

"No." Arjun's mother glided closer to Pippa, her movements quicker than a flash of lightning. "Don't think about what I wish to hear. Answer true, mortal. If you can."

Pippa blinked. "I . . . wanted the life I chose to be an answer, not a question." The instant the words left her mouth, she wanted to shrink into herself. They sounded so trite. She'd often thought such things, but she'd never dared to say them aloud before.

A commotion started from the opposite end of the Great Hall. From her periphery, Pippa watched with relief while Arjun shoved away members of the fey gentry who had gathered around him, obviously with the intention of impeding his path.

Arjun's mother leaned toward Pippa. The scent of evergreen trees and lavender rose from her copper skin. "I'm listening, Philippa Montrose. Speak true."

Pippa bit her lip and chose a version of her truth. "For most of my life, I allowed circumstances to dictate my fate. I don't want to do that anymore." She stared straight into General Riya's intense eyes, their hue so similar to those of her son and yet so different. All at once, Pippa felt that same, strange calm descend on her. The calm she'd experienced the first time she locked gazes with Arjun Desai across the crowded hall yesterday afternoon.

When she searched for a savior and he wordlessly urged her to save herself.

"I am not looking for a partner to complete me," Pippa said. "I want a marriage that brings a sense of peace and understanding. A sense of home." She had hoped to find such a marriage with gentle Phoebus Devereux. But in that instant—for a brief flicker of time—Pippa wondered what it would be like to find her home in Arjun Desai.

"I feel a sense of peace when I'm with Arjun," Pippa said. "And I hope he feels that peace with me."

General Riya continued staring at Pippa in silence, her features unreadable.

Pippa chewed at the inside of her cheek. It was a deliberately vague answer. But she could not trust Arjun's mother with the entire truth. Pure-blooded fey could not lie. Arjun's mother might be forced to reveal their deception to the gentry. What would happen to Pippa if the protection of Arjun's family was taken from her? Would she ever see Lydia and Henry again? Without them, Pippa could never find a home anywhere, in any world.

The general narrowed her gaze.

"Mother." Arjun skidded to a stop right before them, his eyes wide, a bead of sweat on his brow. He caught himself. Smiled at the growing throng of curious onlookers. "What are you doing?" he said through his teeth.

Still the general said nothing. She merely looked from her son to Pippa and back again. Then she inhaled through her nose. "I wanted to meet your mortal bride without your hovering like an insect in the wings, waiting to twist every word to your advantage."

Arjun's smile faltered for less than a second. "Mother, I believe you might—"

"You understand that I suffered for choosing to marry your father," General Riya said.

Arjun nodded. "Yes."

A pause. "You understand that he suffered as well."

"Yes."

"I suppose you suffered, too." She pronounced the last statement in a begrudging tone that surprised Pippa. Shouldn't a mother care about her son's pain?

"Whatever gave you that idea?" Arjun grinned in an easy, unaffected fashion. "Have I not become all that you'd hoped I would become?"

Arjun's mother frowned at her son, her expression pensive.

Relief washed through Pippa's body. Just as Arjun had predicted, his mother would put a stop to this wedding.

General Riya took in a careful breath. "What games are you playing, Arjun?" she asked her son.

"I'm not playing any games." He arched a brow at her, his hazel eyes gleaming.

"I came here with all haste to put a stop to this farce of a marriage, just as you knew I would. It is unfair to this poor mortal girl for you to inflict yourself and this world on her in such a selfish manner." Her voice dropped further. "After all you suffered—your struggle to find a home, a place to belong—you should know better."

"What is it the mortals say?" Arjun wondered aloud, his tone airy. "The apple doesn't fall far from the tree."

General Riya glanced Pippa's way. "Do you want to marry my son?"

"I—I—" Pippa didn't know how best to respond. She looked at Arjun. Bit her lip.

"Of course she wants to marry me," Arjun lied. "Just as I want to marry her. We wouldn't have announced it to the world if we didn't. The only question now is what happens next."

"A lifetime of questions," General Riya said softly. She glanced at Pippa once more. "Searching for answers."

"Well," Arjun joked, "just the right one."

Pippa's nerves were coming undone. Arjun jested as if he knew he'd already won the battle. As if he knew his mother would do precisely as he wanted.

"You are my only son, Arjun," General Riya said. "I do not wish you to join in a marriage rite with just anyone."

"I suppose you would prefer I marry among the gentry," Arjun agreed.

"I've never hidden that desire," she replied. "Just as you've never hidden your wish to defy me at every turn."

Arjun raised a flippant shoulder.

General Riya looked at Pippa yet again. Exhaled as she searched Pippa's eyes for . . . something. "For a mortal, you chose well," she said. Then the general whirled on her heel and vanished into the crowd.

Arjun continued smiling as if nothing had happened. He took Pippa's hand. Followed in his mother's footsteps, purpose in his every movement.

"Arjun," Pippa whispered, the panic starting to rise in her throat. His mother was not going to stop this wedding. "What are you—"

He drew her into an embrace, his breath against her ear, the warmth of his skin bleeding through the thin fabric of Pippa's fairy gown. "She's calling my bluff," he said softly. "I will not turn away first. If our charade is revealed now, they will descend on you like vultures. I refuse to let that happen. I swear on my life that you will be home before the last rays of sunlight touch the horizon."

"But what if she—"

"My lieges, my lords, and my ladies!" Vyr announced from the opposite end of the audience hall. "Shall we *finally* begin?"

Pippa's heart lurched to a stop in her chest.

"Don't fret," Arjun said again, his voice barely audible over the rising din. "She wishes to test me. When it comes time to say the vows, she will stop it. I know her."

Pippa disagreed. If she'd learned one thing from their earlier interaction, General Riya was not one to flinch or turn away. Nor was she as predictable as Arjun professed her to be.

It dawned on Pippa in that moment that General Riya did not really know her son. Did Arjun really know his mother, as he claimed? Pippa had seen true conviction in his mother's eyes. Was it the desire to teach her son a lesson? If so, which lesson?

Arjun threaded his fingers through Pippa's reassuringly, his posture poised. Confident.

Was he right? Would his mother stop them before their vows were made? If Pippa protested—revealed their deception—what kind of horrors would the fey gentry of the Summer Court inflict on her?

Pippa followed Arjun up the dais to stand beside Lord Vyr and Liege Sujee. Between the two couples lay a small table with a covered tray and a wrapped parcel. Her heartbeat rose to a steady thrum.

A tall, slender fey wearing a deep purple raiment, which offset his long plait of white-gold hair, stepped forward and raised his arms, mirroring the set of immense antlers wrapped around the empty throne at his back.

"We begin," he announced. When he opened his mouth to chant, a hush descended on the crowd. The light weaving through the treetops dimmed. Around them, enchanted fireflies sparked to life, hovering in the air like living jewels.

The sound of the chanting filled the warm air. Flowed like a song with an ancient melody. Pippa saw Liege Sujee's eyes close, silent tears falling down their cheeks. Lord Vyr bowed his head in reverence.

Arjun continued staring at his mother, a knowing smirk on his lips. Then the slender fey with the white-gold hair and the purple mantle stopped chanting and, with infinite care, removed the silken wrappings from the small parcel on the table before him.

Inside was a glazed vase, painted with thorns and flecked in gold leaf. Liege Sujee nodded at Lord Vyr, who smiled at his betrothed with clear affection. Then—without a word—he withdrew a small blade from the sleeve of his emerald wedding ensemble and cut a slit down his palm. A moment later, he squeezed his heart's blood on top of the glazed vase.

With a satisfied nod, the fey lord conducting the marriage rite removed the silver dome with a flourish, revealing a plate of food.

Amusement rippled through the crowd. Pippa glanced at Arjun with a look of puzzlement.

Rice? He'd made her rice and . . . vegetables?

"I promise my bride she will never go hungry another night in her life," Arjun said, his words soft as he gazed down at her. As if they were meant for Pippa alone. For a blink of time, all appearance of jest vanished from his features. Pippa saw truth. A glimmer of home.

He'd prepared a meal for her? How . . . wonderful. Warmth blossomed to life behind Pippa's heart. She felt it shudder, as if it were awakening from an age-old slumber.

"Do you have anything to offer?" the tall fey with the white-gold hair asked Pippa.

"She is mortal." Arjun cut his eyes at the fey lord. "It is not customary for—"

"I can sing," Pippa said. Her voice did not waver. She looked at Arjun's mother. When would the general put a stop to this? Pippa waited for General Riya to meet her gaze, but the stoic woman continued watching her son, as if daring him to defy her.

It appeared Arjun Desai had inherited his stubbornness from his mother.

Pippa turned toward Arjun. His eyes met hers the next instant. In their depths, Pippa could see him beseeching her to trust him. He'd done so much to keep her safe. Prepared a meal for her. Even now, he held her palm in his. He would not fail her.

Pippa closed her eyes and decided to trust Arjun.

Nuair a bha mi 'm chaileig ghòraich
Thug mi gaol is gràdh don òigeir
Aig am bheil a' phearsa bhòidheach
'S cha ghràdhaich mi ri m'bhèo fear eile

Pippa listened to the words flow from her lips. Magic wove through each note, until she swore she could hear the melody curling through the trees not just in Gaelic, but in English as well.

> *When I was a foolish young girl*
> *I gave my love to a young man*
> *Who was tall and comely*
> *And my love, for as long as I live, will be for no other*

Pippa sang for her grandmother. For all the lost memories of her happy childhood. Memories drowned in her mother's laudanum and her father's tumbler of whiskey. In the way Lydia and Henry would look to her first before speaking, as if she might spare them from their father's anger or their mother's absence. She sang for her brother and sister. For her best friend, Celine.

Pippa squeezed Arjun's hand.

She sang for him, too.

> *Ach tha mis' an dùil 's an dòchas*
> *Gu'n tig an là 's am bi sinn còmhla*
> *'S ma bhios tusa dìleas dhomhsa*
> *Cha ghàdhaich mi ri m'bheò fear eile*

> *I live in expectation and in hope*
> *That the day will come when we will be together*
> *And if you will be faithful to me*
> *My love, for as long as I live, will be for no other*

Pippa sang the way her grandmother had taught her. It had been so long since she'd sung to anyone besides herself. Even at Mass, Pippa had only mouthed the words. Singing reminded her of everything she'd lost. Of laughter and love and a life of plenty.

She squeezed her eyes shut. The melody flowed with surety, the words no longer soft, but light and bright. Pippa's hands floated from her sides as if they were carrying the song, her fingers untwining from Arjun's of their own volition. Her grandmother used to sing with her hands, and Pippa had always thought it was as if her grandmother were an enchantress, casting spells in a glittering glen. Good magic, filled with warmth and the smell of freshly baked bread. In this moment, Pippa could almost feel her standing close. Nodding in encouragement to Pippa, as Pippa often found herself nodding to Lydia and Henry.

"Dinna sing like a bird," her grandmother would say. "Birds sing from the head. Sing from the heart. Or from your stomach, aye? That way even the saints above know you mean it."

When the last note died on her lips, Pippa opened her eyes. All the fey were staring at her as if they were figures in a painting. When Pippa looked at Lord Vyr and Liege Sujee, she saw fresh trails of tears flowing down Sujee's cheeks, a warm smile on their lips.

Arjun's brow was furrowed, an odd light in his gaze. As if he knew a secret he longed to tell Pippa. Soon. When the time was right. Wordlessly he reached for her hand once more.

"Do you accept Lord Arjun's tribute, Philippa Montrose?" the tall fey presiding over the Rite asked.

Pippa looked first at General Riya. Then at Arjun, who twined their fingers together, like vines around a tree. "Y-yes."

"And do you accept Lady Philippa's tribute, Arjun Desai?" he continued.

Arjun canted his head toward his mother, an odd expression on his face. He waited, refusing to say anything. Then, for the first time, Pippa saw a flicker of concern ripple across his features. He stared at General Riya for a beat. Only to assume a posture of unmistakable defiance.

"Yes," he said with conviction, daring his mother to contradict him.

The presiding fey with the plait of white-gold hair moved closer. He took Pippa's free hand in his. Then he grasped Arjun's empty palm, joining the two together until Pippa faced Arjun, both their hands linked. The entire time, Arjun stared at his mother. Waiting. Dread bubbled in her throat. He wore a look of abject refusal. One that refused to bend or flinch first.

The dread mounted, unseen energy coursing through Pippa's veins, her heart pounding like a battle drum.

The willowy fey paused. Then he raised his own hands in the air in a slow sweeping motion, his lips moving in a soft chant reminiscent of the one he'd used at the beginning of the ceremony. Above the shining dais, notes appeared, glowing like stars. With a quizzical expression, Pippa studied them, only to realize they were the notes she herself had sung only a moment ago. The fey reached toward the music and collected a few of them in the palm of his hand. Without hesitation, he threw the notes into the glittering Mystflame, which sparked in response before crackling to life in a burst of white flame.

His footsteps measured, the fey took a spoonful of the food Arjun had prepared for his tribute. He glanced over his shoulder at General Riya. Pippa desperately wanted to follow suit. To look to see what it was General Riya conveyed to both her son and the presiding fey. But the general stood behind her now, obscured from view.

The next instant, all the color washed from Arjun's face.

The fey threw the silver spoon and the food into the fire. "It is done." Then he lifted Arjun and Pippa's joined hands, and a rosy light began to spread around their fingers. "Now and forevermore, you belong to each other."

Good God.

Was that it? Were they . . . ?

"Are we . . . married?" Pippa whispered.

"You are, my child," the presiding fey said.

Pippa snatched her hands from Arjun's, who continued blinking at nothing, his features wan. Her eyes flitted wildly from side to side. She hadn't known. If someone had told her exactly when the moment would pass—exactly when it would be too late—she would have put a stop to it.

Anger shrouded her mind. She'd been relying on her cursed fiancé the entire time. Her trust had been folly. Anger flashed through her, hot and fast. How dare he leave her future up to such chance? To his idiotic notions of pride and—

"Now," the tall fey crooned in a singsong voice, "we will bear witness to Lord Vyr's tribute." He walked toward Vyr and Sujee when a cold light started to emanate from Arjun's head. It brightened, flickering like star fire, before spreading down his arms and legs.

His eyes widened with alarm. "Mother." He turned in place.

His body flickered again, but this time it was almost as if he were on the verge of vanishing from view. Pippa glanced about wildly, confusion overtaking her anger. What the devil was happening?

"Mother?" he repeated, and General Riya stepped toward him, one hand reaching for his, the other braced on the hilt of her sword.

"No," Pippa whispered when he flickered once more, the light around him an unsteady glow.

If she was not permitted to go anywhere without Arjun, then he could not be permitted to go anywhere without her. Pippa grabbed his hand and held it tight. The glow spread like a flash of lightning, down his arm and into hers. The cold braced her bones. Chilled her blood. Arjun gripped her hand in a sudden vise.

Then everything pulsed around them, and the ground beneath Pippa gave way to an ice-cold abyss.

OUR REVELS NOW ARE ENDED.

THE TEMPEST,

WILLIAM SHAKESPEARE

———◄●●►———

Michael came to an abrupt stop in his trek through the darkening forest. All around him, tiny fireflies danced through the air, casting warm light across the lichen-covered ground.

He glanced down at the ring on his pinkie finger and frowned.

All at once, the arrow that had been pointing north—keeping him on the path to find Philippa Montrose—was spinning about as if it were possessed. Michael shook his hand, hoping the ring had merely been momentarily addled. The tiny, compasslike needle continued spiraling in place.

"What balderdash," he muttered.

He knocked back the hood on his brow and waited a moment in consideration. Trepidation took shape within him, causing his stomach to tighten as if he were bracing himself for a blow.

Michael had been in the land of the fey for several hours, and still he found himself out of sorts, as if he'd woken from a deep sleep. How did his forebears make their home in this place? A part of him wanted to change into a wolf as he wandered through the forest in the Sylvan Vale, but what would he do with the ring or the talisman Valeria Henri had given him? Not to mention how difficult it would be for him to rescue Pippa if he were caught close to dawn and unable to face the moon.

Michael still lacked the skill to change on command, which had quickly become one of the most challenging factors of being a new werewolf. For him, the transformation had to take place beneath the light of the moon. The fuller the moon, the easier the shift. If he transformed into a wolf and did not revert back to his human form before dawn, he would be unable to return without moonlight there to guide him. The longer he was a wolf, the harder it would be to change back.

All at once, the spinning in the ring's center stopped. The tightness in Michael's chest eased. He glanced at the needle embedded in the center of the black stone ring.

Now it was pointing south. The completely opposite direction.

Michael frowned once more. That didn't make a lick of sense. How was it possible for Pippa to travel that quickly? From the way the arrow had remained for the last hour—unmoving and ramrod straight—Michael gathered that he had been very close to finding her only a minute before.

Nonetheless, Michael did an about-face. The arrow again pointed north, though it wavered about in a lazy fashion, which meant Michael still had some distance to travel before finding Pippa. He exhaled. Along the horizon, the top of a snow-capped mountain in the heart of a shadowy land touched the stars.

Michael didn't know much about the world of the fey. But he'd heard enough of the stories to know that if the needle was pointing in that direction, he was being led into the winter land of the dark fey.

The Sylvan Wyld.

That same spark of trepidation reignited within him. His kind had been banished from the Wyld four hundred years ago. Were guards stationed at the border to enforce this banishment? If Bastien had been allowed to travel through both territories, then perhaps it had been long enough that their exile was no longer in effect? Was it worth such a gamble?

Then again. Michael sneered to himself. Bastien had spent his life as the exception to most rules. Undeservedly so.

It did not matter. Michael knew it in his bones. If Pippa was in the Sylvan Wyld, Celine would be close by. After all they'd weathered together—after his proposal of marriage only a handful of weeks ago—Michael had many things he wanted to say to Celine Rousseau. Things she needed to hear.

Come hell or high water, it was time for her to listen.

With a determined set to his brow, Michael marched toward the mountain. At least one good thing could be said about the forever night of the Sylvan Wyld; once he crossed its border, he could assume the shape of a wolf at will.

Perhaps then he would finally feel a sense of home.

———◆◆◆———

O n an outcropping of snow hundreds of feet above Michael Grimaldi, a lone wolf with a coat of rich brown fur lurked beneath the moon. It watched through the flurrying powder as Michael changed directions, shifting toward the mountain in the heart of the Winter Court.

A Winter Court cloaked in lies and misdirection. A Winter Court that would not welcome him. A Winter Court that had no place for vampires or their misbegotten watchdogs.

The wolf on the outcropping watched with satisfaction as Michael moved closer to his fate. Toward the role he'd unknowingly stolen from his cousin a few short days ago, when Michael had fired a shot intended for another and struck down Luca Grimaldi, the leader of their pack.

The wolf huffed, its breath forming a cloud in the brisk air. Then it turned in place and began limping through the shadows, trailing a thin stream of blood from its missing front paw. Despite the makeshift wrapping around it, the wound still refused to heal. The pain the wolf felt with each mincing step fueled a growing fire. One that did not need much kindling to be set ablaze.

Émilie Saint Germain stopped in her tracks when a particularly sharp sensation knifed through her stomach. Another huff of air caused a plume of smoke to obscure her vision. Despite her lupine strength—the strength of the wolf magic flowing through her veins—it was all she could do not to howl in agony.

But she was not angry. No. Truly she wasn't. Not anymore. She'd realized this when she'd watched what transpired on the riverboat that fateful dawn. Vampires and werewolves were weak when they fought each other. Distracted from what should be their greater cause, just as the fey gentry of the Sylvan Vale had always intended.

Weak apart. But perhaps they could be stronger together, as they once were.

With each passing moment Émilie spent in the land of the fey, it became less about revenge. The more she saw of what her kind had lost—the more she realized how much werewolves and vampires did not belong in the darkened corners of the mortal world, squabbling for scraps—she realized it was no longer about vengeance. It was much more than that. Something greater. Something far more powerful.

In the world of humans, werewolves and vampires were relegated to the shadows, cursed to move about in secrecy. In the land of the fey, they had once ruled on high, their court set deep in a bejeweled mountain.

It was time to take back what had been stolen.

Émilie the wolf smiled to herself and vanished into the forest. Promises had been made. It was time for them to be kept.

MY BOUNTY IS AS BOUNDLESS AS THE SEA.

ROMEO AND JULIET,
WILLIAM SHAKESPEARE

———◆◆◆———

Celine bolted upright, startled from her dream. She'd fallen asleep again. There was no telling what time it was, but night reigned supreme beyond the terrace of the treetop chamber she shared with Bastien. The sky was a pale grey velvet, and the immense trees beyond cast long shadows through the torchlight, peppered by the occasional glow of a will-o'-the-wisp.

Celine gazed above and noticed that one rather small, familiar wisp was hovering on the wooden ceiling above her head.

"Has my mother returned from her meeting with General Riya?" she asked the wisp.

The little blue wisp bobbed from side to side, signaling no.

"Perhaps I should have gone with her, as Bastien suggested."

The wisp seemed to hesitate.

Vestiges of Celine's dream clung like the tentacles of an octopus. She tossed her head and rubbed her eyes, trying to recall details that had, only a moment before, seemed so clear.

All at once, the wisp scurried away. Which was a clear sign that Bastien was close by. A breeze riffled through the air, toying with the ends of Celine's long, unbound hair. She gathered her dark curls to one side and wound them around her fist just like she had as a child. From behind, she felt the shadow of Bastien moving through the darkness. The shiver that rippled over her skin in his presence was never from fear. With him, there was only trust. Never mind that he was a vampire. Never mind that blood drinkers were the enemies of her mother's court.

Bastien and Celine were beyond such things. They were night and day. One did not exist without the other. Celine hoped there would come a time in which their union might serve as an example. A way to save her mother's world from the fear and hatred that tore it apart so many centuries ago.

"I don't understand why the wisps are so afraid of you," Celine murmured as he glided closer, like a shadow drifting through a misted wood. He reached a hand to rest on the nape of her neck. She leaned into his touch, his thumb brushing across her skin in a gentle caress. "It's not as if you could drain their blood, for I'm certain they don't have any to begin with." She heard him smile.

"Only today I wondered if I could," he said. "How they might taste."

"Care to hazard a guess?"

"Like champagne."

Celine laughed. "Then they should be very careful indeed."

Bastien sat behind her and wrapped his arms around her waist. She rested her head on his shoulder, and they sat in comfortable silence for a time.

"You had to hunt again," Celine said softly. "That's the fourth time today."

"I didn't realize you'd noticed."

"I always notice when you're gone. Is everything all right?"

Bastien hesitated a moment. "No."

"Tell me."

She felt his head tilt toward the single lurking wisp in the corner. "I wish I could," he replied, his words soundless.

"It's harmless." Celine toyed with the edge of the silk sleeve he wore. A beautiful design, though the fey garments did not suit him. She missed seeing him in the bespoke suits he used to wear. The way the rigid tailoring drew attention to the angles of his body. To his broad shoulders and narrow hips.

"They're not harmless." Bastien held her close. "They're spies, and information is often the deadliest weapon of all. They seem to be multiplying the longer we stay in any one place. I barely noticed them the first time we came to the Vale. Now I see them everywhere."

"They enable my mother to keep abreast of all the happenings in the Sylvan Vale." Celine frowned. "Is that not a good thing? Didn't Nicodemus employ spies of his own to watch over his empire?"

"I suppose so," Bastien said after a time.

Celine wanted to protest further. To encourage him to speak freely. This particular wisp was young and small. Rather sweet and accommodating. It had only arrived in the Moon Rabbit's Grove this morning. Celine couldn't imagine it being a cause of concern. True, it would likely report anything of note to its superiors. Unless she and Bastien planned a violent coup or something of the like, why would it relate the inane details of their conversation? Without a doubt, there were more pressing matters of concern.

But that didn't matter. If Bastien did not feel comfortable speaking in the little wisp's presence, then she would ask it to leave.

Celine looked toward the eaves. "Starlight? Would you give us some privacy?"

The tiny blue wisp trilled in place. Then without hesitation it floated toward the billowing drapes and into the pale darkness that signified night in the Sylvan Vale.

When Celine reached for the length of cloth Bastien had left on the edge of the bed, she found it damp. The crisp scent of Lake Lure wound into her nostrils. "Did you go for a swim?"

"The lake is especially nice at night, though the creatures that reside in its depths are less than thrilled at my presence."

"My mother told me she instructed them not to trouble you."

"I know. But their resentment is . . . palpable."

Celine sat up and faced him. "Do you wish to return to the Ivy Bower?"

Bastien paused again. "Yes. And no."

"You're unhappy here," Celine announced softly. "In the Sylvan Vale." She'd known it all along, but had held fast to the hope that he would grow more comfortable in the land of the summer fey after enough time had passed.

Bastien did not reply at once, as if he were taking a moment to settle his thoughts. To choose his words. Celine did not care for it. She prided herself on being direct and honest with Bastien. She expected nothing less in return.

"It's only been three days. I want to give you all the time you desire to spend with your mother," Bastien said. "I would give anything for the chance to know my mother now. I don't want to take you from her until you're ready." His features hardened. "And until we have a plan in place to deal with the authorities in Paris."

"But . . ."

"But"—Bastien offered her a tired smile—"I don't belong here. And . . . neither do you."

Celine's green eyes went wide. "Why do you think I don't belong here?"

"This place . . . I don't think it's what you think it is. There's a strangeness at work here. As if the entire thing is a house made of cards, destined to fall apart in the slightest breeze. And even though your mother assures us that you are safe in the Vale— safe and welcome—I disagree. They tolerate your presence. It's as Arjun said. An ethereal like him—like you—will always be second-class in Sylvan Vale."

"But how is that different from the mortal world?" Celine asked, her words turning testy. "I'm a woman. I can't vote. My voice does not matter. One day I belong to my father, the next day to my husband. I can't move about that world unless a man paves the path for me. At least in the Vale we have women in true positions of power and influence."

Bastien's cheeks hollowed. He nodded. "I suppose it's convenient that I would forget that." He offered her a bemused grin. "I'm sorry."

"You're a man." Celine rested a hand on his cheek. "That's why you need me. To remind you of the things you can't see."

"Or the things I perhaps, however unwittingly, ignore." Bastien sighed. "I don't want to stay in the Vale forever. I can't. Every day we are among the Summer Court, I grow hungrier. More restless. It's difficult for me to hunt freely here."

"I understand." Celine hesitated. "Perhaps you could—"

"I will not feed from you." Bastien's eyes flashed through the shadows. "That is not a topic for discussion. You are the girl I love, not a bottle of wine for me to drink."

"Are you sure we don't want to ask my mother for a solution?"

"Your mother . . . I'm not ready for her to know about my changing appetites. If the rest of the court were to realize how hungry I am—and the threat that knowledge might pose—they could begin to openly revolt."

Celine hummed in agreement. "It is not only you that causes them worry. Umma has told me they are uncomfortable with the idea of her potentially naming me as her successor, even though she has made no moves to do so."

"You've reiterated that you're not interested?" Bastien's shoulders tensed, bracing for her response.

"Several times. But . . . there are moments when I wonder if I might be able to help in some small way." Celine chewed at the inside of her cheeks. "Perhaps sway their minds into being more tolerant of those who are not like them? Their disdain for mortals troubles me more with each passing day."

"I don't know if it's possible for them to see past their

prejudices." Bastien dropped his voice below a whisper. "Do you ever wonder if it was wise for the fey to cross into the mortal world in the first place? Perhaps things were better before those boundaries were blurred."

Celine pressed her lips into a line. "If the vampires could not have traveled to the mortal world, then what would have happened to them after they were banished? Where would they have gone?"

"I don't know." His expression turned thoughtful. "Perhaps it would have been better if vampires had ceased to exist."

Celine pulled him close, her chin coming to rest on his shoulder. "Don't say that. It upsets me to see how much you despise your own kind." She paused. "May I ask you a question?"

"Don't do that," Bastien said with a gentle smile as he threaded his fingers through hers. "Don't waver. Be who you are. Fearless, at all turns."

She smiled, but it did not touch her eyes. "Even now, after everything, if you were given the chance that night in Saint Louis Cathedral to decide whether or not to become a vampire, would you still have chosen to die the true death?"

"You're thinking about Ali's time-traveling silver."

Celine nodded.

Bastien took her hands in his and pressed a kiss to each palm. "I don't know what I would do. But I do know that I would have regretted losing the chance to love you more."

She kissed the side of his neck, tasting the sweet water of the lake. Almost as if it were made of melting snow and warm honey. Then she nipped at the skin beneath his jaw.

He laughed and pressed her back into the bevy of silk cushions strewn across the counterpane. His lips moved up her neck to her ear. Celine's breath hitched, her pulse moving in time with the rise and fall of her chest. When his fangs grazed across her throat, she sighed.

"You can," she said softly. "I want you to." Her heart pounded through her body, her blood moving hot and fast. "I know you're unhappy with your choice of food in the Vale."

"Unsatisfied. Not unhappy." Bastien traced his nose along the vein in her neck, inhaling as he moved. As if he wished to savor her scent.

"You won't hurt me." Celine angled his chin upward so she could see his eyes. "And no one wants to hear that their lover is unsatisfied," she murmured with a mischievous smile.

When he bent closer—his hands braced on either side of her head—Celine's eyes fluttered shut. Bastien kissed her, and she wrapped her arms around the lean muscles of his torso, her hands tracing his broad shoulders. She reveled in his touch. In the strength she felt beneath her fingertips. In the way his skin felt cool and smooth, like the scales of a snake.

"Your mother could return at any moment," he said, his lips moving along her collarbone. "What if she asks to see you? It's early still. She might want to share a pot of tea."

"No," Celine disagreed. "She won't return until tomorrow. That's what her note said."

Bastien paused. "And where did she go?"

"To attend a court matter. Something about a wedding." Celine gripped the muscles in his arms, her right leg hooking around him so that she might push her hips into his. "Less talking, Monsieur Saint Germain," she said when he muttered in a low voice. "More action."

One side of Bastien's lips curved upward. "La vie est semée d'épines, et je ne connais d'autre remède que d'y passer rapidement," he said in her ear as one of his hands slid down her leg. He pressed into Celine, and her head fell back, their clothing nothing more than a tantalizing barrier.

Voltaire. *Life is thickly sown with thorns. And the only solution is to pass through them quickly.*

Celine opened her eyes to order the blue wisp to take its leave. Then she remembered that she had already told it to go. She hoped it knew better than to return anytime soon.

A pleased smile tugged at Celine's lips. In the past it would have disturbed her to realize how much she enjoyed the feeling of commanding a room. How much she relished impressing her will upon even the smallest audience. From an early age, Celine had possessed an odd relationship with power. She'd been fascinated by it. Intrigued by all its possibilities.

In her wildest fantasies, she'd never imagined that she might be the daughter of an actual fairy queen, with the chance to assume the kind of power a girl like her could never fathom possessing in the world of mortal men. Queen Victoria, for all her power and influence, still needed the permission of the men around her to carry out her duties.

It was too easy for Celine to imagine herself sitting on the Horned Throne. Maybe the fey gentry of the Vale would be angry to see a halfblood elevated to such a position, but after enough time had passed, perhaps Celine could disavow them of the notion that they were her betters. One day, perhaps they might even see her as their equal.

Was it wrong for her to desire power if it meant being given the chance to offer much-needed perspective to a troubling situation?

Men throughout the world were granted carte blanche under less auspicious circumstances. It was easy for someone to say that power belonged to those who didn't want it. If a man didn't want something, how would he know to fight for it? At least he had the choice. Men had been given access to power all their lives. It was their so-called birthright.

Maybe it was time for them to see what a woman could do.

These thoughts raced through Celine's mind.

Bastien pulled back, his expression quizzical. He studied her for a moment. Celine watched the way the darkness receded in his eyes. How his features returned to those of a mortal man. It was something that fascinated her. In the beginning, it was his transformation from human to vampire that captivated her. The way his ears would sharpen into points. The way his teeth would lengthen to fangs. The ink that swirled around his irises, the inhuman set to his brow.

But now Celine was much more enthralled by his transformation back into a man.

"Are you there?" Bastien asked.

Celine nodded. "Sometimes I forget what we both are."

"I prefer it that way."

She squeezed his arms and drew him closer. "I forget the power that flows through our veins."

His gaze swirled into storm clouds. "I'd prefer it that way, as well."

"Is *power* such a dirty word?"

"I've never seen it do anything but corrupt even the good."

Celine pursed her lips to one side as she looked up at Bastien. "I suppose you're right. Now kiss me," she said. "Kiss me and make me forget. Again and again."

He grinned, more than happy to oblige her.

Though her mind continued to swirl, Celine shoved aside her concerns. Let her body surrender to sensation. In Paris, she'd overheard young women talk about la petite mort. The little death. That brief loss of consciousness. That shining moment when every thought was silenced, and the only thing that mattered was feeling.

Celine had experienced these little deaths before. Her own hands, her own shy exploration. Shame had been quick to follow, her heart beating fast, her skin flushed with awareness. The shame of feeling dirty and wanton. Wrong, in all ways. She'd known what God and the nuns would have to say about her actions.

But with Bastien, Celine had come to realize her shame was wrong. Her pleasure was not a thing to relegate to the shadows or cast aside like a soiled garment. Like some wilted flower, used and discarded. No. Her pleasure was a powerful thing in its own right, worthy of attention.

With Bastien, these little deaths reminded Celine so keenly of what it meant to be alive. To know her heart continued to beat in her chest and her lungs continued to fill with delicious air. To experience the blood rushing to her body, warming through her, causing her skin to tingle and ignite.

To share in these little deaths with a creature of darkness—a demon of blood and sin—was thrilling. But then Celine always relished danger.

So she relished it once more, their bodies moving in an ancient rhythm, her fingers wrapping around the vines carved onto the bedpost, the starshine cool on Bastien's bared skin.

SUNAN OF THE WYLD

———◆●◆———

Y ou've dropped them in the middle of a blizzard," Suli pronounced in a flat tone, his voice thin, yet oddly resonant.

"Yes. I have." Sunan's bright eyes twinkled, a knowing grin
tugging at his lips.

Suli sighed. "What if they become sick?" He studied the
moving images flickering in the center of his brother's most
faithful wisp spy.

"They won't. It is only for a moment." Sunan's grin widened
from where he sat, the glowing greystone walls behind him
casting strange shadows across the packed-snow floor.

Suli's lips pressed into a line. "But why are you toying with
them?"

"Because I find it interesting."

Suli exhaled through his nostrils and rubbed his blue chin as
he regarded his elder brother. "It's not quite reassuring that you
find their torment interesting."

"Of course I don't find their torment interesting, brother. It's
their reactions that fascinate me. Earthdwellers in turmoil
often show who they truly are. Don't you think it's easy to be
kind and generous in times of good and plenty?" Sunan mused.

"I find that I see through to the marrow of an earthdweller's bones much more easily when their mettle is put to the test."

Suli frowned as he continued observing the Wyld's newest arrivals, witnessing their panic and confusion unfold in the shadow of the Winter Court's mountain fortress. "And is it important for you to see who they are to the marrow of their bones?"

"Yes. Very. This mortal and this ethereal hold great significance."

"Well, I wish you wouldn't let them suffer." Suli harrumphed. "They will suffer enough once they understand why you have brought them here. Once the Great Lie is revealed."

"I won't allow them to suffer," Sunan said, his goblin features pensive. "Not too much. But a little suffering is necessary. I would know who our guests are at their cores. What makes their hearts beat faster. What they love. What they fear."

Suli toyed with the edge of his weathered sleeve, the roughened wool folding in on itself. "I am glad to know you aren't indulging the playful side of your curiosity."

"Oh no. Not now." Sunan's grin was easy. Gentle. Knowing. "That comes later."

Suli groaned. "What should I expect next?"

"Well, if all goes according to plan . . . a massacre."

E ven before Pippa opened her eyes, her teeth started to chatter.

The wind howled around her, whipping snow and shards of ice into the air. The crystals stung her face in the darkness, causing her to brace into the tempest. To lean against the blizzard.

She attempted to open an eye and regretted it the next second, her fingers struggling for warmth amid the ludicrously thin wedding gown hanging in wind-whipped tatters from her shoulders.

All at once, arms encircled her, pressing her face into a muscled chest that smelled of cinnamon and fresh linen. And just like before—only yesterday, if Pippa stopped to think about it—the nearness of Arjun Desai settled the storm inside her. Pippa almost laughed at the absurdity. From the moment she first met Arjun in a darkened alleyway a stone's throw from the stronghold of the Court of the Lions, he'd been nothing but a source of consternation. On that first occasion, she and Celine had witnessed him pummel a helpless man into the ground, only to freeze him unconscious beside a pile of moldering trash.

Misfortune after misfortune continued to befall Celine after that, and of course Pippa was unable to escape her best friend's spate of bad luck. Why was it that Arjun, of all people, would change the course of Pippa's life in such a drastic fashion? In the matter of a single day, he'd become a source of problems who also served as a solution. Perhaps it was a ridiculous joke. Or maybe it was simply that Arjun was the only person in Fairyland whom Pippa could trust. The only source of familiarity in a place Pippa would never—could never—understand.

Yes. That must be why. As soon as they returned to New Orleans, Arjun would return to being the same nuisance he'd been before. Always ready with a smirk and quip, awaiting the chance to make Pippa feel small and insignificant.

And she would never again think about that kiss they shared beneath a murderous tree.

"W-w-we have to f-find shelter," Pippa stammered through her chattering teeth.

"Is that so?" Arjun shouted over the howling wind. "I was quite enjoying myself."

"Sod off," she replied.

Laughter rumbled in his chest. "Good girl. Stay angry. It will keep you warm." He glanced around them, shuddering from the cold, even as he removed his embroidered jacket and draped it around Pippa. "Now, where would I—"

"L-look for a h-h-hill," Pippa said, squinting through the darkness.

"What?"

She clenched her jaw shut and spoke without opening her

mouth. "Some kind of hill or embankment. We can pile up snow and take refuge in its shadow."

"Right," Arjun said. "I wish I could say I was impressed, but you've always been rather brilliant."

"T-talking will not keep us w-w-warm." Again Pippa felt herself start to sway.

"Don't faint." Arjun's eyes widened. "Damn it all. We didn't eat anything." He snorted. "So much for my promise that you would never go to sleep hungry."

"I won't faint," Pippa yelled through a blast of icy wind. "I w-wouldn't give you the satisfaction of catching me. Also how are you th-thinking about f-food at a time like this?"

He laughed again and tucked her under his arm. All at once, the wind died down around them, the howls silenced in an eerie instant. A stillness descended in the air, the ground before them sparkling with newly fallen snow.

"What in hellfire . . . ," Arjun muttered. The sky above them filled with white light, as if the moon had suddenly appeared from behind a cloud.

They seemed to be on the edge of some kind of forest, the trees skeletal and bare, their bark almost black beneath the night sky, save for the occasional evergreen, its branches covered in dripping frost.

Pippa clung to Arjun, her eyes scanning their surroundings, her posture wary. The sunny side of her disposition wanted to believe they'd stumbled through a tare and were now back in the mortal realm, but the sharpness of the colors—the odd way the storm vanished one second after pummeling them into near oblivion—and the strange way the frost smelled like mint and something Pippa could not identify told her this was most assuredly some other part of the cursed fey lands.

"Where next, poppet?" Arjun asked.

Pippa made a face. "My father used to call me that."

Arjun's eyebrows shot into his forehead. "Well, that'll put paid to it. I take it you were not that close?"

Ignoring his question, Pippa pointed east. At least she thought it was east, given the cast of their shadows in the moonlight. "We should walk in that direction."

"How can you be so sure?"

"I'm not. But I see a shimmer of water through the trees just there. And we need to be near a source of water, do we not?"

"Hmmm. Again, I'm not impressed. You'll have to do far better than that to impress me, wife."

Pippa almost groaned. She wrapped herself in Arjun's jacket, swathing it around herself like a cocoon. "Wife." She sighed. "We are really and truly married, then?"

"In the eyes of the Summer Court, yes." Arjun began walking through the skeletal trees, toward the shimmer of water. "But don't fret; as I said before, I have no intention of holding you to your vows. Once we return to New Orleans, you're free to wed young Master Devereux."

Pippa pressed a palm to her forehead as she skirted a fallen limb, the bough covered in ice and a dusting of snow. As feeling returned to her frozen body, a flash of bewildered fury bloomed in her stomach. "Dear God. What am I going to do? The wedding is tomorrow. How will I ever explain where I was or what

I was doing, much less the fact that I *married someone else?* What will Phoebus' father say?" She kicked aside a mound of snow in her path, her slippered foot sinking deep, almost causing her ankle to turn. "What will God say?" she muttered, struggling to yank her leg free. "Yes, Philippa, I understand that one marriage was made under duress. Yes, my child, it is fine for you to be married to two different men! I see nothing wrong with that." Pippa heaved her foot from the snow, anger heating her blood. Never mind that she was fairly certain her fingers were turning blue. She looked to Arjun and found him watching her, a troubled expression on his brow.

"What is it?" Pippa blinked. "What has gone wrong now?"

He inhaled through his nose. "Nothing. Nothing at all."

"Don't lie to me, Arjun. Please," Pippa said, a knot in her chest. "We promised we would be honest while we were in the world of the fey."

"I should tell you . . . time moves differently here."

Dread swirled beneath her skin, crawling up her throat. "How so?"

Arjun gazed at her sidelong as they walked. "Your wedding date has likely . . . passed."

"What?" Pippa nearly stumbled face-first into the freshly fallen snow. "How is that possible?" She began to shake. "Only a day has passed since I arrived here!" she wailed.

Henry and Lydia. Oh God. What had she done?

"In the mortal world," Arjun continued, his tone nonchalant, "I'd wager a week or so has gone by."

Pippa whirled on him, her blue eyes wide, his wedding jacket falling from her shoulders. "You waited until *now* to tell me that?"

"Don't worry; I'm certain Phoebus will still have you."

"You . . . you cad." Pippa fought the urge to shove him. To wallop him right in the face. To wipe that tense smile off his countenance. The dread was quickly being replaced by her most faithful companion, rage.

Her body quaked harder, her blue eyes flitting from side to side. "No. No. Dear God, no."

"Don't fret," Arjun reassured her. For the first time since she'd arrived in the world of fairies, she sensed a strange emotion buried beneath his words. Something like regret. Or could it be . . . jealousy? "Phoebus weathers disappointment well," he continued.

It was cruel. Too cruel, even in its sarcasm. As if there were pain beneath the words. A barbed insult, meant to leave a mark. In an effort not to launch herself at Arjun in a fit of fury, Pippa bent and scraped snow into her hands. Without hesitation, she flung a ball at his face. Then another.

"You—you miserable arse!" Pippa said as she grabbed fistfuls of snow.

"I told you," Arjun said while dodging her continued attack, "Phoebus will still marry you. I'll never let a soul know of our wedding." He ducked left. "No one will uncover anything untoward. So why are you—"

"You think this is just about Phoebus?" Pippa shouted. "How like a man to believe the only thing that matters to a woman is their approval."

His hazel eyes widened with surprise. "This isn't about marrying—"

"This is about Henry! And Lydia!" Angry tears began streaming down Pippa's face, her trembling worsening. She stomped through the snow to shove him backward. "And every important promise I've ever made. You—and your *goddamned* arrogance— have ruined everything."

Arjun grabbed her by the wrists in an effort to halt her continuing onslaught. "Who are Henry and Lydia?"

"What am I going to do?" She lunged for him, but instead of an attack, it was almost as if she'd flung herself into his arms. Even Pippa could not be certain. All she knew was that she needed . . . something. Some measure of comfort, like a cobra seeking shelter in the embrace of a mongoose. "If anything happens to them, I swear I will—" Her words were swallowed by a shriek.

From the shadows to their right emerged a passel of short, stout warriors wielding weapons of iron, their leather armor burnished from age and use. Their leader wore a strange cap perched on his head at a jaunty angle. At first glance, it resembled a gentleman's smoking cap, its tip pointed and slightly askew. Upon closer inspection, Pippa realized what gave the odd adornment its color.

The hat was stained with blood.

At that, Pippa fainted, keeling right into Arjun's arms.

THE SMALL WISDOM IS LIKE WATER IN A GLASS:
CLEAR, TRANSPARENT, AND PURE.

RABINDRANATH TAGORE

———◆◆◆———

A rjun carried an unconscious Pippa in his arms as he followed the armed goblins through a back entrance of the
Ice Palace of Kur, its blue turrets chiming in an icy breeze.

One of the goblin guards poked and prodded at the hem of
Pippa's tattered wedding garments, grunting to his compatriots
in a language Arjun could not understand. Two of the other
goblins chortled in response.

Whatever they were saying was likely not a compliment.

"Watch it, you grubby twat," Arjun said the next time the
same goblin poked at Pippa's dangling foot. In the distance, he
caught strains of discordant music and the occasional bellow of
a mournful beast. They continued walking down darkened
hallways of solid ice toward the ruckus. Toward the same Great
Hall Arjun, Celine, and Bastien had last encountered in their
recent audience with its ill-tempered king. The same diminutive regent to whom Arjun owed six mortal weeks of service—a
promise he'd made to keep them from being thrown to a passel
of flesh-eating demons.

Blast it all. Of course the fiendish little monarch would
choose now to call due his promise.

Weariness tugged at Arjun's brow. His heart ached with the weight of so many failures. He'd failed in his promise to find a healer for Odette. He'd failed to send Pippa home safely. Failed to put a stop to their wedding. Then he'd even failed to ensure his new wife would never again go to bed hungry.

In all his life, Arjun could not remember failing so spectacularly.

With a grimace, Arjun straightened his shoulders. Cradled Pippa closer, his hold on her tightening with resolve. Now was not the time to wallow in doubt and self-pity.

They neared the entrance to the Great Hall, its iron double doors—blasted through on one side and hanging by a thread on the other—still frozen in place. Once their party darkened the threshold, Arjun caught sight of the same kind of riotous feast he'd witnessed on the last occasion. Immense glasswing butterflies and iridescent beetles the size of his head fluttered among the dangling ice chandeliers in the coved ceiling, and creatures with all manner of dripping fangs and hooked talons and bristled tailbones gathered on three sides of the room, gnashing at bloodied bones and tossing their half-eaten meals to the side in favor of the next steaming course.

The smell of carnage and entrails—of charred meat and blackened bones—almost caused Arjun to retch.

"Wait here," croaked the goblin flanking Arjun. He made his way to the dais at the opposite end of the room, upon which the king of the dwarves sat, enjoying his flagon of dark green wine.

Pippa stirred in Arjun's arms, her long eyelashes fluttering.

"Perfect," Arjun grumbled. With care he set her on her feet, pulling her close so he could speak in her ear.

"Don't startle, love," he whispered. "All manner of beasts are around us. I'd wager you've never seen their like before. If you yell or carry on, you'll draw undue attention." He paused to wrap his jacket tighter around her, and again recalled the story of Draupadi. Well, he certainly wasn't Krishna, though the thought of bloody retribution did give him immense joy.

Her lashes fluttered once more. "It smells like a barn," she grumbled. "And . . . old ha'pennies."

"A barn would offer a far more pleasant holiday than this."

When her eyes flashed open, Arjun was again taken aback. The blue in them appeared even more vivid—more alive—in the depths of the Ice Palace. The cool light of the crystalline walls reflected back at Arjun as he stared into Pippa's face, willing her to remain calm. He'd been on the receiving end of her temper more than once, and he was certain the snaggle-toothed ogre to their right wouldn't appreciate its fire quite as much as he had.

"Are there monsters?" she asked, her lips cracked.

"Always," he replied, drawn to her like a bee to nectar. "No matter where you are. These just happen to be a bit more monstrous."

"Will they hurt us?"

"I won't let them."

"If you're wrong, I'll box your ears."

"If I'm wrong, I'll submit. Willingly."

Pippa straightened. She looked around. Arjun felt her shift against him, her motions unsteady. He moved his hand to the small of her back and felt her shiver.

"Arjun," she whispered, her eyes round.

A gargantuan creature resembling an unholy union between a bear and walrus stood on its hind end and bellowed, droplets of its saliva shooting through the air, raining down around them. Its cry sent the nearby beasts into a frenzy. Another creature with laughter like that of a hyena screeched with glee, its nails scraping across the wooden table as it reached for a mangled bone.

"Look at me, meri pyaari," Arjun said to Pippa when he heard her breath hitch as if she were on the cusp of a scream. "Tell me about the pirate woman. Chang Shih was her name, was it not?"

"I can't—remember."

"Then tell me about the penguins."

She met his gaze and held it, her eyes tremulous. "They mate for life."

"Foolish flightless birds." Arjun shifted his other hand to the side of her neck, waiting for her pulse to steady, his thumb caressing her jaw in a sad attempt to soothe her. If he distracted her with facts, perhaps she would not succumb to fear. And if that did not work, he knew how to make her angry. In a short time, he'd become an expert. Anger, Arjun had learned, was a powerful force when wielded in the hands of Philippa Montrose.

"It's romantic." A furrow gathered above her nose.

"I think it's sad."

"That makes me sad for you," she said as she mirrored his gesture and pressed her palm to his cheek.

Arjun didn't know when her touch had become a balm to his nerves. He closed his eyes and grinned. For an instant, he allowed himself to forget . . . everything.

Booming laughter echoed from the other end of the room. It grew until all the creatures around it fell to silence. Pippa and Arjun turned toward the sound, though Arjun tucked Pippa behind him, each clinging to the other. Under normal circumstances, Arjun would have found the idea of him clinging to anyone amusing. A tad pathetic. But he didn't have time to think about it. Nor did he have time to ponder how right it felt.

"You!" the dwarf king bellowed. "Son of Riya!"

Arjun offered him a half bow and a snide smile. "You called, Your Majesty?"

The king snorted. "You thought you could come back to the land of the dark fey and evade the terms of your promise?"

"Of course not," Arjun replied, his tone blithe. "I had every intention of coming to see you as soon as I put my affairs in order."

"A likely story," the king chortled. He tilted his head to one side like a vulture lurking on a branch, awaiting the death of its prey. "Who is the pretty little morsel you've brought with you?" He sniffed, as if trying to divine her scent through the stench of the Great Hall.

"Oh, forgive my rudeness." Arjun grinned. "I'd like to introduce you to—"

"A mortal?" the king said as recognition dawned on him. "A

mortal morsel?" He laughed again, the sound maniacal. "You've brought me a tribute! I accept. She looks delicious."

A creature resembling a tiny dragon squawked, and the bear-like walrus bellowed once more, its tusks gleaming like newly honed knives.

"I do apologize." Arjun's smile sharpened. "But she is not a tribute. I'd like to introduce you to my wife, Lady Philippa Desai." His expression turned cold. "As such"—he raised his voice—"she is mine, and I am hers. If a hair on her head is touched out of turn, my mother and I will consider it the gravest insult." Arjun let his words ring through the cavernous chamber of ice and monsters. He disliked having to play the hero. Disliked the responsibility. But he would not allow any harm to come to Pippa. She was the only wife he would ever have in this immortal life, and if he couldn't keep her safe, then he would have failed in every way that should matter.

Should. An interesting word. Yesterday, Pippa had simply been a girl Arjun knew. One whom he had encountered on a handful of occasions. At least twice before, Arjun had enjoyed her company. Found her enchanting. She was smart, witty, and loyal. But more than that, Arjun had thought her kind. Kindness was, as his father always said, the one thing that distinguished a good man from a bad one. Arjun didn't know if he believed that, but he never ignored the wisdom of his father.

Kindness had been in short supply after Arjun's mother had brought him to the Sylvan Vale as a young boy. The least Arjun owed his young wife was the kindness of his consideration.

"Hmmmm," the king said. He shifted from his seat and pushed away from the table's sagging center. Step by step, he made his way down the dais as if he meant to take his time.

Finally he came to stand before them.

"You married a mortal?" the king said in a guttural voice. "Does your mama know?"

Arjun nodded.

The king snorted. Then began to laugh. It started as a quiet rumble before growing to a guffaw. He held his stomach and doubled over with laughter, pausing to slap his knee as if he'd heard the most amusing story in the world.

Soon the rest of the beasts and beings in the Great Hall joined in, and the ice chandeliers hanging above quaked from the reverberations, the crystals tinkling. At least one or two of them crashed to the floor, exploding in a thousand tiny pieces, sending unfortunate souls in its path scurrying.

"Very well!" the king said through the laughter. "If you wish to subject your new bride to the terrors of the Sylvan Wyld, I will not stop you. But make no mistake, your service is to this court for a period of no less than six weeks."

"Six *mortal* weeks," Arjun corrected.

"What drivel?" The laughter died on the dwarf king's brow as fury mottled his skin.

"That was the promise I made," Arjun replied, his tone breezy. "Six mortal weeks of service, which I believe is about five or six—no more than seven—days in the Wyld."

The king narrowed his eyes at Arjun, then paced toward the

bear walrus, who continued gnawing on an old bone and watching his regent with rapt attention, as if the creature were waiting for permission to be unleashed.

All at once the king whirled on Arjun. "You damnable summer fey!" he roared.

The remaining laughter faded in an instant.

"How dare you try to trick me," he raged. "I did you a favor because you were General Riya's son. I did not allow my ice sabers to tear you limb from limb for trespassing, and this is how you repay me?"

The crowd around him began to grumble, their agitation palpable. Arjun shielded Pippa with his body and held up a hand in an attempt to stay the regent's ire. "I did not try to deceive—"

"Silence!"

The clanging of weapons being raised was followed by the hiss of swords tearing from their scabbards. Bloodlust emanated through the room, like the low hum of an approaching swarm.

The king paced forward again, a short sword made of iron swinging from his right hand. "I will be the one to decide—"

The bear walrus yanked him off his kingly feet with a single swipe of a claw and tossed the bellowing monarch into its open mouth. The crunch of bones against teeth reverberated throughout the chamber. A single bloody thumb careened through the air, landing with a sickening splat a stone's throw from Arjun's feet.

A blood-curdling scream tore from Pippa's lips. Then the creatures of the court began fighting in earnest, as if a cannonball had exploded nearby or a gun had been fired toward the ceiling. All Hell seemed to untether, iron weapons and meaty fists clanging in the familiar symphony of battle. Above them, tiny pale blue orbs of ice popped in place, as if disappearing.

Arjun spun around, caging Pippa in his arms. They stumbled over the body of a creature with a snout like a pig and horns like a satyr, and Pippa yelled, falling forward onto the frozen floor. Her cheek brushed across newly spilled blood. When it dripped toward her eyes, another shriek of horror flew from her lips. Arjun reached for her, only to be knocked to his knees, one of his hands landing on her breast.

"What are you doing?" she gasped, shoving him away.

"Trying to save you," he shot back.

"Try less." She scrambled to her feet, blood staining her shredded wedding garment. Arjun searched the floor for a weapon, taking hold of a crudely fashioned hatchet. When he turned around, he saw Pippa holding a dented shield and the small sword of a fallen goblin, its blade wavy and misshapen.

Arjun sputtered. "And what do you think that is going to—"

With dizzying speed, Pippa parried a blow from a spear aimed at Arjun's side. Then, before he had a chance to react, she pivoted in place and deflected the downward arc of another iron blade, her movements lithe and practiced, like those of a dancer. Sparks rained around them when metal struck metal.

An incensed creature with fangs like a vampire and a long thin face tinted a green hue snarled at Pippa, and Arjun lunged into its path. It feinted left, attempting to sidestep Arjun on its way to disarm Pippa.

Arjun grabbed the creature by its filthy collar and dragged it close. It smelled of meat and blood and frost, its fangs gnashing together. The creature shoved back at Arjun, its broken nails catching him just beneath the chin. Arjun was certain it had managed to draw blood, but the heat of battle flowed through his veins, so he felt nothing but deep satisfaction when he pressed his bare palm to the hollowed-out cheek of the fanged monster. Up close like this, Arjun saw small rows of iridescent scales along the creature's hairline. He curled his fingers into its thin skin and sent the magic pulsing through his touch.

The creature took a moment to react. But Arjun watched its expression slacken with surprise as the blood iced in its veins. Its body stiffened, settling into stillness. Arjun shoved it aside with a wicked smirk. When it struck the floor, the creature cracked and shattered into pieces, like a crystal vase.

Arjun staggered back, his mouth agape. Pippa leapt to the side with a cry.

"That's . . . new," he said, incredulous. Arjun had never in his short life frozen the water in something and witnessed it splinter into glasslike shards before his eyes.

When the beasts and goblins and winged creatures nearby realized what Arjun had done, they turned on him. Surrounded him. Snarled with barely checked rage.

"Now you've done it, son of Riya." A beast resembling a centaur, with legs like a horse and the torso of a man, emerged at the edge of the crowd, his right eye swollen shut and both fists bloody. "There's no one here to stop them from tearing the flesh straight off your body and licking your bones clean."

His pulse thrumming in his temples, Arjun struggled to keep his face calm. "Pippa," he said under his breath. He'd meant for her to stand in his shadow, so that he might—at the very least—spare her from the worst of their ire. But instead she positioned herself so that her back was to his. So that she was defending him every bit as much as he was defending her.

Something strange—something beyond himself—warmed through his chest.

"But perhaps if you beg, I'll let the girl live," the centaur continued.

"He's lying," Pippa said. "Don't believe a word he says."

Though she spoke with conviction, her small sword raised in the air, Arjun felt her tremble behind him.

He didn't want to die here in the wastes of the Sylvan Wyld. To be eaten by glasswing beetles and flesh-eating hobgoblins and beasts with filthy fangs and remorseless souls. Nor did Arjun want to perish on his hands and knees, begging for the mercy of wicked creatures who were as likely to grant him a boon as they were to offer him a flagon of wine.

If anything, the beasts in the Ice Palace only wished to humiliate Arjun further. Pippa's teeth chattered behind him, though she did not flinch. Brave girl. His bride of a mere moment was formidable. Unflinching. So much more than he'd inexcusably expected at first glance.

"I'll do it," Arjun said without hesitation. "I'll say whatever you want me to say, so long as you let her live."

"N-no," Pippa stammered. "Don't—"

The centaur threw back his head and laughed, his yellow

irises shining with an evil light. The light grew brighter and brighter, taking on a sound and mind of its own. Until Arjun was forced to shield his eyes. Pippa, too, drew back in dismay, the centaur laughing all the while.

They shrank back, their weapons wavering about haphazardly.

Pippa clutched at Arjun's shoulder as the light grew ever brighter. He turned to draw her into an embrace, as if the white light might swallow them both whole. Then it flashed and flickered before fading in a single breath.

Arjun opened his eyes and looked around, his pupils still burning from the brilliance. Pippa stirred in his arms, her dark lashes fluttering.

The entire chamber was empty. No broken, bleeding bodies, no overlarge insects hovering beneath the rafters. No long banquet tables laden with stinking food and drink.

"Hello." A calm voice echoed to Arjun's left.

He whirled around to find two small blue goblins standing side by side. Arjun recognized one of them. It was the one who'd served the king his drink the last time Arjun was in the Ice Palace, juddering with nervousness the entire time.

The small goblin took a step forward, his compatriot watching with an anxious stare.

"Welcome to the Sylvan Wyld," the little blue goblin server said. "My name is Sunan. And you passed my first test."

"Sunan of the Wyld," Arjun said in recognition. The very same Sunan that Bastien had sought so desperately on their last journey through the wintry wilderness.

With a grin, Sunan clapped his hands once, twice . . . and the third time, it echoed like a toll of thunder. Pippa shouted, her palms covering her ears. A flicker of lightning shot through the space, causing the entire ice structure to tremble. The ramparts began to crumble. The ground shook beneath their feet.

When Pippa and Arjun opened their eyes, they were standing in musty darkness. The walls and ceiling were all made of stone, as if they were in some kind of cave.

Sunan grinned. "Are you ready for my next test?"

———◆◆◆———

Pippa gathered herself beside the roaring blue fire, a chipped mug of steaming liquid clutched between her hands. Arjun sat next to her, his features drawn. For a time they did nothing but sip their drinks. Pippa could not even stop to consider that the brew she'd been given might cause her harm. All she knew was that it was warm and it tasted like bitter chocolate and fizz water, with a hint of rosemary. Offhand, it did not sound appetizing. But it was warm and filling as it slid down her throat.

"What is this place?" Arjun asked the little blue goblin who had introduced himself as Sunan.

Sunan twiddled his thumbs, then waved a hand through the air. A small toadstool appeared, upon which he sat. With a sad smile, he conjured another mushroom chair and offered it to the other blue goblin waiting in the wings.

Then he looked left. Looked right. "You are in what remains of the Winter Court," he said quietly.

Arjun froze in place, his mug a hairsbreadth from his lips. "I thought the winter fey held court in the Ice Palace of Kur."

Sunan smiled another sad smile. "That is the illusion we wanted all the summer fey to see. If we appeared ragtag and disheveled—with a madman for a king—then no one would perceive us as a threat, nor would they consider invading our lands." He brushed a hand across his blue chin. "It would seem that we had nothing worth taking."

Arjun's eyes widened. "Do you have something worth taking?"

Pippa nudged him with her shoulder, dismayed that he would ask such a mercenary question. "What are you doing?" she whispered. "Are you trying to anger him?"

"You needn't fear me, Lady Philippa," Sunan said. "I did not bring the son of Riya here so that I could feed him lies. I brought him here in the hopes that he might serve as an emissary to the Summer Court. So that we might . . . work together to improve the relations between the two halves of our world."

Pippa wanted to understand what Sunan meant. From the little she'd seen and heard, she knew the Winter Court and the Summer Court had been at odds for quite some time. That vampires and werewolves had been banished from Fairyland years ago, but she had yet to hear the reason for it. She leaned forward, listening, hoping she might glean an understanding from the conversation that was sure to follow.

Confusion tugged at the bridge of Arjun's nose. "I'm not certain what you think I can do to sway my mother's mind. She keeps her counsel close and does as the Lady of the Vale directs, without question."

Sunan exhaled, his thin lips puckering. Though his brow was heavyset and his skin roughened across his cheeks, there was a gentleness to his expression. Something Pippa recognized in those who had weathered the passage of time with a keen sense of perspective. "Your mother . . . has been capturing Wyld creatures along the border," Sunan said.

Arjun lifted a shoulder. "If they are trespassing on our territory, then that would not be unwarranted."

"It isn't about her capturing them," Sunan continued, his features grave. "It's what is being done to them after they are caught."

"What?" Arjun sat straighter, his eyes narrowing. "What are you talking about?"

"General Riya and Lady Silla are capturing Wyld creatures and using them to test new weapons the like of which I have never seen in all the many years of my life."

Arjun stood. "What kind of weapons?" He shoved his hands in his pockets, a gesture Pippa had come to recognize. Her new husband was uncomfortable.

She pressed her free hand to her forehead. A good wife would stand beside him. Offer her reassurances.

But she was too weary to be a good wife. Too angry to offer him her support.

"I cannot be certain what kind of weapons they are," Sunan said, joining his hands on his lap, his simple garment—a long tunic of homespun cloth and a set of matching trousers gathered at the waist—crinkling on itself. "I only know what the survivors have told us. Those precious few of our ilk that have managed to escape."

Arjun's hands fisted at his sides. Though he looked haggard, his clothing frayed by the harsh winds of the winter storm and hollows forming beneath his eyes, he nevertheless stood tall. "Why should I believe you?"

A kind smile curved up Sunan's face. "Because I've gone to so much trouble to bring you here. To test you so that I might know your mettle. And I believe you and Lady Philippa are worthy of knowing our truth. Without doubt, it is a risk to tell you"—a sadness took shape in his eyes—"but it has become more of a risk to remain silent." Sunan slid from his toadstool seat and took to his feet. At his full height, he came to Pippa's knees.

"I will not accept your word on faith alone," Arjun said after a time.

"My brother cannot lie." The second goblin, who had been silently observing their exchange from his seat in the shadows against a rough stone wall, stepped forward, his voice rife with indignation. "Nor would he, even if it were possible."

"He set a storm on us!" Pippa replied at once. "Let us believe we were in the midst of a massacre deep in the halls of the ice fortress."

The second goblin snorted. "A harmless illusion."

"A deception, by any other name." Pippa lifted her chin.

Sunan grinned. "I would not expect you to believe me on faith alone, Lady Philippa," he said. "And I am willing to show you so that you may see the truth with your own eyes."

"How would we know that this is not another harmless illusion?" Pippa said. From the corner of her eye, she saw Arjun glance her way, a grateful smile on his lips.

"I would swear it," Sunan said. "On my life."

"Sunan," said his brother, "he is the son of General Riya. And she is a mortal with no ties to our way of life. He is a gifted liar in his own right, and she is quick to anger."

"He lies to spare others pain, brother Suli," Sunan replied without missing a beat. "And her anger is righteous. I could not ask for more."

"It is folly," Suli replied, his words soft.

"Perhaps," Sunan said. "But I cannot continue to do nothing." He paced forward, his hands joining behind him. "I've been hoping to find a way to broker a peace. Those who reside within our mountain grow restless. They tire of living such a half-life. Of watching their summer brethren thrive, while they molder. If your mother continues testing weapons on winter fey—weapons that are meant to destroy what remains of our kind—I cannot promise to prevent those remaining few from launching a full-scale assault." Sunan's sadness spread across his features, his shoulders sagging. "I have kept them at bay as long as I can. Sometimes I conjure banquets for them, to make them forget their hunger. Other times I offer them a chance to see the loved ones they have lost. But the illusions are no longer enough. They want revenge."

Pippa chewed at the inside of her cheek. For months, she had longed to see her younger brother and sister. Though she knew an illusion would never suffice, the idea nevertheless tantalized her. "How do you conjure such illusions?" she asked.

"Forgive me, child," Sunan said. "I forget that you are mortal. Long ago, many fey in both the summer and winter lands were able to control some form of elemental magic. With the passage of time, this magic has been all but lost to most of us." He waved his hand before him. "From my mother, I inherited my ability to manipulate air. To conjure images from recollections. I give them shape and form, but they are only images. They do not last. The belly is fooled into being sated for a short time. The touch of a loved one lingers but a moment, leaving behind nothing but cold memory." He sighed.

Arjun remained standing, his gaze leveled at the blue fire crackling in the center of the dark chamber. "Your brother, Suli, is correct, Sunan of the Wyld," he said. "This is folly, for I won't believe anything you show me."

An iron blade tore from the tiny scabbard at Suli's side as he stepped forward. "You dare to—"

Sunan held up a hand. "Suli," he said. "Please." He turned toward Arjun. "My honor is my word, and my word is my bond."

"An old phrase." Arjun pursed his lips.

"I still honor the old ways, Arjun Desai. Do you?" He inhaled with care, the tiny hairs in his blue nostrils trembling. "Or have all summer fey lost any sense of honor?"

Pippa swallowed. She could see Arjun bristling, the muscles in his forearms flexing. "Arjun." She stood and reached for his arm. "Let us hear them out."

His jaw rippled. "He's telling me my mother is harming prisoners. That the Lady of the Vale—Celine's mother—wishes to besiege the Wyld and break the bonds of an ancient treaty." Arjun whirled on Sunan. "Why would they do this?"

"Because the Lady of the Vale's greatest wish is to unite these lands under one dynasty. Her own."

Time passed in weighted silence. Pippa's gasp echoed in the chamber. "You mean Celine?"

Sunan nodded. "It was why I could not have entreated Nicodemus Saint Germain's heir or the only daughter of Lady Silla. It was impossible to know where their loyalties might lie. I took a calculated risk singling you out, Lord Arjun. But I believed your skepticism for the Summer Court and your storied relationship with your mother—which remains fractured by all accounts—would enable you to see the truth."

"It's true I dislike my mother," Arjun said, "but I don't believe she would do something so cruel."

Sunan's expression turned grave. "You said it yourself. She would if her queen—if the Lady of the Vale—asked her." He waited a moment. "Come. Speak to the survivors. Hear what they have to say. If you wish, I will bind my hands in iron and remain at your side, so that you will know I am not conjuring anything."

"Please, Arjun," Pippa tried again. "Perhaps we should—"

"He's been toying with us from the start," Arjun said. "He let us believe we were about to die, all for some ridiculous test."

"We are our truest selves when we are about to die," Sunan said.

"And did I pass your test?" Arjun sneered.

Sunan nodded. "As did your bride." He appeared unperturbed. "It is clear she loves you dearly, as you do her." This last statement echoed into the rafters, the sound reverberating in Pippa's ears.

Her face turned hot. "Wh-what?" she blustered, not even daring to glance toward Arjun. "I—"

"You fought to save him at your own peril," Sunan said. "What I know of mortals tells me that very few of them would fight to defend someone they do not love, at risk of their own lives. Mortals are a rather selfish sort, in my estimation," he continued as if he were commenting on a flower or the clouds in the sky. "As are fey. But at least fey do not fool themselves into thinking otherwise."

"I disagree." Pippa cleared her throat. "The mortals I know are good, kind people. They would not wish ill on others."

"Only a few mortal years ago, in the place known as the land of the free, brothers fought brothers and fathers fought sons, all so that rich humans could keep their fellow humans in chains." Sunan spoke as if he were issuing a quiet admonishment. "I understand this fight because I, too, have seen what comes of it. If the Summer Court continues to hold the Winter Court underfoot, there will soon come a time when the subjugated rise up."

Arjun paced toward the fire while Sunan spoke. Quiet consideration filled the space until the popping of wood sap from the fire took on a life of its own. Pippa thought about Sunan's last statement. His request. His illusions had frightened her. Their vividness had stolen the breath from her body. At this moment, she could not prevent herself from shuddering at the memory. And yet . . . and yet, Pippa could not believe Sunan to be evil.

"Please come and see the truth for yourself," Sunan beseeched them. "Once you've heard the stories these wretched souls have to tell, make your own decision. But I beg of you, please do what you can to sway your mother from this path. It is not a righteous one. Nor is it kind. And it will not be stomached for much longer."

Pippa walked to Arjun's side. Took his hand in hers. "Perhaps we should listen." She flushed when she recalled Sunan's suggestion that the sentiments shared between Pippa and Arjun were those of love.

What nonsense.

Arjun gazed at her sidelong. Squeezed her hand. "I'll listen." His features hardened. "And then I will decide for myself."

THE GREAT WISDOM IS LIKE WATER IN THE SEA: DARK, MYSTERIOUS, IMPENETRABLE.

RABINDRANATH TAGORE

———◆◆◆———

The first thing Arjun noticed was the smell. It was unlike anything he'd encountered in any world. He'd expected the copper scent of blood. The stench of rot and unwashed bodies—however rare in the land of the meticulous fey—was also unsurprising.

But another scent hung throughout the space.

It was the scent of melancholy. Of desperation. Of keening pain. It hung like moldering linen in a forgotten closet, the stale perfume of dust and decay cloying his nostrils.

Never before had Arjun smelled a feeling. With his prized monocle, he'd seen the color of emotions in the mortal world. He'd used the information to his advantage. But he could always remove the lens so that he might witness the world as it actually was.

The smell of this pain was a smell from which he could not escape.

It was old water and sharp vinegar. Tinctures and compresses. Words whispered from cracked lips.

"Dear God," Pippa whispered beside him, her hand coming to her mouth.

Countless pallets lined either side of the cold stone floor. Arjun found himself thankful for the heavy blanket of darkness deep inside this mountain fortress. When he turned in one direction, he noticed a missing eye, the skin of half the poor soul's face blackened and bruised. He looked away and was dismayed to find another victim, the skin on both her legs flayed, leaving raw muscle exposed to the cool air. Holes littered the delicate wings of a nixie perched in the recesses of a wall. He would never fly again, and the knowledge of this loss seemed to pull at his tiny features.

Soft moans and the occasional sharp cry punctured the shadowy silence. A young winter fey with horns and cloven hooves cried out for water, and Pippa scrambled to find a bucket and a ladle.

True to his word, Sunan walked beside Arjun, his hands bound in iron to prevent him from conjuring any images.

Eyes bored at the back of Arjun's skull. He turned in place to see a dark fey glaring at him. She was missing an arm. Half her face had been burned by what appeared to be acid.

Arjun took a deep breath and crouched before her. "Is there anything I might—"

The dark fey spat at him. "I could smell your stench the second you arrived, filthy summer whelp."

A wave of anger rippled over Arjun. He resisted the urge to react. The need to defend himself. He took a careful breath and wiped the fey's spittle from his cheek. "I suppose I'll dispense with the pleasantries as well," he said. "Will you tell me what happened to you?"

"Why?" the wounded fey woman sneered. "So that you might celebrate your success at court? How wondrous your newfangled weapons are at clearing the field?"

Arjun shook his head. "What has happened to you is nothing to celebrate." He braced his elbows on his knees. "Please. Tell me."

"You expect me to believe you'll listen?" Dry laughter spewed from her lips. Arjun could tell she had once been beautiful. There was likely gentry in her lineage. But the weapon used against her—whatever it was—had wrought extensive damage, the kind even the most gifted healer could not conceal. "You expect me to believe you'll hear me when I speak ill of your beloved lady?" she said. "Your celebrated general?"

Arjun's cheeks hollowed at the mention of his mother. He wanted to leave this place. Pretend as if he'd never set foot inside this mountain. He bit down on nothing. Behind him, he heard Pippa rustling among the pallets, her voice soft and soothing. Without anyone asking her—without hesitation—she was there to offer comfort to those who needed it. She did not see weakness. She saw only need.

It was so mortal of her. And Arjun was grateful for it.

Arjun nodded. "I'll listen."

Tears welled in the dark fey's eyes. Her copper hair flashed as she shoved what remained of it back from her bronzed skin. "The first to fall were the children."

─ ❧ ─

Arjun lay in the darkness, his back against the frigid stone floor. Sleep eluded him.

Not that he deserved it. How could anyone sleep when confronted with the horrors he'd witnessed only hours ago?

All his life, Arjun had slept in warmth and comfort. In Bombay, he remembered the way the heat sweltered. How it became a living thing. Then, on the first day of the monsoons, how the heat would join with the rain to rejoice to the heavens. He and his friends would race into the streets, shouting and jumping through the mud, the sweltering heat coiling through his hair, making it stand on end.

In India, even when it rained, Arjun did not know cold.

The first time he'd encountered snow was when he lived in Cambridge. It had seeped into his skin and left him shivering. But even then, he'd been able to afford a coat. To light a merry fire, so that it crackled while it warmed his bones.

He was not used to this kind of cold. This kind of . . . emptiness. It was not just the chill of the floor beneath him or the threadbare quality of his blanket. It was the bracing cold of truth.

Arjun turned in place and shivered, moving carefully, hoping he did not wake Pippa, who slept on the raised rope bed beside him. A part of Arjun had desperately hoped to share in her warmth, but it was presumptuous. Not to mention that he would never, under pain of death, make a young woman uncomfortable in her own bed by insinuating even a drop of entitlement. It did not matter if they were married. It was in name only, and he would not be one of those men who failed to care what their wife wanted or needed.

Even as he closed his eyes again, trying in vain to find the sleep that so eluded him, the image of the burned fey returned to his mind. Of the rotting, blackened burn marks on another dark fey's skin from where a weapon had been fired at their stomach so many times that it had all but sliced them in half. That particular fey was unlikely to live for more than a week. Sunan had said as much as they took their leave. Still another elderly fey with horns and greying temples spoke in hushed tones about a small cannon, capable of firing many bullets at once. Hundreds and hundreds before needing to be reloaded, the tips fashioned of solid silver. The last fey Arjun spoke with—a kobold with shining eyes like those of a dokkaebi—mentioned another weapon made of poisonous gas, formed from a powder of crushed silver and mustard seed, mixed with a kind of acid that burned on contact before filling his lungs and causing him to feel on fire from the inside out.

He told Arjun about watching his family die, one by one.

Sunan and Pippa were careful never to mention that Arjun was the son of General Riya. In truth, Arjun avoided introducing himself at all. And though he would never admit it, he was grateful. If any of these survivors knew who Arjun was, he would not blame them in the slightest for their wrath.

Pippa conversed at length with a water nymph, who spoke of her creek being poisoned. Of underwater darts and traps filled with jagged pieces of silver, meant to explode on contact. A troll shared a tale of his skin being burned by molten silver, only to have the silver ripped away once it had hardened, flaying his flesh with it.

The sight of this particular wound had been too much for Pippa. She had run away, retching.

Arjun turned in place again, bunching the ball of rough cloth that served as a pillow.

Could his mother do such a thing?

He didn't want to believe it. He refused to believe it. His mother was many things, but he'd always seen her as good. As worthy of admiration. She was well-respected. A warrior, through and through. And though her son was an ethereal, she'd never treated him as less than another fey. She'd offered him the same cool disdain she offered the rest of the Summer Court.

The story that haunted Arjun most was another tale told by the same water nymph, who'd been forced to watch her little brother drown in a poisoned creek bed. She'd wanted to save him—tried to save him—but she'd been too weak. It was a miracle she had survived at all.

When Arjun was ten mortal years old, he heard a story of a baby-faced ethereal who'd incited the ire of a member of the gentry. His name was Osin, and his father had been a mortal regent on a far-flung island in the Pacific. When Osin was twelve mortal years old, his mother had brought him to live in the Vale, and his beautiful face charmed the members of court. But Osin's peers were angered by his beauty. One night while Osin slept, three of his fey peers took him from his bed, wrapped him in a blanket like a swaddled babe, and placed him in a boat on Lake Lure as a way to startle him when he awoke. They thought it would provide them with a good laugh, to listen to him cry out in fear, his beautiful, cherubic curls bedraggled.

The boat sprang a leak, and Osin, unable to free himself from his bindings, drowned. None of the nymphs or other water sprites came to his aid, for he was an ethereal, and ethereals were taught to fend for themselves.

This tale haunted Arjun. When he was young, he'd wondered if his mother would have come to save him, were he to suffer Osin's fate. Or if she—like the rest of her kind—would leave him to perish. Whenever he heard movements in the darkness, he sprang awake, ready to attack. He would not find himself wrapped in his own funeral shroud, meant to die an agonizing death.

For Arjun, the idea of drowning was a source of constant terror. It was one of the things he envied most about Bastien and the other vampires in the Court of the Lions. Vampires did not need air to survive.

Only when Arjun decided to live in the mortal world did he know the respite of a restful night. He still remembered the night he first came to New Orleans, a little more than a year ago. The tropical air and the scent of the breeze had filled his lungs and steadied his pulse. He'd walked the streets of the French Quarter before retiring for the evening.

It wasn't Bombay. Not at all. But something about New Orleans made Arjun feel at home. Something about its rawness. Its realness. He paused to have a beignet beneath the light of the moon, the strains of a kind of music Arjun had never heard before fading in the distance.

Of course it wasn't perfect. As it was in India, he noted that those with darker skin served those with lighter skin. When the young boy with brown skin placed the fried doughnut before Arjun, Arjun met his gaze and held it. The boy nodded, and Arjun offered him a smile.

No matter where Arjun went, he could feel the injustice of it all. That feeling never left him, whether he was strolling down the Causeway or taking a turn around the vaunted lanes of Malabar Hill in Bombay. When he was sitting outside the steps of the University Library at Cambridge, waiting until a friend could escort him safely through the stacks, without the fear of being reprimanded by the son of an earl or the next Duke of Marylebone. For nothing more than failing to be born in the right skin.

All the places Arjun ever lived, he'd never forgotten what it meant to be who he was.

But that night in New Orleans, when he'd experienced his first restful sleep, offered a sharp contrast to this moment, the first evening he would spend in the depths of Mount Morag, deep in the heart of the Sylvan Wyld. A shiver raced down his spine, and he tugged the musty blanket closer. As an ethereal, things like extreme heat or extreme cold did not reach into his bones as it did a human's. But still, this was a bitter kind of chill. Arjun longed to light a fire, but, of course, there was no hearth to be found so deep in this fortress of ice and stone.

"Arjun?" Pippa whispered. "Are you awake?"

Her words echoed a conversation they'd shared a world and half a lifetime ago. "Yes."

"I—I—"

"Is something wrong?"

"I'm . . . f-freezing."

Arjun sat up. The instant the threadbare blanket fell from his chest, the chill reached into his body. He sat at the edge of the rope bed and pulled Pippa toward him. Her teeth were chattering, her shoulders quaking. She wrapped her fingers around his shirtfront and pressed her face into his neck. With trembling hands, she moved the covers and tugged him into the rope bed alongside her. Arjun gathered her in his arms as she trembled against him, her fingers grasping the front of his tunic.

Pippa had been shivering this entire time, and Arjun had been too lost in his own thoughts to notice. She buried her face in his arm, and something unfurled in his chest. It settled him, this feeling. As if he'd found something he'd lost long ago.

"I can't sleep," Pippa admitted.

"Nor can I."

She hesitated before speaking again. He could feel it in the way her breaths slowed. "Are you greatly troubled?"

Arjun smiled to himself. Pippa's kindness would be his undoing. "Perhaps it would be easier if I were someone else," he joked.

She sniffed. "Or something else."

"A bear perhaps. At least then, we would be warmer."

"No." Pippa shook her head. "Penguins. I've always liked penguins."

"They mate for life, so I'm told."

She frowned. "Wouldn't you like to be a penguin? They sound so joyful. They play and frolic and swim all day, then they sleep cuddled against each other beneath an aurora of colors in the night sky."

"I suppose I could be a penguin, then," Arjun said. "As long as you were a penguin, too."

Another shiver racked her slender body. Arjun pulled her closer, and she responded by wrapping her arms around him. She smelled of sunshine in springtime. Arjun found himself taking a deep breath. The tension in his stomach eased further. Her warmth touched him, body and soul.

"May I ask a favor?" Pippa said once her trembling began to abate.

"Of course."

"I would appreciate it if tomorrow we pretended as though tonight never happened."

Amusement flared through Arjun, along with a strange pang around his heart. "Of course. I'll take this secret to my grave."

"But you're immortal."

"A technicality, meri pyaari. I don't share secrets with anyone, unless they offer me money."

He swore he could feel her smile.

"Did you know the queen owns all the swans in England?" she said.

"I did. I received that information the day I first arrived on the shores of England," he joked. "Did you know the first bandage ever used by humans was made from a spider's web?"

"Really?" Pippa said. "I didn't know that."

"My father told me."

"I think you love your father a lot."

Arjun did not reply right away. "I did."

"Has he passed?"

"No."

A moment of silence. "But you don't see him?"

"No. I don't." Arjun took a steadying breath. "Which is why I've turned out so poorly," he teased. "I lacked the proper influence."

Pippa sat up to look at him. "You do that often. You make jokes when you're uncomfortable."

"Alas." He narrowed his eyes. "I'm not the only one who avoids difficult conversations."

She averted her gaze.

"Who are Lydia and Henry, Pippa?" Arjun asked.

Her lips thinned into a line, as if she were willing her mouth silent.

"Philippa," Arjun said gently. "You don't have to tell me if you don't wish to tell me. But I'm here to listen when you're ready."

"I want to tell you," she whispered. "And I haven't wanted to tell anyone for a long time." She closed her eyes. "They're my younger brother and sister. I left them behind in Liverpool with my aunt Imogen after promising I would send for them before the year's end. Everything I've done—coming to New Orleans, getting engaged to a proper young man—I've done so that I might bring them to America to keep them safe and provide for them."

"I don't understand why this responsibility has fallen to you. What about your parents?" Arjun said. "Your father is a duke. Should he not have the means to—"

"My father is serving a life sentence for insurance fraud in an English prison outside Yorkshire."

For the first time in a long while, Arjun found himself at a loss for words.

She toyed with the edges of the threadbare blanket and burrowed herself into the crook of his elbow. "I'm the one who made sure he was arrested."

Arjun waited.

"When I was a little girl, he seemed so perfect," Pippa said, her tone wistful. "He played with me and read to me and sang with me. My father had a beautiful singing voice."

"A trait you share," Arjun said.

Her smile was bitter. "As a child, I didn't know that our family's wealth was all but gone. My father was set to inherit a worthless dukedom. I think even he didn't know it until my grandfather passed away. Once he realized how close we were to ruin, he began to drink. The drinking led to gambling. Soon he was spending all his time and what remained of our funds on vices. He chased lightskirts and frittered away the dregs of the estate. I realized not long after that that he was trying to steal from the few friends he had.

"Worse still, he began setting fire to some of our abandoned holdings and declaring art and family heirlooms stolen so that he might collect the insurance monies. The authorities already suspected him. I knew the only good thing our family still had— our name—was going to be tarnished forever. Any hope of my marrying well and possibly sparing my younger brother and sister suffering would be gone. My father would ruin us all, so I . . . I set fire to a warehouse office along the pier and made it seem as if he'd perpetrated arson once more in an effort to defraud his insurers. I went so far as to leave evidence implicating him, which was not difficult for the authorities to uncover."

"That was incredibly brave of you."

"My mother never forgave me. When they took my father away, she became hysterical, and her doctor prescribed laudanum, which she started pouring in her breakfast tea." She sighed. "I thought I had saved us all. But after the scandal of my father's court appearance—for he fought the charges, against the advice of his solicitors—any suitors I might have had disappeared all the same. Our state of affairs became the talk of the town, and no decent family would have me."

"Because your father was imprisoned?"

"No," she said. "Because he blamed me and publicly proclaimed his innocence, all while suggesting that I was the one responsible for the insurance fraud, as well as the thefts."

Arjun held Pippa in silence for a time, his muscles tense. "Family can be a difficult thing."

"Yes, it can be." She paused. "Thank you for not apologizing. I haven't told anyone this story since I left England, but whenever I came across anyone familiar with it back home, they all reacted the same way. They said, 'Oh, you poor dear!' and clucked about, offering me their condolences. Which, by the way, do not provide a place for my brother and sister nor a hot meal. Their apologies made me feel . . . tired." She took Arjun's hand and studied it as she spoke, as if she were giving herself something else to look at. "Tell me a secret, Arjun, and I'll tell you one in return. Tell me something you've never told anyone else."

Arjun studied the way she held his hand. He threaded his fingers through hers as if it were the most natural thing. The way they formed a bond stronger together than they were apart.

"Sometimes when I cook for myself," he said, "I imagine I'm with my father, back home in India. I try to remember how he made things. How he would add spices and crush garlic and stir a pot. As if . . . I'm close to him when I prepare a meal."

"For each of the birthdays we've spent apart, I set a place for both Lydia and Henry at the table." Pippa gripped his hand tightly. "And I talk to them so that I don't feel alone."

Arjun looked down at Pippa. Pippa looked up at Arjun.

And it was enough.

MISERY ACQUAINTS A MAN WITH
STRANGE BEDFELLOWS.

THE TEMPEST,

WILLIAM SHAKESPEARE

———◆◆◆———

Snow pummeled Michael's side. Ice stung his eyes. Though he possessed the ability to turn into a werewolf, as a human he was not immune to the effects of this frozen wasteland. After all, he'd been born and raised in New Orleans. Never before in his life had he experienced such cold.

Anger ignited within him when he consulted the compass ring once more. If Pippa hadn't vanished one second and re-appeared the next in an entirely different location, he would have found her by now. Michael clutched his cloak and bowed into the wind, which responded by knocking him onto his backside. He sank into two feet of newly fallen snow, his boots wet, his face frozen.

Exhaustion tugged at his features and weighed down his bones.

There was nothing to be had for it. He needed to find shelter and rest so he might wait out the storm. The best thing for him to do was to change into a wolf and seek a cavern or a fallen tree trunk somewhere close by.

He supposed the one advantage he had now that he'd entered

the perpetual night of the Sylvan Wyld was the ability to change at will into a wolf. Once Michael had crossed the border, he'd felt the magic course through his veins, there for the taking.

A world of unending darkness. One in which a young werewolf like himself should be in his element. This was the land of his forebears. The source of the lupine magic running through his veins.

Michael searched among the trees until he saw a large hollow in the distance, set beneath the roots of an immense oak tree. He would be able to rest far more easily as a wolf. He'd be warmer, and his ability to fend for himself—along with his instincts—would be at their sharpest.

He made his way toward the earthen outcropping, sending a silent prayer that it would provide a measure of the shelter he desperately sought. Buffeted about by the wind and ice and snow, it took him a full twenty minutes to make his way there. Though he loathed the idea, he had to remove his clothing completely and set it aside so that it would not be shredded beyond all recognition from the violence of the transformation. Into his pocket he placed his watch and the compass ring, before beginning to undress in the bitter cold. He started to shiver as soon as he removed his shirt. Quickly, he collected his garments and wrapped them in his ice-covered cloak. After a moment of hesitation, he tore a strip of cloth from the hem of his shirt and fashioned a loose necklace of sorts, upon which he threaded his watch and his compass ring before tying it around his throat, just below the talisman necklace Valeria Henri had made for him.

They would be safer there than among his things.

Michael looked toward the brightest part of the sky. It was overcast as a result of the snowstorm, but a hint of moonlight still managed to glow beneath the blanket of clouds. He closed his eyes and braced himself.

The pain he expected did not come. The transformation was smooth, the magic rippling down his back in a wave of warmth. In New Orleans, Michael could feel the snapping of every bone when he changed. The way his fangs tore through the skin of his mouth. How his claws ripped the nails of his hands and feet as they grew, like some cruel kind of medieval torture.

He marveled at the ease of his transformation in the Sylvan Wyld. In the blink of an eye, he was a werewolf, his sight perfectly attuned to the night forest before him. The fur along his body provided the warmth he needed. With a contented huff, Michael moved into the shelter beside his neat pile of clothes.

He'd barely begun to drift to sleep when a scent assailed his nostrils. He leapt onto his paws, a growl ripping from his mouth, his dark hackles raised.

Another wolf emerged from the shadows in a nearby grove of trees. It moved with care, its steps a bit mincing. Even from a distance, Michael could see that one of its front paws was missing. But it moved as if it meant for Michael to see it. As if it had been watching Michael all along.

When the wolf drew close, Michael realized it was a female. One with distinct eyes and a haughty demeanor. The wolf walked even closer, not at all threatened by Michael's fighting stance.

Instead it sat before him, waiting for him to stop growling and start listening. Michael knew this was no ordinary wolf. A part of him recognized her, even from a distance.

Émilie Saint Germain. Émilie La Loup. Banished to the frozen wastelands by her own brother, following the events that had transpired on the riverboat several weeks ago.

She'd caused Michael so much pain. And he'd taken her love—his cousin Luca—from her.

Now they faced each other in the darkness. There was no place for either of them to hide a weapon. If Michael attacked her, he held an advantage because of her injuries. If she attacked him, her advantages were age and awareness. The fearlessness of a Saint Germain.

In truth they were equally matched. Which meant they were both at each other's mercy.

He lowered his hackles. Michael knew the path of violence all too well.

I see you've found your way home, Michael Grimaldi.

Michael startled, a fresh growl emanating from his throat.

In the Wyld, wolves can speak to each other without words. Wouldn't this have been a great help to us in New Orleans, when we needed it most?

Michael continued growling, though uncertainty tugged at his heart.

Speak to me in your mind, Émilie continued. *As if you were speaking to yourself.*

Michael glanced down at her missing paw. Her leg trembled as she took a step toward him, her expression keen. *What they did to you was wrong.* Even in his mind, his tone was be-grudging.

It was important for my brother to stake his claim. I took from him. It was natural for him to take from me. Émilie sat down again in front of him.

You are not angry? Michael asked. *I would be angry.*

Of course I am angry. But I am also grieving.

Michael whined. *Please know that I never meant to hurt Luca.*

I know. But this time my grief has taught me a painful lesson. She looked up at the moon. *It has taught me that violence only brings about more violence. More bloodshed. More death. I want to put an end to it all.*

Michael said nothing.

You don't believe me? Émilie asked. *I understand if you don't. It will take some time. But I have proof that the Sylvan Vale is creating weapons to annihilate what remains of the Sylvan Wyld.*

You've seen these weapons? Surprise rounded Michael's lupine gaze.

I've heard of them, from those who've witnessed unspeakable suffering. From those with little to nothing to lose. Michael, you are the best of us. Luca spoke often of your sense of right and wrong. Your intellect astonished him, even when you were a boy. He was always so proud of you. Will you help me put an end to this ridiculous war, once and for all?

Again Michael did not reply, though pain knifed through his chest. Luca had been like an elder brother to him. Michael suspected Émilie of using his guilt as a tool of manipulation, but it did not make her choice of weapon any less effective.

Michael had lost so much. Again his attention was drawn to her wound. What would it feel like for him to lose a hand or a foot? How had she survived in these frozen wastelands with such an injury?

Émilie Saint Germain had lost a great deal as well.

She continued. *It will take you time, I understand. But Luca would have helped me. I hope you will be willing to do what must be done to keep our kind safe, in his memory. For once, I wish to honor the remembrance of someone I loved and lost.* Émilie stood once more as if to leave.

It's cold out there, Michael said. *Would you like to stay here until the storm passes?*

Émilie paused. Then she limped toward him, lowered herself to the ground, and fell asleep.

———◆●◆———

A rjun stared up at the ceiling of the small chamber. In his
arms, Pippa slept, her lips puckering and her brow creas-
ing with concern. He studied her face. The soft sweep of her
long eyelashes across her cheekbones. The way her lips pushed
forward. The curls of hair on her forehead.

Something pulled at his heartstrings. Irritation followed in
its wake.

Damn it all. Arjun cared. He cared about her . . . too much.
And try as he might, he could not banish the memory of Sunan's words.

Was it possible for Pippa Montrose to love him? Did he . . .
love her in return?

She sighed in her sleep, an expression of consternation unfolding across her features.

Before tonight, Arjun had wondered what could trouble a girl
like her. He'd watched them at Cambridge when they came to
visit their brothers or their cousins, their white parasols fluttering and their kidskin boots pristine. These lovely young ladies
from titled families, with storied pasts and promising futures.

At least now he knew what troubled Philippa Montrose.

Just as he knew all too well the pain of losing his family. With each passing year, the memories of his time with his mother and father in Bombay became murkier. As if a haze were thickening around his mind. Perhaps the fog lent itself to rosier remembrances. Maybe his father had not been such a wonderful cook. Maybe his mother had not smiled as much or told him as many fanciful tales. Tales which, Arjun later realized, were likely not the stuff of her imagination.

No. Even if time made his memories fonder, Arjun still cherished his childhood and lamented its loss. For years, he had begrudged his mother. If only she had allowed them to remain in the mortal world. *Why were you unhappy?* He wanted to shout at her. *Why did you have to ruin everything?*

For so long, Arjun had attributed his loss to her ambition. She'd left the mortal world because she could never achieve the kind of influence available to her in the Sylvan Vale. And now his mother was the chief huntress of the Summer Court, second only to Lady Silla. She was General Riya. A begrudging realization began to take shape in Arjun's mind. Perhaps it was wrong for a woman to sacrifice her dreams because society demanded it. Celine and Pippa and Odette and Hortense and Madeleine . . . they deserved to have ambitions of their own.

His mother should be no different.

Pippa stirred on Arjun's chest, a hand coming to rest beside her cheek.

She had already sacrificed so much for the sake of others. She did not deserve to sacrifice her future as well. A sense of powerlessness had settled on Arjun's shoulders after he spoke with the victims of the Sylvan Vale's horrific weapons. Even if he pleaded their case to his mother, what could be done to mend such broken bodies and ravaged souls? It had plagued him well into the night.

But perhaps there was something he could do to help Pippa.

With great care, Arjun rose from the rope bed, the twine creaking as he moved, causing him to wince. Then he made his way into the corridors of ice and stone.

It was not difficult for him to find Sunan's lair. From beyond the weathered door of his chamber, the glow of the blue flame emanated through the ice walls, like a beacon in the night. Arjun stepped into the central room with its domed ceiling and found Sunan waiting, as if he'd been expecting Arjun to seek him out.

"It took you longer than I thought it would," Sunan said.

Arjun stood before him. "I couldn't sleep."

"Nor could I," Sunan admitted. He conjured a larger toadstool for Arjun and gestured for him to take a seat. "Suli did not believe you would be moved by what you saw today. He thought your loyalty to your mother would remain true. Once again, I am triumphant." His laughter was soft and sad. "I do not know why he bothers making wagers with me anymore."

Arjun studied the blue fire sparking in the center of the chamber. It tinged the shadows with an eerie light. "Is this fire real?" he asked. "Or have you conjured it, like the toadstool?"

Sunan lifted a shoulder. "Things are real if you believe them to be."

Arjun snorted. "Spoken like a master of illusion."

"I make no apologies for what I do now, especially given my past," Sunan said, his goblin features darkening. "Many centuries ago, I took things that did not belong to me. I enjoyed my life at the expense of others. When I caused harm, I used illusion to turn leaves into gold and sand into bread and pain into laughter." He sighed. "I gave little thought to how those I left in my wake would be sickened or paupered by my actions. I took and I took, and I cared only for myself and what I wanted.

"Then . . . I came across a warlock with a traveling silver," he continued, his eyes reflecting the blue fire. "When I learned how it allowed its possessor to travel between worlds—between times, even—I knew I had to have it."

Arjun's heartbeat quickened. "It allowed its possessor to travel through time?"

Sunan nodded. "Can you imagine? The ability to change fate. To learn one's future. For a master of illusion, it was too tempting. So I stole the mirror after I orchestrated its master's death." He paused. Sent Arjun another sad smile. "Suli is the only member of my family I have left, for good reason. My eighteen brothers and sisters, their families, my parents, their parents, my lover, our children . . . I lost them all to this mirror." His expression turned grave. "But that is a story for another night. And the lesson does not change: when you toy with the illusion of time, you are no longer the master of anything, for time has mastered you."

Arjun leaned forward with a look of understanding. "This was why Bastien sought your help. With a mirror like this, he could change his fate and no longer be a vampire."

Sunan nodded. "It is possible. But the cost?" He sighed again. "I could not tell you what it might be." He turned to face Arjun fully. "But you did not come to see me because you wished to speak about my past."

"No," Arjun agreed. "I did not."

"Allow me to speak plainly. Will you help me save what is left of the Sylvan Wyld?" Sunan asked. "Will you help us maintain the balance between darkness and light?"

Arjun locked gazes with the tiny blue goblin. Though he tried to corral his thoughts, he could not stop them from wandering. Sunan's mirror intrigued him. A tare through time. That is what it could provide. He could return to Bombay and see his father's memories restored. He could go back and stop Émilie Saint Germain from nearly sending Odette to her final death.

But what other horrors might ensue instead? One disaster averted was just that. Arjun's life had taught him that nothing happened as he'd expected. The last thing he'd ever considered possible when he left New Orleans was that he might travel to the land of the fey and marry a mortal girl.

A girl who—over the span of a few days—had touched Arjun's soul in a way he could never have imagined.

"This mirror," Arjun began. "Can it function as an ordinary tare, from this world to the mortal one?"

Weariness settled on Sunan's shoulders, but he nodded. "It can. But if you wish to toy with time, I cannot—"

"I have no interest in toying with time," Arjun said. "I've learned in my life that there are things I cannot change, for good reason." He stood. "I will speak to my mother as an emissary on behalf of the Sylvan Wyld. If we arrange a meeting in neutral territory, I will do what I can to convince her and the Lady of the Vale that their actions must cease if the tenuous peace between the Summer Court and the Winter Court is to hold." His hands balled into fists at his side. "But I would like to request two things in return."

Laughter bubbled from Sunan's throat. "I would expect no less from the only son of the chief huntress."

"I wish for you to send your most gifted healer through your mirror to New Orleans, so that life can be restored to Odette Valmont," Arjun said.

Sunan pursed his lips to one side of his mouth. "And the second request?"

"I wish to have use of the mirror for personal reasons. Rest assured, I will not use it to bring anyone into the Wyld."

A moment passed in consideration. Sunan pressed his lips from one side of his face to the other. "Once you enter the tare, you will also swear to avoid the Maze of Mirrors?"

"I'm not even certain what that is," Arjun answered honestly.

"As you pass from our world into the mortal one, you will see a garden path of polished blue stones leading to a labyrinth filled with mirrors. Once you enter it, you are bound by its rules, and only time will tell what might become of you."

Arjun nodded. "I understand."

"Then I will agree to allow you use of the mirror, so long as you do not seek to bring us harm." With that, Sunan stood from his seat and paced before Arjun. "But I will make a few requests of my own. You must not divulge the true plight of the Winter

Court to anyone. It is of utmost importance that we maintain the illusion of the dwarf king and the stronghold at the Ice Palace of Kur. I fear our weakness would be too tempting to Lady Silla."

"I understand," Arjun said.

"And I would ask you to promise that neither you nor Lady Philippa will abandon the Wyld before speaking to the Summer Court about how their new weapons threaten the tenuous peace between their land and the land of the dark fey."

"I promise."

———◆◆◆———

Bastien heard the commotion before he saw it. An ear-piercing scream echoed through the twilit trees. He wiped the blood from his hands and mouth, then stopped to listen.

One scream echoed into the next. The sound of laughter followed on its heels. Bastien released the staglike creature in his arms and turned toward its source. As he drew closer, he slowed, no longer blurring with the preternatural speed of a vampire. Instead he crouched in the shadows, prowling, his senses on alert.

The screams turned pitiful. Soon Bastien was able to make out words.

"You will be killed for this," a lamentable creature wailed, its voice cracking from pain. "I swear you will be torn limb from limb."

"You've wandered beyond your borders." Someone tsked, their amusement plain. "Who will save you now?"

"I am the daughter of—"

The twang of a crossbow being loosed drew another scream from the poor soul's lips. Bastien knelt in the thicket and peered from between a set of low-hanging branches. He saw a clearing, with no fewer than six members of the highest order among the Vale's gentry, known as the Fey Guild, circling the injured creature. The Fey Guild was comprised of the families with the most power and influence in the Summer Court. It reminded him of some of the more exclusive social clubs in New Orleans. He recognized the members of the Fey Guild because of the distinctive evergreen emblems they wore on their mantles. On their sleeves. On their hoods. On their jewelry. On any surface that drew attention to their lofty station.

Those in the Fey Guild were considered royalty in the Sylvan Vale. And in Bastien's experience, they tended to behave like the entitled children of wealthy landowners. Cruelty was de rigueur, as was their amused indifference to the plight of those beneath them.

Three of the Fey Guild members carried gilded crossbows. From a distance, Bastien could smell the distinct scent of the silver-tipped arrows. A metal meant to cause grave damage to any night-dwelling creature of the Sylvan Wyld. Meant to bring about harm to Bastien and his kind.

Angling for a better vantage, Bastien soundlessly clawed up the tree into the branches, where he settled in to bear witness to the unfolding scene.

A horned satyr—her hooves bloodied and her chest littered with arrows—swayed in the center of a makeshift circle. "I've"— the satyr nearly stumbled, blood dripping down her stomach and arms—"I've told you what you wish to know. Let me pass."

One member of the Fey Guild, a lady by the name of Laryssa, shook her finger as if she were scolding a little one. "I want to know where they took General Riya's son. Even if Arjun Desai is a cursed ethereal, he still ranks higher than mongrels like you." She spat. "Filthy winter monstrosity."

"I don't know," the satyr cried. "I've told you I don't know where they've gone, only that they were seen entering the Ice Palace known as Kur."

Lady Laryssa shook her head, raised her crossbow, and fired another shot at the satyr's thigh. She shrieked in agony as the arrow's shaft buried deep beneath her fur. Laryssa tugged on the string attached to the arrow, and the satyr tumbled to the ground with a shuddering cry.

Bastien had seen enough.

He landed in the clearing with a solid thud, anger rippling over his body in waves.

"What is the meaning of this?" Bastien demanded in a guttural whisper.

Only one member of the Fey Guild had the sense to gasp in shock and attempt to flee. Bastien blocked his access by blurring into his path. Though he knew it would be seen as a threatening gesture, he bared his fangs. A male member of the Fey Guild pointed his crossbow at Bastien on instinct. Bastien faced him, daring him without words to fire a shot.

"If I were you," Bastien said viciously, "I would be damned certain I didn't miss."

"This is none of your affair, vampire," Lady Laryssa interjected in a nonchalant tone. "If you leave now, we will pretend you did not trespass on matters far beyond your purview."

"This is a creature of the night." Bastien looked toward the satyr, who lay on the ground, her chest heaving. "She is unarmed. You are torturing her for information about General Riya's son." A muscle ticked in Bastien's jaw. "Arjun Desai is a member of my family. I assure you this is very much my business."

Along the edge of the clearing, one of the hooded members of the Fey Guild stepped forward. Bastien struggled to conceal his dismay when the fey lady removed her hood.

"I regret that you saw this, Sébastien," Lady Silla said, her voice calm and her features impeccable, as always. "I find torture to be as disagreeable as you find it to be. But unfortunately, it is effective. Lord Arjun and his new bride were taken from the Ivy Bower on their wedding day, apparently in an attempt by a lord in the Wyld to call due on a promise. Since I know both Arjun Desai and his new bride, Philippa Montrose, are important to you and to my daughter, I thought it prudent to uncover their whereabouts with great haste." Lady Silla moved through the clearing as she spoke, gliding like a swan across the water. "Which, alas, has caused me to resort to such less than savory methods."

Confusion wound through Bastien's mind. Arjun had married Pippa? He did not even realize the two were well-acquainted, let alone attracted to each other. Pippa was engaged to Phoebus Devereux. If a wedding between Arjun and Pippa had taken place, it must have been as a last resort . . . which meant that it was possible the marriage was made under duress. "I wish you would let the satyr go, Lady Silla," Bastien said. "She is suffering and has already answered your questions."

Lady Silla nodded, the pearl powder along her brow gleaming in the afternoon sunlight. "I intend to release her, and of course I will see that she is treated for her wounds. I am not a monster."

Bastien bit down on nothing and swallowed. There was much more that he wished to say. But he knew today what he'd known yesterday: if he defied the Lady of the Vale in her own land, there was no telling what might become of him.

After countless attempts to warn Celine against the folly of being deceived by appearances, he worried her patience with him had grown thin. He understood why. Celine wanted to believe her mother was a benevolent leader. That her blood was the blood of a gracious queen. Bastien knew this because it was precisely the same sentiment he'd clung to for so many years when it came to his uncle Nicodemus. Bastien's unceasing faith in his uncle had been to both their detriments.

Celine's mother was unlikely to listen to Bastien's protests, so he turned his attention toward the satyr. He crouched beside her and began breaking the ends off the arrows with strings still attached to them. The satyr yelped in pain, startled by Bastien's motions. Uncertain of his motivations.

All at once, Bastien heard the sound of another arrow being fitted for a crossbow. Of the spring being tightened. He stood and turned toward it, his fangs bared.

Another member of the Fey Guild—a lord by the name of Vyr—grinned at Bastien. "Give me an excuse, you miserable blood drinker." His eyes shone with a wicked light. "Make it seem as though I had no choice. I beg of you."

"Aim true, Lord Vyr," Bastien said. "Because you won't get a second chance."

"Vyr," Lady Silla said with a clap of her hands. "Put down your weapon at once."

Lord Vyr's silver eyes glittered. He grinned again at Bastien, the crossbow still aimed at Bastien's heart. Then he pointed the weapon toward the ground. "Of course, Lady Silla."

"Let us not part from here with a misunderstanding between us, Sébastien," Lady Silla said in a kind tone. "This unfortunate incident is in service to my daughter. The Wyld creature knew of Philippa Montrose's whereabouts. Celine values her mortal friend's life dearly. I am only trying to help them both. I hope you understand."

Bastien said nothing. He was tired of the Lady of the Vale offering perfectly plausible reasons for deeply troubling behavior. He did not believe Lady Silla, even if the fey were unable to tell a lie. The ruler of the Summer Court relished holding power over even the lowliest of creatures. Whatever deception she offered now was one she herself believed, just as she believed in her own goodness. Her own twisted sense of righteousness. But Bastien had seen the gleam in her eye on more than one occasion. The suggestion that violence as an answer was not a distasteful notion, but a desirable one.

"If Arjun Desai and Pippa Montrose are trapped in the Winter Court, it is because Arjun promised a period of service to a dwarf king in an attempt to save me and Celine," Bastien said. "I would like permission to go to the Ice Palace and barter with this dwarf king to ensure their freedom." It grated on Bastien to ask Lady Silla for permission, but he knew it was the correct path forward, if he wished to take his leave of the Summer Court under favorable terms.

If he ever wanted to come back.

Lady Silla's smile unfurled slowly. "Return to the Moon Rabbit's Grove. I will speak to you and my daughter shortly."

―◦―

"They must have been forced to marry." Celine paced across the curved floor beside the long table in the dining room, anger causing her cheeks to flush. "If they were forced, there must be some way to annul it." She stopped short, her long fey robes swirling about her slippered feet. An exasperated cry burst from her lips. "Damn it all! Only yesterday I learned how permanent such unions are among the fey. They are allowed to wed once in their immortal lifetimes. Just once. I can't imagine why Pippa—let alone Arjun—would ever agree to such a thing!" She whirled on Bastien, her rich amethyst skirts spinning in the opposite direction. "If they are being held against their will, we must rescue them." Determination flared in her green eyes. "These cursed winter fey must learn they cannot toy with us in such a brazen manner."

It was one of the many reasons Bastien had fallen in love with Celine: her unwillingness to turn away from the things that mattered to her, even in the face of grave danger. But for the first time since Bastien met Celine, her unflinching gaze caused a knot of discomfort to tighten in his throat. He swallowed, refusing to allow it purchase.

Her strength—her loyalty—was an asset. A quality he would always admire in her.

Never mind that she sounded like her mother.

"Cursed winter fey?" Bastien said softly.

Dismay softened her features. "Of course I don't mean you."

"Of course." Bastien crossed his arms. "Just the winter fey who don't matter."

"That is . . . unfair of you to say." Celine started to chastise him further, then stopped herself. She reached for Bastien, the jewelry around her wrists—large amethysts encircled by flawless diamonds in a design distinct of the Summer Court—flashing with each of her movements. "I don't want to fight with you," she continued. "Especially not when our family is in trouble."

Bastien took her hands. Kissed her palm, pausing to inhale the scent of her skin, never once forgetting what they both were. "I've already spoken to your mother." He framed her face between his hands. "And even if she doesn't grant me permission, I intend to leave within the hour."

Celine blinked. "Why would she not grant you permission?"

Bastien exhaled with care. For less than an instant, he considered sharing his true thoughts. How Lady Silla's best attempts had failed to fool him. But there would be time for that later. Now it was of far greater importance that they come to Pippa's and Arjun's aid. "Your mother is a . . . complicated woman, Celine," he said. "She rules a land of capricious fey. Every action she undertakes must be careful. Calculated. It isn't possible to maintain order as she has without being . . . uncompromising at times. I don't begrudge her this."

Celine wrapped her palms around his wrists, her shoulders sagging. "Has my mother offended you in some way, Bastien? Please tell me. Each day you seem to grow more distant, and you frown whenever she enters the room."

Bastien hesitated. He despised hesitating with Celine. He wasn't sure if she was ready to hear the things he'd heard or see the things he'd seen. Worse yet, he wasn't certain if Celine would be willing to believe any of it. "Your mother and I come from very different worlds."

"Don't be a politician. Not with me." Celine sneered. "I've seen the way you charm people into your confidence by giving what amounts to nonanswers."

The knot in Bastien's throat tightened further. It was a similar charge to one he'd levied at her own mother less than an hour ago. "Perhaps my true discomfort arises from the similarities I share with Lady Silla," he admitted.

"You dislike her," Celine said, accusation underscoring each word.

Bastien bit down on nothing. He caressed the side of Celine's face with his thumb. "Yes."

"Why?"

"Because she hides who she is from you," he said. "If she's hiding parts of herself, it's because she knows you will not be pleased to see them."

"She's been kind to us," Celine said. "Welcoming of you, despite the animosity of her court. Why are you so incapable of believing she loves me?"

"I believe she loves you," Bastien said. "Sometimes even the wickedest creatures are capable of the greatest love." His grin was dark. "I should know."

Anger twisted Celine's face. "You are—"

"Celine," Lady Silla announced from behind Bastien. When Bastien turned around, displeasure took root in his chest. Ali was in Lady Silla's company, his silk fey garments stained a dark purple.

A match for Celine's robes. Bastien met Lady Silla's gaze. A knowing smile curved her lips.

Celine brushed Bastien aside and moved toward her mother with resolute strides. As if she were intent on proving Bastien wrong. "Mother, if Pippa and Arjun are prisoners of the Winter Court, I wish to journey there with Bastien and beg for their release."

"Of course you do," Lady Silla said in a kind tone. She pushed back a lock of black hair from her daughter's forehead. "And of course you should go. You do not need my permission, my dear. Though I must insist that you take a few members of my personal guard with you. If the Winter Court were to capture you and discover that you were my daughter, you would be a prize indeed."

Ali frowned. "That . . . does not seem wise, Lady Silla."

The Lady of the Vale's slender eyebrows shot into her forehead.

"I beg pardon," Ali said with a small bow, his hand resting on the jeweled hilt of his curved sword. "But it seems unduly dangerous for your only daughter to travel into the land of your sworn enemy without an extremely good reason."

"My best friend is trapped there," Celine cried. "What could be a better reason?"

"Are there no diplomatic solutions?" Ali said. "My father is in a position of authority at home, and I know he would not risk journeying to an enemy's territory unless all other avenues were first explored." He placed a hand on Celine's shoulder. "I apologize for interfering, Celine, but I don't wish to see you hurt or taken hostage."

Bastien watched this scene unfold with sharp interest. He said nothing, though objections and opinions lodged in his mouth, begging for release. He knew if he acted against Celine's mother now, he would seem petulant. Argumentative.

But the Lady of the Vale's choice to include the time-traveler Ali in these discussions was far from happenstance.

Lady Silla was the furthest thing from a fool. And Bastien did not believe in coincidences.

He decided the best course of action was to agree with Ali for the time being, no matter where his true opinions might lie. More than anything, he wanted Celine to go with him to the Wyld. To take her away from her mother to a place where they might both clear their heads. But now was not the time to say so. "I agree with Ali, Celine," Bastien said.

A flicker of surprise ghosted across Lady Silla's face. Satisfaction warmed through Bastien's veins at the sight of it. "Perhaps you and your mother could arrange a meeting with the dwarf king so that we might negotiate for Arjun's and Pippa's release. In the meantime, I could travel to the Wyld and see what might be done from there."

Celine clenched her fists at her sides. "I don't want you to leave without me," she said. "I've told you before how much I dislike you facing danger alone."

"I understand," Bastien said. "But Ali has made an important point."

At that, Celine's mother reached for her daughter's hand. "Aga, perhaps we should listen. I would be happy to try whatever I can to negotiate for your loved ones' release. And of course I would want you to be involved in every aspect of it."

Celine hesitated. Then squeezed her mother's hand. "Umma, if you would agree to meet with them on neutral ground, I will remain behind to make the journey with you so that we might entreat with them together."

If Bastien weren't so disturbed, he would admire how adeptly Lady Silla played the hand she was dealt. Undoubtedly, her greatest design was to separate Bastien and Celine, which she had just done with very little effort on her part.

Bastien sighed to himself. Lady Silla and he were more alike than he cared to consider.

"And if it would help mollify your concerns, I would be honored to accompany Bastien to the Sylvan Wyld," Ali said.

This was not to be borne. A muscle rippled in Bastien's jaw. This time-traveling pissant was not going anywhere with him. Bastien would not have his every thought or action reported to the Lady of the Vale.

Bastien said, "As kind as that offer is, I must—"

"Your counsel would be of far greater use to us here, Ali," Lady Silla said with a serene smile.

"I must agree," Bastien said.

Celine pursed her lips in irritation, first at her mother, and then at Ali. Finally she settled on Bastien. She glided before him and pressed her forehead into his chest. "Be safe. If you don't find them in two days, come back to me." She tugged him toward her by the collar of his shirt, her voice dropping to a whisper. "Or I will come find you myself."

AND THE MORAL OF THAT IS—"OH, 'TIS LOVE,
'TIS LOVE, THAT MAKES THE WORLD GO ROUND!"

ALICE'S ADVENTURES IN WONDERLAND,

LEWIS CARROLL

———◆◆◆———

Pippa faced the magic mirror in the darkened chamber of blue ice and grey stone, her eyes wide. "Back to New Orleans in the time it takes to brew a cup of tea," she murmured to Arjun, her words soundless. "Are you sure it's safe for us to use?"

"I used it twice this morning and once last night," Arjun assured her. "If we go directly to New Orleans and disregard any other paths along the way, we will be safe. But we must return by mortal nightfall because I promised Sunan that we would not abandon the Sylvan Wyld until our meeting with the Summer Court tomorrow at dusk."

Pippa nodded. She reached a tentative hand toward the worn surface of the traveling silver. At her nearness, the mirror began to undulate, a low hum filling her ears. Pippa pulled back, chewing at the inside of her cheek, her stomach tensing. "Can we trust the Lady of the Vale to honor the terms of that meeting?"

Arjun riffled a hand through his dark hair. "The plan is to gather along the border of the Wyld and the Vale. There is a bridge that unites both lands. Centuries ago, it was built with the promise of unity. Ever since I can remember, it has been treated with deference. It is as appropriate a place as any to serve as neutral territory."

Pippa nodded. "It would be unseemly to engage in violence there."

Arjun's lips thinned into a line. "It would be foolhardy for either side to put an end to a peace that has existed for centuries." He paused. "But the fey are unpredictable, so it is wise for us to be prepared for anything." With a halfhearted smile, he attempted to change the course of their conversation. "We should be on our way soon. There are people waiting for us back home in New Orleans."

Pippa nodded once. "Phoebus," she said. "Odette and the Court of the Lions." She folded her hands before her.

It troubled Pippa beyond words that she was not excited to see her fiancé. Phoebus was a good man. He deserved to have her reassurance that all was well. That she wished to marry him as soon as possible.

Arjun reached his hand toward her and smiled. "Shall we?"

Pippa closed her eyes. She knew the reason she wasn't thrilled at the prospect of being reunited with Phoebus Devereux.

Arjun Desai. Her half-fey . . . husband.

She threw back her shoulders. Of course she was attracted to Arjun. He'd come to her rescue countless times. Risked his life to keep her safe. Offered her warmth and compassion and companionship.

They'd shared a single, thrilling kiss.

But a handful of days together in a realm of near-constant danger did not make a marriage. It did not matter if that moment they kissed tilted her life. Turned it upside down for an aching instant. Phoebus was reliable. Pippa knew what to expect of a marriage with him. He would take care of her and of Lydia and Henry. Perhaps he would be a senator or even governor one day. They might have a few children of their own. Phoebus would retire to his garden, and Pippa would paint and read to her heart's content.

It would be a lovely life. It was greedy of Pippa's heart to expect more. To want ... another tilted moment of passion. Arjun Desai's world was filled with the unpredictable and the unknown. It was not the right place for Pippa or her brother and sister.

With that, Pippa opened her eyes and pressed forward. This mirror was different from the one in Arjun's flat. The instant her skin touched its surface, ice-cold air blasted around her. Pippa stepped through the looking glass into a world of white. Snow fell in soft flakes around them. To their left was a path lined with stones, leading to a black tower. To their right was a winding lane of blue cobbles just beyond a gleaming garden. Something chimed in the air, as if the shining hedgerow were beckoning to them.

Arjun's grip on her hand was firm. They continued walking in a straight line through the gently falling snow, toward what appeared to be an arched door, the wood stained a dark mahogany.

Once Arjun turned a handle, he motioned for Pippa to step across the threshold first. The familiar heat and scent of a New Orleans summer wafted around Pippa as she moved into the thick darkness. Her eyes began to adjust as the light in the room brightened.

They were at the Hotel Dumaine in the middle of the afternoon. Though Pippa had only ever seen the extravagant lobby of black and white marble, she recognized the fluted columns and the delicate scent. The perfume of lilies and vetiver. An elegant table covered in white linen stretched the length of the narrow room, its walls replete with intricate crown molding and trimmed with white shadow boxes.

Three place settings lay at one end of the table.

The beat of Pippa's heart stuttered for a second. Three cups. Three plates. Three smiles.

"Is Phoebus meeting us here?" Pippa asked. When Arjun did not respond right away, Pippa turned toward him. Both his hands were in his pockets.

"No," Arjun admitted. "He is not."

Her brows drew together. "What? I thought—"

"Pippa, I . . . don't want to stand in your way," Arjun said, his voice gentle. "Nor do I wish to put undue pressure on you. I only"—he took in a breath—"I want you to have choices."

"Arjun, what are you talking about?" Confusion tugged at Pippa's features.

"You said you were marrying Phoebus to protect your family. I don't think any young woman should have to sacrifice her dreams or her hopes for her own future. Not for anyone." He paused. Closed his eyes, as if he needed a moment to gather himself. When he looked at her once more, Pippa felt her world start to tilt again, ever so slowly.

"Your family became my family that day in the Ivy Bower," Arjun said. "And my family will never know want for all their lives, no matter what happens." When his voice thickened on the last word, Arjun cleared his throat, his hazel eyes bright. "Pippa, be with the one you choose. Be with no one. It is your decision." He kept his distance, his hands remaining in his pockets, his words careful. "And if you still wish to marry Phoebus, I will be there to celebrate your wedding. But if you change your mind . . . I am here. I will be here."

Pippa's pulse continued to stutter, her world spinning upside down. A feeling of dizzying awareness washed through her, flushing her skin, causing her face to turn hot. She knew what Arjun had done. She knew it. But she dared not believe it.

The door at her back opened, sending a shaft of amber sunlight across the polished marble floor.

"Pippa!" a familiar voice cried, followed by another high-pitched shriek and the joyful barking of a corgi puppy. Two sets of shoes and four paws trampled toward her, and still Pippa could not turn around.

What if this was all a dream? What if she woke in the next breath?

Silent tears glazed her cheeks. Arms latched around her legs, and a familiar set of small hands wrapped around her waist. Pippa dropped to her knees and gathered her brother and sister to her, their heads of tangled blond curls joining with hers. They laughed while she cried, Queen Elizabeth trembling with happiness beside their feet.

Through her tears, she looked for Arjun.

But he was already gone.

—∾—

Hours later, Pippa studied her reflection in a cracked mirror, the icy walls of the lone bathing chamber in Mount Morag—the Winter Court's fortress—sending a chill over her damp skin. Her wet hair hung loosely about her shoulders. The hollows in her cheeks were pronounced, her eyes still red from happy tears.

She'd stayed with Lydia and Henry until her brother and sister fell asleep on a bed of luxurious linen in a room on the top floor of New Orleans' finest hotel. Their bellies were full. Pippa could have fed herself alone on the sight of their contented smiles.

It had been difficult for Pippa to leave them behind again, but it was for less than a day, and Arjun had promised Sunan that he and Pippa would return to the Wyld before the gathering along the border tomorrow.

And Arjun had more than earned Pippa's trust.

On the journey back through the mirror to the Winter Court, they said little to each other. Pippa's emotions ran wild through her mind. Words continued to fail her, for she could not seem to find the right ones to say. For his part, Arjun maintained his distance.

At least twice, Pippa hoped he would draw closer. Or at the very least, take her hand.

But she knew he was simply honoring his word not to put undue strain on Pippa or press her to make a decision.

Funny thing, that. For Pippa, there was no decision to be made.

The threadbare garment she wore of homespun linen clung to her damp skin. In any other light, it would be scandalous for her to be clad in something so meager. It concealed less than her undergarments. The hem barely reached her knees. A casual observer would be able to discern her figure even if she stood in the shadows.

The girl she'd been only a few days ago would have protested. Instead Pippa stared at herself without flinching. A sense of freedom—of understanding—settled on her shoulders.

It wasn't that she wished to do away with propriety. No. She was far too English for that. Its structure offered a kind of safety. She knew where to go and how to dress and what to say in any given situation. Her family's ranking at court had given them a wide berth within society.

The confines of propriety were familiar to Pippa, like a pair of old gloves she could not bring herself to discard.

But—perhaps for the first time in her life—the path that lay before Pippa was clear. Unimpeded by indecision or uncertainty. She reached toward the mirror, wondering if it, too, harbored any magic. When her fingers grazed across its cool surface, she found herself touching her own cheek. Pippa closed her eyes. Imagined that her hand was his hand. That Arjun touched her everywhere she wished to be touched, in every way she wished to be touched.

Arjun had brought Pippa to her family. He'd brought Lydia and Henry to a place of safety, under the watchful eyes of the Court of the Lions. He'd given them a home to call their own.

Beyond that, he'd given Pippa the gift of choice. The chance to chart the course of her own future.

No one in her life had ever done something like that for her.

Conviction blazed in her eyes. This was not a decision Pippa made lightly. Arjun had told her that she could return to her life with Phoebus. That he would not stand in her way.

But Phoebus would never be her home. Not anymore.

Pippa turned from the mirror toward the door of the spartan bathing chamber. Her heart pounded as she made her way down the darkened, craggy corridors, so different from the resplendent halls of the Ivy Bower. In this moment, something about these misshapen walls seemed perfect to Pippa.

Home could be many things. It did not have to be a place. It could be a person. Or perhaps a feeling.

She did not knock on the door to their shared room. With a deep breath, Pippa pushed it open. She found Arjun sitting in darkness, save for a single candle. In one hand he held a tiny notebook. With a pencil the size of her thumb, he wrote inside its pages, his handwriting neat. Careful. Pippa had first noticed it the day Michael Grimaldi had interviewed her and Celine following a gruesome murder at Jacques' several months ago. She'd found Arjun's habit of taking meticulous notes interesting. A part of her had wondered what he wrote.

"Pippa?" Arjun asked, a brow rising into his forehead. When the candlelight struck the hem of her nightshift, his eyes went wide. He cleared his throat.

"I have a question," Pippa said. "How did you ever persuade Aunt Imogen to let you take Henry and Lydia from Liverpool?"

A stranger might have found Arjun's answering smile a bit smug. Perhaps a touch condescending. But Pippa recognized his humor for the shield it was. The way it concealed something deeper. Something truer.

"A family of vampires does have its advantages," he joked.

"You didn't."

He laughed. "No threats were levied. But glamour can be an asset in such cases." Arjun leaned back in his chair with another broad smile. "There was a time last year when Boone—"

She crossed the small room and placed a hand over his mouth. He stared up at her, the light of the single candle flame dancing across his chiseled features. Pippa shifted her hand to caress his jaw. To let her fingers twine through the dark waves on his head. He closed his eyes, the tiny notebook and the pencil falling from his grasp.

His hair was damp, too. He smelled of warm spices.

Pippa moved onto his lap. She settled her knees on either side of his hips.

"What are you writing?" she asked.

His palms came to rest on the small of her back. "About my day."

"You keep a journal?"

"Of sorts." He offered her a crooked smile. A real one. "It's to ensure my memory is never taken from me."

Pippa nodded. "They stole Celine's memory after what happened in the cathedral."

"Yes." Arjun paused. "My father's memory was forfeited, as well."

Pippa blinked. "When?"

"When I was a boy, my mother came to bring me to the Vale. He asked her to take away his memories and move him to another city where no one knew him so that he wouldn't be faced with the pain of losing us."

Pippa bit her lip. "So you never saw your father again?"

"I saw him," Arjun said softly. "He was . . . much older." He met her gaze. "He did not know who I was."

"I'm sorry," she whispered.

He raised a shoulder. "There's nothing to be had for it. I've learned to accept it."

"Nothing about that is acceptable." Pippa framed his face with her hands. Placed a kiss on his forehead. Then on the tip of his nose. "You . . . are loved, Arjun Desai," she said softly. "So loved."

Arjun swallowed. He pressed his brow to hers. "As high as the sky, and as deep as the ocean," he said. "That is how much you are loved." Then he caught her by the chin and kissed her.

Pippa melted into his embrace. She felt his hands slide up her back. Felt the hem of her thin nightshift rise above her hips. She did not care. She returned Arjun's kiss, her fingers curling into his shoulders, grasping at him as if she were hanging on the edge of a precipice.

His lips traveled the length of her neck, sending a shiver down her spine. Arjun yanked his tunic over his head, and Pippa arched into his bare skin.

She knew what she wanted.

Pippa straightened. Looked at Arjun. Saw herself in his eyes.

In the way their chests rose and fell together. She did not avert her gaze as her hand trailed down his chest. Lower still. The beat of her heart became a steady thrum in her ears.

Lower still. Her fingers did not shake.

Arjun took a sharp breath. He did not look away either. "I've never—"

"Nor have I," Pippa said.

"Are you certain?"

Pippa nodded. "You are mine." Her breath hitched as he lifted her. As he raised the hem of her shift even higher.

"And you are mine," he said in her ear. He stood in a fluid motion, bracing her in his arms, her legs wrapped around his waist.

They made it as far as the closest wall, Pippa's back thrust against the ice. She gasped at the sensation of the cold on her shoulder blades. The contrast it served to the heat of Arjun's skin.

When they joined together, Pippa's world tilted sharply, then righted itself. Everything spun slowly as the ice melted down her spine. As they rose and fell in tandem, their breaths shared, their sight hazy.

The candlelight dimmed, and Pippa slipped through ice and fire into the skin—into the life—she'd chosen for herself and no one else.

WHAT, DRAWN, AND TALK OF PEACE?

ROMEO AND JULIET,
WILLIAM SHAKESPEARE

———— ◆•◆ ————

B astien stood in the darkness along the border of the Sylvan
Wyld, waiting for Arjun, his mind . . . unsettled.

A moment later, his brother emerged from the grove of skeletal trees at the edge of the wood.

Arjun spoke first. "There's time still for you to go back."

"It's not in me to be a coward."

"Yes," Arjun agreed. "But I'm certain the events of today will
be more than you bargained for when you decided to cross into
the Wyld last night."

"Perhaps." Bastien continued staring at nothing.

"Nonetheless." Arjun turned to face him. "I'm glad you found
us."

"It wasn't terribly difficult," Bastien joked in a morose tone.
"After all, the dwarf king and I still have a score to settle. He
threatened to eat Celine, if you remember."

Arjun snorted. "That he did," he said softly.

Bastien frowned. "But do you truly think the Summer Court
will come here today?" Doubt creased his brow. "And to what
end? It is folly for the tiny regent to think he has anything to

gain in this exchange. Lady Silla is a deft bargainer. She will not give unless she intends to take far more."

"I don't know if the Summer Court will come." Arjun sighed. "And my mother operates in a similar fashion." His expression turned morose. "It's a wonder she and Lady Silla work well together," he joked.

The two young men studied the bridge before them in silence. "What happens if they don't come as you requested?" Bastien asked.

"I will have fulfilled my end of the bargain to the dwarf king, and we may all take our leave." Arjun continued staring at the bridge.

It arched over tumultuous waters. This was the second time Bastien had attended a gathering in this particular place. On one side, the shore appeared sunny and bright, the surface of the river smooth, the waves lulling as they lapped at the tall grass.

On the side of the bridge closer to the Sylvan Wyld, sharp crags of ice and stone littered the banks. Errant flakes of snow cascaded from a shadowy sky. The waters churned, bubbling against the shore like the contents of a cauldron.

Bastien glanced at Arjun sidelong, sensing there was more he wished to say. "Is there something you're not telling me, Arjun?"

Arjun exhaled slowly. "If I were concealing something, what would be the reason, Bastien?"

Bastien's eyes narrowed. He nodded. "I understand."

"All will be revealed soon," Arjun said softly.

"If you are in need of aid, you have but to ask," Bastien said.

"I know." Arjun turned to face him. "Just keep Philippa safe. If something goes awry, take her back to New Orleans as soon as possible."

"You have my word," Bastien said. He canted his head to one side. "It's a tragedy to fall in love, is it not?"

Arjun snorted. "One of epic proportions. As if your heart is dancing along a cliff with a smile on its face, ignoring all your warnings."

"But I would have it no other way."

"Yes," Arjun said. "I too would have it no other way." He nodded. "Bastien . . . do not trust everything your eyes see today. There is . . . more to the story. Much more. Please believe that what I say—what I do—I do in service to both the Sylvan Vale and the Sylvan Wyld."

He nodded once. "You have my trust, Arjun Desai."

"Now say a prayer to your vampire gods that my mother listens to me."

THE MISTRESS WHICH I SERVE
QUICKENS WHAT'S DEAD.

THE TEMPEST,

WILLIAM SHAKESPEARE

———— ◆◆◆ ————

M ichael was at his wit's end.

Since yesterday, he'd transformed twice from beast to man and back again. The prior afternoon, his compass ring had failed him yet again. It had spun about, first wildly, and then in a lazy circle.

His attempt to find Philippa Montrose—as well as Celine Rousseau—was falling once more beyond his grasp.

This morning, he'd changed into a wolf as soon as the ring pointed steadily in one direction again. But Michael no longer trusted it. Such things began to lose their power once they were outside the reach of their maker for too long. Already the ring had failed him twice. It was not possible for a human girl like Pippa to be one place in one moment and travel such a distance in the next unless—

Pippa must have access to a magicked mirror as well.

Which meant that she was fully capable of returning to New Orleans at any time, just as Michael was. And if Pippa had access to a traveling silver, Celine did as well. Which *then* meant that Celine's disappearance was likely of her own design.

His mind continued to spin about like the arrow in his useless compass ring.

Michael huffed to himself in frustration, trying his best to determine his next step forward. It was easier for him to suspect that Bastien was the villain in all that had transpired. Bastien wore this mantle well. But was it possible Celine herself was the villain? The one who had fled like a coward into the night?

If Valeria Henri could hear Michael's thoughts, she would know how grossly he'd lied to her. Nothing Michael had done was for the benefit of anyone but Celine. Of course he wished to keep Pippa safe, but his greatest desire was to find Celine and speak with her face-to-face.

Perhaps Michael was foolish to believe that a young man who offered his hand in marriage deserved more than to be cast aside without notice or consideration. He wanted to hear her say the truth with her own lips. Michael needed to hear it for himself, so that he could start to forget.

So that he could let her go.

You haven't eaten yet. Émilie Saint Germain emerged from the snowy thicket carrying a creature that resembled a hare in her mouth. Without another word, she set the lifeless animal down in front of Michael.

Michael snorted. *I'm not hungry.* He still wasn't used to the idea of eating as a wolf.

Eat because you need your strength. Émilie nudged the hare closer. *I've learned something about the blond young woman's whereabouts that might be of interest to you.*

Suspicion clouded over Michael's mind. *How?*

A nymph I spoke with by the river told me a large gathering is supposed to occur between the Summer Court and the Winter Court on the border bridge today near dusk.

And why would she tell you this?

Because she knows it is of interest to me. Émilie sat on her haunches. *Especially now that I've confirmed my suspicions about the weapons I mentioned before.*

Michael began to eat. *What have you confirmed?*

I suspect the Summer Court to be working with a weapons manufacturer, a mortal one.

Unease cut through Michael's stomach. *Why?*

They have a weapon similar to a battery gun. It is capable of firing hundreds of silver-tipped rounds before needing to be reloaded.

Horror set Michael's blood ablaze. *Do you think they would bring such a weapon to this meeting today?*

I don't know. The meeting is meant to be a negotiation, I suspect for the release of the blond girl you seek. She paused. *Given her love for the blond girl, I would not be surprised if Celine Rousseau is present today.*

Michael stood at once. *If a weapon capable of such destruction is used, many innocents might die. We must—*

Don't worry, Michael. Émilie yawned. *We are always there to keep those we love safe.*

————◆◆◆————

They gathered on the border between the Sylvan Vale and the Sylvan Wyld in calm silence.

Celine stood with her mother in the warm sunshine near the bridge. A silken canopy hung above them for shade, members of the Grey Cloaks positioned strategically around them, intent on keeping their queen and her daughter safe.

To the right and left of where they stood, thirty members of the gentry milled about in their finery, as if they'd dressed for a special occasion.

Though Celine found it odd for them to accompany her mother to a simple negotiation for Pippa's and Arjun's release, the smiles of the lords and ladies and lieges, along with their easygoing manner, lent a spirit of lightness to what would otherwise be a somber occasion.

Celine stared across the water toward the churning banks on the other side. Even through the darkness she could see the familiar gathering of the dwarf king's court. The immense creatures with their moldy tusks and stained garments, along with the centaurs who stomped their hooves and tossed their hair about with wild abandon.

She heard their king's arrival before she saw him. The ale-drinking regent was carried on a litter by four three-eyed ogres. He laughed and drank without a care in the world, as if he'd already won the day, the same pair of tiny blue goblins trailing in his wake, their terror plain.

Miserable little tyrant, Celine thought to herself. *How dare he kidnap my friends and expect anything but a harsh rebuke in return?*

Just as Celine was about to say something to her mother, the Lady of the Vale reached for Celine's hand and squeezed it tightly in her own.

Across the way, Pippa and Arjun stepped into view, their hands joined as if in solidarity.

Celine's heart began to pound. She walked with her mother and General Riya toward the bridge, a pair of Grey Cloaks trailing closely in their wake.

Arjun and Pippa strolled from the darkness in the direction of the light. Celine bit her lip as they moved closer to her side of the bridge. Closer to safety. Behind them waddled a single hob-goblin with a spear twice his height, who prodded Arjun to stop directly at the halfway point along the arched bridge.

There they stood, half in shadow and half in light.

"Arjun Desai," Lady Silla said with a smile. "It is good to see you looking hale and hearty."

Arjun offered her a small bow, his expression weary. "I have not been mistreated."

"And Pippa?" Celine exclaimed before she could stop herself. "Have you been harmed in any way?"

Pippa sent her a tired smile. "Not at all."

"We are only cold," Arjun said, "especially at night."

"I suppose it is what you deserve," General Riya said in a curt tone. "Striking a bargain with such creatures."

The hobgoblin gnashed his teeth and waved his spear about.

"Very well, then," Lady Silla said. "What are the king's terms for your release?"

Arjun cast the Lady of the Vale a searching gaze. Celine tried to divine the emotions swirling within his eyes, but she did not know him well enough. Just like the time he'd offered his help when Celine was questioned by the police, he gave away very little of himself.

Then Arjun turned toward General Riya. "Mother," he began, "what are you doing to these poor creatures?"

Celine felt rather than saw the general startle. The next instant, General Riya's features hardened. "Whatever you have heard was said to sway you unjustly. It is not the full story."

"General," Lady Silla interjected. "There is no need for us to explain ourselves." She reached a hand toward Arjun. "Please do not believe—"

The arrow struck Celine's mother without warning. She fell to the ground the next instant.

DEATH IS NOT EXTINGUISHING THE LIGHT; IT IS ONLY PUTTING OUT THE LAMP BECAUSE THE DAWN HAS COME.

RABINDRANATH TAGORE

———◆◆◆———

A rjun was allowed only one breath. One single breath. Then pandemonium broke loose.

His mother yanked him toward her in the same instant the Grey Cloaks circled Celine and the fallen Lady Silla. Dark blood flowed from a ghastly wound on the Lady of the Vale's left side. Celine screamed as she was carried away.

The arrow jutting from Lady Silla's body was made of iron. Like all the weapons in the Winter Court.

"Arjun," his mother demanded, yanking him closer once more. "Seek cover before you, too, are struck by the winter vermin."

His shock melted away at his mother's words. "Pippa." He pivoted on his heel, only to have his mother haul him backward and thrust him toward the Grey Cloaks, all while barking orders.

"Keep my son's hands away from your skin," she shouted over her shoulder. "Bind them if you must."

On both sides of the bridge, awareness began to take the place of their collective shock. Arjun yelled for Pippa to run, and the ogre beside the dwarf king bellowed. All at once, Sunan turned in Arjun's direction, a look of horror settling onto his goblin features. Pippa's blue eyes went wide, her expression fixed in fear.

Though the hobgoblin with the long spear yanked on her wrist, drawing her back into the shadows, Pippa stretched toward the light, her hand grasping at nothing but air. "Arjun—"

The hobgoblin snarled as he dragged her back. Three redcaps leapt onto the bridge from the icy reaches to face the line of Grey Cloaks, their weapons pointed in warning.

Arjun struggled against the Grey Cloaks, foul insults collecting on his tongue. Before he could utter a single one, a weapon began firing from the side of the bridge that was bathed in light. A weapon that froze the blood in his veins. Silver-tipped bullets started to fly from the sunlit shore toward the dark world of snow and ice, faster than the military tattoo of a snare drum. Again he shouted to the Grey Cloaks restraining him, demanding to be set free. Instead they covered his bound hands with a length of cloth, preventing him from freezing them in place.

"Pippa!" he yelled again. A third Grey Cloak glided forward to hold Arjun steady. At his mother's signal, they began yanking him from the bridge toward the terra firma of the Sylvan Vale's shore.

"Arjun," Pippa screamed across the bridge as the redcaps flung her onto the icy shore and pressed her back toward the frozen forest.

A thick fog of darkness descended along the frozen riverbank, and Arjun was certain Sunan conjured it in an attempt to spare the lives of the winter fey moving about in a panic.

Frantic, Arjun twisted toward General Riya, his shoulder contorting from the strain of his captors' grip. "Mother, you must stop this at—"

"They struck down our lady at a gathering made in peace," General Riya spat. "If you are not going to defend our own, then I will have you removed from my sight. Take care that you are not branded a traitor along with everything else."

Never before had Arjun seen his mother so angry. "The winter vermin have broken the treaty. Cross the bridge into their territory," she ordered a handful of Grey Cloaks. "Find the one who fired upon the Lady of the Vale. Show them no mercy."

All at once, a low growl emanated from the darkness on the opposite side. It was followed by several more snarls. Six wolves emerged from the thick fog to crouch along the edge of the ice-covered bridge, daring any of the summer fey to cross their way.

Bullets continued flying, though frustration took hold among the ranks of the Summer Court. They muttered to themselves, irritated that the show of bloodshed they yearned to see had been stolen from their view by Sunan's illusion.

Gratitude raced through Arjun's veins. Hopefully the winter fey would have scattered to—

The ogre bellowed once more. Its mournful baying hung through the air like a warning.

The fog began to lift just as it had come.

Horror descended on Arjun when he realized why. The illusions along the winter embankment were starting to flicker and fade.

Sunan had been struck down.

The Summer Court stopped firing its gleaming golden weapon,

the machine stuttering to a halt. Confusion rippled among those of the summer gentry who remained. In less than a minute, the gathering of winter fey along the embankment had diminished by more than half, their counterparts vanishing without a trace. What remained was a ragtag assemblage of broken, twisted creatures, many of them fallen, their bodies bleeding into the snow.

Bastien rose to his feet from where he'd been helping one of the fallen, his eyes wide, his features filled with rage.

A figure moved in Arjun's periphery, darting between the bewildered masses of the Winter Court, weaving through the dismayed redcaps and the momentarily distracted wolves. Even through the smoke, Arjun knew it was Pippa. She threaded through the thinning crowd, her eyes locked on his. A mixture of elation and fear gripped Arjun's chest. She was trying to get to him. It was foolhardy and dangerous and—

Another volley of silver bullets showered onto the banks of the Sylvan Wyld. Arjun's heart leapt into his throat. Pippa settled behind the trunk of a tree a stone's throw behind the vanguard of immense werewolves. Arjun silently begged her to remain where she was, though blood stained her hem and sleeve, and he longed to search her for signs of injury.

When her eyes met his again, he knew Pippa planned to make a run for the bridge. Without thought, Arjun tore himself free, his shoulder popping in place, his hands still bound behind his back. He raced to meet her as she broke from the shadows, bullets flying into the snow and sending shards of splintered wood through the air.

The wolves struck Pippa first. They snatched her by the arm as she attempted to skirt past them. She screamed a scream that tore through Arjun. The red wolf threw Pippa into the air before another dark-haired beast clamped its jaw around her leg, drawing rivulets of blood. Pippa screamed again as they hauled her toward the forest like a rag doll.

Arjun didn't realize he was shouting until his mother took hold of him. Until something struck him in the back of his head.

Then everything fell to darkness.

WHERE CIVIL BLOOD MAKES CIVIL HANDS UNCLEAN.

ROMEO AND JULIET,

WILLIAM SHAKESPEARE

———◆◆◆———

Hours later, Celine could not stop shaking. Her mother had yet to wake from her wound. The healer had mentioned—his expression grave—that it was possible Lady Silla might never open her eyes again.

Pippa had vanished into the forest in the jaws of a wolf. The sound of her screams continued to echo in Celine's ears.

And Bastien?

Bastien had not returned from the Winter Court.

Celine sat on the edge of the dais just below the Horned Throne, her body trembling like leaves in a summer storm.

She heard Ali's quiet footsteps as he drew near, his gait familiar, his sword hilt striking his hip with every other step. He sat down beside Celine and waited. Her shaking did not abate. Celine gripped the edge of the dais with both hands, her fingertips turning bloodless. After a time, Ali reached for her right hand.

"Don't touch me," Celine said as she snatched her hand away, her teeth chattering.

"As you wish." His reply was one of infinite patience. "I am here whenever you need anything. Whenever you need to talk."

Celine said nothing for quite some time. "My mother?" she asked, her voice gruff.

"The same," he replied with a weary glance her way.

"How"—incredulity bloomed across her face—"how could they fire on her at a peaceful assembly?"

"I . . . don't know."

A fresh wave of fear overtook Celine, a shudder rolling down her spine. "What if my mother never awakens? What if—what if Bastien never returns? What if something happened to him?" Her eyes darted toward the ceiling of curved branches, the leaves above whispering an unfathomable response. "Pippa." Celine's voice broke.

"Don't lose heart," Ali said. "You are a brave young woman and, from what I hear, very resourceful. At times you remind me a great deal of my own mother." He smiled to himself. "You don't know what a comfort that has been."

All at once, Celine's trembling stopped. "Your mother," she whispered.

Ali crooked a brow at her, his tiger eyes wide. "Celine?"

"That's the answer, Ali," she said, jumping to her feet. "We can fix all of this. We can make sure Bastien never leaves for the Wyld and my mother is never struck by an arrow. We can return Pippa back to New Orleans safe and sound!"

Ali shook his head. "That is not—"

"We must find that maze of mirrors, Ali. We *will* find it." Celine took both his hands in hers, desperation seeping through her words. "I swear to you, all the resources of the Summer Court will be used in search of it."

He stared into her eyes and then nodded. "Very well. If we are to begin our search in earnest, then I should probably introduce myself."

"What?" Celine released his hands. "Ali, I—"

"My name is Haroun al-Rashid. I am the firstborn son of Khalid Ibn al-Rashid and Shahrzad al-Khayzuran." He bowed. "It is my very great pleasure to meet you, Celine Rousseau."

Epilogue

D ark blood dotted the snow on one side of the bridge. Along the other, Lord Vyr stood alone, waiting.

In the river, a creature surfaced, its deep green hair flecked with bits of sharp metal.

Lord Vyr and the nymph waited for a time.

Soon the wolf emerged from the bank of shadowy trees. It limped toward the shore, its missing front paw slowing its progress.

One by one, the wolf, the nymph, and the fey lord acknowledged one another with a nod of their heads.

Then they returned the way they'd come, their plan nothing short of a rousing success.

YOUR GUIDE TO RENÉE AHDIEH:

SEE WHERE
CELINE AND
BASTIEN'S STORY
BEGAN

Excerpt on Page 375

READ MORE FROM
THE BEAUTIFUL
QUARTET

Excerpt on Page 385

CHECK OUT RENÉE
AHDIEH'S FIRST
SERIES

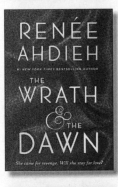

Excerpt on Page 395

STILL CRAVING
MORE RENÉE
AHDIEH?

Excerpt on Page 409

TURN THE PAGE FOR AN EXCERPT OF:

———◦◇◇◇◦———

New Orleans is a city ruled by the dead.
I remember the moment I first heard someone say
this. The old man meant to frighten me. He said there was a
time when coffins sprang from the ground following a heavy
rain, the dead flooding the city streets. He claimed to know of
a Créole woman on Rue Dauphine who could commune with
spirits from the afterlife.

I believe in magic. In a city rife with illusionists, it's impossible to doubt its existence. But I didn't believe this man. *Be
faithful,* he warned. *For the faithless are alone in death, blind
and terrified.*

I feigned shock at his words. In truth, I found him amusing.
He was the sort to scare errant young souls with stories of a
shadowy creature lurking in darkened alcoves. But I was also
intrigued, for I possess an errant young soul of my own. From
childhood, I hid it beneath pressed garments and polished
words, but it persisted in plaguing me. It called to me like a
Siren, driving me to dash all pretense against the rocks and
surrender to my true nature.

It drove me to where I am now. But I am not ungrateful.

For it brought to bear two of my deepest truths: I will always possess an errant young soul, no matter my age.

And I will always be the shadowy creature in darkened alcoves, waiting . . .

For you, my love. For you.

NOT WHAT IT SEEMED

———◦◦◇◦◦———

The *Aramis* was supposed to arrive at first light, like it did in Celine's dreams.

She would wake beneath a sunlit sky, the brine of the ocean winding through her nose, the city looming bright on the horizon.

Filled with promise. And absolution.

Instead the brass bell on the bow of the *Aramis* tolled in the twilight hour, the time of day her friend Pippa called "the gloaming." It was—in Celine's mind—a very British thing to say.

She'd begun collecting these phrases not long after she'd met Pippa four weeks ago, when the *Aramis* had docked for two days in Liverpool. Her favorite so far was "not bloody likely." Celine didn't know why they mattered to her at the time. Perhaps it was because she thought Very British Things would serve her better in America than the Very French Things she was apt to say.

The moment Celine heard the bell clang, she made her way portside, Pippa's light footsteps trailing in her wake. Inky tendrils of darkness fanned out across the sky, a ghostly mist shrouding the Crescent City. The air thickened as the two girls listened to the *Aramis* sluice through the waters of the Mississippi, drawing closer to New Orleans. Farther from the lives they'd left behind.

Pippa sniffed and rubbed her nose. In that instant, she looked younger than her sixteen years. "For all the stories, it's not as pretty as I thought it would be."

"It's exactly what I thought it would be," Celine said in a reassuring tone.

"Don't lie." Pippa glanced at her sidelong. "It won't make me feel better."

A smile curled up Celine's face. "Maybe I'm lying for me as much as I'm lying for you."

"In any case, lying is a sin."

"So is being obnoxious."

"That's not in the Bible."

"But it should be."

Pippa coughed, trying to mask her amusement. "You're terrible. The sisters at the Ursuline convent won't know what to do with you."

"They'll do the same thing they do with every unmarried girl who disembarks in New Orleans, carrying with her all her worldly possessions: they'll find me a husband." Celine refrained from frowning. This had been her choice. The best of the worst.

"If you strike them as ungodly, they'll match you with the ugliest fool in Christendom. Definitely someone with a bulbous nose and a paunch."

"Better an ugly man than a boring one. And a paunch means he eats well, so . . ." Celine canted her head to one side.

"Really, Celine." Pippa laughed, her Yorkshire accent weaving through the words like fine Chantilly lace. "You're the most incorrigible French girl I've ever met."

Celine smiled at her friend. "I'd wager you haven't met many French girls."

"At least not ones who speak English as well as you do. As if you were born to it."

"My father thought it was important for me to learn." Celine lifted one shoulder, as though this were the whole of it, instead of barely half. At the mention of her father—a staid Frenchman who'd studied linguistics at Oxford—a shadow threatened to descend. A sadness with a weight Celine could not yet bear. She fixed a wry grin on her face.

Pippa crossed her arms as though she were hugging herself. Worry gathered beneath the fringe of blond on her forehead as the two girls continued studying the city in the distance. Every young woman on board had heard the whispered accounts. At sea, the myths they'd shared over cups of gritty, bitter coffee had taken on lives of their own. They'd blended with the stories of the Old World to form richer, darker tales. New Orleans was haunted. Cursed by pirates. Prowled by scalawags. A last refuge for those who believed in magic and mysticism. Why, there was even talk of women possessing as much power and influence as that of any man.

Celine had laughed at this. As she'd dared to hope. Perhaps New Orleans was not what it seemed at first glance. Fittingly, neither was she.

And if anything could be said about the young travelers

aboard the *Aramis*, it was that the possibility of magic like this—a world like this—had become a vital thing. Especially for those who wished to shed the specter of their pasts. To become something better and brighter.

And especially for those who wanted to escape.

Pippa and Celine watched as they drew closer to the unknown. To their futures.

"I'm frightened," Pippa said softly.

Celine did not respond. Night had seeped through the water, like a dark stain across organza. A scraggly sailor balanced along a wooden beam with all the grace of an aerialist while lighting a lamp on the ship's prow. As if in response, tongues of fire leapt to life across the water, rendering the city in even more ghoulishly green tones.

The bell of the *Aramis* pealed once more, telling those along the port how far the ship had left to travel. Other passengers made their way from below deck, coming to stand alongside Celine and Pippa, muttering in Portuguese and Spanish, English and French, German and Dutch. Young women who'd taken leaps of faith and left their homelands for new opportunities. Their words melted into a soft cacophony of sound that would—under normal circumstances—soothe Celine.

Not anymore.

Ever since that fateful night amid the silks in the atelier, Celine had longed for comfortable silence. It had been weeks since she'd felt safe in the presence of others. Safe with the riot of her own thoughts. The closest she'd ever come to wading through calmer waters had been in the presence of Pippa.

When the ship drew near enough to dock, Pippa took sudden hold of Celine's wrist, as though to steel herself. Celine gasped. Flinched at the unexpected touch. Like a spray of blood had shot across her face, the salt of it staining her lips.

"Celine?" Pippa asked, her blue eyes wide. "What's wrong?"

Breathing through her nose to steady her pulse, Celine wrapped both hands around Pippa's cold fingers. "I'm frightened, too."

TURN THE PAGE FOR AN EXCERPT OF:

The Awakening

—≈—

First there is nothing. Only silence. A sea of oblivion.

Then flashes of memory take shape. Snippets of sound. The laughter of a loved one, the popping of wood sap in a fireplace, the smell of butter melting across fresh bread.

An image emerges from the chaos, sharpening with each second. A crying young woman—her eyes like emeralds, her hair like spilled ink—leans over him, clutching his bloodstained hand, pleading with him in muffled tones.

Who am I? he wonders.

Dark amusement winds through him.

He is nothing. No one. Nobody.

The scent of blood suffuses his nostrils, intoxicatingly sweet. Like lechosa from a fruit stand in San Juan, its juice dripping down his shirtsleeves.

He becomes hunger. Not a kind of hunger he's ever known before, but an all-consuming void. A dull ache around his dead heart, a blast of bloodlust searing through his veins. It knifes through his stomach like the talons on a bird of prey. Rage builds in his chest. The desire to seek and destroy. To consume life. Let it fill the emptiness within him. Where there was once a sea of oblivion, there is now a canvas painted red, the color dripping like rain at his feet, setting his world aflame.

My city. My family. My love.

Who am I?

From the fires of his fury, a name emerges.

Bastien. My name is Sébastien Saint Germain.

BASTIEN

───── ≈ ─────

I lie still, my body weightless. Immobile. It feels like I'm locked in a pitch-black room, unable to speak, choking on the smoke of my own folly.

My uncle did this to me once when I was nine. My closest friend, Michael, and I had stolen a box of cigars hand-rolled by an elderly lady from Havana who worked on the corner of Burgundy and Saint Louis. When Uncle Nico caught us smoking them in the alley behind Jacques', he sent Michael home, his voice deathly quiet. Filled with foreboding.

Then my uncle locked me in a hall closet with the box of cigars and a tin of matches. He told me I could not leave until I finished every single one of them.

That was the last time I ever smoked a cigar.

It took me weeks to forgive Uncle Nico. Years to stomach the smell of burning tobacco anywhere in my vicinity. Half a lifetime to understand why he'd felt the need to teach that particular lesson.

I try to swallow this ghost of bile. I fail.

I know what Nicodemus has done. Though the memory is still unclear—fogged by the weakness of my dying body—I know he has made me into one of them. I am now a vampire, like my uncle before me. Like my mother before me, who faced the final death willingly, her lips stained red and a lifeless body in her arms.

I am a soulless son of Death, cursed to drink the blood of the living until the end of time.

It sounds ridiculous even to me, a boy raised on the truth of monsters. Like a joke told by an unfunny aunt with a penchant for melodrama. A woman who cuts herself on her diamond bracelet and wails as drops of blood trickle onto her silken skirts.

Like that, I am hunger once more. With each pang, I become less human. Less of what I once was and more of what I will forever be. A demon of want, who simply craves more, never to be sated.

White-hot rage chases behind the bloodlust, igniting like a trail of saltpeter from a powder keg. I understand why Uncle Nico did this, though it will take many lifetimes for me to forgive him. Only the direst of circumstances would drive him to turn the last living member of his mortal family—the lone heir to the Saint Germain fortune—into a demon of the Otherworld.

His line has died with me, my human life reaching an all-too-sudden end. This choice must be one of last resort. A voice resonates in my mind. A feminine voice, its echoes tremulous.

Please. Save him. What can I say that will make you save him? Do we have a deal?

When I realize who it is, what she must have done, I howl a silent howl, the sound ringing in the hollows of my lost soul. I cannot think about that now.

My failure will not let me.

It is enough to know that I, Sébastien Saint Germain, eighteen-year-old son of a beggar and a thief, have been turned into a member of the Fallen. A race of blood drinkers banished from their rightful place in the Otherworld by their own greed. Creatures of the night embroiled in a centuries-long war with their archenemy, a brotherhood of werewolves.

I try to speak but fail, my throat tight, my eyelids sealed shut. After all, Death is a powerful foe to vanquish.

Fine silk rustles by my ear, a scented breeze coiling through the air. Neroli oil and rose water. The unmistakable perfume of Odette Valmont, one of my dearest friends. For almost ten years, she was a protector in life. Now she is a sister in blood. A vampire, sired by the same maker.

My right thumb twitches in response to her nearness. Still I cannot speak or move freely. Still I am locked in a darkened room, with nothing but a box of cigars and a tin of matches, dread coursing through my veins, hunger tingling on my tongue.

A sigh escapes Odette's lips. "He's beginning to wake." She pauses, pity seeping into her voice. "He'll be furious."

As usual, Odette is not wrong. But there is comfort in my fury. Freedom in knowing I may soon seek release from my rage.

"And well he should be," my uncle says. "This is the most selfish thing I've ever done. If he manages to survive the change, he will come to hate me . . . just as Nigel did."

Nigel. The name alone rekindles my ire. Nigel Fitzroy, the reason for my untimely demise. He—along with Odette and four other members of my uncle's vampire progeny—safeguarded me from Nicodemus Saint Germain's enemies, chief among them those of the Brotherhood. For years Nigel bided his time. Cultivated his plan for revenge on the vampire who snatched him from his home and made him a demon of the night. Under the guise of loyalty, Nigel put into motion a series of events intended to destroy the thing Nicodemus prized most: his living legacy.

I've been betrayed before, just as I have betrayed others. It is the way of things when you live among capricious immortals and the many illusionists who hover nearby like flies. Only two years ago, my favorite pastime involved fleecing the Crescent City's most notorious warlocks of their ill-gotten gains. The worst among their ilk were always so certain that a mere mortal could never best them. It gave me great pleasure to prove them wrong.

But I have never betrayed my family. And I had never been betrayed by a vampire sworn to protect me. Someone I loved as a brother. Memories waver through my mind. Images of laughter and a decade of loyalty. I want to shout and curse. Rail to the heavens, like a demon possessed.

Alas, I know how well God listens to the prayers of the damned.

"I'll summon the others," Odette murmurs. "When he wakes, he should see us all united."

"Leave them be," Nicodemus replies, "for we are not yet out of the woods." For the first time, I sense a hint of distress in his words, there and gone in an instant. "More than a third of my immortal children did not survive the transformation. Many were lost in the first year to the foolishness of immortal youth. This . . . may not work."

"It *will* work," Odette says without hesitation.

"Sébastien could succumb to madness, as his mother did," Nicodemus says. "In her quest to be unmade, Philomène destroyed everything in her path, until there was nothing to be done but put an end to the terror."

"That is not Bastien's fate."

"Don't be foolish. It very well could be."

Odette's response is cool. "A risk you were willing to take."

"But a risk nonetheless. It was why I refused his sister when she asked me years ago to turn her." He exhales. "In the end, we lost her to the fire all the same."

"We will not lose Bastien as we lost Émilie. Nor will he succumb to Philomène's fate."

"You speak with such surety, little oracle." He pauses. "Has your second sight granted you this sense of conviction?"

"No. Years ago, I promised Bastien I would not look into his future. I have not forsaken my word. But I believe in my heart that hope will prevail. It . . . simply must."

Despite her seemingly unshakable faith, Odette's worry is a palpable thing. I wish I could reach for her hand. Offer her words of reassurance. But still I am locked within myself, my anger overtaking all else. It turns to ash on my tongue, until all I am left with is *want*. The need to be loved. To be sated. But most of all, the desire to destroy.

Nicodemus says nothing for a time. "We shall see. His wrath will be great, of that there can be no doubt. Sébastien never wanted to become one of us. He bore witness to the cost of the change at an early age."

My uncle knows me well. His world took my family from me. I think of my parents, who died years ago, trying to keep me safe. I think of my sister, who perished trying to protect me. I think of Celine, the girl I loved in life, who will not remember me.

I have never betrayed anyone I love.

But never is a long time, when you have eternity to consider.

"He may also be grateful," Odette says. "One day."

My uncle does not reply.

TURN THE PAGE FOR AN EXCERPT OF:

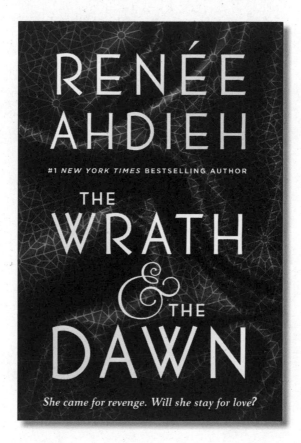

RENÉE
AHDIEH

#1 *NEW YORK TIMES* BESTSELLING AUTHOR

THE
WRATH
&
THE
DAWN

She came for revenge. Will she stay for love?

PROLOGUE

Iᴛ ᴡᴏᴜʟᴅ ɴᴏᴛ ʙᴇ ᴀ ᴡᴇʟᴄᴏᴍᴇ ᴅᴀᴡɴ.

Already the sky told this story, with its sad halo of silver beckoning from beyond the horizon.

A young man stood alongside his father on the rooftop terrace of the marble palace. They watched the pale light of the early morning sun push back the darkness with slow, careful deliberation.

"Where is he?" the young man asked.

His father did not look his way. "He has not left his chamber since he gave the order."

The young man ran a hand through his wavy hair, exhaling all the while. "There will be riots in the city streets for this."

"And you will put them to rout, in short order." It was a terse response, still made to a somber stretch of light.

"In short order? Do you not think a mother and father, regardless of birth or rank, will fight to avenge their child?"

Finally, the father faced his son. His eyes were drawn and sunken, as though a weight tugged at them from within. "They will fight. They should fight. And you will ensure it amounts to nothing. You will do your duty to your king. Do you understand?"

The young man paused. "I understand."

"General al-Khoury?"

His father turned toward the soldier standing behind them. "Yes?"

"It is done."

His father nodded, and the soldier left.

Again, the two men stared up at the sky.

Waiting.

A drop of rain struck the arid surface beneath their feet, disappearing into the tan stone. Another plinked against the iron railing before it slid its way into nothingness.

Soon, rain was falling around them at a steady pace.

"There is your proof," the general said, his voice laden with quiet anguish.

The young man did not respond right away.

"He cannot withstand this, Father."

"He can. He is strong."

"You have never understood Khalid. It is not about strength. It is about substance. What follows will destroy all that remains of his, leaving behind a husk—a shadow of what he once was."

The general winced. "Do you think I wanted this for him? I would drown in my own blood to prevent this. But we have no choice."

The young man shook his head and wiped the rain from beneath his chin.

"I refuse to believe that."

"Jalal—"

"There must be another way." With that, the young man turned from the railing and vanished down the staircase.

Throughout the city, long-dry wells began to fill. Cracked, sunbaked cisterns shimmered with pools of hope, and the people of Rey awoke to a new joy. They raced into the streets, angling their smiling faces to the sky.

Not knowing the price.

And, deep within the palace of marble and stone, a boy of eighteen sat alone before a table of polished ebony . . .

Listening to the rain.

The only light in the room reflected back in his amber eyes.

A light beset by the dark.

He braced his elbows on his knees and made a crown of his hands about his brow. Then he shuttered his gaze, and the words echoed around him, filling his ears with the promise of a life rooted in the past.

Of a life atoning for his sins.

One hundred lives for the one you took. One life to one dawn. Should you fail but a single morn, I shall take from you your dreams. I shall take from you your city.

And I shall take from you these lives, a thousandfold.

MEDITATIONS
ON GOSSAMER AND GOLD

T HEY WERE NOT GENTLE. AND WHY SHOULD THEY BE?
After all, they did not expect her to live past the next morning.

The hands that tugged ivory combs through Shahrzad's waist-length hair and scrubbed sandalwood paste on her bronze arms did so with a brutal kind of detachment.

Shahrzad watched one young servant girl dust her bare shoulders with flakes of gold that caught the light from the setting sun.

A breeze gusted along the gossamer curtains lining the walls of the chamber. The sweet scent of citrus blossoms wafted through the carved wooden screens leading to the terrace, whispering of a freedom now beyond reach.

This was my choice. Remember Shiva.

"I don't wear necklaces," Shahrzad said when another girl began to fasten a jewel-encrusted behemoth around her throat.

"It is a gift from the caliph. You must wear it, my lady."

Shahrzad stared down at the slight girl in amused disbelief. "And if I don't? Will he kill me?"

"Please, my lady, I—"

Shahrzad sighed. "I suppose now is not the time to make this point."

"Yes, my lady."

"My name is Shahrzad."

"I know, my lady." The girl glanced away in discomfort before turning to assist with Shahrzad's gilded mantle. As the two young women eased the weighty garment onto her glittering shoulders, Shahrzad studied the finished product in the mirror before her.

Her midnight tresses gleamed like polished obsidian, and her hazel eyes were edged in alternating strokes of black kohl and liquid gold. At the center of her brow hung a teardrop ruby the size of her thumb; its mate dangled from a thin chain around her bare waist, grazing the silk sash of her trowsers. The mantle itself was pale damask and threaded with silver and gold in an intricate pattern that grew ever chaotic as it flared by her feet.

I look like a gilded peacock.

"Do they all look this ridiculous?" Shahrzad asked.

Again, the two young women averted their gazes with unease.

I'm sure Shiva didn't look this ridiculous . . .

Shahrzad's expression hardened.

Shiva would have looked beautiful. Beautiful and strong.

Her fingernails dug into her palms; tiny crescents of steely resolve.

At the sound of a quiet knock at the door, three heads turned—their collective breaths bated.

In spite of her newfound mettle, Shahrzad's heart began to pound.

"May I come in?" The soft voice of her father broke through the silence, pleading and laced in tacit apology.

Shahrzad exhaled slowly . . . carefully.

"Baba, what are you doing here?" Her words were patient, yet wary.

Jahandar al-Khayzuran shuffled into the chamber. His beard and temples were streaked with grey, and the myriad colors in his hazel eyes shimmered and shifted like the sea in the midst of a storm.

In his hand was a single budding rose, its center leached of color, and the tips of its petals tinged a beautiful, blushing mauve.

"Where is Irsa?" Shahrzad asked, alarm seeping into her tone.

Her father smiled sadly. "She is at home. I did not allow her to come with me, though she fought and raged until the last possible moment."

At least in this he has not ignored my wishes.

"You should be with her. She needs you tonight. Please do this for me, Baba? Do as we discussed?" She reached out and took his free hand, squeezing tightly, beseeching him in her grip to follow the plans she had laid out in the days before.

"I—I can't, my child." Jahandar lowered his head, a sob rising in his chest, his thin shoulders trembling with grief. "Shahrzad—"

"Be strong. For Irsa. I promise you, everything will be fine." Shahrzad raised her palm to his weathered face and brushed away the smattering of tears from his cheek.

"I cannot. The thought that this may be your last sunset—"

"It will not be the last. I will see tomorrow's sunset. This I swear to you."

Jahandar nodded, his misery nowhere close to mollified. He held out the rose in his hand. "The last from my garden; it has not yet bloomed fully, but I wanted to give you one remembrance of home."

She smiled as she reached for it, the love between them far past mere gratitude, but he stopped her. When she realized the reason, she began to protest.

"No. At least in this, I might do something for you," he muttered, almost to himself. He stared at the rose, his brow furrowed and his mouth drawn. One servant girl coughed in her fist while the other looked to the floor.

Shahrzad waited patiently. Knowingly.

The rose started to unfurl. Its petals twisted open, prodded to life by an invisible hand. As it expanded, a delicious perfume filled the space between them, sweet and perfect for an instant . . . but soon, it became overpowering. Cloying. The edges of the flower changed from a brilliant, deep pink to a shadowy rust in the blink of an eye.

And then the flower began to wither and die.

Dismayed, Jahandar watched its dried petals wilt to the white marble at their feet.

"I—I'm sorry, Shahrzad," he cried.

"It doesn't matter. I will never forget how beautiful it was for that moment, Baba." She wrapped her arms around his neck and pulled him close. By his ear, in a voice so low only he could hear, she said, "Go to Tariq, as you promised. Take Irsa and go."

He nodded, his eyes shimmering once more. "I love you, my child."

"And I love you. I will keep my promises. All of them."

Overcome, Jahandar blinked down at his elder daughter in silence.

This time, the knock at the door demanded attention rather than requested it.

Shahrzad's forehead whipped back in its direction, the bloodred ruby swinging in tandem. She squared her shoulders and lifted her pointed chin.

Jahandar stood to the side, covering his face with his hands, as his daughter marched forward.

"I'm sorry—so very sorry," she whispered to him before striding across the threshold to follow the contingent of guards leading the processional. Jahandar slid to his knees and sobbed as Shahrzad turned the corner and disappeared.

With her father's grief resounding through the halls, Shahrzad's feet refused to carry her but a few steps down the cavernous corridors of the palace. She halted, her knees shaking beneath the thin silk of her voluminous *sirwal* trowsers.

"My lady?" one of the guards prompted in a bored tone.

"He can wait," Shahrzad gasped.

The guards exchanged glances.

Her own tears threatening to blaze a telltale trail down her cheeks, Shahrzad pressed a hand to her chest. Unwittingly, her fingertips brushed the edge of the thick gold necklace clasped around her throat, festooned with gems of outlandish size and untold variety. It felt heavy . . . stifling. Like a bejeweled fetter. She allowed her fingers to wrap around the offending instrument, thinking for a moment to rip it from her body.

The rage was comforting. A friendly reminder.

Shiva.

Her dearest friend. Her closest confidante.

She curled her toes within their sandals of braided bullion and threw back her shoulders once more. Without a word, she resumed her march.

Again, the guards looked to one another for an instant.

When they reached the massive double doors leading into the throne room, Shahrzad realized her heart was racing at twice its normal speed. The doors swung open with a distended groan, and she focused on her target, ignoring all else around her.

At the very end of the immense space stood Khalid Ibn al-Rashid, the Caliph of Khorasan.

The King of Kings.

The monster from my nightmares.

With every step she took, Shahrzad felt the hate rise in her blood, along with the clarity of purpose. She stared at him, her eyes never wavering. His proud carriage stood out amongst the men in his retinue, and details began to emerge the closer she drew to his side.

He was tall and trim, with the build of a young man proficient in warfare. His dark hair was straight and styled in a manner suggesting a desire for order in all things.

As she strode onto the dais, she looked up at him, refusing to balk, even in the face of her king.

His thick eyebrows raised a fraction. They framed eyes so pale a shade of brown they appeared amber in certain flashes of light, like those of a tiger. His profile was an artist's study in angles, and he remained motionless as he returned her watchful scrutiny.

A face that cut; a gaze that pierced.

He reached a hand out to her.

Just as she extended her palm to grasp it, she remembered to bow.

The wrath seethed below the surface, bringing a flush to her cheeks.

When she met his eyes again, he blinked once.

"Wife." He nodded.

"My king."

I will live to see tomorrow's sunset. Make no mistake. I swear I will live to see as many sunsets as it takes.

And I will kill you.

With my own hands.

TURN THE PAGE FOR AN EXCERPT OF:

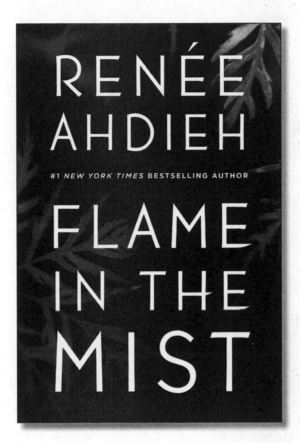

RENÉE
AHDIEH

#1 *NEW YORK TIMES* BESTSELLING AUTHOR

FLAME
IN THE
MIST

The Beginning

———✳———

*I*n *the beginning, there were two suns and two moons.*

The boy's sight blurred before him, seeing past the truth. Past the shame. He focused on the story his *uba* had told him the night before. A story of good and evil, light and dark. A story where the triumphant sun rose high above its enemies.

On instinct, his fingers reached for the calloused warmth of his *uba*'s hand. The nursemaid from Kisun had been with him since before he could remember, but now—like everything else—she was gone.

Now there was no one left.

Against his will, the boy's vision cleared, locking on the clear blue of the noon sky above. His fingers curled around the stiff linen of his shirtsleeves.

Don't look away. If they see you looking away, they will say you are weak.

Once more, his *uba*'s words echoed in his ears.

He lowered his gaze.

The courtyard before him was draped in fluttering white, surrounded on three sides by rice-paper screens. Pennants flying the golden crest of the emperor danced in a passing breeze. To the left and right stood grim-faced onlookers— samurai dressed in the dark silks of their formal *hakama*.

In the center of the courtyard was the boy's father, kneeling on a small tatami mat covered in bleached canvas. He, too, was draped in white, his features etched in stone. Before him sat a low table with a short blade. At his side stood the man who had once been his best friend.

The boy sought his father's eyes. For a moment, he thought his father looked his way, but it could have been a trick of the wind. A trick of the perfumed smoke curling above the squat brass braziers.

His father would not want to look into his son's eyes. The boy knew this. The shame was too great. And his father would die before passing the shame of tears along to his son.

The drums began to pound out a slow beat. A dirge.

In the distance beyond the gates, the boy caught the muffled sound of small children laughing and playing. They were soon silenced by a terse shout.

Without hesitation, his father loosened the knot from around his waist and pushed open his white robe, exposing the skin of his stomach and chest. Then he tucked his sleeves beneath his knees to prevent himself from falling backward.

For even a disgraced samurai should die well.

The boy watched his father reach for the short *tantō* blade on the small table before him. He wanted to cry for him to stop. Cry for a moment more. A single look more.

Just one.

But the boy remained silent, his fingers turning bloodless in his fists. He swallowed.

Don't look away.

His father took hold of the blade, wrapping his hands around the skein of white silk near its base. He plunged the sword into his stomach, cutting slowly to the left, then up to the right. His features remained passive. No hint of suffering could be detected, though the boy searched for it—felt it— despite his father's best efforts.

Never look away.

Finally, when his father stretched his neck forward, the boy saw it. A small flicker, a grimace. In the same instant, the boy's heart shuddered in his chest. A hot burst of pain glimmered beneath it.

The man who had been his father's best friend took two long strides, then swung a gleaming *katana* in a perfect arc toward his father's exposed neck. The thud of his father's head hitting the tatami mat silenced the drumbeats in a hollow start.

Still the boy did not look away. He watched the crimson spurt from his father's folded body, past the edge of the mat and onto the grey stones beyond. The tang of the fresh blood caught in his nose—warm metal and sea salt. He waited until his father's body was carried in one direction, his head in another, to be displayed as a warning.

No hint of treason would be tolerated. Not even a whisper.

All the while, no one came to the boy's side. No one dared to look him in the eye.

The burden of shame took shape in the boy's chest, heavier than any weight he could ever bear.

When the boy finally turned to leave the empty courtyard, his eyes fell upon the creaking door nearby. A nursemaid met his unflinching stare, one hand sliding off the latch, the other clenched around two toy swords. Her skin flushed pink for an instant.

Never look away.

The nursemaid dropped her eyes in discomfort. The boy watched as she quickly ushered a boy and a girl through the wooden gate. They were a few years younger than he and obviously from a wealthy family. Perhaps the children of one of the samurai in attendance today. The younger boy straightened the fine silk of his kimono collar and darted past his nursemaid, never once pausing to acknowledge the presence of a traitor's son.

The girl, however, stopped. She looked straight at him, her pert features in constant motion. Rubbing her nose with the heel of one hand, she blinked, letting her eyes run the length of him before pausing on his face.

He held her gaze.

"Mariko-*sama*!" the nursemaid scolded. She whispered in the girl's ear, then tugged her away by the elbow.

Still the girl's eyes did not waver. Even when she passed

the pool of blood darkening the stones. Even when her eyes narrowed in understanding.

The boy was grateful he saw no sympathy in her expression. Instead the girl continued studying him until her nursemaid urged her around the corner.

His gaze returned to the sky, his chin in high disregard of his tears.

In the beginning, there were two suns and two moons.

One day, the victorious son would rise—

And set fire to all his father's enemies.

Acknowledgments

This was the most difficult book I've ever written. With other books, I often thought that to be true, especially when I was stuck in the weeds, my feet six inches deep in mud and my brow soaked with sweat.

But this one was different in so many ways.

This is the first book I drafted as a new mom. The first book I wrote during a pandemic and quarantine. The first tale I penned during a failed insurrection. The first story I pieced together when my creative well was all but dry.

When I look at it now, I feel a surge of strange emotions. But above them all, I feel pride.

So much pride.

There are few things as resilient as the human spirit. Around me, I am fortunate to have so much love and support. These wonderful people listened to me yell and cry, helped me wrangle words from chaos, laughed with me in the darkness, and smiled at my son over FaceTime. They fixed my mistakes, shared memes via text, and sent dinner to us, the addled parents of a colicky newborn.

Without them, this book would not exist.

B, thank you for being a true friend and an excellent human being. The next steak dinner in NYC is on me. It will be soon, dammit. It's been too long.

Stacey, with each book we work on together, you push me to try harder and write better. Gratitude is an insufficient word for what I feel. Thank you for making the life I have now possible and for being the best advocate and editor I could ever hope to have.

To everyone at Penguin: Your passion and creativity make our dreams possible. I am thankful every day for the privilege of working with you. A special thank-you to Jen Loja and Jennifer Klonsky for all your fierce support. Thank you so much to my publicists, Olivia Russo and Tessa Meischeid. To Caitlin Tutterow for your kindness and consummate professionalism. To Carmela Iaria, Shanta Newlin, Felicia Frazier, Christina Colangelo, Alex Garber, James Akinaka, Shannon Spann, Venessa Carson, Emily Romero, Felicity Vallence, Kara Brammer, the entire marketing and publicity teams, as well as the fantastic teams in sales and school and library, every part of this experience is made more wondrous by each of you. These past two years have shown me more than ever how important our work is. It is an honor to do this with the best team in the business.

To Cindy and Anne: Even in the eleventh hour, you manage to uncover ways to make my books better and more seamless. Also, bless you both for knowing what tense to use in any given situation and keeping track of the seasons. Your humor and grace and professionalism are an inspiration.

To IGLA, Maggie Kane, Heather Baror-Shapiro, Mary Pender, and the team at UTA: Thank you so much for championing my work so tirelessly.

To my assistant, Emily Williams: Thank you so much for keeping my jumbled life in order.

To Alwyn and Rosh: Thank you so much for the gift of your friendship, as well as making sure the French and Hindi are correct in this book. To JJ and Lemon: I am so grateful for both of you.

To Sabaa: I miss drinking tea with you late at night and laughing about nothing. Here's to many more years of touring our books together and watching movies until the wee hours of the morning. So much love to you.

To Elaine: Thank you for fixing the Spanish in this book, for being the best titi Cyrus could ever have, and for twenty (!) years of unflinchingly standing by my side.

To Erica: Every day the gratitude I feel to have you as a sister only grows. Without you, these past few years would have been so much harder. Your support and enthusiasm and the love you have for my son mean everything to me. I am so thankful for you and for Chris.

To Ian, Izzy, and Maddie: So much love to you three as you embark on a new chapter together. I hope this is the best year yet.

To Mama Joon, Baba Joon, Umma, and Dad: Thank you for staying safe and healthy and for never hesitating to play with a screeching toddler who throws his food in your face. We love you so much. To Navid, Jinda, Ella, Lily, Omid, Julie, Evelyn, Isabelle, and Andrew: I am so thankful for all of you and for our family.

To Mushu for being the best little doggie in the world.

To Victor and to Cyrus: You are everything. My life is so much richer and fuller because of you two. Also, Victor asked me to add one more line about him to these acknowledgments:

I love you.